MARLA MONDAY WAS A USER.

Beautiful, talented and depraved, she let nothing stand in the way of her ascent to stardom. From the men and women in her life, she took what she could use and discarded the rest. . . .

Vandy, the Machiavellian millionaire she bled until he was reduced to pushing drugs to meet her demands . . .

Gil LaFarge, the brilliant director whose masterpiece she threatened to destroy . . .

Neva Morgann, the lovely young actress whose part she stole, and finally . . .

Rick Steele, the golden boy who sacrificed his career for hers before she left him an alcoholic tennis bum with no future beyond the next bottle. He might have stayed down, too . . . if someone hadn't killed Marla and blamed it on him.

Rick had to take a scary trip through the debris of his past, turning over the rocks one step ahead of a sadistic cop to prove he wasn't guilty—to himself. . . .

FREEZE-FRAME

Great Horror Fiction from SIGNET

FREEZE-FRAME

by
Arthur Hansl

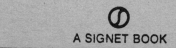

A SIGNET BOOK

NEW AMERICAN LIBRARY

PUBLISHER'S NOTE

This novel is a work of fiction. Names, characters, places, and incidents either are the product of the author's imagination or are used fictitiously, and any resemblance to actual persons, living or dead, events, or locales is entirely coincidental.

SIGNET, SIGNET CLASSIC, MENTOR, PLUME, MERIDIAN AND NAL BOOKS are published by New American Library, 1633 Broadway, New York, New York 10019

First Printing, April, 1985

1 2 3 4 5 6 7 8 9

PRINTED IN THE UNITED STATES OF AMERICA

For Nicole

Acknowledgments

Heartfelt thanks to Bill Dozier for generously sharing his expertise, to Ann Rutherford Dozier for her enthusiasm and encouragement, and to Barbara Wilkins for getting it off the ground.

Oh, what a tangled web we weave,
When first we practice to deceive!

—Sir Walter Scott

1

Marla Monday lived like the star she was in a huge bastard-Mediterranean mansion she had wrested from her third husband in the days when a California divorce cost a rich man dearly. The estate was at the end of Antelo Drive, a cul-de-sac rising above Mulholland, and it covered six acres overlooking the San Fernando Valley. Lonely to the point of isolation, it suited Marla admirably, for she was afraid of nothing and could have a full-bore Roman orgy complete with the spectacle of Christians and lions up here without inviting complaint or interference.

When she arrived home alone before midnight, still high on cocaine and champagne, newly sated by the hard flesh of her current lover, she was wearing something off-the-shoulder, white and Greek, diamond earrings, a gold chain looped around her waist, thonged sandals. The firm, tanned flesh of her body testified to no more than half of her forty-five years and her fine-boned oval face framed by cropped black hair confirmed the lie. Sooty, uneven brows were arched over ebony eyes that gave away none of her secrets, and her movements were as lithe and sure as a teenager's.

She left her car in the driveway and paused before the high portal of her entrance, reluctant to leave the velvet darkness that smelled of night-blooming jasmine with a tangy hint of the desert. How pleasant it was out here breathing the Santa Ana wind, still feeling the length and strength of her lover within her. But morning came early, the start of a special day. She kicked off her sandals, leaving them behind as she moved toward the big door.

Inside she padded barefoot across the cool tiles of the antechamber under a high, dimmed chandelier that served as a night light, stepped down into a sunken living room, and stopped dead, one delicately arched foot poised just above the thick pile carpet.

A visitor sat in semidarkness on her long, low sofa. Someone known to her but still very much an intruder. Marla was not used to unannounced guests and in no mood for surprises. It was a jarring note at the end of an evening that had flowed. Still, she decided not to show consternation; that gave away the advantage. Masking her annoyance, she completed her step into the well of the living room.

"Exactly how did you get in here?" she asked, calmly enough.

A shrug. "I have a knack."

She nodded. That would be true. "You didn't ring for Dieter." It was a statement, not a question. Her servant had separate quarters across the lawn at the far end of the estate.

A shake of the head in confirmation.

Marla said, "Of course not. He would have stayed." This was an interruption of her schedule, her disciplines. She had things to do before going to bed. "It's late. What do you want?" she asked, knowing full well.

"I think you can guess."

"Yes, I think I can, and nothing's changed. You're wasting our time."

"I thought you might reconsider. You've had some time to think."

"I didn't need it. I know what's right for me. Look, I've got a big day tomorrow."

Her visitor sighed and nodded, yet showed no signs of leaving.

Marla had arrived home exuberant. She wanted to retain the edge, let nothing and no one interrupt it, this fool least of all. Tonight was over and tomorrow was everything. She had to block out the unwelcome presence and prepare for it. She could have summoned Dieter, ill as he was, but it wasn't really necessary. What was ignored often went away, and contempt was among her favorite weapons. It might even prompt an amusing reaction.

She unslung the gold chain around her waist and dropped it, shrugged easily out of the simple, elegant white garment and let it puddle at her feet, stepping away from it to stand completely nude. "I'm going outside," she said. "I don't think there's anything more to talk about. You found your way in and you can find your way back out." She moved the sliding glass doors giving onto the patio, pressing the buttons that flooded the exterior with light. Just before stepping out, she looked back and smiled. She had been right.

Beyond the patio a pool formed a simple blue rectangle seventy-five feet long and designed for serious swimming. At its far end a cottage commanded a view of the San Fernando Valley. It was furnished as an elegant guest house, but Marla used it for servants' quarters. Two luxuriant coral trees with massive trunks loomed on either side of the pool area, shading it by day and rigged with light to cast shifting rose-colored patterns around it by night.

On the lawn, beyond the range of the lights, she had embedded a set of gym equipment, the same tangle of bars used by competing acrobats. She worked out on them in the morning and, schedule permitting, again in the afternoon before taking a half-mile swim. Dangling from the bars was a pair of gravity boots, padded hooks designed to be affixed to the ankles and slung over a bar so that the body can hang down full length, stretching the spine and speeding blood to the brain.

Marla clamped the boots to her ankles, leapt to catch the intermediate bar, and swung expertly into position. She dangled upside down, naked and utterly relaxed, eyes closed and a smile on her lips, feeling the rush of blood and cocaine to her head. Tomorrow would be her first day on camera playing the role of Jana in *Starcrossed*, the part Gilbert LaFarge had written for a twenty-five-year-old girl (his own mistress, of course) and done everything he could to deny her. She had had to use all her power to prevail. Well, fuck LaFarge. Abruptly she felt a surge of anger recalling his hurtful comment—that her close-ups would have to be shot through linoleum. He would pay for that; he had already begun to pay. With an effort she pushed the offending memory from her mind and concentrated on feeling the sensual caress of the warm breeze that played along her thighs, thinking that all care and stress would be leached away if she could only stay here, like this, forever.

Sensing a presence, she opened her eyes to see the inverted form of her visitor standing in the lush damp grass before her, and the feeling of well-being faded. It had not occurred to her that a clear dismissal might be ignored. Marla had grown too accustomed to command.

"Are you still here?" It was an inane question, prompted by a sudden feeling of vulnerability. She bit back an angrier remark, acutely aware of her position, more uncomfortable than alarmed.

"So it seems." The face stared down at her, featureless in the night.

Marla was still determined to regain the glow, to let nothing upset her. "Get away from me," she said softly, between her teeth. "Get out now and we can forget about this."

"In just a moment."

Then the visitor knelt swiftly beside her, and catching the short, thick hair in one hand, used the other to draw a sharp saw-toothed knife hard across her throat, leaping back to avoid the sudden gout of blood, bending again to wipe the blade clean as Marla's life flowed out of her onto the grass just a few feet away.

2

By five-thirty on the following afternoon, much of the world knew about Marla Monday's murder. Richard Steelegrave, her second ex-husband, did not as he walked out of the Malibu Tennis Club to his car. All day he had disguised a monumental hangover as he plowed through his teaching schedule with the usual assortment of students, plodding and promising, male and female, young and old. After his last class, he had forced himself through two strenuous sets with the only club member who could make him sweat, and followed this workout with a long swim in the fifty-meter pool. The exercise had left him drained, free of hangover, and ready to start over, if he chose. But today he strode firmly past the bar, determined to lay off the booze. Well, maybe some wine with dinner, nothing more. Last night had scared hell out of him. Because he could remember nothing at all about it.

Steelegrave was a medium-tall, compact man with whitening blond hair that went well with his tan. At first glance, he looked much younger than his forty-eight years, an impression that did not survive closer scrutiny. But if time and life-style had altered the coin-clean profile of his youth, they had also etched his face with interesting lines and planes that had been missing from the bland good looks of Rick Steele, star of TV and motion pictures. Even as Steele had been typical of the handsome young leading men of his generation, Steelegrave was well-cast as the

genial tennis pro at an exclusive club. That he had once
been a celebrity athlete and a Hollywood star did not hurt
his standing with the membership at all, but he avoided
getting too bombed at club functions, where decorum was
required, and he usually sidestepped the wife or daughter
who made an indiscreet run on him. Usually. Exceptions
merely confirmed the rule.

His classic '57 T-Bird waited top down under a eucalyp-
tus tree in the reserved parking area of the club, its rich
British racing green reflecting eight coats of burnished
lacquer which trapped a kaleidoscope of golden highlights
if examined closely enough. The seats were snow-white,
the chrome immaculate, the wide white-walled tires a memory of yesterday. Like its owner, the car was handsome,
well-tuned, and aging.

In contrast, the large dog sprawled indolently along the
length of the seat, one tawny paw hanging over the side,
was yellow-fanged, notch-eared, and mud-colored. Of un-
traceable lineage, he might have been descended from a
timber wolf and a mongoose if judged by his temper. At
least, now that he ate well, his coat was healthy and
tightly stretched over a rangy, muscular body. His name,
when he acknowledged it, was Junkyard, and he was
supposed to be a watchdog.

Junkyard had been saved from absolutely certain death
two years before by Steelegrave, whose apartment had just
been robbed. In the market for some four-legged protection,
he strolled into the Santa Monica Animal Shelter late one
afternoon with the laudable idea that a dog obtained here
was an animal saved, not to mention a hell of a lot cheaper.
Steelegrave was drunk at the time, a condition not unusual
for him and quite undetectable to anyone who didn't know
him well.

Jason Wiley, a lean old black man in a crisp tan uniform,
was on duty, and since things were slow, elected to show
the visitor around in person. The cages were clean and
odorless, with egress to a dog run out back, and there were
no more than two dogs per living space, accommodations
Steelegrave felt might be envied by some humans who
found themselves guests of the county, as he had on one
occasion.

The dogs came in all shapes, sizes, and ages. Some were apathetic, while others were noisy. The smart ones were charming, as though they knew that a good performance here was absolutely essential to a secure future, or indeed any future at all. A handsome red setter licked Steelegrave's hand through the bars and looked soulfully at him—a waste of talent, since this dog was just waiting to be picked up by his owner.

In the very last cage skulked an animal that was, unsurprisingly, billeted alone. As Steelegrave and Jason Wiley drew abreast, it hurled itself heavily against the bars, yellow fangs snapping, weird eyes blazing, shaggy hackles standing on end. It was gaunt and dun-colored with a mangled ear, a broken tail, and a ruff of hair behind the chops that suggested an infusion of wolf or, optimistically, of husky. Steelegrave stepped back in alarm, and Wiley seemed embarrassed.

"That old boy just don't like to be looked straight in the eye," he explained. "Don't nobody want to take him, either."

"No kidding? Well, if nobody wants to take him, what will they do with him. Put him to sleep?"

"No, sir. They gonna kill him."

"Oh."

"He ack like that 'cause he been abused," said Wiley, as though he knew the feeling. Then he added, in the teeth of all the evidence, "He a good dog."

Steelegrave stared at Wiley. "Why don't you take him, then?"

"I already got eleven at home."

Steelegrave looked back at the dog to find the animal's strange amber eyes glued to his own, lips writhing back from awesome fangs, ears pinned to the skull. The card affixed to his cage claimed that this was an abandoned "German shepherd" of indeterminate age, unnamed and free of inoculation against rabies or anything else. A red-ink marker had been used to circle the word "available."

Later Steelegrave couldn't remember whether it was the challenge, or because of pity, or just because he was about half-ripped, but he'd suddenly experienced a feeling of

kinship with this appalling creature. "I've been looking for
a watchdog," he heard himself say.

Wiley beamed. "You found him, sir!"

"I've found a dog that needs to be watched."

"Heh-heh!"

"He hasn't had his shots. Can you do that here?"

Wiley shrugged. "Sorry."

Steelegrave lit a black cigarette. "I'm not taking this
fucking killer out of here without his shots."

This sounded like a commitment to Wiley and he grinned.
"Got an emergency kit here. I can give him rabies and
distemper. Ten bucks."

"Done."

Muzzled and choke-chained, the dog was hauled out of
his cage, injected with the required drugs, and deposited
on the T-Bird's seat next to Steelegrave. Wiley slipped off
the muzzle and sold the choke-chain to Steelegrave for
another ten bucks. Man and dog drove away from the
Santa Monica Animal Shelter staring stolidly ahead, in
mutual distrust.

Junkyard never barked, but he did attack. Four days
after his rescue from the pound he attacked his new
master, upon the latter's return home late at night.

Without making a sound, the dog sprang to sink his
fangs into the man's leg. Fortunately, Steelegrave was
wearing his mid-calf western boots and in the instant it
took Junkyard to seek a more vulnerable hold, the man,
who was quick and strong if far from sober, reached down
and caught the dog by the loose skin over his knotty
shoulders and hauled him off all of his feet. He carried the
heavy animal at arm's length to a door leading to an
enclosed yard and flung him out into the night, slamming
the door behind him.

Then he went to his bar to build a drink and think
things over. After a while, he opened a broom closet and
took out the machete he had bought on a trip to Mexico.
He turned on the yard light and walked out, unopposed
by Junkyard, who sensed the enormity of his error. Carefully he sliced a three-foot length from a perfectly good
garden hose and proceeded to belabor his dog about the
back and shoulders. Junkyard yipped and howled but,

wisely, did not fight back. Next day, he took a small revenge by chewing up the hose and eating most of it. Steelegrave trimmed the segment that remained intact, belted the dog with it once, and hung it on the back fence by a thong. Thwarted, Junkyard retreated into apparent compliance, but he had remained very much his own creature.

"Have a nice day? Digging up the flowerbeds and pissing on people's tires?" Steelegrave asked, swinging in behind the wheel of the T-Bird as the dog made room for him with a yellow grin. He hit the starter and listened with familiar pleasure to the rich mutter of the big engine, thinking once again that they just didn't make them like this anymore. He shoved a cassette into the dashboard stereo, choosing some trumpet classics he had taped selectively. All of his music ranged from the early thirties to the middle sixties; none of the new sounds, acid rock or computer disco, held any charm for him.

To the superb Bunny Berrigan's "I Can't Get Started," Steelegrave drove out of the tennis club and down the hill to the coast highway, where he turned south toward Santa Monica. The sun was dipping toward the horizon, gilding the ocean and staining the smog bank, driven far out to sea by the desert wind, a sinister orange. He went by the Malibu Colony, an entity apart, and past the tacky motels and eateries that squatted between elegant beach homes along some of the most expensive oceanfront real estate in the world. Someday, when the developers managed to outflank the locals, a solid phalanx of Holiday Inns and Marriotts would mushroom here, an eventuality that depressed Steelegrave, who hated progress in most of its forms. He judged the quality of life to be declining and suspected that things would grow worse, never to recapture the grace of that less complex era when his world had been young. Once, while driving north up the coast, past Trancas, where the countryside hadn't changed much over the years, he'd been overwhelmed by a feeling of *déjà vu*, convinced that it was 1958 and he was driving to Santa Barbara, where he would go to the house of Louann MacIver and meet Malcolm Webley. . . . He'd pulled over and stared out at the ocean, trying to hold on to the moment, but it quickly dissolved, as such illusions do. It was something he couldn't explain to Erin, these visits he paid to the past. She would lose patience and sulk, too young and without regret to give a damn about yesterday.

3

When he got out of the army in 1955, the Los Angeles *Times* sports page headlined "RICHARD STEELEGRAVE IS BACK" over his smiling likeness, military cap at a jaunty angle, first lieutenant's bars gleaming on his shoulders. The article went on to say that the top-seeded amateur tennis champ planned to turn pro and should go all the way, an opinion fully shared by young Steelegrave himself.

Two years later he realized it was not to be. The victories at Forest Hills and Wimbledon, in Rome, Australia, and Mexico City were history never to be repeated. The big cups he'd won were worth their exact weight in silver, he discovered when he went to sell them. Somewhere he had lost control of the powerful serve; his legs had less spring at the net. He couldn't go the distance. In his mid-twenties he was washed up as a contender for the big bucks. True, he finished in the money now and then, but mostly he was living on residuals from endorsements and TV commercials. As the demand for his name dwindled, even this source of income dried up. Suddenly, chillingly, he became aware that he would fulfill neither the expectations of the L.A. *Times* nor his own.

At first he tried to convince himself that the army years had taken the edge off his game, but deep down he knew this to be bullshit. It had a lot more to do with the death of McReedy, his slave-driving coach and mentor. Without the dour Irishman to enforce discipline, Steelegrave indulged his taste for the *dolce vita*. Late nights, booze, and sexual excess sapped his energy on the courts and ruined his timing, nullifying the long hours of training. McReedy had recognized these tendencies early and acted to head them off. In awe of his coach, Steelegrave had responded well to the whip. As long as McReedy was around, he had played superb competitive tennis.

He was the top-ranked amateur when the army drafted him. There was still a war on in Korea. Though he hadn't finished college, his name got him an appointment to officer-candidate school and, once commissioned, kept him busy playing exhibition matches rather than running up and down the decidedly dangerous hills of Korea. He hadn't angled for his privileged position, nor had he protested it. Sometimes he fantasized about the glory of combat, casting himself heroically at the head of his platoon. But the casualty count showed a fellow could definitely get killed over there, and McReedy had him programmed for better things. When he got out he would train hard, turn pro, and start working toward the big money. But the hard-living, chain-smoking McReedy died of cancer before his discharge, and no one could be found to take his place. It had been a special relationship. On his own, with no capacity for self-discipline, Steelegrave drifted into self-indulgence, oversampling the joys of civilian life, basking in the diminishing glow of past accomplishment. His comeback effort never really got off the ground before it became evident that he had been a short-lived phenomenon, never really geared for the long haul.

His failure led to some attempt at self-evaluation. He considered the possibility that he was simply not hungry enough. Steelegrave had not been raised in a ghetto or barrio, as had so many ultimately successful athletes. His father was a well-heeled San Diego attorney, his mother a gracious lady of varied community and clubhouse interests. He was a late-in-life only child, the apple of their eye. He had learned tennis on the family court, gone to an Ivy League prep school, then on to USC for two years before dropping out to pursue a career in tennis. True, his parents had died insolvent, having lived up to their considerable means. Killed together in a crash with a pickup truck full of drunken Mexican laborers between Rosarito Beach and Tijuana, they had left their son no legacy other than a mortgage on the spacious house in Mission Hills. Richard Steelegrave Sr. would not for the world have left his son in dire financial straits, but he tended to think of himself as immortal and had not counted on the peculiarities of Mexican drivers.

The boy, who was attending USC at the time, could have finished his education on an athletic scholarship, but by then McReedy, scouting the campus for exceptional talent, had taken one look at his tennis game and recruited him on the spot. The coach had painted an attractive picture of amateur and eventually professional tennis. There was plenty of under-the-table money to finance the talented amateur, and promising financial rewards for a top-ranked pro. Why not get paid for what you liked to do most? He made it sound a lot more interesting than farting around a college campus waiting tables or pumping gas to pay for the necessities.

"But you've gotta be *hungry* for it, kid," the leathery trainer told him. "Or you're just another Joe College who plays a little tennis."

Steelegrave believed he had once had that hunger in quantity. Certainly he had enjoyed the trappings of success; that was his problem. Maybe he had just burned out after seven years of the grind. Or a lazy streak had surfaced after the long army layoff; exhibition games didn't really count. Maybe you had to be raised poor like Pancho Segura, but Bill Tilden had never been poor. Only one fact emerged unarguably. At twenty-five years old he was finished with ranked tennis.

In April 1958 he got an offer to be resident tennis pro at a big private club near Santa Barbara. It was a tentative offer; they wanted to look at him. It seemed an improvement over his current job as an Orange County lifeguard, so he drove north from his rented beach shack near Laguna and checked into the Santa Barbara Hilton, having long since learned the value of a good address. It was Sunday afternoon and his meeting with the club athletic director wasn't until the following morning. Faced with time on his hands, he suddenly remembered Louann MacIver.

Louann MacIver had become Steelegrave's sponsor when he was a top-seeded nineteen-year-old. Her hobby was tennis players, not tennis. She liked them young, handsome, and winners. He remembered her as a raven-haired woman in her late thirties who took a little bit too much sun and a lot too much liquor. Still, she had introduced him to the infinite possibilities of sex, becoming teacher and playmate in an endless variety of erotic games, some of which he had previously, and foolishly, considered perversions. Once initiated, he became a dedicated satyr and, after a weekend with Louann, often walked on the court drained and spaghetti-legged. McReedy stepped between them before Steelegrave's game actually began to falter. Firmly he rationed Louann's access to his charge, a restriction she accepted out of necessity but with poor grace. Though generally a woman of varied and fickle romantic habits, her obsession with Steelegrave lasted for two years. She bankrolled his career and gave him expensive gifts, such as the Mercedes convertible he had regretfully sold only a few months ago. She traveled with him to Rome and London, where he had won the big ones—and stayed in separate quarters on McReedy's orders. MacIver and McReedy loathed each other but the coach was shrewd enough to realize they needed this wealthy and generous libertine to ease their life on the circuit, and Louann sensed that without the Irishman her golden young athlete might not be such a big winner.

"Richard!" Louann's whiskey voice was slipping toward a true baritone. "How splendid! Wherever did you disappear to? I never read about you anymore! Well, never mind. . . . You couldn't have called at a better time. I'm having a thing this afternoon. Come out to the house right away! I don't have to tell *you* how to get here. . . ." Her throaty laugh ended in a hacking cough.

Steelegrave drove up to the lush highlands of Montecito where Louann lived. He was casually elegant in polo shirt and summer-weight blazer, but the dented old Ford he drove spoke eloquently of the decline in his fortunes. A gate guard at the familiar entrance motioned him on impassively when he gave his name, and he chugged up the long driveway under a protective canopy of trees that engaged each other overhead like an honor guard crossing swords.

Louann's house was a Spanish mansion built around a central patio the size of a village plaza. Aztec gargoyles spouted water from each of the four corners. Beyond the house, lawn, pool, and tennis court were several acres of rare trees that could flourish in California, imported from all over the world by Commodore MacIver, Louann's father. Steelegrave remembered squeezing the poisonous, milky sap from the fruit of a curare tree, while Louann laughingly told him she painted her fingernails with the stuff.

At the graveled parking circle, he would have liked to hide the Ford among the Porsches and Caddies anonymously, but a Mexican in a red jacket leapt out to take it. Steelegrave ignored the front door and found his way through a labyrinth of manicured hedges to the back lawn, where he knew the party would be under way.

The guests gathered around the pool and spread out over the vast lawn, a hundred or so sleek Santa Barbarans, graying men, dapper in light jackets and ascots, their ladies in long flowered dresses under wide floppy hats. The younger generation congregated apart, cool and watchful, as though waiting for later, when something might happen. A trio of Mexican *cantantes* in traditional custome sang the sad ballads of their homeland while Mexican waiters in white jackets circulated with canapés and anything anyone might want to drink. Long wooden tables assembled for the occasion held a lavish buffet of beef, game fowl, and seafood.

Steelegrave snagged a gin and tonic from a passing tray and drank gratefully. He was sipping his second by the time he saw Louann bearing down on him. At her heel trotted a tall, dark young man in tennis gear, who looked familiar.

"Darling Richard!" she rasped, kissing him on both cheeks, then holding him at arm's length for inspection. "You look divine, a trifle more mature, but just divine!"

"You too," Steelegrave lied. Louann had aged badly, as though her passage through time had been over unpaved highway. Her skin had coarsened and the pull and tuck of cosmetic surgery had given her face a scraped-bone appearance. Her breath reeked of gin and cigarettes. Of decay.

She tugged on the dark-skinned boy, who showed a great many teeth in a winning smile. "This is Paco Avila," she said proudly. "I'm sure you've heard of him." Steelegrave had; a top-ranked amateur, Avila was going to be second-seeded in Paris next month. He was a handsome lad, strong-limbed with a bush of shiny black hair. A prime candidate for the MacIver seal of approval.

"Everyone! Everyone!" she called, attracting a small, desultory group already in the vicinity. "I want you to meet Richard Steelegrave! He used to be very, very big in tennis!" "Used to be" is what she said.

She stepped between the two of them, reaching up to bury one hand in Richard's yellow hair and the other in Paco's black thatch. "My two darlings! I think I'll call them 'Night' and 'Day.' Oh, do let's have a picture!"

Someone with a camera was already there, and the three of them grinned into an almost instantaneous flash.

"How about this?" Louann dropped her hands and hugged them both around the waist. Flash. "Now I have a marvelous idea!" She waved the photographer away. "An exhibition match! Between Paco Avila and Richard Steelegrave! Right now!" There was some interest, a patter of applause.

Shit, thought Steelegrave, starting to sweat. He leaned close to Louann, showing as many teeth as Paco, and said, speaking through them, "I'm not ready for this, Louann. Out of shape."

"He'd be delighted!" she translated, clapping her small brown hands and turning to Avila. "Take him up and find him the right things."

With a little shove, Steelegrave was dispatched toward the big house behind Paco. In the master suite upstairs, Paco opened a closet to offer a selection of tennis outfits. The Mexican's clothes were hanging exactly where his once had and they fit almost as well, right down to the shoes.

"Just one set, okay, Paco?" he said, pulling on socks.

The boy shrugged and smiled. "Sure."

A crowd had gathered by the time they reached the courts. Louann gave Paco a special little hug, wriggling against him. Steelegrave thought she might tie her kerchief to his racket as a sign of her favor. Or maybe around his cock. He regretted going along with her game, resented her pressuring him. He hadn't played for weeks, killing time by drinking and partying, while this kid was clearly in top shape.

They volleyed briefly and Steelegrave won the toss for serve. He also won the first game on the strength of that serve, conceded to be one of the hardest in professional tennis when it was under control, as it was now. Paco came back to take the second game easily, covering the court as swiftly as anyone Steelegrave had ever played against. Still, he managed to win his service against the kid in the third, in spite of a double fault and several changes of advantage. After that it was mostly downhill for Steelegrave. He won one more game by reaching into the bag of tricks he had learned through long experience, but the kid soon caught up with his drop shots and was fast enough to get back under the clever lobs in time to put them away where Steelegrave couldn't reach them. The gin and tonic sloshed around in his stomach and he felt too queasy and rubber-legged to chase the hard ones. He was afraid he would collapse. Or vomit. Finally it was over— six-three in favor of Avila. Steelegrave put on a loser's game smile and shook the kid's hand, ruffling his hair and punching him on the arm. The crowd applauded the sporting gesture and Louann ran up to plant a consolation kiss on his cheek.

"It was an honor to play you," Paco said, seeming to mean it. "You were my idol when I was a boy." Steelegrave, who was twenty-five, winced.

"Be sure and talk to Malcolm Webley before you go," Louann croaked in his ear. "He asked me and I told him all about you. He's the agent, you know." Then she spun away from him and plastered herself against Paco, nuzzling the brown column of his throat.

Steelegrave strode across the lawn toward the big house, still wearing his stiffening smile but seething inside. He would have destroyed that kid just a few short years ago. Of this he was certain.

At poolside, he peeled off shirt, shoes, and socks and

dived into the water, still wearing Paco's shorts. To hell
with it. He swam two slow underwater lengths and then
hauled himself out, feeling somewhat refreshed. Upstairs,
he stood under a needle shower in a sunken tub of blue
lapis lazuli, the site of numerous sexual encounters with
Louann in his formative years. He remembered how she
had associated orgasm with water—running water, drip-
ping water, still or rushing water. He had accommodated
her in Acapulco Bay, in the Malibu surf, at high tide on
the French and Italian rivieras, and in an assortment of
brooks and lakes where it had sometimes been just too
damn cold for him. A small price to pay for a liberal
education.

When he went below, the party was shifting gears.
Older people were leaving and younger ones were coming
alive. The *cantantes* gave way to Elvis Presley and other
contemporary sounds. Lights were coming on over both
patios and most of the guests elected to stay outdoors in
the mild spring twilight.

Hungry, Steelegrave stood by the buffet, dipping prawns
in a rich sauce, washing the food down with good California wine.

"I lost a small wager on you," said a voice at his
elbow. "You hadn't much stamina."

He turned to find a small man wearing a tweed jacket and
the ubiquitous ascot standing beside him. He had cream-
colored hair, wavy around the ears, thinning on top. His
thick mustache curled upward and his plump cheeks were
ruddy with good health. Or high blood pressure. He looked
like a diminutive Colonel Blimp.

"Too bad," said Steelegrave. "You shouldn't have bet on
me."

"Louann tells me you were one of her . . . ah . . . young
gentlemen." Seeing the look on Steelegrave's face, he quickly
held up his palm. "No offense meant. I know of you on
your own merits, of course. I only duffer at tennis, but I
do read a lot. You were one of the best. Should have
beaten that lad handily."

"I wasn't ready to play. Louann kind of hustled me."

"I'm Malcolm Webley," said the small man, sticking out
his hand. Steelegrave correctly guessed his British accent

to be fraudulent. Once known as Max Weber, he had become a devout anglophile when he traveled to England as a public-relations officer near the end of the war. He had taken the name "Webley" from the British service revolver and loved to tell how he had been "blitzed" when one of Hitler's buzz bombs had strayed within a few miles of him near the end of the conflict.

"Yes, I know. The agent."

"Rather more than an agent, actually. Personal manager. I supervise every aspect of a client's career. Love interests, publicity, all that sort of thing. Keep a bit more of his money, as well." Webley chuckled, piling steak tartare on a piece of rye bread. "Louann said I should take an interest in you. I think she might be right, for once."

"I'm not an actor."

"No matter. Come, let's sit down for a bit." He led the way to a pair of deck chairs near the apron of the pool. People milled around the outdoor bar, but the pool was dark and silent.

"To be an actor one needs no more than a modicum of intelligence and the sincere desire to be one," Webley said. "My mother-in-law is old, has a goiter, and she is ugly enough to frighten a bulldog away from a meat wagon. Given the proper material and a good director, I have no doubt she could excel. The Italians take people off the streets and make them into actors. The problem is not how to play a part, but how to get a part." He pulled a briar pipe out of his pocket and made much of packing and tamping it.

"Now, if you happen to be young and handsome, or beautiful, and you have a certain indefinable quality sometimes called 'presence' which can be captured by the camera, you can be something far better than an actor." He puffed at his pipe until it glowed in the night. "You can be a star."

"I thought talent had something to do with it."

Webley dismissed talent with a wave of his pipe. "Very little, actually. The Hollywood hills are full of stars with very modest talent, to give them the best of it. Not many around like Larry Olivier. Most of them think *Hamlet* is a story about a little pig. Oh, I shall admit they are often

performers, but then so are you, like many athletes. I
watched you closely out there on the court—the self-
deprecatory gesture when you missed a shot you should
have put away, the way you managed to patronize the
boy, even while you congratulated him. All actors' tricks."

Steelegrave laughed. "You learn to do that after you lose
a few. To keep from looking too much like a horse's ass."

"You're through with professional tennis," Webley said
flatly. It was too dark now to see his face. In the sudden
silence, a splash and a giggle came from the pool.

"Maybe," Steelegrave acknowledged finally. He restrained
himself from telling the pompous little man off, recognizing the simple truth of his statement.

"There may be something better for you. Our meeting
today is quite providential, you see. Next season, King-
crafts studio will bring out an action series for TV about a
spy who masquerades as a tennis player. They are looking
for a star who plays the game extremely well, and that is
not so easy to find. They are leaning toward a new face
rather than a big name. I have been trying to provide
them just that. You seem to be tailored for the part, as we
say."

Steelegrave lit a cigarette to cover his excitement. "I've
never done anything except commercials. Suppose this
'presence' you talk about doesn't show up on camera?"

"My instincts are seldom wrong in these matters. In any
case, we shall find out, if you're interested." Webley rose
to his feet and handed him a card. "I must get along.
Think it over. I'll make time for you midday on Wednesday.
Please call my secretary the day before to confirm your
appointment." Then he was gone, leaving Steelegrave with
the card in his hand, peering into the dark after him.

For a while he sat there smoking, his mind roiling with
new images implanted by the agent. The man was right:
he was through with pro tennis. And with all its discipline
and self-denial. He marveled that he hadn't thought about
acting himself, after all the years he had been in front of
cameras. They were like old friends. Tomorrow he would
cancel his appointment at the club, pleading illness, to
leave the door open a crack. But it wouldn't be necessary. . . .

The underwater pool lights sprang on in front of him,

scattering his fantasies and trapping the naked figures of Louann and Paco in a bright blue glare. Louann, who had lost none of her penchant for aquatics, clung to the apron of the pool while Paco applied himself, holding her around the waist. The crowd at the bar turned toward the tableau as a single unit. Someone dropped a glass; someone else brayed with laughter. Probably the clown who had hit the switch.

"Turn off that fucking light!" yelled Louann, as Paco disengaged himself in horror. Mercifully, someone complied.

Staring at the darkened pool, Steelegrave felt a sudden kinship with the boy. He had a picture of himself long ago, clutching a younger, slimmer Louann in some similar body of water, paying for the Mercedes, the gold cigarette lighter, the suite at the Ritz or in Acapulco, not by his unique skill at a gentleman's sport, but by a simpler talent that was the basic coin of her circle.

He got out of the deck chair and walked away from the party, clutching the business card in his hand as if it were a winning lottery ticket.

Malcolm Webley's offices were on Beverly Drive near Olympic Boulevard in a single-story old Spanish building of solid construction. Steelegrave walked under an arch smothered in ivy and along a tiled passageway to Webley's suites. The inner office seemed more suited to the man. His massive desk was decorated by both British and American flags, a framed picture of Webley in an American major's uniform shaking hands with King George, and a photo of a handsome patrician woman who might have been his wife. It was definitely not his mother-in-law. The walls were hung with signed glossies of prominent clients. Steelegrave, impressed, tried not to stare at them.

Webley stoked and lit his briar before tossing a thin sheaf of papers across the desk to him. "This is an exclusive personal-management contract that ties you to me for seven years as long as you earn, under my auspices, the yearly minimum specified within. On the other hand, I can drop you at any time. You may take time to read the document if you wish, or show it to your barrister if you have one."

Steelegrave glanced through the papers swiftly. The amount of money mentioned surprised and pleased him. He couldn't think of anything he had to lose. On impulse he said, "I'll take your word that the contract is fair. But just for the hell of it, why doesn't the termination clause work both ways?"

Webley nodded, puffing. "I'm glad you asked. Shows wit. But first, let me ask you something. Can you afford a new car? A decent apartment here in Hollywood? Do you know how to ride a horse? Fence? Act, for that matter?"

"I have five hundred bucks in the bank. I don't know how to fence or ride well. I thought the series was about tennis. And you told me a star doesn't need to be a great actor."

"For Christ's sake, boy, you shall be doing more than this series! You will do all manner of action films, westerns, pirate pictures, anything that keeps you moving, which I suspect is when you look your best.

"I shall buy you a car and pay for your rent, your riding, fencing, and acting lessons, your wardrobe, your publicity. Yes, I said acting lessons. You need not be a great actor, but you must know how to behave in front of a camera. So you see, I shall be making rather a large investment in you in terms of both time and money. You shall repay me when—note I say 'when' and not 'if'—Kingcrafts puts you under contract for the series. Meanwhile, our contract protects me. In view of all my efforts and expenses, I shall not want you to be decamping to some other agency. All actors are whores, you know."

"Don't take it for granted," said Steelegrave, offended. "My word is as good as anyone's."

"That's what you say now. Before you're up there."

"I had some small success at tennis. Got in the papers and everything."

"The picture business is different. For a part or a price or just to see his name in lights, any actor would bugger his very own mum. You'll come to that, too." Webley held up a hand to fend off the younger man's reply. "There's more. 'Richard Steelegrave' gives the impression of a man some fifty years old. All the up-and-coming lads today have names like Rock Hudson or Tab Hunter or even, for

God's sake, Rip Torn. We'll call you Rick Steele. There's a proper name for a star!"

"Hell, Webley! 'Richard Steelegrave' meant something in tennis. Why wouldn't it work for me now?"

"*Mister* Webley, please. We shall give out the news that Richard Steelegrave wants to start his film career with a clean slate. No trading on his popularity as an athlete! D'you see? You gain sympathy and a name that will fit on the marquee at the same time."

Steelegrave considered it. Well, why not? "Rick Steele" had a nice-enough ring to it.

"Another thing," the manager continued. "You will work hard at your classes; your schedule will be very busy. But some of your obligations will seem pleasant. I will arrange for you to escort some of the most beautiful girls in Hollywood. Young starlets, reaching for the top like yourself, and some established stars when I can manage it. You will not assault or molest any of them, unless they absolutely insist. Moreover, you will not go sodding about town drunk or belligerent. . . ."

Jesus! Shades of McReedy. "What do you take me for?"

"Every informed source assures me that you drank and screwed your way out of an outstanding career in tennis. I do not wish to preside over a repetition of failure. Believe me, if I hear of any scandal, I shall wash my hands of you." Webley rubbed his chubby paws together by way of illustration and leaned back in his upholstered chair, firing up his cold pipe. "Can we agree?"

Steelegrave stared at the man while he fished for cigarettes. He felt he needed to gain some control over the situation. "I think so. One or two things, though. I know you're a lot more than the obnoxious little fart you seem to be. At least, I give you the benefit of any doubts. So don't treat me like a simple-minded tennis bum, even if you think that's all I am. And don't call me a whore or a motherfucker unless you smile so widely I know you can't mean it. Other than that, I guess we can agree."

It was Max Weber who answered, without a trace of the droll British accent. "You get my respect when you earn it. It's a meat market out there, kid. I package and sell prime cut, not hamburger. Now, there's two ways to do this—my way or not at all. Your move."

Steelegrave had to smile. Well, he'd tried. "Let's see how it works out your way."

Webley rose, his jolly self again, and held out his hand. "Call me Malcolm from now on. Makes me feel bloody younger."

Steelegrave shook the hand and laughed out loud. He'd seen this kind of performance before. It was as if the spirit of McReedy had returned to squeeze itself into Webley's small frame.

4

Distracted by his memories, Steelegrave ran the light at Topanga Canyon, nearly sideswiping a tiger-striped van that was turning onto the coast highway. The bearded, ponytailed driver leaned on his horn so Steelegrave, who disliked hippies, gave him the finger and Junkyard turned on the seat to growl.

Bunny Berrigan gave way to the clean, clever horn of Harry James playing "When the Angels Sing" as Steelegrave pulled off the highway onto the parking lot of the Guardrail, a cool, dark tavern he used as a regular pit stop. It was one of the last places that still made Moscow Mules—iced vodka and ginger beer served in chilled copper mugs, garnished with a cucumber stick.

He had come to a full stop before he remembered that he wasn't going to drink today. And maybe never again. Last night's loss of memory had scared him. It was a symptom of the hopeless alcoholic, the wet-brain. Torn, he sat in the hot breath of the Santa Ana wind, sweating despite the arid heat, imagining he could hear the chime of ice cubes against glass and the intimate chuckle of the barflies. . . . What harm could a single drink do? Especially since there wasn't a living soul to witness his sacrifice if he passed.

With an effort, he wrenched the T-Bird into gear and peeled out onto the highway, jaw firmly set and eyes narrow, regretting the absence of a camera to record the moment (high angle shot on man and car, zooming to close-up). As he drove up Santa Monica Canyon the trumpet of Harry James reached the climactic finale of "When the Angels Sing" and Junkyard threw back his head to howl, not out of appreciation but because the high notes hurt his ears.

Steelegrave lived across Ocean Avenue from Palisades Park, a bluff overlooking the Pacific Coast Highway and the sea. He occupied one of six archaic bungalows that crouched amid a lot of greenery between a pair of towering, glassy condominiums. The units were thick-walled with high beamed ceilings giving the impression of space. Each had a yard in back hedged in by a fence of weathered wood smothered in ivy. Under an umbrella of olive trees that grew tight against the cottages and among the unkempt jungle spillage that threatened to overrun the walkways between, inhabitants could almost ignore the modern sentinels looming on either side. The owner was a very old party who cared nothing for additional wealth, but the little enclave would be doomed by his death, when his heirs planned to sell out, making room for yet another hulking condominium. Until then, the place was called "Wisteria Manor," though not a trace of that shrub could be found on the premises.

Steelegrave parked behind the buildings, where each tenant was assigned an open carport giving onto a narrow asphalt lane that bisected the block. He started to take out the tarpaulin he used to protect his car from the salt air, when it occurred to him that he might later visit Erin, if she were in a forgiving mood. So he closed the trunk again and walked to his door with Junkyard at his heel.

"Mr. Steelegrave?" A man stepped from behind the hedge directly into his path, making him stop abruptly and causing the dog to show his teeth. The man was faceless in the dark, wearing a light-colored suit.

"Yes?"

"I'm Cosgrove. West Los Angeles Police Station."

He proffered an open wallet displaying his badge and I.D., holding them at arm's length under the light by Steelegrave's door. Steelegrave looked at them carefully.

The man was indeed Detective Sergeant Ryan Cosgrove of LAPD.

"May I come in?" asked Cosgrove. In the light he was a ruddy man over medium height and heavily built with thinning orange hair. His suit fitted indifferently and his shoes were cheap, as if he felt such things didn't matter. The dye job seemed to be his only concession to vanity.

Steelegrave opened the door and gestured him in, but Cosgrove stepped carefully back and let the other man and the dog precede him. Once inside, he barely glanced at Steelegrave's furnishings—a few fine massive Spanish pieces, relics of another time, another place, that were incongruous here—before returning full attention to his host. He declined a chair, so Steelegrave remained standing with him, hoping it might somehow shorten the visit.

"You were married to Marla Monday," said Cosgrove, making it a flat statement.

"A long time ago, yes."

"Have you been listening to the radio this afternoon? Watching any TV?"

"No." Steelegrave began to feel uneasy. "What's the matter?"

"She was murdered. It's been all over the news for the last couple of hours. We don't yet have a suspect in custody."

Steelegrave moved automatically behind the bar. Without conscious thought, he poured Russian vodka into a glass and added ice cubes. He peeled a twist of lemon and dropped it into the drink. The detective watched him closely. His eyes were mere slits creased into the heavy face.

"When?"

"Late last night or early this morning. The coroner's people can't tell exactly. There wasn't enough blood left in the body."

"Jesus! What killed her? A vampire?" Steelegrave regretted the words the instant they were out.

Cosgrove stared at him. "She was found hanging naked upside down from some kind of ankle straps. The coroner says someone used a jagged knife to cut her throat. Slaughtered her like an animal."

Steelegrave blanched and sat down on a stool behind the bar. He drank down half of the vodka. He couldn't imagine anything like that happening to Marla. He had thought her indestructible. "Quit trying to spare my feelings and tell it like it is," he muttered.

Cosgrove shrugged. "Your attitude prompted mine. The coroner will probably make the official statement, since she was a star. He might put it more delicately. But I'm not here just to bring you a death notice, Mr. Steelegrave. I have some questions to ask."

"Am I a suspect?"

"You were once her husband and you are now her sole heir. We have a clear duty to investigate. There was no robbery, so we must consider other motives."

Steelegrave's jaw must have fallen open.

"You didn't know you were her heir?"

"No. . . ."

"The will was drawn less than a month ago. Dieter Greim, he   whatever, witnessed it. He also found the body   d called us. He's a naturalized citizen of German desc nt. Intelligent type."

"I remember Dieter and Lotte."

"His wife's dead now. Diabetes, he told me. Anyway, it's quite an estate your ex-wife left you—that mansion, a yacht, cars, stocks, cash. . . . We already have a rundown from her lawyer."

"Why would she leave it to me?" Steelegrave said, mostly to himself, and gulped the rest of the vodka. He reached for the bottle to pour more. "Care for a drink?" he asked as an afterthought.

Cosgrove shook his head, but something shifted behind his eyes. Steelegrave recognized it for what it was. Thirst. "Now, that's what we wondered," the detective went on. "Why an ex-husband, long since divorced? It would seem more logical if she left it to her kid, wouldn't it? Except she didn't approve of his life-style, Greim says. Can't say I blame her. He's a weirdo. Queer as a square grape. Lives in a dump in Venice."

"I haven't seen him since we were married. Then, maybe three times. He was eight or nine. Marla fired him off to private school in winter and camp in summer. Shy, good-looking little kid. I tried to get close to him, but he wanted no part of me. There was never enough time anyway."

"He remembers not liking you. Doesn't recall his father at all."

"I asked Marla about him once. She said he was a fisherman and he was lost at sea. She was married to him when she was pretty young."

"The kid is bitter about the inheritance going to you. He thinks you'd kill for it." Cosgrove's slitted eyes were unreadable, the pupils invisible behind pods of flesh.

Steelegrave managed a shrug. "I didn't even know about it. Anyway, I don't think I'll sign it over to him." He still couldn't bring himself to believe any of this. This great hulking cop would turn into a practical joker with a dimestore badge any second now.

"Of course, it won't do you much good if you killed her. Or if you come under indictment. The city administrator will get an order to padlock the house, inventory all assets, put the estate under his own or a proxy's administration until a legitimate heir can be found." The detective's gimlet eyes never left Steelegrave.

"That seems fair enough." Spoken as an innocent man. The liquor was taking hold.

"Where were you last night?"

Steelegrave looked at him blankly. Where, indeed? "Right here," he said, recovering. "I had some drinks. Watched a movie."

"What movie?"

"An old one of mine." He pointed at the Betamax next to his TV set, slightly embarrassed. "I play them once in a while for laughs."

That, at least, was true. He remembered shoving in the cassette after a lot of drinks, watching the beginning of *Fall Guy*, starring Rick Steele and Beverly Blaine, and introducing Marla Monday. . . .

The detective went over and took the cartridge out of the videotape recorder, staring at the handwritten titles. Marla's name did not appear. "I've seen some of your pictures, but not this one."

"It looks pretty dated now."

Cosgrove put the cartridge back. "I used to watch *Love-*

Forty. It was a good series. You could like it even if you didn't give a damn for tennis. Why did you change your name back to Steelegrave? Was it the accident?"

"That can't have much to do with your investigation." Steelegrave couldn't talk about the accident.

"Maybe not. But this does. Who can testify that you were here last night? All night."

A good question, that. "Sergeant, if I'm a suspect, then I'm entitled to an attorney. Either arrest me or let me go and piss." Steelegrave stood up.

Cosgrove barely nodded. Steelegrave could feel the detective's eyes on the back of his neck as he strode out of the room. Inside the bathroom he urinated copiously, then splashed cold water on his face and combed his hair to gain time. Everything was moving too fast for him. Marla murdered and himself a suspect! Where the hell had he been last night? Of course, he hadn't killed Marla, but Jesus, it would be nice to know for sure. He had alternately loved and hated her enough at one time or another to do just about anything.

In the bedroom, he found a pack of Nat Sherman's and lit one before coming back out. There was no one in the living room except Junkyard, lying watchfully in front of the hearth. For an instant Steelegrave thought Cosgrove must have gone outside; then he heard a grunt from the kitchen as though someone had been punched in the stomach. The detective emerged holding a knife cushioned on a handkerchief. From where he stood, Steelegrave could see that it had a serrated blade about five inches long, the kind used by commercial fishermen. And that the blade was not clean.

Cosgrove turned the knife over, gazing down at it. "Stains that look like blood. You did a lousy job of cleaning it. Just racked it up along with your kitchen knives. That's really sick, Steelegrave."

"That thing isn't mine."

It isn't? Well, then, who delivered it to your kitchen, the tooth fairy?"

"I'm telling you I haven't got any knives like that."

Cosgrove came closer to him. He extended the knife,

handle first, his tiny eyes fixed on Steelegrave. "You could be mistaken. Maybe you'd like a closer look. Go ahead . . . take it."

Steelegrave didn't move. "I don't need to. I can see it's not mine."

The detective carefully rewrapped the knife in his handkerchief and dropped it into a pocket. "I'm going to have to take you in."

"You can't just walk in here without a warrant or anything," Steelegrave ventured, hoping he was right.

"Maybe not in the movies." Cosgrove produced handcuffs from a leather case at his belt. "Get your hands out in front of you."

Steelegrave balked. "Look, you don't need those things—"

"Get those hands out!"

Steelegrave stood still. Menace seemed to emanate from the heavy man. It would be dangerous to be his prisoner, chained and helpless.

"Are you resisting arrest?" Cosgrove said very softly, his hand moving toward his belt again.

In that instant Steelegrave thought he saw everything. This had to be some kind of a setup. He took a step forward. "Christ knows why, but someone planted that goddamn knife!"

Cosgrove let the handcuffs fall with a clatter and pulled out his service revolver. He jerked it up, aiming for the heart.

"Freeze!"

Steelegrave stared at the gun, appalled. With no sound other than the scrabble of his paws seeking purchase on the parquet floor, Junkyard launched himself at Cosgrove and caught the offending arm that held the revolver between his jaws. The detective cried out and staggered back, his arm forced down by the weight of the animal. The thirty-eight fell on the floor next to the handcuffs. Junkyard, who had obviously been trained as an attack dog with an antipathy for firearms at some time in his past, hung on to Cosgrove's arm, staring him straight in the eye between glances back at his master for further instruction.

"Get him off me," Cosgrove said in a deadly voice, but

he stood still and wisely made no move to recover his revolver.

"Look, I didn't even know he could do that. . . ."

"Call him off!" Cosgrove tried to pull free.

Junkyard growled and shook his massive head until the detective subsided.

"You're a dead man," said Cosgrove.

"Shit," said Steelegrave, and plunged out the front door.

He ran down the concrete pathway between the bungalows and skidded around a corner to the carports, rejoicing that he had left the tarp off the T-Bird. He leapt behind the wheel without opening the door, fired the engine, and backed wildly into the narrow lane. Just before he shot forward, a great weight landed clumsily on the seat and he turned to see his dog scrambling for balance beside him. Which meant that Cosgrove was free.

As Steelegrave roared down the alley toward the street, he heard a sharp explosion behind him and the metallic impact of a bullet against some part of his car. He fought back an impulse to dive under the dashboard and cranked the car through the turn onto the main street, bouncing over a curb before he could straighten out and shove the gas pedal to the floor.

Far behind him Cosgrove stood cursing, gun in hand. He was dismayed that he had fired his weapon in a populated area other than in self-defense. Thank God the round had hit the car rather than going wild. But the son of a bitch had loosed a goddamn dog on him!

An elderly man who had come out to investigate poked his head around the corner, saw Cosgrove standing there with the gun, and trotted back to his bungalow. Cosgrove holstered his weapon and walked rapidly back to Steelegrave's unit. He phoned the station, giving terse orders to have the suspect picked up, describing the man and his vehicle. Then he searched the place thoroughly. He learned that Steelegrave had a fine wardrobe, drank good liquor, and collected photographic memorabilia of what must have been a colorful career. He took an album of pictures and the cassette of *Fall Guy* with him when he left.

*   *   *

Steelegrave sped along San Vicente Boulevard feeling painfully exposed in the conspicuous car with the big dog sitting beside him. He was stunned by the events that had conspired against him. An hour ago he had nothing more than a hangover to worry about; now he was a fugitive people felt free to shoot at! There was only one place he could go, and he might not even be welcome there. But he couldn't turn himself in, either. Not while he couldn't remember anything about last night. . . .

Yesterday (was it just yesterday?) had been Sunday, his day off. He arose at nine, late for him, and lounged around reading the paper. He had nothing to do until late afternoon, then just a movie and dinner at a Japanese restaurant with Erin. Hot as it was, he decided to get some exercise.

Muscle Beach was a patch of sand near the Santa Monica pier that had once been a training area for body builders. Now it provided a place in the sun for local characters, bums, and a variety of hustlers and pushers. But the high bars, parallels, and rings were still in place, sunk in concrete so they couldn't be stolen, and Steelegrave used it as an outdoor gym.

He had the equipment to himself in the midday heat. An old bag lady shuffled past, checking the trashcans; a derelict slept it off in the shade of a ratty palm tree. The hot wind from the desert, unusual this late in the year, had blown the smog out to sea, where it lurked over Catalina, leaving the air around him clear and dry. Steelegrave did an hour of gym routines and then ran for four miles along the water's edge. He finished his workout with a swim and drove home, refreshed.

By the time he had showered and changed, it was after one o'clock. He was hungry and the Santa Ana wind made him feel restless, so he drove down Ocean Avenue toward Venice to have lunch and watch the street people. A rare parking place opened up on Washington Avenue near the beach and he slipped into it. In front of him sprawled a saloon called the Lair that looked as though it were built entirely out of driftwood, and he went in for a drink. Just one.

The place was gloomy and smelled of urinal deodorant.

It was barely cooled by the ceiling fans, and the few customers looked like hard-core drinkers. Steelegrave sat at the bar and lit his first cigarette of the day. The bartender had never heard of Moscow Mules, so he settled for a vodka-tonic. The stool next to him was empty, but a shot of whiskey and a bottle of beer waited on the bar.

A moment later a tall, beefy man came out of the toilet buttoning his fly and sat down next to Steelegrave. He had a pale, sweaty face, a fringe of ginger-colored hair, and close-set round blue eyes. He downed the whiskey, chased it with half of his beer, looked around, and belched. The blue eyes finally came to rest on Steelegrave and studied him carefully for a full minute.

"Rick Steele, ain'tcha?" the man finally asked. The question didn't surprise Steelegrave. He was still occasionally recognized in bars and restaurants.

"Richard Steelegrave," he answered.

The other stared awhile longer. "One and the same, though. Right?"

"Yeah."

The man finished his beer and pounded his mug on the bar for service. The bartender, who had been reading a paper, walked over in slow motion.

"Gimme another Seagram's and a beer. And a drink for my friend here."

Steelegrave held up his hand. "No, thanks."

The bartender went to fill the order. Again the round blue eyes peered steadily at Steelegrave. When the man's drinks were served, he said to the bartender, "You know something? Most celebrities are snotty pricks. They don't like to drink with working stiffs like you and me."

No one said anything. Steelegrave sighed. He had been through this before.

"Especially," the man went on, "ex-celebrities. You know the kind. Has-beens. Fuck-ups."

Steelegrave considered finishing his drink and leaving, then changed his mind. This slob was not going to run him out.

"What I mean, has-beens are assholes. Or they wouldn't be has-beens. Take, for instance, a tennis bum with a pretty face that gets lucky and goes Hollywood. Makes big bucks for a few years. Because some folks get off on faggoty-looking guys with pretty faces. But then he fucks up and goes down the tube. Now, that's gotta be an asshole. Am I right?"

The bartender turned his back and walked away. No one at the bar was paying attention. Deprived of his audience, the big man addressed Steelegrave. "You run over anybody lately?" he sneered.

Steelegrave felt the shock ripple through his body, but didn't let it show. "Got me an old nun trying to make it across the street the other day," he replied pleasantly. "But that's only worth about two points."

He picked up his drink and walked to a small table, sat down, and lit another cigarette. The bastard was making him smoke.

It was no use. The big man followed him, towering over the table, fierce blue eyes staring out of the meaty red face. As Steelegrave turned in his chair to face him, he said, "You know, there's only one thing I hate more than a faggoty has-been tennis player, unless maybe it's a faggoty has-been actor, and that's a goddamn murderer!"

Steelegrave let the cigarette fall from his fingers to the floor. He slipped out of his chair and knelt as though to retrieve it, shifting his weight carefully. Then he clenched his fist and brought it up, followed by all of his weight, into the crotch of his tormentor. The fat man folded over upon himself, clutching at his genitals, his mouth forming the letter O. Steelegrave looked down at the folds of porcine flesh above the man's collar with total hatred. He raised his fists above his head, crossed his wrists, and brought his arms down with all his strength. The big man collapsed, his head coming to rest on Steelegrave's Gucci-clad foot. Steelegrave moved back in distaste, turned, and walked to the bar. He took out a ten-dollar bill and proffered it to the bartender.

"You wanna leave an address or anything?" the bartender said, making change for the money. "You know, in case he's dead or something?"

Steelegrave left two dollars on the bar and walked out. He was shaking by the time he reached his car. At that moment he fervently hoped the bastard *was* dead, no matter what the consequences.

He drove up the coast to Malibu, home territory. The Guardrail, of course, made excellent Moscow Mules, but he hardly tasted them. He drank several, feeling secure in familiar surroundings but not wanting to talk to anyone. He should have known better than to go to a dive full of deadbeats in Venice. There had been this kind of trouble before.

He recalled sitting at a table alone, drinking and watching the sun set, suddenly remembering that it was time to pick up Erin. Even at this stage, he was sober enough to realize that he was much too drunk to go out with Erin. Or even talk to her on the phone. Erin would not be tolerant of his condition; there would be an argument, a scene. Better to wait until tomorrow, think up an elaborate story to tell her. He didn't want to hurt her feelings. He loved her . . . or something like that. She had certainly suffered enough because of him. Dwelling on his mistreatment of Erin, that decent, lovely girl, made him swallow hard. He called for another drink. Just straight vodka on the rocks this time. Stolichnaya, please. . . .

Then he was at home, stumbling around the kitchen under Junkyard's disdainful gaze, trying to prepare his dog's dinner. He almost certainly had another vodka after that. To hold him while he watched the movie. *Fall Guy.* His first feature film—and introducing Marla Monday. He remembered shoving in the cartridge, watching the film up to the part, early in the picture, where he comes home and catches her with another man. He beats hell out of the other guy (Steelegrave noticed that the fight scene was well-choreographed and would hold up even by today's standards) and tosses him down the stairs. Then, before walking out himself, he slaps the girl. Just before the slap, he remembered freezing the frame—right there at the moment of conflict—trying to recapture something.

That was his last recollection. Had he passed out? Not likely. Not in the living room, at least, for he had awakened in bed the next morning, naked. And where in hell had that knife come from? It was no use. He was still drawing a blank.

He drove east on Sunset, more sedately now to avoid attention, but he still felt like a slow-moving target. The word would be out to pick him up by now. He probably had only minutes to get where he was going. If only he had never met Marla Monday. . . .

5

Rick Steele's early career was accurately if unoriginally described by the tabloids as "meteoric" and "explosive," an authentic overnight success. By the summer of 1958, two months after meeting Malcolm Webley, he had a bachelor apartment in Hollywood, a ~~~~~-made wardrobe, and the bright green T-Bird (Wel~~~~ had balked at buying the Jag he would have preferred, all courtesy of his manager. In August it was announced that he would star as "Hawke" in King-crafts' new hour-long series to be called *Love–Forty*, and the popular press as well as the trades featured his face everywhere. True to his word, Webley provided a handpicked selection of starlets and established actresses to parade through his public life. As agreed, he neither assaulted nor molested any of them. Unless they absolutely insisted.

He had only one problem. A chilling one. For a while, it seemed that he couldn't act.

Webley had placed him with Stella Harvey, an acting coach with an impressive alumni of stars, for a crash course in learning his new art. He took private lessons five mornings a week and joined her intermediate and advanced classes on every other evening. Afternoons were given over to riding and fencing, skills Rick mastered quickly, being a natural athlete. Acting, however, was a different challenge altogether.

For a while, he didn't think he could do it. Neither did anyone else.

Stella Harvey's teaching system blended technical acting with heavy doses of the "method." With the Strasberg school being the current fad, there seemed no escaping the grunt-and-scratch approach favored by Marlon Brando and his ilk. Having to perform improvisations, portraying a falling leaf or a snowflake, producing hysterical laughter or tears on demand, brought Rick to the edge of panic. He sweated profusely, or turned white, or simply froze. He took to wearing baggy chinos instead of fashionably tight jeans to hide the shaking of his legs. His peers, who had held him in awe as a famous athlete tapped to star in a series, delighted in scourging him during the oral critiques that followed individual performances. Worst of all, he couldn't understand this weakness in order to solve it. Competitive tennis, whether pro or amateur, was a high-stress game and he had always played well under pressure. He couldn't seem to play this new game at all.

He stood in the glare of stage lights, facing a hostile class seated before him in a semicircle of descending rows. Stella Harvey, waving her ever-present cigarette, presided from the center of the top row. Next to him stood Melody, the lovely extrovert with whom he had just performed an improvisational exercise.

"Do you have any thoughts on this to share with Rick and Melody, Lorraine?" said Stella Harvey by way of opening the commentary.

"It was a good improv for you, Melody," said an earnest girl with close-set eyes. "I got your intention right away. You wanted him to stay home tonight and make love to you instead of going out with the boys. Lots of meaning and strong motivation. I really got off on it." She looked at Rick. "Rick . . . I just don't know what to say. You looked trapped. Like you were scared or something and just wanted to get away. . . ."

Amen, thought Rick.

"He was shaking like a dog shitting razor blades," observed someone, provoking moderate laughter.

"That's not constructive, Dwayne," said Stella Harvey from her perch, blowing cigarette smoke at the offender.

No one else was allowed to smoke in class. "But Lorraine has a point, Rick. I couldn't tell where you were going either. . . ."

There was more, in the same vein.

Conventional assignments were no easier. He stumbled through a scene from *Death of a Salesman*, playing Biff, one of Willy Loman's sons, dropping a football he was supposed to handle with dexterity and then scrambling around the floor to find it. After that, he drew a blank and lost his lines.

"You're never going to get closer than that to perfect casting," said Dwayne, a youth with acne and a weight problem, during the postmortem. "Biff is just like you— the all-American Jock, good-looking, and not too bright. You should have been able to reach down into your own guts and come up with Biff. But, Jesus, you just stood there. . . ."

Rick stared past his tormentors at the tiny brunette who never criticized him or anyone else. Secure in her own unquestionable talent, used to hearing herself praised in superlatives by everyone including Stella Harvey herself, she just didn't give a damn about the others. She was witnessing his humiliation indifferently, a trace of amusement in the curve of her pretty mouth. Her coarse black hair was worn carelessly short and she had lovely, chiseled features, a dimpled chin and dark eyes under uneven brows that gave her a slightly skeptical look. Rick resented her fully as much as he did the others.

She caught up with him after class as he slunk out of the studio onto LaBrea Avenue, darkly determined never to return.

"I have an idea that might help you, friend," she said. Rick saw that she barely came up to his shoulder.

"Your trouble is nerves," the girl went on, stating the obvious. "So you need something that will eliminate them or kind of put them in limbo while you're out there naked in front of the world."

Rick looked down at her. "My, you are a small one, aren't you?" he said. Small but in exquisite proportion, he noticed.

The girl shrugged, unoffended. "So is Elizabeth Taylor.

So is Natalie Wood. Look, I'm trying to help. My advice is to get yourself some Miltowns. M-i-l-t-o-w-n-s. Take a couple half an hour before you go on. It will help with the shakes."

"Is that what you do?"

"I don't need to." He watched her walk away and get into a battered little Volkswagen.

The same night he called Malcolm Webley. "Get me out of that flaky class," he begged his manager.

"Now, now," Webley soothed him. "Keep a stiff upper lip, my lad. Everything is going swimmingly, right on schedule. But Stella Harvey tells me you need help and she can provide it. We haven't a great deal of time to dither about, you know. So kindly apply yourself. There's quite a lot at stake."

Rick groaned and hung up.

In the morning, he drove up into the Hollywood Hills for his scheduled session with Stella Harvey. Her house, a vintage stucco painted flamingo pink, was near the summit of Crescent Heights Road. Instead of sending the Mexican girl who kept house, she greeted him at the door herself, wearing only a floor-length dressing gown. Her hair was brushed down over her shoulders, softening her face, and she crushed out her cigarette before coming over to stand close to him.

"Maid's day off," she said. "It's just as well. We aren't going to have our regular class today." Just over forty now, she had been a B-picture actress until a decade ago, when she found that her real talent lay in teaching. She had done well. Important producers came to audition her showcases and her name was respected in the film industry. The anteroom they stood in was hung with autographed pictures of former pupils who had gone on to greater glory.

Divested of her tailored suit and the strict upswept coiffure, she seemed remote from the disciplinarian who presided over his onstage agonies. She was plump with a shallow curve of belly, but her breasts were firm against his chest, as were the haunches he caressed under the satin gown. Her lips were yielding, without the hard urgency of Louann MacIver's. What had made him think of Louann? The age factor, he supposed. It was enough to make him hesitate. He had sworn off women like Louann.

"Don't tease me, Rick," she murmured against his mouth, reaching for him, making it easy for him to persuade himself she really had nothing in common with Louann.

They moved together to her bedroom, where she pushed him back on a canopied four-poster the size of a playground. "Lie still," she said.

Rick did so, making only the moves necessary to help her undress him. She removed his clothes slowly, making the act a ritual.

"Now," she breathed when she had finished, "try to stay . . . uninterested, for as long as possible. No matter what I do. Think of it as an exercise, an improvisation we are doing together."

"Now who's teasing?"

She didn't reply and he accepted the scenario, intrigued. He closed his eyes so as not to see her nakedness, which, far from being gross, was lush and sensual. He imagined himself on the tennis court at Forest Hills, getting ready to play a sudden-death point, going for the big one.

Her fingers and lips played across his body, feather-light, like warm snowflakes to begin with, then gradually becoming ever more insistent. A faint whimper began far back in her throat and it was less her practiced ministrations than the sound which began to undo him. He felt himself rise and harden, felt her lips descend on him, and heard her delighted giggle.

He sat up and caught her hard by the shoulders, pushing her over and pinning her beneath him. "You win," he said.

As he brought his weight down, she opened to him, as ready as he for the last act, the rhythmic, pulsing climb toward a moment of intense mutual pleasure.

"Let's talk about you," she said through the smoke of her postcoital cigarette.

Rick said nothing.

"I don't understand you," she went on. "You have all the tools—looks, physical grace, reasonable intelligence. You've been in the public eye for years. Yet you stiffen up and become practically catatonic in front of my class. How can they intimidate you so?"

Rick thought about it. He reached for her cigarette and took a deep drag. "They don't. I get disgusted with myself. I played tennis for years. And I was good at it. I concentrated on the game, to hell with the people in the stands."

"Then do the same thing in class. I couldn't ask for more."

"It's not the same. In tennis, win or lose, I never felt like a fool. Clowning around in front of those snotty bastards in your class makes me feel like a complete horse's ass. I just can't laugh or scream or cry when someone tells me to."

"Don't take it out on my kids. They are serious and talented or they would not be in the class. You're an exception, a special case. They resent you because you've had a career handed to you. They think they've got more talent than you'll ever have, and they know they will never, never have your kind of chance. So they don't make it easy for you."

"Set it up so I can go three rounds with Dwayne Upmann right there onstage and I'll give you a memorable performance."

She rolled over and propped her chin on her hand, bringing her face close to his. "You've got to take this seriously. I don't put you through these exercises to make you look foolish. I'm trying to make it possible for you to release yourself and present more than one dimension to an audience."

"I've read all about the character I'll be playing. He's pretty one-dimensional. At least he never breaks into tears or runs around screaming like a demented pansy. Why can't I work within the character I'll be doing? The biggest stars on screen play themselves. Over and over. It seems to work."

"Yes, but *you* can't play yourself. In person, you've got that X quality every producer looks for. It made me want to go to bed with you. I didn't do that to give you confidence, as I'd like to pretend. I did it because I wanted to, from the beginning. And I cringed to think you would reject me for being older, or for some other reason.

"But onstage you seize up like a vapor-locked engine.

All the assignments that seem so bizarre to you are designed to make you turn yourself loose so that your quality can come out. Gable, Cooper, even John Wayne—the stars that just seem to play themselves—all have their character at their fingertips. They can turn it all on in an instant and make it look easy. It isn't. It takes work and motivation."

Rick sighed, dejected. She was right, of course. But it didn't help to know that, if he couldn't bring himself to shed the panic and self-consciousness he felt when called upon to perform.

To change the subject, he stroked the slight swell of her belly and felt her shudder under his touch. "Let's work on today's assignment. I want to get it right."

She moved so as to be above him, and remained poised there for a moment, grasping and stroking him with her free hand. Then she lowered herself upon him slowly . . . up and then down again, luxuriating.

"Oh, yes," she said, many times more than once.

When he was miscast as the half-witted Lenny in a scene from Steinbeck's *Of Mice and Men*, he followed the dark-haired girl's suggestion and took two Miltown tablets chased with several bottles of beer just before going to the studio. He was made of rubber by the time his scene was called.

At least he didn't get the shakes. He staggered and drooled and mumbled, but he didn't shake. When the scene was finished and he stood before the class wearing an idiot's grin, the spittle drying on his chin, everyone thought he was still playing Lenny and there was general applause.

"That was very interesting, Rick," said Stella Harvey, clearly puzzled. "Broad, too broad, perhaps. Lenny was a simpleton, not a psychopath. But you're giving us something we haven't seen from you before. Something of yourself."

"Far-out. All the way out," said Lorraine, meaning it as a compliment.

Dwayne Upmann said nothing.

Rick, intent on remaining upright, received his very first kudos as an actor calmly. He looked around for the black-haired girl, but she was not there tonight. What the hell was her name? Marla something. . . .

He never came to the class again. It was time to go to work.

The pilot of *Love–Forty* was shot in November and December of 1958 in the form of a one-hour TV show and then lengthened by the insertion of largely superfluous action scenes to qualify it as a full-length feature. This innovation on the part of King-crafts studios gave the film much more exposure and profit potential and was soon to be emulated by the competition.

On the first day of shooting, there was considerable tension on the set. The producer, the director, the cast, and Malcolm Webley (from the sidelines) were in a state of suspense wondering whether Rick Steele, an unknown quantity, would be able to carry the show.

Lars Vincent, the director, started him out easy. The morning was spent shooting a tennis sequence, which presented no problem for Rick, who felt at home in motion. After lunch he was slated for a short confrontational scene coming off the courts with Lang Desmond, a veteran of the early talkies who was costarring as his boss.

It took all afternoon. Rick was uneasy and it showed. They were shooting on location and the amount of equipment and personnel involved was daunting. There were vehicles for sanitary facilities, wardrobe, and commissary, a jungle of cables and reflectors, the scurrying crew of technicians. As an athlete he had ignored camera crews. They were an entity somewhere in the stands with the sole function of following his play. Now he had to romance the camera, hit his marks accurately, languish between setups. It seemed a hell of a lot more time was spent catering to the equipment than to the actor.

They finally got through it by favoring Desmond on camera most of the time, and the older actor easily stole the scene. No one criticized Rick. But when they wrapped for the day, Desmond followed him back to the trailer King-crafts had provided for his comfort. The older man produced a flask from his pocket and poured Jack Daniel's into a pair of coffee cups.

Lang Desmond was a handsome man in his early fifties who still resembled the swashbuckler Rick remembered from the films of his youth. His face was somewhat eroded by drink but the dark hair was still thick, parted near the middle and sleeked back in the fashion of a bygone generation of stars.

"To success, pappy," said the older man, draining his cup. "For your success is my success. And all of our success."

"Success." Rick barely wet his lips. His stomach was tied in knots.

"*Love–Forty* can go forever," Desmond went on. "It has good scripting, a big budget, production values, and a hell of a director in Vincent."

"But in the end it's up to me, is that what you're saying?" Rick finished the bourbon and grimaced.

"Yeah."

"I'm gonna do my best."

"Which gives you an A for effort, sport. But what I saw out there this afternoon just ain't gonna fly. They practically had to shoot around you."

Rick didn't know what to say.

Desmond sighed. "I hear you went to one of those cockamamie acting schools that turn out a bunch of fairies like Brando and Montgomery Clift. Now, their stuff might work onstage or in movies with a long shooting schedule, but for TV we work damn fast. You haven't got time to lock yourself in the crapper and jack off or flog yourself or whatever it is they teach you to do to work up your motivation. Your motivation is you're getting over two grand a show. So first you're going to have to forget all the Actor's Studio bullshit you ever learned."

He flashed a sudden charming smile that took the sting out of his words, and poured liquor into their cups. "Then I'm going to try to resist doing all the stuff I did to you this afternoon like stepping on your lines, blocking your light, or diverting attention from your big scene by scratching my balls or staring off into space—all the stuff that comes natural to me because I've been doing it since before you were born."

"Thanks. I'd appreciate that."

"But that won't help you with George Barth, who plays the heavy. You haven't met old George yet, but I've worked with him before and he's a sly fox. Give him a chance, he'll wipe you off the screen."

"How do I handle something like that?" asked Rick when they had downed their drinks.

"You've just got to learn to dominate the scene. Try this. When you're eyeball to eyeball with old George, assume you're carrying a club and he's a snake. Soon as he crawls all the way out of his hole, you're going to smash him flat. That gives you an attitude that shows in the eyes."

"That sounds like Actor's Studio to me." Rick held out his cup and Desmond filled it.

"Whatever works, use it." Desmond raised his cup. "Here's to squashing old George, the snake."

"To George."

They drained their cups. Rick felt the liquor working within him, untying the knots. "I'm gonna flatten him."

"Fucking A."

"Act circles around him."

"No." Desmond leaned forward. "I'm going to teach you a lot of actors' tricks, but it's not going to make you an actor. I'm not an actor either, and I've got over a hundred pictures to prove it. Leave acting to pansies like Brando and Clift. You're going to be a personality. You're going to be Hawke! Actually become him. See? You're going to talk like him, think like him, live like him!"

"I'm gonna be Hawke."

Desmond poured the last of the bourbon, and they finished it. "You're already Hawke," said Desmond. "And I'm Travers, your boss, who can't control you. You know, you really piss me off sometimes, Hawke."

"I piss *you* off? Your dumb ideas get me in dangerous situations. A guy could get killed listening to you."

Desmond got up and grabbed Rick by his shirt collar, hauling him out of his chair. "You get in trouble because you always got to do it your way instead of going by the book. Now, hear this! I run this outfit and I'm tired of taking crap from you."

Rick broke his grip and shoved him back, bouncing him

off the thin skin of the trailer. "You're a feather merchant,
Travers, a lightweight. You're twenty years out of date.
I'd operate a lot better with you out of my hair."

Desmond aimed a punch at his chin, but Rick ducked
and charged, tackling the older man around the waist and
slamming him against the door, which gave way, spilling
them both out onto the wet ground in front of the trailer.

The grips who were striking the set stopped work to
stare at them. Lars Vincent came running over in alarm.

Rick rolled onto his knees and drew back his fist.

"But remember that way down deep, you love me as a
father," Desmond said hastily. "We have a lot of laughs
together, and once I saved your life."

"What the fuck is going on here?" cried the director,
standing over them. Vincent was rarely profane.

Desmond raked the dark hair out of his eyes. "He's just
getting into the part, Lars."

Rick dropped his arm and sat back in the dirt, grinning.
"I think I'm going to like being Hawke," he said.

At the end of the first week of shooting, everyone who
had anything to do with making *Love–Forty* breathed a
collective sigh of relief. Rick Steele, who had been reduced
to panic in Stella Harvey's classes, was remarkably effective on film. The rushes revealed a confident man, tough
but charming and not without humor, who could appeal to
both sexes. He had no trouble with Barth or any other
actor; he challenged them, staying on top of every scene as
Desmond had taught him.

Rick found he could handle the camera, as he could not
a live and critical audience. Moreover, he had an able
director, skilled writers, and a supportive cast, all of whom
had every reason to want the series to succeed. He had the
security of retakes, the protection of camera angles, clever
editing.

Lang Desmond stayed close to him, teaching him the
techniques of the craft, drinking and chasing girls with
him. To each other they were always Hawke and Travers,
making a game of it.

Love–Forty was released in the autumn of 1959, a slick
hour-long series that captured the public imagination im-

mediately and climbed rapidly in the ratings. Rick found himself a star overnight, as much an idol of the teeny-boppers as Robert Wagner or Troy Donahue. In addition to youthful good looks, he had a mature quality that gave him wider appeal, and *Love–Forty*, cynical and sexy for its day, was primarily adult fare.

Gradually, without conscious effort, Rick began to integrate the character of Hawke with his own. He started to pattern his speech after Hawke's dialogue, adopt mannerisms the writers had created for the character he portrayed. He used his own wardrobe and car when playing Hawke on screen. The green T-Bird became a trademark around Hollywood and Beverly Hills and he had to use the Jag he had bought on his own when he wanted to travel less conspicuously. He and Hawke became indistinguishable.

Desmond, caught up in their game, encouraged the fiction. He felt a proprietary interest in Rick's success, and anyway, knocking around town with a new star made him feel young again.

Rick earned $2,500 an episode—each episode taking ten days to shoot during the off-season hiatus. It seemed like good money to him and like peanuts to Webley. With the series doing so well, the manager was already looking forward to renegotiation. He also wanted to find a vehicle that would introduce his client to the big screen. Gilbert LaFarge, a talented young writer with some good credits, had a script called *Fall Guy*, a tight little action story about an army officer who returns from Korea to find his beautiful young wife with another man. He leaves her but she is immediately murdered and he becomes the prime suspect. Webley wanted to change the title to *Hawke* and let the story chronicle the adventures of that character before he became a government agent masquerading as a tennis bum. LaFarge agreed to everything but the title change and rewrote the principal charactor as Hawke. Lars Vincent was persuaded to direct, and Lang Desmond (with his hair slightly mussed) was signed to play Sergeant Dade, Hawke's wartime buddy. Beverly Blaine, an established talent, was cast as his true love, the girl he should have married in the first place. Rick Steele was launched into feature films with a script tailored for him, surrounded by familiar faces, with all the advantages—just as Malcolm Webley had planned it. Diversity of roles could come later, when Rick was established and ready to handle it. Webley was taking no chances for the time being.

Fall Guy also introduced a young actress in the small but excellent part of the unfaithful wife. Malcolm Webley had discovered her in a Stella Harvey showcase. Her name was Marla Monday.

6

Erin Englund shrugged the straps from her shoulders and peeled the mauve leotards down over her exquisite dancer's legs the moment she got home, marched into the shower, shampooed her casually cut auburn hair, and let the hot needle spray play over the small of her back and roll down the cleft between her firm buttocks. She stayed in the shower much longer than usual hoping the drilling heat would act as therapy.

It didn't do much good; she was still profoundly depressed. For once the small house, usually a reliable source of joy and sanctuary, seemed merely a lonely place. Toweling herself in the living room, she looked at the only ashtray in the house, placed, for Richard's convenience, next to the comfortable leather chair he liked to sit in. It made her as angry at herself as she was with him to realize that, unworthy as he was, he could upset her so.

She had nursed her anger all through the unending day, giving her classes in a desultory manner that could not have passed unnoticed by her students. It was not that she was in love with Richard Steelegrave—no one could accuse her of such an excess of bad taste—but she had become used to him. And it seemed reasonable to believe that he had some feeling for her. That he should simply overlook her, without so much as a phone call to tell one of the lies that came so easily to his lips, was more than her pride was ready to bear. Last night would have marked exactly one year since

they had met, and they were going to celebrate the occasion.
Nothing elaborate, just dinner, a few laughs, and perhaps
some protracted lovemaking. He had neither shown up,
nor called, nor answered his telephone.

Erin stalked naked into the kitchen and poured herself a
glass of Dubonnet, a sure sign of her agitation, since she
never drank alone. She left that to Richard, a hopeless
alcoholic by her abstemious standards. Worse still, he
smoked cigarettes, a habit he struggled bravely to control
in her presence, but nonetheless one that polluted his own
body and the air around him. So she had been dealing
with an unreliable, mendacious alcoholic almost twenty
years older than she who smoked cigarettes and had, as far
as she could see, a very doubtful future. It was common
knowledge, though he never spoke of it to her, that he had
forfeited his career and fortune in a drunken automobile
accident years ago. Ironically, she had mourned for him
herself at the time, as no doubt had a majority of teenage
girls in America. Had anyone told Erin Englund at fourteen that she would someday be the lover of Rick Steele,
she would have swooned. Well, she would be glad to
testify to the difference between illusion and reality.

Almost exactly a year ago, Erin had been invited to play
tennis at the Malibu Tennis Club by her friend and pupil
Marjorie Meeker. Marjorie was a wealthy lady in her
forties who had grown children and little else to do but
indulge her passion for athletics. She was a ropy, nut-
brown woman who managed to look awkward even while
excelling at any given sport. Aware of her problem, she
attended Erin's dance class and strove fervently to attain a
measure of grace. She accomplished all the movements and
exercises with ease—while giving the impression that she
was about to fall on her face.

Erin was a strong player, making the women a good
match for each other, but Marjorie was finally able to win
a tie-breaker after a long, hard set. They left the court in a
pleasant state of weariness and were heading for the clubhouse and some refreshment when Erin noticed the pro on
a nearby court giving lessons to an obese teenage boy. He

was lobbing balls patiently at the teenager, who batted them clumsily in all directions.

"Don't slap at the ball," the pro called, "and don't get caught off balance. Position yourself so you can walk into the ball, arm back and ready to follow through. . . ." He was a tall blond man who moved gracefully and looked somehow familiar to Erin.

"Remember Rick Steele, the actor?" said Marjorie at her elbow. "The one who got in all the trouble? Well, he's our tennis pro now. He's gone back to using his own name. Richard Steelegrave."

"I had a terrible crush on him when I was about twelve," said Erin, amazed that he should look so young. He seemed hardly to have changed since she had watched him on TV as a child.

"He has to fight off the female membership. And their daughters. He doesn't fight very hard."

They showered and changed, then sat over iced tea on the glassed-in veranda of the clubhouse, chatting and losing track of the time, until the sun touched down on the Pacific, looking like an orange tennis ball in the cloudless sky. Richard Steelegrave came into the nearly empty room at five-thirty, proceeded to the bar, and ordered a Moscow Mule. He had changed into an alpaca pullover and white duck trousers, looking every inch the tanned and fit sportsman.

Marjorie, an instinctive matchmaker, saw Erin watching him and raised her glass in casual invitation. The tennis pro sauntered over carrying his drink and sat down between them after introductions had been made. Erin saw that he had gray eyes under thick dark blond brows but that the hair on his head was going white. She revised her original estimate of his age by five years.

"What's that?" she asked, touching the beaded copper mug in his hand.

"A Moscow Mule. Vodka and ginger beer. An elixir that was all the rage around the time you were born." She had an uncanny feeling that she had regressed a generation and was watching *Love–Forty* again. The bantering tone, the mannerisms of speech were exactly the same.

"And Richard is solely responsible for its revival here at the club," Marjorie put in.

"It took a board meeting to talk them into getting the right mugs. You see, a copper mug is part of the ritual." He turned to Marjorie. "Is this young lady a prospective member? I'll be glad to give her a guided tour. In depth."

"Sounds interesting, but I can't afford to join."

"Then I can show you what you're missing." He raised his hand to signal for more drinks. Erin could find in his manner no hint of the fact that he was an employee of the club.

"Not for me," Marjorie said. "I've got to run. Raymond has a timetable, even on weekends. My fate is having to conform to it." She stood up.

"Oh, then I'll have to go too," Erin said with some regret. "You've got to drop me off, remember?"

"I could do that," Steelegrave remarked. "Where do you live?"

"In Santa Monica. Near Bundy. I don't want to put you out."

He shrugged. "Not at all. In fact, you're geographically desirable."

The smug assumption irked Erin. "Living in Long Beach would disqualify me, then?"

"Well, there's a twenty-mile limit, you know. But it wouldn't be strictly interpreted in your case. Marjorie, you ought to tell Raymond to switch from golf to tennis. He'd lose some of that gut he's lugging around."

Marjorie's eyes narrowed for an instant. She was very conscious of her husband's physical shortcomings. "You tell him," she said shortly, and stalked out.

"She didn't like that," Erin observed after a moment.

"I merely spoke the truth. Raymond looks like a sack of laundry with a rope tied around it."

"Sometimes it pays to be diplomatic."

He raised an eyebrow at her and lit a cigarette while she wrinkled her nose. "You're thinking that my attitude might jeopardize this plush job I have here as tennis pro. Well, that's part of my plan." He lowered his voice and leaned closer to her. "You see, I'm reversing Horatio Alger's pet theory. I started at the top and I'm working my way down. For my next move, I've got my eye on the caretaker's job. He's a half-blind Mexican and I figure he can't last much longer. After that, I'll replace my own assistant. And so forth. I'm calling my autobiography *From Riches to Rags*. What do you think?"

It was said without bitterness, and she had to laugh. "It'll make a lot of money and you'll star in it. Defeating your purpose."

He talked her into a Moscow Mule. She seldom drank anything stronger than wine, but the vodka blended with ginger beer was tart and refreshing.

By the time Steelegrave signed the check it was dark and they walked out into a night that was clear by local standards. In the parking area, a huge dog reared up from the seat of a convertible as they approached, and Erin jumped back in alarm.

"I forgot about Junkyard," Steelgrave said, holding the door for her. "Go ahead and get in. He'll move over for you."

The dog moved only reluctantly, keeping his yellow eyes on her. He was sullen of demeanor and high of smell. "This looks like the same car you used in *Love—Forty*. It was my favorite show when I was a little girl." Once again, that sensation of having retrogressed in time.

"It's one of them. We had a twin for stunt driving. It didn't survive."

"And you've kept it all this time."

"Call it a souvenir." He put on a tape of Harry James's "Flight of the Bumblebee," keeping the volume low.

It was mild enough to leave the top down and they drove into Santa Monica crammed into the small cockpit of the T-Bird, the great unkempt dog staring at Erin with his wolf's eyes. She was relieved when they stopped and the animal bounded out over her to the ground. Steelegrave led the way through a maze of walkways threatened by a riot of greenery to one of a cluster of aging bungalows shielded from each other by the shrubbery. Inside, he fed his dog while Erin roamed through the rooms looking at the clutter of outsize furniture that obviously belonged somewhere else. The rooms were separated by Spanish arches and thick, solid walls.

"The stuff comes from a big place I had up in Topanga Canyon when I was married," he said, reading her thoughts.

"I had to sell it, finally, but I rescued a few pieces of furniture."

He went behind the bar and poured Russian vodka into a glass, adding only a few cubes of ice. She shook her head at his offer of a drink, marveling that he could consume so much alcohol without apparent effect. She felt light-headed on her single Moscow Mule.

It emboldened her to ask, "You were married to Marla Monday, weren't you?" She was curious to know what it had been like. There had been so much written about them.

"Yes. Now let's talk about you. My life's an open book to anyone who's read the *Enquirer*."

She shrugged, disappointed at having failed to draw him out. "If you insist. But it'll never make a movie."

"I insist."

"I live in a tiny house in Santa Monica that my parents built just after the war. They moved to the valley long ago and kept the place rented until they let me have it so I could be closer to UCLA when I was going to school. I still take some social-science courses and I also have a studio in Venice where I give dance classes. My big adventure was going to New York at nineteen to be a model. I got a little work but someone finally let me know, tactfully, that my bones were too big and my face was too round for high fashion. So I guess I'm a provincial type."

"Thank God. High-fashion models look like graduates of Buchenwald to me."

She hesitated, disturbed by his choice of words. "I once wanted to join the Peace Corps, but I was too young at the time, and I did a lot of marching and protesting at college. Sometimes I think I should have studied medicine and then practiced in some ghetto a world away from Beverly Hills. I didn't do it and it's pretty late now. I have a slightly guilty conscience. Helping rich ladies keep their figures by dancing isn't all that fulfilling."

He actually stifled a yawn. "Nothing is too late at your age," he murmured.

"I'm twenty-eight. A spinster as far as my mother is concerned. Look, I'm not keeping you awake or anything, am I? I warned you my story wouldn't make a screenplay, but you asked for it."

"So I did, so I did. Ask in haste, repent at leisure," he misquoted. "I had in mind more vital statistics. For instance, I gather you're not married. Do you have a boyfriend who's bigger than I am? A dowry? A kinky nature?"

"You're in no danger in any case. I usually date men my own age who don't drink or smoke." She was barely holding on to her temper now.

"Except maybe a little grass."

"Except maybe a little grass."

"Which is okay, of course."

"In moderation."

"I'm more comfortable with old-fashioned vices. For instance, I never do grass unless I'm staying home. It makes me jam on the brakes at green traffic lights for fear they'll turn red before I can get through. Every car behind me is a cop or a jealous husband."

"A classic case of paranoia."

"Perhaps. But I must admit the stuff is kind of fun when you're in bed with the right person."

She looked directly at him. "*If* it's the right person."

"Perhaps we have found something we have in common." He grinned and refilled his glass with vodka. "Whereas we've stablished that you're not overly fond of jaded old parties who drink and smoke, and I've had very little to do with commies and women's-libbers who obstruct traffic and commerce marching around with their cretinous signs and slogans, we have now discovered that we both have an affinity for smoking grass under intimate circumstances. At least it's a beginning."

His grin was disarming and his gray eyes glinted with mischievous challenge. She was learning that he was a classic tease, that he had a perverse need to provoke anger or at least controversy.

Moreover, he was totally unlike anyone she knew. Her friends and her lovers were almost invariably young and concerned, steeped in gloom over the erosion of the environment, the gathering threat of nuclear holocaust, the injustices they felt were heaped on the poor and the minorities. Lately, although she shared their commitments and ideals, their pessimism had begun to pall on her. She needed to laugh and to feel lighthearted, to be reassured that more awaited her than their bleak, doomed world.

Richard Steelegrave was clearly egotistical and insensitive, but there was something paradoxically refreshing about his utter lack of conscience and his cheerful hedonism. She considered the old saw about opposites attracting. Certainly she was physically attracted to him, even while his values and life-style repelled her. There was about him a whiff of tarnished glamour.

At least, there was no danger of an emotional involvement such as the one she was presently withdrawing from. Steven, the moody young intern with whom she had considered sharing a life dedicated to good works among the needy, had damaged himself inestimably in her eyes when he was busted for pilfering and marketing a staggering amount of drugs he had found lying around the UCLA medical facilities. His claim to be a victim of the reactionary fascist police had failed to convince her. Now she needed an antidote for her disillusionment. Why not a man she could enjoy as she would a good meal or a strenuous dance session? Someone who would act as a cathartic for her dammed-up energies. She decided at that moment to have an affair with Richard Steelegrave. A short one.

Steelegrave had two more drinks, claiming that he couldn't eat on an empty stomach, and a fog as thick as cotton batting had moved in over the cliffs of Santa Monica by the time they left his bungalow to dine. He put the top up on his old car and drove them down Ocean Avenue to a small, shabby building not far from the pier. The neon legend above it, blurred by the fog, proclaimed "Chez Jay." Inside, the bar was crowded, the floor littered with peanut shells, and there were few tables, but the food was surprisingly good. They feasted on steamed clams and swordfish and drank white wine. The proprietor, a burly man with a pepper-and-salt spade beard, greeted Steelegrave familiarly, as did the bartender and several patrons. Erin guessed the bistro was one of his regular hangouts, a place where he was recognized and catered to.

After the meal, Steelegrave ordered brandy for himself (she declined) and lit one of his black cigarettes. One blond brow went up and the gray eyes, only slightly glazed by the formidable amount of alcohol he had consumed, studied her with meaning. He opened his mouth to speak.

It wasn't hard to guess what he would say, and even easier to beat him to it, using fewer words. "Your place or mine?" she asked.

Erin considered it a year wasted.

She went into the living room, grabbed the ashtray and tossed it into the garbage, a consciously symbolic gesture, for she had just decided to get rid of Richard, if indeed he had not already gotten rid of her. It made the little house seem more her own again, turning it back into the retreat it had always been for her. She carried her drink into the bedroom, where she pulled on tight white shorts and a T-shirt as a concession to the unseasonable heat. Never a vain girl, she used a minimum of makeup and dressed for comfort, even if her outfits did tend to favor those splendid legs. If she had dreamed of an exotic career as an actress or a model when she was very young, the realization that it might be beyond her reach did not unduly sadden her. Other options appealed more to her now—a husband and family, her studies and some useful work that would reinspire dedication.

Richard leered at her from a poster on the far wall, no part of her plan. He was wearing a dinner jacket and holding a gun, an impossibly smug expression on his face. The onion-shaped mosques of Arabia were depicted by an artist's rendering in the background. Some old picture of his filmed in Morocco. She put down her glass so that she would not throw it, and went to pull the poster off the wall, hiding it out of sight in a closet. She looked around for further evidence of him, but there was none. He was banished.

Not that she would never miss him; Richard could be fun. He was a frequent and inventive lover whose libido matched her own merry, uninhibited approach to sex. He could be appealing and was possessed of an ageless little-boy grin that could melt her heart, even when she suspected it was an actor's trick he practiced coldly in front of his mirror. His outrageous stories of Hollywood a generation ago held her rapt, for he debunked all her idols, including himself, knew where all the skeletons were hidden.

"Oh, he couldn't have been gay!" she cried, defending one of her favorites, then adding quickly, "Not that I have anything against gays. But he just couldn't have been. And it was so sad. Dying so young, just by falling down and cracking his head!"

"Well, he was wearing high heels and he tripped over his skirt. He was on downers, too, so he wasn't navigating."

"Oh, come on, Richard!"

"Just showing you our feet of clay." But he never spoke of the incident that had brought him down.

When he got a few dollars ahead, they would fly down to the beaches of Mexico, avoiding the tourist traps like Acapulco, sailing by day and scouting the local scene at night. He knew where to go—the old hotels, the hidden stretches of sand, the good restaurants. Traveling with him was never a bore. Of course, he drank too much, but he never became abusive or lost control. Liquor made him caustic, sarcastic, infuriating, but seldom dull or maudlin. He was easy to hate but hard to dislike.

Well, she was immune to him now. Of one thing she was certain. The man she settled down with would be nothing like Richard. Which made Luis leap into mind.

She had met Luis last night after she had given up on Richard and left her house in anger. She knew that Bergin's was a hangout for singles and she took a seat at the bar with absolutely no intention of spending the evening alone. Even so, she rejected out of hand the first man to approach her. His graying temples and smooth good looks reminded her too much of Richard. The young Latino named Luis far more suited her mood. He was no more than her own age, with hot dark eyes and casually mismatched clothes. He was studying to be an attorney, almost ready to take his bar exams, and doing paralegal work for undocumented (illegal) aliens in his spare time. It soon became apparent that he was a radical, dedicated to the very causes she had embraced so passionately during her activist campus days. The same causes Richard derided so cynically that she had finally suppressed her convictions when they were together and had even grown away from her most heartfelt ideological commitments. With Luis she was back on familiar ground. She even managed to expunge from her mind the slight but disturbing resemblance he bore to Steven, the medical student who had fallen from grace. His dark eyes (so different from Richard's ice-gray ones) warmed her, and they sipped wine and talked far into the night. . . .

With a squeal of tortured tires, a car swung into her driveway, shafting her picture window with its high beams. She recognized the unmistakable sound of the T-Bird's engine, a sort of sustained, genteel chuckle that stopped abruptly as the car door slammed. Before she could summon any reaction, Richard Steelegrave had walked through her front door with his great rusty dog a pace behind him.

Erin gathered herself and stood very straight. She raised her arm and pointed over his shoulder at the night beyond. "Out," she said. "You and the hound, both."

Richard looked pale under his tan. A lock of fair hair hung over his forehead and a muscle twitched alongside his jaw. "Hear me out, Erin. I've got a real emergency."

"I'm not interested."

Richard looked at his watch. Then he walked around the unbending figure of Erin and turned on the television set, tuning in Channel Two. Dan Rather was talking about Poland on the CBS evening news.

"I don't want you in my house, Richard," said Erin from behind him. "I'm not big enough to throw you out, and if I was, I suppose your damn dog would attack me. But if you have an ounce of class, you'll just leave."

Dan Rather finished dealing with Poland, glanced down and then up again. "Famed movie actress Marla Monday was found brutally murdered this morning on the lawn of her Bel-Air mansion by her longtime chauffeur and manservant. Her nude body was discovered hanging from a set of gymnasium equipment; her throat had been savagely slashed.

"Los Angeles police authorities are keeping silent at this point regarding possible motivation or suspects. The coroner's office also remains cautious, stating only that death was caused by a sharp object. Coroner Thomas Noguchi, a controversial figure who has sparked resentment in the past with his speculations concerning the death of famous stars, has clearly decided to remain close-mouthed in this case, saying only that a full report will be issued later.

"Marla Monday's career spanned two decades and was still going strong. She was due to begin a new film—*Star-crossed*—on the very morning following her death. Producers of the movie cannot be reached for comment on whether *Star-crossed* will be canceled or not. . . ."

Erin stared at the likeness of Marla Monday superimposed on the screen next to Rather. She felt her anger draining away, to be replaced by confusion. It was ghastly, of course, but Richard seemed upset out of all proportion. He had been divorced from the actress years ago, and he had every reason to despise her. . . .

"I don't know what I can say or do, Richard. It's horrible . . . but you haven't seen her in years, have you?"

Richard turned off the set. "No . . . I mean, I don't think so." He drew a deep breath. "No, I haven't."

"Well, have you or haven't you?"

He exhaled. "The cops think I killed her. One of them came to my place just now, less than an hour ago, to ask questions. He found a knife in the kitchen that I never saw before, and he was going to arrest me. When I objected, the wild bastard pulled a gun on me, for Christ's sake! Junkyard jumped him and he dropped the gun. I got the hell out of there and came here."

She looked at him with disbelief. "Do you mean to tell me you ran away from the police?"

"Well, yes. . . ."

"Richard, you're crazy! Now, you just use my phone to call them up and turn yourself in. You can say you ran because you were all upset. . . ."

"I can't do that."

"Why for God's sake not? You didn't kill her, did you?"

Richard sat down on the leather chair and ran his hands through his hair. He reached into his pocket for cigarettes and lit one. "Have you got a drink around here?"

"No."

He looked pointedly at the glass of Dubonnet on the coffee table. "Even some of that stuff would help."

She sighed and walked into the kitchen for the bottle.

She also got the ashtray out of the garbage and brought it to him. Then she placed the phone in front of him. "Call the police."

"It's not that simple." He filled a glass with Dubonnet and drained half of it, wincing at the unaccustomed sweetness.

"Richard. If you don't call the police—if you don't stop acting like that half-assed character you used to play on television—then I want you out of here. Now!"

"Listen to me. I don't know where I was last night. I had some trouble in the afternoon and I drank too much. That's why I didn't call you or pick you up. I didn't want you to see me bombed out. You can be pretty goddamn intolerant, you know. Anyway, I had some kind of a blackout that lasted from early last night until I got up this morning. I don't remember anything."

"That doesn't mean you killed her, you idiot!"

"I can't prove that I didn't."

"They have to prove you did. That's the way the law works."

"What about the knife? Suppose it's the one used to kill her?"

"How could it be?"

"Well, someone could have planted it. Or else . . ." He pushed the unthinkable from his mind.

"Now, you listen to me. Why should you have killed her? You've been divorced for fifteen years. The way I heard the story, she walked out on you when she figured you were finished, and married your friend. That's not reason enough to kill. Maybe in the heat of anger, when it was all happening, but not after all those years. I mean, I know you're pretty unstable, Richard, even flaky at times, but I'd like to think you wouldn't butcher someone just because she left you years ago."

"Your faith in me is touching."

"Well, then?"

He finished his Dubonnet and refilled the glass. "There was more to it than that. . . ."

7

Rick married Marla Monday because she fascinated him. But when Sheila Graham put the question to him over drinks at the Polo Lounge, he replied, "For the fun of it." When she turned to ask the same thing of Marla, the new bride simpered and said, "Because he's got a big cock and knows how to use it." The remark never found its way into Sheila's column but it got around anyway, since they were a party of six at the table. It wasn't the kind of publicity that did Rick any harm at all.

Part of what fascinated Rick was that you never knew what Marla would do or say next. She delighted in shocking the more jaded denizens of the film colony, but that didn't make her vulgar. She could be a nun or a blind virgin who played cello with equal ease. Her performances were calculated to prompt the reaction of a specific audience. She was, above all, a marvelous actress.

Marla's gift became apparent for the first time in *Fall Guy*, and there followed a concerted rush for her services. Malcolm Webley rationed her out sparingly, keeping the demand for her keen. He let her do another picture with Rick called *Riptide*, and they were good together. It established her name and made them a popular team. *Riptide* barely scratched the surface of her talent; her performance soared above the mediocre vehicle, while Rick simply played Hawke with a different name. It was clear that Marla was destined for better things. Webley began to move her toward a higher plane.

In the meanwhile, Rick was almost fully absorbed with *Love–Forty*. After two years the ratings merited a renegotiation of his contract, doubling his salary to five thousand dollars per episode. By 1963, when the original contract expired, Webley renewed for twenty-five thousand per. *Love–Forty* was the highest-rated show on TV after *Gunsmoke*. And Rick still had the spring hiatus to make one feature a year. Webley carefully filtered the scripts that were submitted, never letting his client extend himself beyond the somewhat limited area within which he excelled. It reduced the possibility of career error and guaranteed the loyalty of his fans.

As soon as he could afford to, Rick bought a rustic house in Topanga Canyon. To get there he had to turn off Topanga Canyon Road and follow a primitive dirt trail, cross a homemade plank bridge spanning a brook, and wind along until the track dead-ended at the house. Every couple of years heavy rains would swell the brook to an angry river that invariably swept the bridge away, isolating Rick if he happened to be home or cutting him off from the house if he had been out. In addition to floods, he had barely survived two major fires during his tenure. Rustic beauty did not come without a price in California.

Rick barely gave a damn. If he were burned or flooded out, he could always buy another house. There was plenty of money. In the meanwhile, he enjoyed his privacy, despite any inconvenience to the occasional young lady who drove into the creek while trying to navigate the bridge or couldn't turn her car around when it was time to go home.

The house had enough elevation to afford it an ocean view, and an enormous plank deck stretched out toward the Pacific to take full advantage. Rick sank a big redwood tub in the deck and ran plumbing out to service it. He liked to soak in hot water at the end of the day and study his script with a drink at his elbow. Now and then he invited a nymphet or two to wallow around and watch the sunset with him.

This afternoon only Marla shared his tub. They had

been an item on and off screen since *Riptide*. To the public, they were Hollywood's golden twosome, especially since Robert Wagner and Natalie Wood had broken up. To each other, they were territory not yet fully explored. After two years, an element of mystery remained. Perhaps because they were still uncommitted to each other, on parallel but separate courses. Malcolm Webley contrived to keep them that way. Married stars lost the appeal of eligibility.

From her side of the tub, Marla watched him worry his script, mouthing some of the lines silently, a Moscow Mule within easy reach. Though it was still light, a pale crescent moon had risen in the clear sky.

"This is really romantic, Rick," she said. "Here we are—naked in this hot water, everything touching. I'm all aroused and you're sitting there memorizing that drivel."

Rick mumbled something and raised the script, blocking her out. For seconds Marla stared at the blank folder; then she carefully stubbed out the marijuana cigarette she was smoking, took a deep breath, and slipped under the surface of the water. He didn't notice for a moment, lost in the material he was reading. Then he gasped and dropped the script into the tub. He said, "Jesus!" and scooped the sodden paper swiftly onto the deck. After that, there was nothing to do but surrender to the moment, and he lay back with a groan. He wanted to howl at the premature fingernail moon above them.

She broke the surface all too soon. "I can't hold my breath that long!"

He reached out and caught her by the arms, lifting her almost out of the tub to set her upon himself. Water sloshed over the side onto the deck as she settled, shifting, accommodating. Her face remained close to his throughout, her eyes studying every nuance of emotion that crossed his. Marla held that sex was largely cerebral and the eyes mirrored the subtlest and therefore the most erotic aspects of the act.

Afterward he said, "Look what you did to my script." It lay on the deck, a pulpy mess.

"Depart from it. Improvise. Ad-lib. Do something exciting for a change."

"Sure. They love surprises on that show."

"That's the trouble. No surprises. It's a dull show. Why don't you expand beyond it? Do something different?"

"Because while money may not buy happiness, it does buy some of the most interesting substitutes."

"During hiatus, then. Look at some new material."

"I'll talk to Malcolm."

"Malcolm won't help. He doesn't think you can play anything but Hawke and all those clones of Hawke you do in features. Maybe he's right, but I'd think you'd want to find out."

"What do you suggest?" Rick asked, stung.

"If it were my career, I'd diversify, grow. You've been Hawke for six years—almost as long as Arness has been Matt Dillon. You're locked into one part, stereotyped."

"I've got a contract. Anyway, I do a feature a year."

She looked at him from under her uneven brows, water still streaming from the crisp black hair. "I'd break the contract, tell them to stuff it. They may not let you do television for a while. Maybe never. What of it? You can make good features. And have time to play."

He lit a cigarette, thinking about it. It was very tempting. The series was ball-breaking work; he had little free time. How pleasant it would be to do a couple of features a year for top dollar, as he now surely could, and travel or play the rest of the time. And tell King-crafts to stuff it. He looked at the determined line of Marla's delicate jaw. She would do exactly that, having more balls than most men, figuratively speaking.

"I read something that would be great for both of us, luv," she enthused, circling his neck with her slim wet arms. "Luv" was an endearment she had picked up from Webley and applied to everyone. "It's a comedy called *All for the Money* and it's funny as hell. It'll give you a whole new dimension, prove you can be something more than a G-man with lockjaw. Do it right and it can open up a whole new world for you."

"Malcolm would soil his laundry. And he's got script approval on all my stuff, you know."

"He might even approve. But if he doesn't, you can

insist. I'll back you up. Between the two of us, we're his meal ticket."

Malcolm Webley did not approve.

Marla sent him a copy of *All for the Money* as though it were a project she was considering for herself alone and waited until he had read it and pronounced it "delightful." Then she came to his office with Rick and they told him they wanted to do it together and that Rick wanted out of *Love—Forty.* The manager blanched and fumbled for a nitroglycerin capsule. Ever since his doctor had diagnosed mild angina a year earlier, he had used the capsules more as props than as medicine. Some people suspected they were just that.

"Aw, come on, Malcolm," Rick pleaded. "Give it a chance. It could work beautifully."

"You ought to try amyl nitrite," Marla suggested. "Poppers are really fun."

Malcolm's face flushed, proving the pills were real. "You really can't do this, you know."

"You loved the script," Marla reminded him. "You thought it was hilarious."

"It was!" Webley burst out. "But is he?" He swept a hand toward Rick.

Rick scowled. "Hawke has his humorous moments."

"True, he does," the manager conceded patiently. "But it is a restrained, ironic humor that you can handle because it reflects your own personality. This script calls for you to excel at farce comedy, an element that may not be in your repertoire."

"He's supposed to be an actor," said Marla. "Give him a chance to prove it."

"That is a challenge I would like to avoid!"

"You are condemning him to mediocrity!"

"I am being realistic!" Webley got himself back under control. "Anyway, this discussion may be academic. Who is going to cast Rick Steele in a big, expensive comedy?"

"So far, only Universal and Warner," Marla told him. "I've done my homework, Malcolm. I optioned the script before I went around with it. The studios love the story and they want me badly, so they'll work with Rick. He's box office. Why don't you just go along with us? You can write some fat contracts."

Webley shook his head sadly. "All this is beside the point. Immaterial. If you break your contract with Kingcrafts, Rick, you are out of television. They won't just let you go. They won't let you buy out for any price you could ever afford to pay. They'll just blackball you. You won't work in TV again. Ever. And television is the medium of the future. You are throwing it all away to snatch at the unlikely chance that you are the next Cary Grant." He took a deep breath. "You are pissing against the wind."

He sighed. "Will they work with his schedule?" he asked Marla hopefully. "Shoot it during the spring hiatus?"

"No way. They'll need him for months. This picture shoots all over Europe. You read the script."

"Then I'm telling you to finish out your contract, Rick. Just three more years. After that, you can do as you like. With my blessing."

"You don't think I can do sophisticated comedy or any other goddamn thing except Hawke," Rick said. "Well, I have a better opinion of myself. We'll do this one our way, Malcolm."

"You realize you are in violation of our personal contract," Webley said quietly.

"Then drop me. You have that option."

"I shouldn't want to do that yet. You may get away with this somehow, though I doubt it." Webley reached for his pipe and began to stuff it. "You're making me smoke. Doctor told me not to, y'know."

"Oh, really, Malcolm." Marla rose as if to leave, then turned back. "There is one more thing, so you'd better get another one of those caps out."

Webley looked as if he were expecting a blow.

"We're getting married."

"Jesus fucking Christ!" exploded Max Weber. Then he gathered himself together and produced a wan smile. "Bless you, children," said Malcolm Webley.

There was time for a honeymoon before *All for the Money* started shooting. Rick had walked away from *Love–*

Forty amid veiled threats and hard feelings all around. There would never be a better time for him to get out of town.

They flew to Rome, arriving in the middle of the pope's Ecumenical Conference, and the city teemed with clergy decked out in the trappings of their respective orders, in addition to the tourists and natives. Monks in what looked like brown army blankets trod the streets on sandaled feet, bowed under the weight of enormous silver crucifixes, the crowns of their heads shaved bald. Loftier churchmen in flowing black robes relieved only by red sashes and skull-caps glided through the crowds, sometimes hand in hand, and an occasional cardinal resplendent in scarlet and gold could be glimpsed passing in a limousine. Along the fabled Via Veneto tall, handsome young men wearing tri-cornered plumed hats and white shoulder belts crisscrossed over swallowtailed military tunics strolled aloofly in pairs, tasseled sabers dangling by their polished knee boots. Rick was reminded of a lunch break at a major studio that was doing several costume epics at the same time.

He and Marla watched the passing parade from a sidewalk table in front of the Café de Paris. *All for the Money* had about two weeks of preproduction still to go, so much of their time was free. They were staying at the new Parco Dei Principi Hotel, in the heart of the city but away from the din by virtue of being located in the middle of the park after which it was named. It was an island of calm in the midst of confusion, but they spent little time there. When Rick had been in Rome to play tennis, he was in training and McReedy had practically kept him locked up. He was making up for it now.

"Who are they?" Marla asked, watching two of the uniformed Adonises saunter by. They returned her look with quick smoldering glances, then resumed their practiced mien of arrogant condescension.

Umberto Ugolini shrugged but Rick saw the flicker of interest as his dark eyes lingered on the young men. "They are sort of honorary *carabinieri*, chosen for their family names and good looks. They must be over six feet tall and wear a uniform well." He sneered. "Aristocrats who serve as tourist attractions."

Umberto Ugolini, the Italian co-producer of *All for the Money*, was handsome in a soft, decadent way. He had heavy sensual lips, hooded eyes, and patent-leather hair in the style of Juan Perón. He wore silk shirts with mono-grammed French cuffs and his manicured nails were brightly polished. His constant companion was his "secretary," a young man with a profusion of black curls and a wardrobe of wasp-waisted jackets that never quite covered his butt. After one long, calculating look at Rick, Ugolini focused his oleaginous charm on Marla, appointing himself their guide and mentor in Rome. He got as much publicity mileage out of their early arrival as he could, too, arrang-ing for his favorite *paparazzi* to ambush them in clubs or discos. Rick could find nothing to like about the man, but Marla thought it was good politics to go along with him. Besides, she claimed he amused her.

Rick looked at the cars inching their way along the Via Veneto with horns blaring and the farting little Lambrettas darting in and out between them. At the intersection, a cop with a salami sandwich stuffed into his pistol holster stood on a yellow fuel drum directing traffic. As Rick watched, a Fiat sedan ignored his signal to stop, gliding right under his imperiously outstretched arm. The cop shrilled his whistle and yelled a curse after the driver, who then stopped abruptly, bringing traffic to a complete standstill, and leapt out of his car in a rage. He was a big, florid man in an expensive silk suit and he moved with theatrical determination until he stood before the cop, still perched on his yellow can. The big man raised both hands, palms up with the fingers bunched together, and waved them a scant inch beneath the official's nose. They screamed at each other for fully three minutes while everyone else leaned on their horns. Rick shook his head. It was a comic-opera city.

"Is the traffic always this bad?" Marla asked.

"Worse, when it rains," said Ugolini. "Then the police run away and hide in the coffee shops and everything stops. *Maledetti fascisti*," he added. Fascist bastards. De-spite his bourgeois background, his wealth, and opulent life-style, Umberto Ugolini was an avowed Communist. So, Rick learned, were a number of Rome's film elite, including Visconti and Vittorio de Sica. This seemed to him to put them at cross purposes with themselves, but then, that was symptomatic of most Italians he'd met. Their right hand was oblivious of what the left was up to.

To get away from Ugolini and the September heat in the city, they rented a small Fiat and drove south. But the beaches near Fiumicino airport were lined with miles of cabañas and eateries built side by side to accommodate the sweltering Romans. The crowded restaurants served mediocre food indifferently, and when they reached the water, it was murky and smelled suspect. Rick remembered it as clear and inviting little more than a decade before, when he ran the empty beaches as part of his training program.

When Ugolini urged them to accept an invitation to the film festival in Taormina, Sicily, they didn't hesitate. Even when they learned that the producer, his nance secretary Guido, two publicity flacks, and a makeup artist were going along as part of their entourage.

Taormina was a short hop by plane from Rome, then less than an hour's limousine drive up the coast from the airport in Catania. Sicily lay bone dry under cerulean skies without a trace of cloud. Brown, burned hills rose inland of the narrow coastal road, but on the other side the beaches were wide and empty, the sea blue and tempting. The locals they passed looked as lean and desiccated as the land itself, stained dark by the merciless sun and their Carthaginian ancestry. Rick saw no friendliness in their black eyes, and their donkey carts gave way only grudgingly before the honking limo. He'd heard that Sicilians were a breed apart from their softer Roman cousins, as tempered as the blades they were known to carry and use at the slightest provocation.

The village of Taormina tumbled out of the foothills to the coast, the old traditional section occupying the high ground. The steep streets were made of cobblestones, and an ancient amphitheater perched at the apex of the town. The amphitheater was one of the reasons Taormina was chosen to host the film festival, Italy's answer to Cannes. The final screening was always held there, and the biggest stars attending the event were exhibited on its stage.

Rick and Marla were booked into a modern hotel close

by the sea. Their balcony overlooked a little rocky cove with the clearest water they had seen anywhere. Other guests of the festival were staying there too. Lana Turner and her current husband, Robert Eaton, had the suite next to theirs; on the other side Umberto Ugolini and Guido shared quarters. Yul Brynner and John Huston were supposed to be around somewhere, but Burton and Taylor, with the perks of royalty, would arrive only on the last day of the festival and stay in private accommodations.

Rick lounged on the balcony breathing air that was like champagne and idly watching a trim sloop tie up at the short pier down on the bay. The sleepy resort was a perfect antidote for the hectic bustle of Rome. A place to rest up and get in shape for the picture.

"Will you look at this!" Marla called. "Someone just shoved it under the door."

Rick turned and walked back into the suite where she was staring at several sheets of paper she had just shucked out of an envelope. A dark-skinned maid was padding around unpacking and putting their clothes away.

"It's a schedule," said Marla. "A full page for each of the three days we'll be here. I know we're expected to make a few appearances, but this is ridiculous!"

Rick looked over her shoulder at the typewritten pages. It accounted for their time from nine A.M. until midnight every day, allowing about an hour for siesta.

The phone rang and he picked it up.

It was Guido. "*Buona sera.* Signore Ugolini is expected you to dine with him. Eight o'clock on the terrace."

"Tell him thanks, but no thanks. We'll have something sent up. This is supposed to be a honeymoon, chum." He hung up.

It wasn't that easy. By ten o'clock the next morning they had already been herded through breakfast and were out on the crystalline waters of the little bay in a flat-bottomed rowboat with Rick at the oars, a hot sun beating down on them from the cloudless sky. Another craft, rowed by a taciturn native, wallowed nearby, carrying a still photographer, a publicity clown in a black suit and pointed shoes, and Guido in a jockstrap bathing suit. Rick wore trunks, having declined to be photographed in an outfit like Guido's, and Marla was in a scant bikini. She hadn't allowed the makeup girl to touch her and Rick thought she looked like an incredibly precocious teenager with her arched black eyebrows and crisp short hair.

"We gonna row aroun' to da grotto!" yelled Guido, gesticulating across the distance that separated the boats. "You gotta go aroun' that pile-a rocks and then-a you gonna see it!"

The grotto lay just beyond the rocks that marked the entrance to the bay. The mouth of the cave wasn't impressive, just an opening big enough to allow passage to one of the small boats at a time. Outside the protected basin the sea was choppier and Rick had to maneuver with some care to glide in without scraping against the rocks. The other craft followed, aptly handled by the oarsman, who disdainfully ignored a flurry of shouted instructions from Guido.

Inside, the water was still once more and of a clear blue so transparent they could see every detail of the ocean floor. Schools of multicolored fish darted back and forth, and sea urchins clung to the smooth rocks. By some trick of light the vaulted ceiling reflected the shimmering sea so faithfully that the passengers of the boats themselves took on a bluish hue. It was surprisingly light in the cave.

The photographer, who worked for an Italian magazine called *Oggi* ("Today"), was fiddling with his camera equipment—filters, light meters, or whatever. The flack in the black suit took out a notebook and tried to look essential. "Now, get inna water," called Guido. "Swim aroun' like you having a good time!"

"Another frustrated director," Rick muttered, but they jumped in and splashed around obligingly while the photographer clicked away. Rick dived to the bottom, which seemed to be six feet below but was nearer twenty. The water was surprisingly cool considering the heat of the day.

Marla threw her arms around his neck when he surfaced. "This would be heaven without these vultures," she said. "I feel like a trained seal."

"This is only the beginning. Then there's lunch in the

country, back to the hotel for interviews, cocktails and dinner with the gang, a movie on the other side of the goddamn island. I leave anything out?"

She slid her leg between his thighs as they trod water. "Let's play hooky."

"Shit, we're trapped."

"We'll find a way."

Luncheon was held twenty miles up the coast at the seaside villa of Don Aldo Fattore. Rick and Marla shared one of a caravan of limos with Ugolini and the ever-present Guido.

From a distance the villa looked like an oasis on the arid coastal plain, but close up it was no tropical paradise. The palms were ratty and the grass was struggling despite all the watering Don Aldo must have done. The building itself was authentic enough, with the original atrium preserved or restored to form an impressive entrance hall. Ugolini suggested it had belonged to some ancient Roman noble in disfavor or exile, for who else would live in Sicily?

They were met and shown in by servants, but Rick saw two heavies lurking in the background carrying sawed-off shotguns. Don Aldo greeted his guests at the entrance surrounded by a bevy of women sharing a family resemblance who were all dressed in unrelieved black. They were of different ages, but in contrast to the lean peasants of the countryside, they were invariably fat, a condition that kept them from looking like crows.

"Sows," said Ugolini *sotto voce* to Marla. "In the provinces it is a sign of wealth and prominence to be fat as a pig. You will find no Roman chic here."

Don Aldo bowed over Marla's hand and leered at her approvingly. He was a small man, quite old, with sparse hair clinging to his leathery brown scalp. The hand he gave perfunctorily to Rick was square and hard, as though it had known peasant labor. He hawked, swallowed something he had brought up, and spoke some rapid Italian in a high-pitched voice, never taking his reptilian eyes off Marla.

"Don Aldo is entranced by the *signora* and would be

honored to have a private word with his most beautiful guest before the afternoon is over," Ugolini translated.

Marla managed not to grimace, but she did look a little glassy by the time they got away. "Ugh," was all she said.

The party was not at the villa but on the wide beach before it, in a black-and-green-striped tent big enough to house an Arab League convention. There were tables loaded down with food, much of it cold fish and meat jellied in aspic. Waiters circulated with trays of wine. Out here the women were neither fat nor dressed in black, but more often sleek starlets from Rome, some in bikinis still damp from the sea. Rick didn't see any of the bigger names from the film festival but he spotted an actor who used to play Tarzan and was now doing the currently popular Italian muscle epics and a rangy ex-cowboy who had lost his western series and gone into exile after punching out a studio head. The former Tarzan, who wore a short-sleeved crew-neck shirt showing off enormous biceps and pectorals that resembled an old Roman breastplate, was surrounded by more girls than Vittorio Gassman, also lounging nearby. He left his entourage and strolled over to Rick and Marla.

"Hi, Rick," he said, twinkling his eyes at Marla. He had been a guest star on *Love–Forty* a few years ago and he looked as boyish as ever, though he must have been nearly forty. "I see you're here with that *stronzo* Ugolini, queen of Italian westerns. If he goes swimming, he'll leave a ring around the Mediterranean."

"Well, if he drowns we can find him by the oil slick," said Rick. "Why are we here anyway? Who's this Aldo Fattore, a patron of the arts?"

"Naw, a *mafioso*. Biggest gun between here and Palermo. This is kind of a command performance. He calls up guys like Ugolini and says round up a few stars and lots of girls. This one and that one. He screens a lot of pictures out here and he's got his favorites. It's all the old fart can do anymore."

"What are you doing here, then? Did he really like *Hercules Versus the Molemen?*" Gwila Mars had sidled into the conversation. She was a perennial ingenue whose middling years were finally becoming apparent under her makeup.

The big man narrowed his eyes at her. He didn't enjoy jokes at his own expense. "He likes your old silents, too, Gwila. But that's only because he can't hear anymore."

The actress said coldly, "I'll still be around when you're back chasing sand crabs on Muscle Beach."

"My, aren't we testy today! I'd say it was that time of the month, but you don't get those anymore, do you?"

Gwila Mars paled and raised her hand as if to strike, but something in the actor's eyes gave her pause and she confined herself to hissing, "Bastard!" before she whirled around and stalked away.

"Imagine that!" He looked after her with mock astonishment. "And half an hour ago the old dirtbag was trying to get me out in the ocean with her for a quickie."

Marla caught Rick by the hand. "Let's get out of here," she said.

As they left the tent the hags in black arrived to make a concerted attack on the mounds of food. They elbowed each other and anyone else who got in their way.

Outside, the beach stretched endlessly in either direction, mounded with white sand dunes. They took off their shoes and walked north, the direction away from Taormina. When the sand became too hot, they walked along the surf line, letting the tide lap at their feet.

Marla finally said, "Halfway around the world to hear the same rot you have to listen to back home. And that slimy little mobster!"

Rick looked longingly at the blue waves rolling in, topped with white froth. He took his jacket off and threw it in the sand. The gaudy tent was a speck in the distance. "You know how to ride waves?" he asked her.

"No."

"Come on, I'll show you."

They stripped off their clothes and ran into the surf. Rick taught her to catch the swells and ride them in to shore, keeping her body stiff so she could plane in like a surfboard. She caught on quickly and they frolicked in the ocean for half an hour, then baked their salty bodies in the sun. She began to cover him up with sand.

"Hey!" he protested. "It's too hot for that."

"Come on, let me. I've never done this before, I never had time to be a kid."

He let her cover him up to the neck, though it wasn't comfortable. Then she molded two huge breasts onto him and placed a sprig of dead sea fruit over his crotch. "God, I wish I had a camera!" she exclaimed, and collapsed next to him laughing.

They dressed and decided to take the road back rather than slog through the sand again. It was a potholed two-lane blacktop that handled the sparse coastal traffic made up of trucks, ancient buses, donkey carts, and an occasional Fiat. While they were pulling on their shoes, a singularly decrepit bus shuddered to a stop near them to pick up a small clutch of peasants carrying straw market bags.

For a moment Marla watched the women in black climb aboard. They were not fat like the ones back at the villa, but sinewy and prematurely aged by hard labor. They belonged to a world that existed on the fringe of her memory. Impulsively she grabbed Rick's hand. "Come on!"

"It's going the wrong way," Rick protested.

"That's the idea."

They boarded the doorless conveyance as it was pulling away, and Rick fumbled in his pockets to discover only lire in high denominations. Marla had some coins in her bag and they moved down the lurching aisle to find room on the hard slat benches that served as seats. Unwelcoming black eyes followed them curiously, taken aback or even affronted by the sight of the glamorous woman with short, mannish hair and the blond man in a tailored ice-cream suit. Tourists slumming, no doubt, making a lark of sharing the sorry conditions of their everyday lives. Rick smiled tentatively at an old crone sitting across from them, cradling a piglet in her lap. She glared back and spat on the worn floorboards between her feet.

"Well, okay, hon." Rick lit cigarettes for both of them. "Where to?"

"Anywhere. Wherever this thing takes us. Knowing would spoil the fun. That's how you play hooky."

The bus rattled through several villages and finally broke

down in a slightly larger town. While the cursing driver lifted aside the cowling to examine the expiring power plant, Rick and Marla got off gratefully, stiff and sore from the long jolting ride. The place was no tourist mecca but it looked marginally more prosperous than others they had passed through. The shops were well-stocked and there were a few tourists around, including Germans wearing backpacks and *lederhosen*. They wandered the streets until sundown, and then, finding they were very hungry, went into a small trattoria near enough to the sea to hear the surf.

There wasn't a menu. A waiter, no surlier than any other Sicilian, brought them *pasta al burro*, a tough *bistecca*, and finally fresh fruit and goat cheese. Marla ate ravenously and drank the rough red wine with gusto.

"Admit it," she said. "This is fun."

He conceded that it was. She rubbed her knees against his under the table and looked at him over the single guttering candle set in an old wine bottle. A warm breeze stirred the candle and reflections danced in her eyes. She had never looked lovelier to him.

"Let's not go back for a while," she said. "We don't go to work for a week."

The idea was tempting. Especially with this girl. Away from Hollywood and the likes of Umberto Ugolini, another Marla was emerging. The glib, brittle facade she'd raised against the peculiar stresses of that other existence was fast falling away, and he liked the metamorphosis.

But there were practical considerations. "The passports are back at the hotel, Marly. So are my wallet and the credit cards. I just grabbed some lire as we went out."

She put out her small hand. "How much?"

The sum total of the thousands of lire they had between them added up to less than two hundred dollars. "A fortune!" she exclaimed.

"But no passports."

"We'll improvise."

If Signore Enzo Parlapiano ran his small hotel by the book, it was because the authorities, who could be bribed in simple matters concerning smuggling or murder, were deadly strict on the subject of guest registration. No passport, no accommodations, he told them with sincere regret, looking at Rick's gold Rolex and Marla's simple string of pearls. To deny hospitality to such rare birds wrenched at his very soul. They were obviously rich and as gorgeous as movie stars. He had had American guests before, because he spoke English, but none such as these.

"*Signore*," Marla entreated the tubby proprietor, "we have been robbed and now we have no place to sleep!"

Parlapiano hardened his heart. "Then you have no money."

"Oh, yes, we have money! Show him the money, Rick. They were pickpockets and they only got the passports because they were sticking out of my husband's pocket."

Rick displayed his roll of lire to bolster Marla's eloquence.

"Then you must go to the police station, the *questura*," the innkeeper said sadly, his eyes on the fat wad of bills. "The loss of a passport must be reported."

"But we are tired." Marla placed a hand delicately against her brow and even contrived to totter. "And I'm not feeling well. We'll go to the police tomorrow."

Parlapiano could only shake his head. He was corpulent for a Sicilian because he did no manual labor and was as fond of wine as of money. His prominent nose hosted a cluster of broken blood vessels and his eyes were small and cunning.

As Rick and Marla turned to leave, he called out, "Wait"— an idea having struck him.

They looked back at him hopefully.

"There is a cottage that belongs to my cousin and his wife who are in Rome to see that pageant of priests, the idiots. It is a small place and there are no services, but it is by the sea. It is not part of the hotel, you understand, but perhaps we can come to some arrangement. Unofficially of course . . ." Parlapiano laid a thick finger against his empurpled nose and assumed a sly expression.

The tile-roofed cottage was small and clean, built of something like adobe and whitewashed inside and out. There was an ample kitchen equipped with crude utensils and a dining table. The living room was furnished with bulky pieces of rough-hewn wood and the bedroom had a soft, sagging feather mattress and a large wooden crucifix on one wall. The plumbing was primitive but, to Rick's relief, at least indoors. Marla exclaimed in delight over everything and after he'd paid over what seemed like an exorbitant sum to Signore Parlapiano, the fat proprietor bustled away with ill-concealed glee.

Marla put down the shopping bag she had purchased in town and took out the toiletries and change of under-clothes she had bought, including swim trunks for Rick. There was also a bottle of wine, which they opened and poured into thick mugs they found in the kitchen cupboard. Then, drawn by the murmur of the surf, they wandered outside.

The lights of the town were strung out along the coast in the distance and the full moon and stars looked close enough to touch in the clear night. Rick set down the wine bottle and lay back in sand that was still warm from the heat of the day. He lit an Italian cigarette and inhaled the harsh smoke contentedly.

"I think we've found it," Marla said, settling down next to him.

"What?"

"The perfect place for lovers."

Rick scanned her face in the starlight for signs of facetiousness, and found none. Marla seldom spoke of love. She had always been casual about their relationship, prompting him to respond in kind. Which suited him well enough, for he had never been in love, discounting the painful adolescent crushes of his teen years, and wasn't sure he wanted to be. It was enough to be with someone who was beautiful, talented, and never boring. Someone he could enjoy without totally committing himself.

He realized he knew very little about her; she would never talk seriously about the past. He knew she had a son by a teenage marriage, a handsome little tyke who was always ensconced in boarding school or summer camp. He had met the boy only twice, and failed to establish rapport. The father had been a commercial fisherman who drowned at sea, she said. Beyond that, she was evasive. Once when they were in Mexico together he learned that she spoke fluent Spanish and asked her about it. "You never told me," he said.

"A girl has to have her secrets."

"You've already got too many."

"All right," she relented. "Great-grandfather was a Spanish grandee who bedded an Aztec princess when he came to the new world. Together they founded a ruling dynasty that lasted until the revolution, when our lands were confiscated and our family murdered or driven into exile. My relatives fled with nothing but the jewels they could carry. We're planning a counterrevolution, though, to put us back in power."

"Sounds like a Mexican soap opera," he grumbled, giving up.

Rick remained curious, but he didn't push her. He'd married her for fun, hadn't he? And out of lust, of course. What mattered was now. And until now, it had been enough. But the new Marla was burrowing deeply under his hide. He felt a tug at his heart to think that this burgeoning feeling might be mutual, but he held himself in check. "You used to say it was tacky to be in love with your own mate," he reminded her lightly.

"I'm thinking of making an exception of you." Her eyes were unreadable in the dim light, but there was that tug again.

Still, all he said was, "I'll try to be worthy," in his usual bantering tone. It wasn't at all what he wanted to say, but he couldn't bring himself to go further. Because then she would have him.

He looked at the crisp dark head she laid against his chest and thought: What the hell, why do you need to say the words anyway, when the deed speaks so eloquently? He buried his hand in the thick black hair and brought her face up to his.

Rick got up early the next morning, without waking Marla. He had slept well, which surprised him, for the bed was much too soft. He pulled on his new trunks and slipped silently out of the cottage onto the beach.

The sun had barely risen and the air was still cool. He stretched out the kinks inflicted by the pulpy mattress and began to jog toward the town, a mile or so away. As he got closer, he passed fishermen returning with their predawn catch. They were dragging their sturdy boats up on the sand, packing the fish onto donkey carts for market, and spreading their nets to dry. They watched without expression as he ran by, no part of their world or concern.

The town was wakening, and commerce stirred in the streets as he jogged along parallel to the coast road. There were Lambrettas here, too, along with trucks, wheezing buses, and the inevitable donkey carts. Rick kept going for at least a mile beyond the town before heading back. He felt no fatigue; his body craved exercise after the relative physical inactivity imposed by travel. Seeing a fruit stand on the road, he wished he had thought to bring some lire. Sicilian fruit was renowned as the most luscious anywhere, though he wondered where they grew it in this arid land.

A quarter of a mile short of the cottage, he saw a woman approaching across the sand. She trudged toward him carrying a market basket and wearing a long, full skirt, a peasant blouse, and a black shawl over her head. He nearly ran past her before he recognized Marla.

"Hey . . ." He pulled up abruptly.

"*Buon giorno*," said Marla.

Her transformation was astonishing. In that costume, with the shawl covering her short hair and not a trace of makeup on the olive skin, she could pass for a comely native.

"What's with the disguise?" he asked.

"I'm going to market."

"But the clothes . . ."

"They were in that armoire. Along with some men's things."

"Doesn't mean we have to wear them."

"Ugolini's bound to have the police looking for us by now. I'm blending into the population. We need food, you know." She grinned, enjoying the intrigue.

"You've got to know more Italian than 'Buon Giorno' to buy food."

"I'll just point at what I want."

"Suppose people talk to you? Ask questions?"

She made a quick, graceful gesture toward her mouth

and ears. Anyone would know it meant she was deaf-mute. He shook his head in admiration. "Want me to go along?"

She shook her head. "You're not right for the part. Just be a good Latin husband and loaf around till I get back."

He watched her walk away with a sturdy peasant gait and felt a touch of pride. She was indeed a girl for all seasons, as adaptable as a chameleon. She could become anything she truly thought she was. For the time being that was a beautiful deaf-mute Sicilian housewife.

The day warmed up rapidly. Rick swam out past the mild surf into the ocean. There were no waves big enough to ride here, possibly because a long breakwater made up of huge rocks protected the beachfront on either side of town. He stroked over to the rocks and looked down at the clusters of sea urchins that clung to them. It gave him an idea.

In the kitchen of the cottage he found a rusty but serviceable knife. He swam back to the rocks with the thing between his teeth, reminded of a scene he'd done in *Riptide*, his second picture with Marla. It wasn't easy without flippers, face mask, or weight belt, but he managed to stay down long enough to pry several of the prickly creatures off the rocks, working carefully to avoid their poisonous spines.

Ashore, he breakfasted on two of the sea urchins, simply turning them over and scooping the meat from the exposed belly with his knife. They were as delicious as he'd heard, and he placed the rest of them in a bucket of salt water for later.

When Marla came back he was napping in the noonday sun. She had bought pasta, vegetables, fruit, cheese, and a fish. Wine, too. He noodled around watching her prepare the meal as if it were a familiar daily chore.

By the time everything had been stewed, spiced, broiled, and simmered, it was late afternoon and they had finished the first bottle of wine. They sat down to their feast with enormous appetite and Marla exclaimed over the sea urchins, making him feel like the best hunter in the tribe. Afterward they repaired to the sagging bed for a long, innovative siesta.

In the evening they strolled hand in hand along the beach they had come to think of as their own. The sun was sinking behind the stubby, bald hills, gilding the ocean with its last rays.

"What would happen," Marla wondered at one point, "if we just stayed here?"

He knew it was just the wine—of course, Marla lived for her career—but he pretended to think about it. "Nothing," he said finally. "Nothing at all."

"Well, that might not be the worst thing in the world."

"Then what would we do? We don't know how to be anything but movie stars."

"We could buy the cottage from that grubby little man. I'd learn Italian and gradually stop being deaf and dumb. Then people would think it was a miracle and make me a saint."

Rick decided to pursue the fantasy. "If we started to run out of money, I'd get a boat and fill it up with sea urchins to sell in town. Soon I'd be a big wheel with a lot of boats and all the fishermen working for me. The Mafia'd try to horn in, but I didn't used to be Hawke for nothing."

She giggled, a sound he'd never heard her make, then said solemnly, "If the Mafia got you, I'd never remarry. I'd wear black widow's weeds and become deaf and dumb again. I'd be a tragic figure in town. An object of great respect."

It was darkening fast and they were almost back to the cottage. He stopped and caught her arms, turning her to him. "We'll never do any of this, Marly, but I want you to know I wouldn't mind."

"Neither would I. . . ."

Four men were waiting for them in the cottage, hidden in the darkness until Rick found the light switch. Three strangers and Signore Parlapiano, who was standing because there was nothing left to sit on.

The oldest intruder, a stocky, hard-looking man about thirty-five, seemed to be in charge. At least he sat in the only comfortable chair. The other two, younger men, lounged on the wooden banquette. One of them looked like a snake with his long neck and narrow head poised as if about to strike. He had slanting green eyes above high cheekbones and hair that was cut off in bangs just above the eyes. When he leaned forward Rick saw the shoulder holster under his arm. Instead of a salami sandwich, it held a Colt .45 automatic.

Rick froze with his hand next to the light switch. He heard the sharp intake of Marla's breath, but when he looked he saw no further sign of fear. She stood well-planted on her bare feet, still in the loose cotton dress she had worn to market. Had he been alone, he might have hit the light, ducked back out the door, and bolted. As it was, they were trapped.

"What the hell?" he said, looking at Parlapiano.

The proprietor shrugged and spread his hands eloquently. "*Scusi,*" he said.

" '*Scusi,*' my ass. Tell them to get the hell out of here. *Fuori!*"

There was a burst of Italian from the man in the chair. He wore a zippered nylon jacket with black trousers. The others had similar jackets with varying trousers. The Snake, for instance, wore tight American jeans.

"You must go with them," Parlapiano translated.

"Why?"

"They are . . . ah . . . the authorities."

"Police?"

"Well . . . ah . . . they have similar duties."

Rick looked at Parlapiano with disgust. The little bastard had certainly sold them out. To whom seemed to be the only question. He went over and took Marla by the arm. "Okay, hon. Let's see if we can just walk away from this."

Not likely. The Snake uncoiled in a single lithe motion and placed himself between them and the door.

"Passports please!" The stocky man in the chair grinned, revealing a gold tooth and the only English he had.

"They were stolen," Marla told him.

Parlapiano said something by way of translation, and the stocky man replied.

"You must go with them," Parlapiano repeated.

The stocky man stood up, as did his confederate on the banquette, a large, expressionless youngster with hooded eyes. The Snake slid out the door and waited outside. Marla was permitted to take her handbag with her.

"You prick," said Rick to Parlapiano as they went out.

Hawke would probably have kicked the Snake in the nuts and taken the other two out with karate chops, but Rick walked meekly enough to their car. It was no police vehicle, which gave him an additional chill, but an old black Fiat sedan that looked like a hearse. They were crowded in back with the Snake, while the stocky man rode shotgun and the younger one drove.

"God, Rick," said Marla in a small voice.

"They're just some kind of plainclothes guys," Rick reassured, taking her hand. "That little shit turned us in because we didn't have passports. Probably makes himself a buck that way."

But he didn't believe it himself. Even in Sicily they wouldn't have cops like this. These were hard-case punks if he'd ever seen them.

"Maybe they'll let us go if we give them our jewelry. Your watch and my pearls." Her voice was tight with growing fear.

Rick held up his wrist to show the stocky man his Rolex. "*Per lei*," he said. "For you."

Greed showed in the man's eyes, but he merely grinned, displaying his matching gold tooth, and shook his head. He can always take it later, Rick thought. Jesus!

The car hurtled down the pitted coast road through the starry Sicilian night.

"*Bene!*" Umberto Ugolini snapped, and slammed the phone back on its cradle.

He lounged back from the desk in his hotel suite and looked at his secretary with heavy-lidded, brooding eyes. One corner of his plump mouth quirked downward petulantly, the other rose. Guido interpreted this to mean that while his *patrone* was still in a towering rage, he had found some ameliorating circumstance in which to take satisfaction.

"*Dio*, how I loathe Americans!" the producer exclaimed, and Guido smirked as though he had heard something new or at least moderately funny.

"And yet I must deal with them, eh? Massage their egos, toady to their peculiar concepts of individuality. But when the time comes, I must be like steel! One first flatters and cajoles, then one strikes! You will see, little friend, how these people must be dealt with. A lesson for you, eh?"

When Rick and Marla were let into the suite, followed by their Sicilian escort, Ugolini leapt up and ran around the desk to Marla. Ignoring Rick, he swept her into a quick embrace. "*Cara!* You are all right? You have not been harmed?" He stood back, holding her at arm's length, examining her as he would a precious commodity. He was wearing a brocaded robe over silk pajamas and smelled like a medium-priced Parisian whore. "Why, that dress is terrible!" he cried.

"We're fine." Marla regarded him coolly. "In spite of your friends."

Ugolini said something in Italian and gestured languidly at the Sicilians, who started for the door. The Snake glided out last, with visible reluctance.

Rick took a step toward the producer, his eyes narrow. "So you sent those punks after us—"

"Rick . . ." Marla's tone stopped him. "Let me try first."

"I'll give you about two minutes."

"When you disappeared, I was desperate!" cried Ugolini, looking only at Marla. "Here in Sicily, you understand, anything can happen. Kidnapping for ransom is common!"

"We weren't kidnapped until tonight," Marla said levelly. "Who were those men?"

"Associates of my friend Don Aldo. When you disappeared . . . well, I had to find you." He spread wide his arms, the picture of a reasonable man. "You could have been in terrible danger, and my responsibility—"

She cut him off. "We left to enjoy a tour of the island on our own."

Ugolini took a step backward in mock surprise. "On your own? Leaving me to explain your absence? You were to be presented tonight, if you remember. I was greatly embarrassed when I could not produce you." He whirled on Rick. "What are you trying to do? Destroy her? These are important functions. You are totally, unforgivably irresponsible."

"What makes you think it was his idea?" asked Marla.

Ugolini permitted himself a sneer. "In Italy, a man is in control of his woman."

"How would you know?" Rick put in.

Crimson spots appeared on the producer's sallow cheeks, and Guido tried to hide a smile. Ugolini turned and stalked back behind his desk, where he sat down and rested his jowls on steepled fingers, composing himself. "I will not work with this man," he said to Marla.

"Then stay away from the set," Rick suggested.

Ugolini slapped the desk with a pudgy beringed hand. "*Sporca miseria!*" he hissed. "It is you who will not be on the set!"

"Really, Umberto," Marla said calmly. "This is all nonsense. I control the property. The contracts are signed."

Ugolini smiled unpleasantly. "Contracts? In Italy? I can withdraw from this project and it will founder. You will have to begin all over. As for contracts, you may present your case to the courts. In perhaps five years there may be room on the agenda. I doubt it, but you could try." He leaned back, making conciliatory gestures with his fluent hands. "However, *cara mia*, I do not wish this to happen. I have found a far better solution." His self-satisfied expression suggested that everything was settled.

When no one said anything, he continued, "I spoke to William Holden some time ago about *All for the Money* and he was most interested. Unfortunately, your husband was already involved. Yesterday, when my disillusion with Mr. Steele became complete, I called him again. He is in Switzerland and he is available. There would be a delay of no more than a few days. I don't have to tell you he has a proven talent in light comedy, which Steele does not." Ugolini leaned forward again, trying to compel her with his eyes. "My dear Marla, you must consider your career. You and Holden! Think of that combination! The decision is yours!"

She looked at the seated man for a long time. At least it seemed long to Rick, who was holding his breath. Marla was a veritable calculator when it came to gauging her own best interests. Finally she smiled at Ugolini. "Nice try, Umberto. But no."

The producer scowled and ran a hand through his greasy hair. "I warn you. I can terminate this film."

"But you won't, Umberto," said Marla, as if speaking to a child. "Tonight you had us kidnapped. Everyone in the lobby saw those three hoodlums bring us here. With me in this 'terrible' dress, as you call it. However, I don't have to prove anything to your silly Italian courts or wait to be put on their agenda. I will just scream 'kidnap' and if necessary 'rape' and 'torture' at your hands. Think of the publicity! Between Rick and me we'll convince the industry and, incidentally, the world that you are an unbalanced lunatic who would contract violence to gain a business concession. You'll never co-produce with America again. Why, you'll even smell to high heaven in Rome, where double-dealing is an art form. You'll be back making pasta westerns, if you're lucky." She smiled at him and shook her head. "Now, I'm tired, Umberto. And angry. Make up your mind before I change mine and start screaming."

Ugolini let the heavy lids of his eyes droop, masking any alarm he might have felt. He assumed an expression of peevish disdain and fluttered a hand at her. "You have rejected a proposal that would have assured success for the film and yourself."

"Oh, I'll succeed."

On the way out, Rick stopped in front of Guido. "Get us two tickets to Rome on an early flight tomorrow like a good fellow." He patted the young man's cheek.

In their suite he opened the French windows to the warm night and they stepped out onto the balcony. Running lights from small craft in the bay winked at them and waves slapped at the gravelly shore.

"I can hear the surf here, too," Marla said at last. "But it's not the same.

"We'll go back someday, Marly."

But they never did.

8

All for the Money premiered at the Pantages Theater in Hollywood in the spring of 1965, a year and a half after Rick and Marla were married. On hand were the custom limos to transport the stars, the familiar cluster of searchlights stabbing the sky as though tracking enemy aircraft, the usual seething crowd of mindless juveniles to be cordoned off for the safety of arriving luminaries.

Marla, wearing a silver lamé gown cleft to the navel under a white mink wrap, provoked a general howl as they alighted from their car. Rick in dove-gray evening dress and frilled shirt had his own shrill following, and even his guest and longtime friend Justin Evander III, who had nothing to do with pictures, rated an ovation because he looked like a star. Malcolm Webley, with his tall, stately British wife, completed their party as they walked along the red carpet between the ropes and cops that parted the straining mob, submitted to the obligatory interview, and passed into the theater.

Rick had downed a quantity of vodka as an antidote for his nerves. *All for the Money* had not been a happy picture. It had come in late and over budget. European winter weather and a lack of rapport between the American money men and the Italian co-producer had accounted for some of the delay, but it was Rick's inability to deal with broad comedy that called for a revision of the script after the picture had started shooting. As a result, radical surgery had been performed on his part. He retained top billing according to the terms of his contract, but it was Marla's picture. Her genius as a comedienne was widely regarded as the only hope the film had of making it. Rick was judged a liability.

He had seen a rough cut and not liked it at all. It gave him the first visceral twinge of panic he had known since facing Stella Harvey's class in another life. Of course, he told himself, it's only a rough cut. How the hell could anyone judge anything before editing, dubbing, or music? Editors were capable of miracles. Still, it had cost so goddamn much money! If it bombed he would make a legion of enemies. They were waiting for him after he broke his contract with King-crafts.

He watched the screen poker-faced as the action unfolded. It was an elegant picture, a perfect showcase for Marla's beauty and talent. He had fared less well. With dismay he watched himself being wiped off the screen. The editors, in their wisdom, had left as much of him as possible on the cutting-room floor, and the footage that survived showed him stumbling awkwardly through the part, as though unaware of what was going on around him. His comedic attempts could best be described as leaden. Rick watched the debacle, horrified. He searched frantically for a redeeming moment, for one really good scene (perhaps the love scene on the Spanish Steps featuring the back of his head?), but could find little to take comfort in. He wished that he had never done the picture, that he had listened to Malcolm. He wished that he had a drink.

Finally it was over. The limos were waiting, along with a clutch of stragglers still hoping to catch a glimpse of Hollywood royalty. Rick snarled at a kid trying for an autograph and ducked quickly into the lead car after Marla.

"Well, then, fuck you, man!" the lad called after them as they drove away.

"No way to treat the fans, chum," said Vandy, turning back from the front seat with a grin. He was a swarthy, rakish man with dark eyes and black hair that curled back from a pronounced widow's peak, giving him a slightly satanic air. That Rick's discomfiture should amuse him was nothing new. Their friendship had always included an element of rivalry.

The post-premiere party came together at the newly built Beverly Hills mansion of Umberto Ugolini. The place was an egregious mix of cathedral architecture and Mussolini modern, with vaulted ceilings propped up by pillars, frescoed walls, and a half-acre or so of the marble floors Italians can't seem to live without. Aside from some lewd statuary, there was no furniture as yet, so it was like standing around a metropolitan railway station being served food and drink by an army of uniformed waiters. Those of Hollywood's finest who could stomach Ugolini attended, the rest having gone their own way after the premiere. But there were second-echelon celebrities in abundance, mixed with the producer's own hard core of hangers-on.

Rick broke out of the admiring circle around Marla after enduring a number of gratuitous compliments paid him by sycophants trying to find something nice to say. He got a glass and a bottle of Russian vodka from a service bar and carried them out onto the terrace, another meadow of marble featuring an Olympic-size swimming pool that steamed in the night air. He sat down in a damp wrought-iron chair and poured a drink. Scenes from *All for the Money* flickered relentlessly across a screen behind his eyes. He played each scene well—just as he would if he could do it all over again.

"Mind if I join you, old son?" said Malcolm Webley from behind him. "Can't have you drinking alone."

Rick held up a hand without looking around. "You don't have to say 'I told you so.' "

"Wouldn't dream of it."

"I should have walked right around this party. Vandy could have taken Marla."

Webley shrugged, pulled up a chair, and sat down. "Better you're here. Showing the colors. Nailing the flag to the mast, so to speak."

"Balls."

The older man sipped at his glass of champagne and sighed. "At least Berto serves good bubbly, I must say."

"Yeah. Hard to believe he's a Commie."

"Not really. The Italian Reds are a breed apart. They

are theoretical rather than practicing Communists. Determined to divvy up the other chap's boodle. Never their own."

"You should see his place in Rome. He's got a fence made out of iron spears and a yard full of Dobermans to keep out the common folks. At parties, there's a liveried footman behind every chair to light your smokes and another one in the head to hold your dick while you piss. Literally."

"I've heard say he's a weird one."

"You could say that. Girls, boys, low-flying owls—anything goes."

They sat in silence for a moment.

"How bad is it?" Rick asked finally.

"The picture? I dunno. No matter how well or badly it does, it can't help you or hurt Marla."

"I don't mean the goddamn picture. I'm talking about my situation. My career, if you like."

"Sticky wicket."

"Talk American, will you, Malcolm?"

"You are on thin ice. When King-crafts had to drop the series because they couldn't replace you, they became vindictive. The industry hates actors who break contracts and will be glad to see you fall on your arse."

"I'm sorry I asked."

"I think you can survive it, but you must be very careful. I shall cast about for just the right thing and, with luck, you shall be on your way again." Webley drank off his champagne. "Dare I suggest you let me be the judge of your material in the future?"

Rich was touched. He felt a surge of gratitude toward the dapper little man. He had hardly earned such loyalty. "Thanks, Malcolm." His throat felt constricted and he drank some of his vodka.

"Stiff upper lip, old son."

"What the hell, you can always go back to tennis." Vandy stepped silently out of the shadows, his white teeth flashing. Rick was reminded of Marla's comment. "He doesn't walk," she'd said. "He prowls."

Justin Evander and Rick had attended the same Ivy League prep school twenty years earlier and had stayed in touch ever since. Vandy was indecently rich; the family had pioneered in electronics. He had homes and offices strewn around two continents and an older brother to look after business or, at least, delegate authority. That left Vandy free to dedicate his life to less mundane pursuits. Currently he was mildly obsessed by Marla and, typically, making little effort to disguise his lust.

Rick looked up at him, suppressing an urge to bounce one off his chin. But it didn't pay to let Vandy know when he'd touched a nerve. Instead, he smiled. "What would you do for a pimp, then?"

"I'd quit slumming around with you and go back to high society where I belong."

People began to drift out onto the terrace, including a group surrounding Marla and Umberto Ugolini. They were passing joints back and forth, scenting the evening with cannabis. The producer was flanked by a rosy-cheeked body builder and a little rat of a man named Marcos Marx, who had earned instant celebrity by killing a cop who tried to prevent him from pouring red paint over draft cards at an induction center. Released after serving four years in comfortable isolation, he had become the darling of the antiwar movement, written a book about his ordeal with the aid of a ghost, and was preparing to star in the screen version—to be produced by Umberto Ugolini.

Webley nodded in his direction. "The archtypical antihero, that one. Small, dark, and greasy, with hypnotic eyes. He's the leading man of the future, Rick. Your competition for the next ten years."

"You blond Nazis are on the way out," Vandy agreed. "How would you like to handle me, Malcolm?"

"You're too pretty. They want them dark and ugly. Also smaller and slightly unclean."

Vandy watched Ugolini casually stroking Marla's smooth flank. "Maybe you'd better go rescue your lady, Rick. He's showing an unhealthy interest."

"He likes beefcake better. Anyway, look who's talking." Rick finished his drink, feeling the vodka reach for his extremities.

Vandy contrived to look offended. "I treat her as my own sweet sister," he protested.

"So your sister tells me. And your mother, too." But

Rick was too depressed to banter with Vandy. "Let's collect Marla and get out of here."

"Oh, let her enjoy her moment, old man," said Webley, adding wistfully, "the party girls will soon be leaping into the pool. Starkers, no doubt. And me here with m'lady."

"Let's pitch a couple of the little darlings in now, Rick, and get things started early," suggested Vandy, his pirate's eyes roaming the terrace in search of candidates.

Rick's heart was not in it. The mocking images of what could have been began their parade before his mind's eye again. If it hadn't been for a pansy director who could hardly speak English. And Ugolini skulking around yelling for script changes every hour. "Hell with it, amigo," he said to Vandy. He shook his head to clear it and stood up, setting down his glass. "Except for a few semipros, this is Boys' Town. You can do better down on the Strip. Let's get Marla away from those creeps before she catches something. See you later, Malcolm."

Followed by Vandy, he worked through the group around Marla until he stood in front of her. "Shall we go, my sweet? I'll send a gladiator for your wrap." He looked pointedly at the curly-haired tower of muscle standing beside Ugolini.

Marla made a disappointed little moue of her mouth and shrugged almost imperceptibly. "Whatever you think best, luv."

The producer looked at Rick with a malicious smile. "For your wife, this is an important evening. Surely you will let us share her triumph a little longer. Do not be selfish, Reek."

"Marla is used to triumphs."

"A habit you can envy, eh?" Ugolini looked at Vandy with frank appraisal. "And your friend. Is he not enjoying himself?"

"I'm waiting for the donkeys to rape the virgins," said Vandy.

"Oooh! I love it when they come on so tough," snickered Marcos Marx, who was going through a lavender phase for the benefit of his patron.

Marla made the introductions, straight-faced. "Justin Evander, Umberto Ugolini. And, of course, Marcos Marx."

"Ugolini the weenie-genie," said Rick, making Vandy laugh.

The producer looked confused, but the muscle-bound youth beside him scowled. "That's not funny, you," he said. His name was Jody, and Ugolini was going to take him to Italy and make him a movie star. Sure.

Rick smiled at him. "Snake off, Fruitcup," he said.

The ensuing silence was broken by someone's nervous giggle. Rick saw the glint of anticipation in Marla's eyes and knew she would love to see this one played out. But finally pragmatism won out and she simply said to the boy, "Would you be a dear and fetch my wrap?" No bad career moves for Marla.

Rick decided not to let it alone. "Well, what are you waiting for?" he snapped at the kid.

Jody's face reddened and the veins stood out on his neck.

"Heavens, don't cry!" Vandy feigned alarm.

Jody started forward, but Ugolini raised a languid hand, stopping him in his tracks.

"You nearly ruined my film," he said to Rick with measured venom. "Now you would ruin my party as well."

Rick reached for him, catching him by his soft neck with one hand. "Say again?"

Jody cried out and flung himself on Rick. Vandy reached out to try to pull him off, but the muscle man placed a hand against his chest and shoved, sending him backpedaling into an occupied table, where he sprawled on his back, carrying everybody down with him in a welter of spilled liquor and broken glass. When he tried to get up, a stubby actor with a notorious temper rose from the floor, announcing that this was too fucking much, and punched him alongside the head, knocking him down again.

Rick felt himself torn away from Ugolini by incredibly strong hands and flung away into a knot of onlookers, who promptly pushed him back toward the enraged Jody, who was advancing with flailing arms.

"Nail the sissy sumbitch!" yelled Vandy from the floor. "He fights like a girl!"

Rick avoided a couple of wild swings, took a numbing

punch on the shoulder, and counterattacked. He had not been in a real brawl for a long time. Hawke's fights were carefully choreographed and preprogrammed for him to win. He swung a photogenic punch at Jody's midsection, stepping in nicely, getting a lot of shoulder into it.

It was like hitting a washboard. The kid swarmed in and reached for his throat with his weight lifter's hands. He picked Rick up off the floor and shook him.

"In the nuts! Kick him in the nuts!" yelled Vandy.

Rick heeded the advice, lashing out with his foot just as everything began fading to black. Caught squarely, Jody dropped him to step back and clutch at his groin. Rick struggled up off his knees and swung at the exposed nose. The big fellow lifted a hand to his face and brought it away red.

"Blood!" he screamed. "My blood!"

Then he sat down on the floor and began to weep in earnest.

Rick stood swaying, fingering his tender neck. He could hear Ugolini shrieking in Italian somewhere out of his line of vision.

"What is this?" a sweet-faced blond wanted to know. "Some kind of time-out?"

"Aiiieee!" As if to negate her fears, Marcos Marx broke out of the crowd waving a wine bottle, which he swung at the back of Rick's head. "You goddamn shit!" he screamed.

Alerted, Rick ducked and caught the blow painfully on his injured shoulder. Vandy scrambled up and launched himself at Marx, throwing a very creditable body block that propelled the revolutionary author of *A Martyr for the People* through a plate-glass partition into Ugolini's vast ballroom. Marx bounced back up, apparently unhurt, shaking off glass as a dog sheds water, spewing obscenities in the direction of his assailant.

"Cut out that dirty talk!" bawled the stocky actor who had slugged Vandy. "Can'tcha see there's cunts around?"

Rick turned to find Marla standing next to him. She seldom drank more than a little wine, but her eyes told him she was pretty stoned on pot. "I just can't take you anywhere," she said with a grin. Then, in apparent fury, she slapped his face and cried, "How can you humiliate me so!" adding softly, "Just in case anyone's watching."

"Oscar performance, babe," said Rick, rubbing his cheek.

Webley was there too. "An appalling spectacle. And most ill-advised." The manager looked at him coldly.

Vandy appeared with Marla's wrap. "That's enough reviews. I hear tell someone called the cops. Is anything keeping us here?" A siren keened in the distance, giving weight to his words. No one prevented them from leaving.

Outside, a few limos still waited for business, the uniformed drivers standing around together smoking and listening to the approaching siren. One car, a vintage custom-built Cadillac convertible, stood apart from the others. It looked half a block long, with four doors and fender-mounted spare tires, and it belonged to Umberto Ugolini.

"Oooh!" Marla exclaimed, pointing. "Let's take that one!"

Rick went over and peered inside. "The key's in it," he announced, getting behind the wheel. "Pile in."

Marla and Vandy got in back as he fired it up. With a yell, one of the chauffeurs flung aside his cigarette and charged toward them. Rick slewed the big car around to miss him by about a foot and shot out the gate, spraying gravel against the side of a police unit that was just turning in from the street, using red light and siren. The Caddy plunged across the road and laid tracks over a neighboring lawn before Rick could wrestle it back on course.

He took evasive action in case of pursuit and they careened through a maze of quiet tree-lined streets before ending up on Sunset Boulevard. No one seemed to be following them, so they went to Scandia and ordered smoked salmon, beer, and aquavit. Both Rick and Vandy looked disheveled, but they had on neckwear, the house requirement, so it was all right. Ken Hansen himself showed them to a booth somewhat removed from the stargazers.

"I'm going to say you both kidnapped me," Marla decided, stuffing herself with salmon. Grass gave her a voracious appetite. "Umberto is going to be very angry."

"It was worth it. I haven't laughed so hard since the pigs ate my little brother," claimed Vandy.

"It's not your problem. You're not in the business," she told him.

"You think my old amigo shot himself in the foot?" Vandy asked Marla. "Bracing Ugolini like that?"

She looked at Rick sadly. "I think more likely between the eyes."

"No one likes Ugolini," said Rick. He drank some aquavit and chased it with beer. It rekindled warmth and confidence.

"He's a toad," Marla agreed. "But tonight a lot of what passes for important people in this town saw you out of control. They saw sour grapes and maybe panic, and that scares them."

Rick shook his head. "It wasn't panic, it was poison. I had to get it out of me. All those weeks in Italy working with those comic-opera clowns. We had a director named Malatesta, Vandy. That means 'headache' in Italian. It should have been pain in the ass. He acted like he was directing a circus, gibbering away in two languages, neither of which anyone could understand. And that Commie scumbag Ugolini sneaking around the set, cutting my part and changing the dialogue so there wasn't a white page left in the script. . . ."

Marla looked at him steadily. "Fool the others, Rick. Try to fool Vandy or me, but never, never kid yourself. You couldn't handle the material."

She turned to Vandy before Rick could reply. "Did you know I had a kid, Vandy?"

"No. . . ."

"He's nine now, a beautiful boy with melting brown eyes. He looks like Rick must have looked at the same age, except he's dark. I put him in private school when Rick and I got married. I know I'm a lousy mother, but then, we've been traveling almost ever since making *All for the Money*.

"Anyway, one day a couple of years ago, he looked into a toy-store window and saw some electric trains going around a track, through tunnels and so forth. I thought his nose was going to grow through the glass. I got him home, but it was all he could talk about, so I went back and bought a train for him. I got him the old-fashioned frontier model with a tall smokestack because I thought it was quaint and maybe because it was a little cheaper, costing around two hundred dollars at that. I wasn't rich then. Well, it turned out he wanted the sleek Super Chief, so he just got out his ball bat and smashed the train to pieces. He could have had a lot of fun with that train, but it wasn't exactly what he wanted, so he destroyed it. You see, Eric has more in common with Rick than just good looks."

"I may be drunk, but I don't quite see the analogy," Rick lied.

"Then I'll belabor the point. You're very good at playing Hawke, alias Rick Steele. *All for the Money* was too much of a stretch for you. You crashed and burned. . . ."

Rick leaned forward. "It was you who wanted that picture from the beginning. For both of us. You conned me into dropping the series, which is what burned the fucking bridge. . . ."

"I did, but I was wrong. Malcolm was right. I'm sorry, but we had to know, didn't we? It's just that you were a star before you were an actor.

"But back to my point. You could have handled it gracefully tonight. Did you break your racket and punch your opponent every time you lost a tennis match? I'm sure you must have lost some. I mean that you could have laughed and gone on doing your own thing. Maybe not Hawke, but something like it. Everyone would have said, 'What a sporting fellow.' " She shook her head. "But no, you've got to rain on the parade if you can't lead it. Well, you just broke your train, luv. I hope it can be mended, because you're not going to get the other one."

Rick tried and failed to be angry with his wife. It was easy to rage at Ugolini, whom he despised. Wrecking his party had purged his bile, left him feeling good. But he knew that Marla never dissembled with him, simply called the shots as she saw them. Her instinct in second-guessing the film industry was uncanny, which made her verdict disturbing. He drank more aquavit to counter his malaise and said, "It'll all work out, Marly. They were mostly Ugolini's joy-boys around when we kind of cut loose."

"But not all." Marla leaned forward, putting her hand

over his as if they were alone, ignoring Vandy's foxy
smile. Her pupils were slightly dilated, but there was no
distortion of speech or thought. "Listen to me. I hope it
will be all right, but let me tell you something. I won't be
a party to your death wish if you destroy yourself. I won't
leap on your pyre, no matter how I feel about you. I've
worked too hard and come too far."

"Shit, this is turning into a wake," Vandy commented,
shifting in his seat. "Tell you what! Let's go down to
Emerald Bay. We can take the *Satyr* out tomorrow and
cruise down to Mexico for a couple of days. Far from
prying eyes. I'll send the dago's car back in the morning."

Vandy had a beach house in the exclusive Emerald Bay
section of Laguna Beach. The *Satyr* was his big ocean
cruiser, a party boat of international repute that hoisted a
cocktail flag featuring a red fist with middle finger extended on a white field above the legend "*Digitus Impudicus.*"

Marla let go of Rick's hand and reached into her purse.
She came out with a rolled joint, which she put between
her lips and lit, a fairly daring public act at the time. "I'll
smoke to that," she said.

Ken Hansen was back over like a shot, before a dozen
noses could wrinkle, begging her to put it out. This was
interpreted by Marla as an act of inhospitality if not downright *lèse-majesté*, and they left literally and figuratively
under a cloud, Vandy carrying the bottle of aquavit.

The freeway was deserted at that late hour and Rick
drove fast, taking an occasional pull at the bottle Vandy
passed over from the backseat. Beside him Marla fiddled
with the stereo, trying to find music to suit her mood,
which seemed to be manic-depressive, alternating between
bursts of laughter or song and prolonged dark silences.
Within an hour they were on a lonely stretch of coastal
road between Newport Beach and Laguna, racing along
parallel to the surf. The interior of the car reeked of
marijuana and aquavit, and Rick felt a sudden need of
fresh air. He released the snaps anchoring the top and
punched the button that would put it down.

The Cadillac, which was hitting seventy, slowed percepti-
bly when the canvas rose with a thin whine, instantly
becoming a sail. There followed a staccato ripping sound

as the material peeled away from the frame to whip back and billow around in their wake.

"Shit!" cried Vandy. "Stop the car!"

"What for?" Rick yelled back.

"Gotta piss, for one thing! Then maybe I'll walk home."

Rick pulled over onto the shoulder of the road. He could hear the surf but could not see it, for they were in a depression between two small hills and the fog was dense. He got out, shivering in the damp chill, and staggered, hanging on to the door, feeling as though his knees could bend either way. Marla scooted over the seat to stand next to him. They could hear Vandy urinating on the roadbed somewhere in the night.

"This is very romantic, luv. I hope you've had a good time, because tomorrow is another day and you're not going to like anything about it."

"I didn't like anything about this one, either."

Vandy appeared, working his way cautiously toward them by clinging to the car. "Cheer up, it's not over yet. We should have some more drinks, maybe smoke some more dope." He peered at the skeletal remains of the top, halted in mid-erection. The canvas was back on the road somewhere. "We're going to have to send this thing back to Ugolini in a brown paper bag if you keep this up."

"Rick isn't driving anymore," said Marla.

"It's only a couple more miles," Rick protested.

"How many people think Rick can still drive?" Vandy wanted to know.

Rick's hand rose alone.

Marla got in behind the wheel and adjusted the seat to her smaller frame. "Get in, both of you. I want to get home before I freeze."

Rick got in beside her and Vandy returned to the backseat. They would have reached Vandy's place in less than five minutes. Emerald Bay nestled in a cove just north of Laguna Beach, and they were already well south of Corona del Mar. But Marla wanted a cigarette and Vandy lit it for her, puffing on it a few times before leaning forward to pass it over. Marla reached up, but she had been smoking the other stuff all evening and her coordination was considerably impaired. Her fingers brushed the tip of the cigarette, dislodging the glowing ember so that it fell down her neckline into the valley between her naked breasts. She cried out in pain and released the wheel to clutch at herself with both hands.

The big Caddy was taking a gentle curve toward the ocean, holding well to the right-hand side of the road. When Marla lost control, it drifted across the median line into the oncoming traffic lanes and Rick could see the dim, close-set headlights rush out of the fog directly at them. Later, in his dreams, the yellow orbs seemed to float slowly toward him, allowing all the time in the world to alter course and avoid disaster, had he not been paralyzed. But in reality, it happened fast. He reached for the wheel, but his own motor reflexes were sluggish from the long night's drinking, and the best he could do was spare them a head-on collision. As it happened, the Cadillac struck the other car heavily with its massive left fender, then swerved to the right, overcompensating from Rick's desperate tug at the wheel, and skidded to a stop in the shrubbery beyond the shoulder of the road as Marla found the brake. The behemoth survived the crash intact, the shock easily absorbed by its heavy frame. Marla, shaken but unhurt, stared uncomprehendingly along the beam of the surviving headlight, which pointed aimlessly at the bushes. Vandy bounced off the back of Rick's seat on his way to the floorboards. He hauled himself up at once. "Aw, goddamn! Now what?" he yelled.

Rick opened the door on his side and stumbled out onto the grass. He got up and peered around in the night for the other car. It was about twenty yards away and well off the road, judging by the little tongues of flame that licked at its carcass. He ran through the fog toward the fire, tearing off his dinner jacket, seeing the little Volkswagen on its back, wheels still spinning in the air. He flogged the sinister little orange daggers with his coat until he had smothered them, leaving himself in darkness, unable to see more than the contours of the wreck.

"Sweet Jesus Christ!" Vandy stood at his shoulder, swaying and breathing heavily. He snapped on his cigarette lighter, adjusting the flame to maximum height, and crouched down. Rick knelt beside him.

The short, sloping hood of the car had been smashed back into the cockpit, displacing the single occupant, a young woman as far as they could tell. Her head and upper torso had gone through the windshield, shatterproof or not. Brown hair mercifully masked most of her face, but one dead, open eye was visible in the feeble light, looking at nothing in particular. Rick never knew a human body contained so much blood. Her hair and dress were matted with it, and still it flowed. From the severed arteries of her neck, from the crushed skull, from everywhere.

Vandy let the lighter flicker out; they didn't need to see more. Rick got to his feet, gulping deep breaths of night air, fighting back his nausea. The jolt of adrenaline which had carried him across the highway with such purpose had subsided, leaving him merely confused and shaken. He tried to marshal his thoughts, to gather energy for the next move, but overcome by sudden weariness, wanted only to lie down.

"We've got to get out of here," he heard Vandy say.

"What?"

"She's dead, man. There's no way to help her. We've got to get out fast." He caught up Rick's smoldering jacket and shoved him toward the Cadillac. Rick tottered across the road, trying to bring everything into focus, battling the lethargy that enveloped him. Marla materialized before him like a phantom in her white gown, the pale oval of her face featureless in the dark. She caught his arm, stopping him.

"Go back," Vandy grated at her. "There's nothing you can do."

"Tell me," she said to Rick.

"She's dead."

"Oh my God!"

"We can't just stand around here," Vandy insisted. "Someone can come along any second."

"If we're caught leaving the scene . . ." Rick began, still struggling for lucidity.

". . . we say we were going for help," Vandy finished for him. "But it's two-thirty in the fucking morning and my place is about three miles away." He turned to Marla.

"If this gets out, you're finished, kid. You won't even be able to make skin flicks."

"But it was an accident," Marla said in a dazed, faraway voice.

"You're full of dope, never mind champagne. They can tell by your eyes and they've got tests they can give you that'll show dope in your system just like they can show alcohol. Now, let's move!"

He shoved past them and got behind the wheel of the Cadillac. "Get in, dammit!" He started the engine and tried to drive back onto the highway. The rear wheels spun, digging down into the sandy soil, but the car wouldn't move. He shoved down the accelerator, cursing, succeeding only in burying the wheels deeper.

Rick walked around the long hood through the beam of the headlight and peered closely at the crumpled left-front fender. Having borne the brunt of the impact, it was jammed back solidly against the wheel. "Forget it," he said.

Vandy jumped out and tried to pull the heavy metal free of the tire, but Ugolini's Cadillac had been put together when solid steel rather than light alloy was used for sheet metal. Even pulling together, they couldn't budge it. From the direction of Corona del Mar, a set of headlights grew in the distance.

"Shit," said Vandy.

Marla stood at the edge of the road, gazing at the approaching lights like a fawn caught in the hunter's beam. The car came on relentlessly, its brights effectively limning persons and vehicles like players and props on an abruptly floodlit stage. The driver slowed almost to a stop, as though taking meticulous inventory, then speeded up and drove off into the night in the direction of Laguna Beach.

"That does it," said Vandy. "He'll call the cops."

Marla went to sit in the car, slumping against the seat. When Rick came close to her, he could see the despair on her face in the jaundiced light from the dashboard. "He's right," she whispered. "He's right."

Rick fumbled for cigarettes and lit one. The smoke made him feel dizzy. "We'll come up with something. There are three of us."

"Three witnesses on drugs and booze," said Vandy from behind him. "Anyway, they can tell from the skid marks we were on the wrong side of the road."

"We'll get the best lawyer. Christ knows we can afford it. Belli or Ivan Carstairs."

"Then she probably won't do time. But it's still the end of her career. Finis. Kaput."

"Then shut up, Vandy. What the hell are you trying to do?"

Vandy walked around to face him. "Trying to show you that there *is* something to do. That you can save her."

"Then just come out with it. How?" But his mind was clearing and Rick already knew what Vandy would say.

"Tell the cops you were driving."

Rick, looking at Marla, saw the change in her face, the unmistakable flicker of hope. But she said, "Don't be ridiculous, Vandy."

Vandy ignored her, speaking directly to Rick. "You can handle it better than she can, amigo. And you've got a hell of a lot less to lose, especially after tonight. But she could be the biggest star in the world! If they bust her for dope on top of causing a fatal accident, it's all over, believe me."

Rick looked at Vandy with sudden hatred. This greasy, fucking Iago with his simple, logical solutions. He had been a cajoler, a coaxer, a blandisher since childhood. This should be an obvious sacrifice for Rick Steele to make, he seemed to say. Small loss to the world, or to himself, such a modest talent. And hey, old buddy, you know you'd fuck up sooner or later, anyway. . . .

"You could say you were driving, Vandy. Since it's your idea."

Vandy answered without hesitation. "I would if she were mine." Then he had the grace to bow his head.

Rick turned away from Vandy and caught the leaping hope in Marla's eyes again. She was so tiny, his wife. Never helpless, not that, but somehow diminished and vulnerable. He reached down for her, caught her by the arms, and pulled her up easily. "Get away from us," he snarled aside at Vandy, who retreated, Rick could have sworn, with just the hint of a bow.

"I can do this, Marly," he said to her, his face against her cheek. "Is it what you want?"

Her small, surprisingly strong arms snaked out around his neck. He could feel her tears against his flesh, the flutter of her lashes. "I can't face it," she said, weak for the first time since he had known her, needing him, really needing him for the first time. "I just can't lose everything over this."

Lose everything. A ghastly vision of the dead woman across the highway intruded, threatening to make a mockery of the moment. He suppressed the image, chased her ghost away. She was dead, after all. Out of it. This one, whom he loved, was alive and desperate.

Presently they heard sirens in the distance. For the second time that night.

The dead woman was one Meade Lacey, a twenty-three-year-old Mormon schoolteacher of single status who occasionally augmented her income by moonlighting as a baby-sitter and had been returning home from just such work when she was struck and killed by the wayward Cadillac. She had been active in her church, loved children, and donated her spare time to charity work around Orange County. A national contest could not have turned up a more innocent victim, never mind a sampling of Southern California. Facing charges of vehicular manslaughter in her death was a jaded actor from the Sodom and Gomorrah of Hollywood who was found to have enough alcohol sloshing around in his veins to fell a quartet of L.A. Rams and who had been driving a car reported to be stolen. The Orange County prosecutor was out for blood.

After considering Melvin Belli and F. Lee Bailey, Rick engaged Ivan Carstairs, successor to Jerry Geisler as a defender of Hollywood stars, to represent him. Carstairs was lanky, Lincolnesque, and melancholy (whereas Geisler had been short, dapper, and dynamic), a master at lulling the opposition into thinking he was a bit dim-witted despite his awesome reputation, thus giving him the advantage of dealing with a relaxed, unwary antagonist whose words subsequently became his or her own coffin nails.

People said he could have gotten the Boston Strangler off with a reprimand, and he did not come cheap.

During the legal proceedings against him, Rick's driver's license had been suspended and he remained secluded in the Topanga Canyon house. Marla was finishing a picture and though she dutifully came home at night to cook for him and temper his deepening depression, the days passed slowly. He had no desire to venture out and face the media-bred hostility he felt sure lurked waiting for him, no urge to see the looks of admiration turned to contempt. He spent hours pounding tennis balls against the backboard of the court he had just recently built, and began the cocktail hour measurably sooner each afternoon.

His last meeting with Malcolm Webley offered no comfort. The little manager had undergone a change. Missing from his desk was the picture of his regal wife, who had just died, to be replaced by a full-color eleven-by-fourteen glossy of the tarty little redhead he now lived with. Tweed jackets and ascots had given way to polyester jumpsuits and gold chains nesting in exposed chest hair. The new getup was out of harmony with his baggy eyes and liver-spotted hands. He clung to the pseudo-BBC accent and his sang-froid, however. "Silly little twat." He waved a negligent hand at the photo of the redhead. "Keeps me young, though."

Unable to agree, Rick said nothing.

Webley, typically, pulled no punches. "Briefly said, you're finished," he stated, his small hands at work loading his pipe, the lone prop to have survived the sartorial revolution. "You've really torn it this time. Remember what happened to Humpty-Dumpty? 'All the king's horses and all the king's men . . .' and so forth, if you follow my meaning? There's nothing I can do for you, old son. You have become the proverbial leper at the feast."

"You're overreacting, Malcolm. I'm not convicted of anything yet."

"You will be, but that's neither here nor there. It seems you have slain Orange County's own version of Joan of Arc and the Virgin Mary rolled into one. The press has painted you as a true son of Babylon, and since you ran roughshod over the sensibilities of the film industry in your heyday, you have built up no equity of goodwill. There will be no fund-raiser to help you meet expenses, no angel to offer you a part when you get out of the slammer."

Rick paled at the mention of incarceration. "It won't come to that," he said quickly, and changed the subject. "Listen, Malcolm, people forget. They forgot that Mitchum was busted for dope, that Walter Wanger shot a guy. They'll forget a car accident. I'm only asking you to hang in with me. Find me something to keep me alive. We'll build back from there. . . ."

Webley shook his head. "I'm not interested anymore. You have jettisoned two successful careers as blithely as fuck-all. You are as self-destructive as a lemming. Do you recall that I told you years ago I would wash my hands of you if you as much as involved yourself in scandal?" The little hands rubbed each other in a remembered gesture. "Well, you've gone all that a tad better, haven't you? I'm very angry with you, Rick. You have cost me a great deal, as well as yourself. You're a bloody suicidal idiot!"

"I've made you a fortune, Malcolm!"

Webley glared at him, puffing on his pipe until Rick had to fan the smoke away. "More's the pity it can't go on! I've warned you and I've coddled you and I've nursed you! All a great bloody waste!" He leaned back in his deep chair with a sigh. He didn't seem to have anything more to say.

Rick got up to leave. "What the hell, Malcolm, we had our moments."

Webley rose too. "We had a few laughs at that." He put out his hand and Rick took it, just as he had at the beginning of their long relationship. He had almost reached the door when the manager spoke. "You might try Europe," he suggested.

Rick turned back, bitterly amused. "The graveyard of failed American actors?"

Webley shrugged. "I can't think of anything else."

When Marla's picture wrapped, she stayed home with Rick and shared his exile, exhibiting domestic qualities he had forgotten she possessed. She adapted, chameleonlike, to his frequent changes of mood, anticipating his every need. She surprised him with the excellence of her cooking, a chore she had seldom performed since the brief idyll in Sicily. If he sulked, she jollied him out of it; if he sometimes made love to her with a violence that suggested punishment, she accepted and seemed even to enjoy it, as though in this way she could acknowledge her debt to him.

. But she did not appear in court with him during his arraignment or during the subsequent preliminary hearing, despite the pleas of Ivan Carstairs, who felt that her visible support would strengthen his client's position. Malcolm Webley insisted that she maintain a public distance from the pariah Rick had become, lest she be too much associated with his crime and thus tarred by the same brush. Rick agreed with this stance. Having already forfeited his future to ensure hers, it made no sense to imperil this considerable sacrifice for the comfort of having her at his side in the courtroom. The extra credibility it would lend him seemed nebulous, in any case.

They no longer socialized, except for infrequent visits to Vandy's mansion above Mulholland Drive. Marla would drive them in her agile little Porsche, with Rick, his wings clipped, riding beside her in humiliation. On these occasions Vandy was the essence of good humor in an obvious attempt to buoy Rick's spirits, but the warmth had gone out of their relationship and his best efforts seemed forced. When in residence, he lived alone save for an enigmatic German couple named Dieter and Lotte Greim, who serviced the estate, and whatever girl (he called them his little darlin's) was currently servicing him. The little darlin's all had nicknames such as the Beef Trust, a girl of Junoesque proportions, the Dairy, whose mammary endowments were such that Lotte despaired of serving her at table, being unable to find space in front of her for the plate, and the Spinner, a miniature blond even more compact than Marla. They were all invariably young, sexy, and very attentive to Vandy.

Except, possibly, for the Leopard, who was introduced lounging bonelessly on the apron of the pool one Sunday afternoon. Her voice was a throaty purr and she had tawny hair cut in bangs just above a set of amber eyes that fastened unblinkingly on Marla and remained there for the duration.

They were, as was customary when Rick and Marla were invited, a group of four. Refreshments in the form of tall drinks and strong grass were brought by Dieter, a giant of a man with fair hair brushed straight back over his scalp and an explosion of scar tissue on one cheek. He held his right arm slightly bent, as if he could not straighten it, and though his manner was impeccable, his demeanor was not that of a servant. The first time she saw him, Marla looked at him with instinctive curiosity and interest.

Vandy, who was thoroughly stoned, sipped his drink and grimaced. "Dieter, you goddamn Nazi, I said soda water, not tonic."

The huge German took the offending glass and dumped its contents unceremoniously into the pool, where the ice cubes and wedge of lime bobbed around in a cluster. He rebuilt the drink with the requested ingredients from the service bar, handed it to Vandy, bowed, and stalked away across the lawn.

"That was a deliberate act of defiance," Marla laughed. "I think you hurt his feelings, calling him a Nazi."

"If I remember it, I'll fire him tomorrow. He looks like a Nazi, and I don't like Nazis. But I don't discriminate. I don't like niggers, wops, hebes, frogs, spics, dagos, hunkies, limeys, or micks, either."

"That narrows it down," commented Marla.

"You look kind of like a dago yourself," Rick pointed out. He closed his eyes against the last rays of late-afternoon sun, his head spinning from the combination of booze and grass. He was not ordinarily a doper and the drug was wasted on him. It scrambled the circuits in his brain and hopelessly distorted his sense of time. Worse, it brought him down or even induced a state of paranoia, but nowadays he would try anything.

"Greek," Vandy corrected him. "Greeks are beautiful. My mother is Greek."

Rick remembered his mother from boyhood, and she had indeed been beautiful. A Greek opera singer who had married an American tycoon to introduce a little color into a bland dynasty. Vandy worshiped her.

"I'm the other way around," purred the Leopard. "I love everybody." But her eyes were fastened solely on Marla. She had crept along the border of the pool on her tanned belly until she could lay her tawny head on the actress's thigh. Marla neither responded nor rejected her. She took the fresh joint Vandy handed over, toked deeply from it, and passed it on to the recumbent girl.

"Not too much," Vandy cautioned, stroking the Leopard's flank. "This stuff is different."

He took the joint from her and placed it between Rick's lips. Rick inhaled without opening his eyes, no longer caring about the source of nirvana. The smoke was acrid and chemical to his taste. It assaulted his lungs fiercely and numbed his fingers. His eyes shot open as he spat out the offending weed and tried to bring the world back into focus. "What the hell was that?" he managed to ask.

Vandy retrieved the joint and stubbed it carefully. "Angel dust. A little bit goes a long way."

Rick struggled to his feet just to prove to himself he could do it. It seemed to take a long time. His thoughts roiled in confusion, branching away from any central theme he might try to grasp. The simplest act needed enormous concentration. He began a long trip toward the pool gleaming a dozen feet ahead of him like a blue oasis of sanity and refreshment. Somehow he reached the edge and managed to stumble gracelessly in, feeling the overheated water close over his head. He thrashed back to the surface, realizing to his horror that he could not swim, that his limbs would not respond to the weak signals from his drugged brain. Nor could he make more than a gagging sound, for his mouth and throat were full of water. With a desperate lunge he caught hold of the gutter, drew his body along until his feet could find the bottom, and then held tight to the edge of the pool. He spat out the water and could have yelled for help, but now there seemed to be no need to. A cunning idea came to mind. His back was to the others and they obviously had not noticed his predicament, his moment of sheer panic. Well, they need never know; he could hang on here forever. Ex-lifeguards simply didn't drown in six or seven feet of water or cry for help like babies. He giggled at the thought, his shoulders shaking with mirth. Careful now, they mustn't see him laughing; they'd think he was nuts. He tried to control his hilarity, but it bubbled up out of him until he cleverly covered it by pretending to cough. There now, he finally had it battened down, only an occasional snort escaping. He clung to the edge of the pool, his eyes closed tight against vertigo, and tried to will himself back to lucidity. The trick was to stay awake, not let the heated water lull and eventually claim him. He rubbed his face against the cooler tiles of the pool or bit the inside of his cheek when he felt himself slipping. He never knew how long he stayed that way. He felt as though it could have been seconds or hours.

When he opened his eyes he knew it hadn't been hours. There was no direct sunlight and the air was cooler, but he could easily make out the color of the pool tiles and the grass beyond. Tentatively he tested his systems and found them to be functioning. He moved through the water at the shallow end of the pool as if wading through quicksand, and emerged on the apron. Remembering that he was not alone, he hauled himself swaying to his feet, looking around for the others.

They were at the other end of the pool among the lengthening shadows, grouped now in a dim cluster. Rick got prudently down on all fours, judging this to be the safest means of locomotion, and crawled toward them. Approaching as slowly as a snail on Valium, he was gradually able to make out more detail.

They were all completely naked. Marla lay on her back, the perfect breasts jutting up, nipples dark and pointed. Her eyes were closed and it was impossible to tell if she was in ecstasy or simply unconscious. Her white legs were incredibly lovely even sprawled loosely apart as they were with the Leopard's mane tucked firmly between them. Vandy rode the Leopard, whose perfectly formed posterior reared up and pushed back to meet his every thrust. It was, in all, a well-choreographed performance, a bit of rhythmic pornography presided over by a director who knew from long practice how to handle his players.

Rick drew closer, peering at the erotic tableau in awe. No one seemed aware of his scrutiny. With his perception heightened to the approximate degree that his intellect was diminished, he saw at first only a graceful tripling of strangers enhanced by the beauty of the bodies entwined, any blemish or crudity erased by the onset of twilight. The temptation was to recline there in contemplation, perhaps eventually rouse himself to join the party. Everything was seen as though through a rose filter lens.

Gradually the mist cleared and the actors took on character; the cast began to fall in place. Riding tall in the saddle was Vandy, whom Rick realized he had begun to dislike. He felt nothing much about the Leopard other than an abstract lust inspired by the perfection of her writhing body. But below them lay Marla, who, for all he could discern, might be the victim of the piece, in the process of being violated while helpless or unconscious. He remembered Vandy's penchant for casual perversion, and a red ball of rage began growing behind his eyes. The bastard had drugged him to get him out of the way while he played mixed doubles with the odd-man-out. Rick could have fucking drowned for all Vandy cared! Well, he had fooled the son of a bitch and survived. He had returned from the Black Lagoon with the strength of ten and driven by vengeance. When Vandy arched up and threw back his head in a silent scream of pleasure, Rick reached for his neck.

Rick's court appearances were anticlimactic after the sensational media hype that preceded them. They took place in Orange County, a bastion of conservatism in those days before Mexican and Asian immigration (both legal and otherwise) netted Democratic politicians an army of new voters and, incidentally, reintroduced tuberculosis to America. Then, county residents had nothing more sinister to contend with than a glut of summertime hippies along their coastline, and Hollywood was, figuratively speaking, a world away. Judge Herb Rickley, the jurist in charge, did not tolerate a circus atmosphere in his courtroom, the locals turned apathetic when they discovered Marla Monday would not be on display, and even the tabloid press lost interest when they learned there would be no full-scale trial. It was as if the defendant were already a forgotten man.

Charges of grand theft auto were dismissed against Rick when one of Umberto Ugolini's retainers reminded him that his Cadillac, which had just been sent over from Europe, had a heavy drug stash secreted between its door panels and might not bear close inspection if introduced into evidence. Ugolini gnashed his teeth and changed his story, leaving Rick free to plea-bargain on the remaining charge. Ivan Carstairs, a brilliant trial attorney, felt himself wasted in his diminished role as a mere negotiator. He changed Rick's plea from innocent to guilty of vehicular manslaughter under extenuating circumstances, obviating the need for a trial. The hard-nosed prosecutor was somewhat mollified by the generous restitution the defendant agreed to pay—and perhaps relieved not to have to face Carstairs before a jury. After a notably undramatic hearing that was ill-attended by the press, Judge Rickley handed Rick a three-year suspended sentence, this period to be spent on probation, the terms of which limited his driving to daytime hours and required him to check in regularly with a probation officer.

Restitution to be paid the victim's family was decreed at a quarter of a million dollars, and Carstairs' fee for his minimal effort came to nearly as much. Rick liquidated his assets and put the Topanga Canyon house on the market. He retained for himself only his personal items and one car, the old T-Bird. Like his father before him, he hadn't been interested in saving money. There was always time to make more.

Rick became more and more reclusive. After the incident that left his host hospitalized for a week, he saw no more of Vandy. Even the enormous Dieter had been unable to haul Rick away from the naked man before he had inflicted a concussion by banging Vandy's head against the apron of the pool. It was not yet common knowledge that the drug called angel dust could turn the user into a violent sociopath capable of remarkable feats of strength, so no one, including Rick himself, knew what had gotten into him that afternoon. For her part, Marla claimed she recalled nothing that happened after Rick had jumped into the pool.

The Topanga Canyon house sold and went into escrow, and still Rick remained there, apathetic as to his next move. He hit tennis balls for hours, watched daytime television aimlessly, and drank formidable amounts of vodka. Whereas he had been a party drinker, he now became a steady, sodden drinker. But no amount of alcohol banished the recurring dream of yellow headlights emerging slowly out of the fog directly at him, coming on so slowly that he had all the time in the world to get out of the way. If he had not been paralyzed. During waking hours he sometimes became confused and forgot that he had not actually been behind the wheel at the time of the accident. After all, he had admitted guilt so many times. And what the hell, he had failed to prevent it.

Marla was rehearsing a play at the Ahmanson Theater in the new Music Center complex downtown and she seldom got home before Rick had gone to sleep or passed out. She had long wanted to go onstage, and the project occupied all her energy, leaving no time for a remote, sullen husband, now an industry untouchable, who would neither talk shop nor even read the trades. They grew swiftly apart.

One afternoon she came home early to tell him she was leaving him.

9

Erin interrupted for the first time, outraged despite herself. "How could she do that? After you saved her miserable career. How could anyone?"

Steelegrave shrugged and smiled. "Marla wasn't just anyone. She was like a primitive organism totally dedicated to its own survival. Anyway, I remember as if it were yesterday that she came home early and caught me sober, probably planned it that way. 'I can't stay with you anymore,' she said. 'It just isn't right for me. You'll drag me down like an anchor.' Marla always thought in terms of what was 'right' or 'wrong' for her.

"I just stood there, stunned. You know how you think of all the things you should have said and done when it's too late? But then, what the hell was there to say? 'You rotten bitch, after everything I've given up for you!' Or maybe, 'Couldn't you at least wait a decent interval, old girl?'

"But it gets better. Next, she actually said, 'You don't have any reason to believe this, but I care for you more than I ever have for any man, and I will miss you. I can't say I love you. I don't think I know what that is all about. But I do care, and someday, somehow, I'll try to make up for this.' She was capable of feeling guilt, you see. I should have laughed at her or slugged her, but I still couldn't react. The whole thing was unreal. I guess I took her for granted because I'd put it all on the line for her and figured she owed me. Of course, by then I should have known her better.

"It was as if she were trying to convince herself. 'I'm almost thirty,' she said. 'I've got to move fast if I'm going all the way. Life isn't some kind of a rehearsal, it's just once around the track and I've got to go for it.' Or words to that effect. I still didn't do anything, not even reach for a prop like a drink or a cigarette and that seemed to annoy her. She said, 'You might as well know that I'm going to marry Vandy when our divorce is final.' "

"Why didn't you at least go public and tell the truth about the accident?" Erin cried.

"Oh, come on, kid. With Vandy the only other witness? At least that goosed a reaction out of me, I remember. 'I could kill you,' I told her. 'That would really slow down your career.' She wasn't afraid at all, just shrugged it off as if I were being childish. 'Then we'd both be finished,' is all she said. She was a very gutsy lady, was Marla. She might have guessed I wouldn't kill her, but she couldn't know for sure. I sure as hell thought about it. Then and later."

"She wasn't very brave that night on the highway," Erin said disgustedly. "When she fell apart and let you take the blame." Suddenly she hated the dead woman for squeezing Richard dry, for destroying the substance of him and leaving her only the shell.

He said, "I've often wondered if that wasn't just another performance. She was good enough to fool me. But I'm not talking about moral courage, anyway. What Marla had was the physical kind. I walked over to her and showed her my fist. 'I don't have to kill you,' I said. 'I could just break your face. In a few minutes I could make you into an object that small children would run screaming from in the streets.' She never even blinked. Just looked at me kind of sadly. I stood there mentally measuring the distance between my fist and her delicate little jaw, lifted up like a target while she watched me. Of course, I couldn't even hit her. She was a great beauty, you know." Steelegrave looked glumly at the empty bottle of Dubonnet and fumbled for a cigarette.

"If you couldn't kill her then, you couldn't have killed her last night," Erin said.

Steelegrave didn't seem to hear the remark. " 'Why Vandy?' I asked her, just for the record, because it wasn't hard to figure. Vandy had money and power. 'He'll back *Lady of the Lake*' was her answer. That was Marla's pet project, a script the studios didn't think would fly even with Marla Monday. They were right, too. It turned out to be one of those critical triumphs that bomb at the box office. Vandy lost his ass. Over two million, a lot of money back then." Steelegrave smiled at the memory. "Anyway, she wanted me to understand about Vandy. 'It's a business thing for me,' she said, as if that made everything all right. 'He seems to be fascinated with me for some reason, and you know how Vandy is, he'll pay any price for what he wants. I think he's kind of a shit, actually. Well, perhaps we have something in common at that. He'll pay anything for me and I'll do anything to make *Lady of the Lake*.'

"I think Marla wanted to make me hate her, playing the cold, calculating bitch. I think she wanted to make it easier for me in a way, you see."

"I think she was being herself."

"One of her selves. She was as multifaceted as a high-priced diamond. Well, I saw that I couldn't keep her and I couldn't kill her. I was afraid I might start begging if I just stood there, so I went out onto the deck and looked at the view that wasn't mine anymore. I kept my back to her so she couldn't see my face. After a while she touched me and I jumped because I hadn't heard her come up. 'I told you how it was with me once, remember?' she said. 'That I wouldn't stick if something happened to you, something that could bring me down too. Even after what you did for me. Maybe they just left something out of me, I don't know. But I can't let myself fail, I just can't.'

"I told her to get out, that I would ship her things. As far as I can remember, I never saw her again."

It seeeemed to Erin that she was looking at Richard for the first time, and she liked what she saw. She wasn't used to thinking of him as a man capable of making such a sacrifice, no matter how misguided. Gone was the casual cynicism, even the arrogant lift of eyebrow or curve of mouth that could infuriate her so, all erased by his remembered desolation. Suddenly she was sorry for him and felt she could understand the elaborate facade he had built around him to disguise any trace of vulnerability.

"You loved her, then," she said. "In spite of everything."

"I suppose I did. Life with Marla was never dull. It was all peaks and valleys. No plateaus."

His answer angered her unreasonably, considering that the woman was dead and she knew she was not in love with Richard. To change the immediate subject, she asked, "What happened between her and Vandy?"

"Oh, she left him after *Lady of the Lake* bombed. She took him for a million-plus and that big house she was living in. Not to mention what *Lady* cost him. That was before they rewrote the California divorce laws. In those days they used to divide everything in half and then give both halves to the wife. Well, I'm exaggerating, but I read that she did very well. Sure, he could afford it financially, but it must have really put a dent in his megalomania."

"But she finally failed, after all. Her movie was no good."

"Marla never failed and *Lady* was an excellent picture. It got an award at Cannes and the critics drooled all over Marla. It just lost money because murky medieval costume dramas weren't taking off that year. But it never hurt her, only Vandy. He picked up the tab and Marla said goodbye. She didn't need him anymore."

"It seems to me he had almost as much reason to kill her as you did. Why didn't they send the police after him?"

"Maybe they did if he's even in California." Steelegrave got up and released Junkyard into the backyard. The dog was growing restless. "But in my case, they have an up-to-date motive. The cop who came after me said that Marla changed her will less than a month ago. She left everything to me." He bowed slightly in her direction. "You are looking at a very wealthy man."

"She did *what?*"

"Made me her sole heir. Rather a waste if I end up in the gas chamber, don't you think?"

"And you didn't know she did that?"

"No." Steelegrave looked at his watch. "Listen, I'd better not stay too long. They might link us up somehow and come looking here. I was hoping you might keep the dog and lock my car in your garage. Say you didn't know anything at the time if they find it."

Erin got up and went over to him. "Richard, I can see why you ran. Anyone would have panicked. But if you keep running, it will be much worse when they find you. And you know damn well you can't hide forever."

Steelegrave prowled away from her, circling the room. "If it's the wrong knife, I can come in. But even if they say that in print, how can I believe them? And if it's the right knife, Jesus, they've got me no matter what really happened. Can I say the cop brought the goddamn knife with him and planted it? Why the hell would he? Or that Vandy killed her and hid the knife in my kitchen because he hates me?"

"*He* hates *you?*"

"That he does, and I wouldn't want it any other way. I damaged his precious body and humiliated him in front of a servant, not to mention the women. You don't know Vandy. He is one vindictive son of a bitch. And imagine how much he hated Marla! She nicked him for millions, took him to Dump City, and then probably laughed at him, knowing her. That would really have rattled his cage. None of which proves anything, unfortunately."

Abruptly he stopped pacing and turned toward Erin. "There might be a way I can come in now. . . ." He looked at her with measured hope. "It's asking a lot from you, I know, but suppose, just suppose you say I was with you. All evening and all night. Then I could just hang tough, run a bluff."

Erin said nothing, just looked at him unhappily.

"I know it's a hell of a thing to ask . . ."

Erin sighed. "It's not that, Richard. Not at all. But I just . . . can't do it."

Steelegrave nodded. "I know, you're right. It's asking you to perjure yourself."

"No! Listen to me. I would perjure myself cheerfully if I could, but I can't. I wasn't alone last night."

He stared at her. "Well, okay. Maybe it doesn't have to

include the evening. Just, say, from midnight on. That seems to be the earliest she could have . . . died."

Erin could only shake her head.

Steelegrave's eyes narrowed. "Do you mean," he asked quietly, "that you had . . . company all night long?"

She nodded.

"I see." His eyebrow shot up and his mouth curved sardonically in a remembered way. He said lightly, as though amused, "Get laid?"

Suddenly she was furious. How dare he make her feel guilty, as though she were failing him, when his own lack of simple consideration had driven her to act as she had? "As a matter of fact, I did! When you didn't show up—or even call—I went out and found someone. We had a ball!"

He held up a hand in mock protest. "Spare me the details. So he could contradict your story, which we don't need." He added in the familiar bantering way that irritated her most, "I'm assuming it was a 'he.' "

"Very much so," she replied icily.

"Well, then, how jolly for you." She recognized a slightly British version of Hawke. Or was he doing the Saint this time? Either way, he was back in character, being himself by being someone else. He sauntered toward the door.

"Richard . . . where are you going?"

He turned back, face set and eyes steely, all the way into the part now. "It's better for you if you don't know."

"Oh, shit! You're going to play detective, right? It's *Love–Forty* all over again. What are you going to be when you grow up, anyway?"

"Someone kills your wife, you ought to do something about it. Even if she dumped you a hundred years ago."

"Stop it! That's almost word for word out of an old Bogart picture that was made before I was born. I just saw it on late TV."

"Well, I didn't," lied Steelegrave, embarrassed. "Look at it another way. If I can't find out who really killed her, or at least stay clear until somebody does, they'll just grab me and look no further."

Erin sighed, giving up. "Look, Richard. I'll keep your dog and hide your car. You can take mine. I'll get a rental or whatever." She looked at his white trousers, navy polo shirt, and tennis shoes. "There are some things in the closet you left after we came back from the desert that time. It might be a good idea at least to change, don't you think?"

In the bedroom closet, Steelegrave found a pair of tan chino slacks, a matching windbreaker, and a straw hat. He put them on, wondering idly what his poster was doing crammed in the closet instead of up on the wall. Then the phone on the bedside table gave him an idea. Vandy had always had three addresses in California—Evander Electronics in Culver City, a penthouse in Beverly Hills, and the beach house in Laguna. Excluding the Antelo Drive mansion that went to Marla, of course. He still remembered the number for the beach house if it had not been changed, so he dialed it first.

"Hello . . . ?"

The voice was unmistakably Vandy's. Steelegrave cradled the phone gently.

Bingo!

Before he left, he found the snub-nosed revolver he had given Erin for her birthday, checked to make sure it was loaded, and slipped it into his pocket.

10

Detective Sergeant Ryan Cosgrove stood before the desk of Captain Fletcher Strickland, the officer in charge of the West Los Angeles Police Station, getting his ass chewed. He stood with his thick legs spread apart and his massive stomach thrust forward, giving away by his demeanor nothing of what he felt. His great slash of a mouth remained tightly shut and he stared stoically a foot above the captain's head.

"Now, let me see if I've got this straight," said the captain in a wondering tone. "You want to stay in charge of the case, right? After all, all you did was bungle the arrest of a red-hot suspect in the murder of the year and discharge your piece in suburban Santa Monica, where you could have hit some little bitty old ginch in the left ear while she was watching the idiot lantern in her retirement home, the slug to have emerged along with her brains from the right ear. . . ."

"He loosed a dog on me, Cap'n. He was getting away—a red-hot suspect, like you said. . . ." Cosgrove had admitted firing his weapon only because the act had been witnessed.

" 'Suspect' is exactly what he is. Until we get a lab report, he could have been cleaning a fish with that fucking knife."

"He ran away. I had every reason to presume guilt. The knife has a serrated blade like the one the coroner says killed the victim."

Strickland pushed back from his desk with a sigh. Cosgrove was his most effective officer and had the best arrest record in the division. Moreover, he liked Cosgrove, which was more than he could say for most white men. Not that he disliked white men, he just didn't actively like or really trust most of them. For that reason he tried to be scrupulously fair and never, never called them honkies. He suspected that Cosgrove had all the inherent prejudices of his Texas roots, yet Strickland liked to have him around and did not want to lose him. Losing Cosgrove was always a distinct possibility, for the sergeant lived on the periphery of disaster, ready at any time to fall into the deep shit.

Strickland felt that Cosgrove was a seething mass of contradictions. He limped from a felon's bullet that had severed a ligament, held two departmental citations for bravery balanced by two suspensions for unnecessary use of brutal force. Though he was a law-school graduate with a keen analytical mind and could debate brilliantly on such diverse subjects as theology and the subtler aspects of criminal law, it was common knowledge that he would rise no higher than his present rank. The department, in its discretion, had long since deemed Cosgrove emotionally unfit for command, a decision he was unregretfully aware of. It left him free to remain the consummate loner, doing his own thing.

"Cos," said Strickland, "I hope this bastard killed his ex-wife deader'n hell and that we catch him real quick. I hope he's not already in Canada or Mexico. Most of all, I hope, for both our sakes, he's not innocent. That's because this is going to be a very well-publicized case, every crack and corner exposed to merciless light. And there you are, Cos, shooting up Jane Fonda-land, where the entire city government thinks nobody except hoods should have guns on account of they are underprivileged and have to be able to defend themselves against us fascist police.

"And you want to remain in charge of the case. Shit, I oughta issue you a rubber gun and put you in charge of Lost and Found."

Cosgrove realized he shouldn't have tried to run a bluff past Strickland. The captain was sharp and above all a valuable ally with whom he could not afford to lose credibility. "I guess what I'm trying to say, Fletch, is I'd like to make amends for fucking up the arrest."

Strickland took no offense at Cosgrove's use of his first name when they were alone. The men had been friends a long time, since they were both sergeants in Hollywood Division. They were both physically big men, another tie that bound them, although Strickland was rangier, with much less belly. There had been a time when they liked to go over to the police gym, put on the gloves, and beat the shit out of each other. Strickland had been a Golden Glover, a tough inner-city kid who had planned to pound his way to the top before he changed tactics and joined the cops. He was a faster, trickier boxer than Cosgrove and he could pretty much chop the slower man to pieces at will. The trouble was, Cos could take an unlimited amount of punishment and keep moving in, and when he hit you, Jesus, how it hurt! Even if the punch only landed on an arm or shoulder. At the end of three rounds, Cosgrove's face looked like raw meat and he was just beginning to get pissed off. Strickland always called time after three rounds. He wanted neither to bloody Cosgrove further nor to absorb more damage to himself.

Furthermore, Strickland enjoyed plumbing the depths of Cosgrove's mind. Self-educated by necessity, he had had little exposure to erudite companions. Cosgrove's mercurial switches from locker-room cop humor or street talk to scholarly dissertation never ceased to fascinate Strickland, who soaked up lore like a sponge. Back when Cosgrove could still hold his liquor, they had hoisted many a glass together and Strickland had learned among many other useless facts that Alexander the Great was a pansy and so were most of the Spartans, but they could all fight like hell. He learned that a bunch of Africans from the empire of Carthage led by a dude named Hannibal crossed the Alps and kicked the bejesus out of mighty Rome. Using elephants as troop carriers.

"Cos," Strickland said, more kindly, "there's an all-points out on this guy. It's not just our problem anymore. They'll probably grab him a long way from L.A."

Cosgrove shrugged. "Someone's got to do the legwork

anyway. Check his contacts. If he didn't skip, he could surface around here."

Strickland wondered how he could make Cosgrove's situation clear to him. Lately the man just didn't seem to be tracking. He decided to tell it straight. "The fact is, Cos, I'm going to suggest you take some time off. I know for a fact you've got three weeks' paid leave of absence coming and I'm ordering you to take it now. Go fishing. Go to the Riviera."

Cosgrove's wide trap of a mouth tightened with shock at the captain's words. He had not expected this. "I don't want to take a leave of absence now, Cap'n. Especially not now. I'm asking for a chance to rectify an error."

"Then," said the captain softly, "you can take a suspension. You know what a third suspension means, right? Probably three strikes and you're out. I've got to cover my ass with the commission, some members of which like you not at all. If they start asking about you and you're out of town, unavailable, on leave—then maybe they'll walk around it and you'll come out all right. If you're here, we could both get knocked down, me for not taking disciplinary action, especially if the Santa Monica city council starts to scream. The old bastard who saw you shooting is yelling no one's life is safe from trigger-happy cops.

"So, can you see now, Cos, that I'm trying to save your ass but that I will expose my own cheeks only so far to do it?"

Cosgrove concealed his contempt for Strickland. The captain was a gutless wonder after all, he thought. Abruptly his features creased into a totally disarming grin. "Okay, Fletch. You're the boss and I bend to your will. 'Blessed are the meek, for they shall inherit the kingdom of God.' "

"Yeah. Amen."

Watching Cosgrove's massive back lurch out through his office door, Fletcher Strickland felt a twinge of misgiving. He had a gut feeling that someday he would regret covering for the big sergeant, who was behaving ever more erratically, like he wasn't too tightly wrapped. There was an aura of pent-up mayhem about him.

As a black officer responsible for the prosperous lily-white enclaves of Brentwood and Bel-Air, among others,

Strickland was in a sensitive position. He regarded his job as no more than a stepping-stone to becoming police chief or mayor, as had his hero, Mayor Tom Bradley, and it often amused him to know that some people were just waiting for him to make a wrong move. He had no intention of giving them that satisfaction, for he was confident of his judgment and of his ability to avoid the kind of mistake that could scuttle a very upwardly mobile career. He knew he was young and ballsy enough to go a long way.

At the same time, he was aware of his vulnerability and he knew it didn't take a very big mistake when people were laying for you. You only had to remember Watergate. A two-bit burglary that had busted a President elected by a landslide—and loathed by a vengeful few. Strickland experienced an uncharacteristic moment of doubt. Maybe he should have shit-canned Cosgrove long ago. He sure as hell didn't need a rogue cop at his station. Just thinking about it brought a dew of perspiration to his forehead.

Cosgrove went out the bright red-tiled entrance of the West Los Angeles Police Station in a state of controlled rage. The night outside was starry, washed clean by the Santa Ana wind, but he felt only the dry heat that blew relentlessly against his body, jangling his nerves as he limped to his car, his old injury exacerbated by fatigue.

Inside his dusty, aging Olds, he thought about taking a drink. He pictured a tumbler three-quarters full of Jack Daniel's with a couple of ice cubes and a lemon twist, surrendering for a moment to the agony of his thirst. Why not? He was on leave of absence, relieved of duty by that turd Strickland. For several years Cosgrove had allowed himself alcohol only on the rare occasions when he was off duty for an extended period of time. That was because once he took the top off the bottle, he was gone for three days. The first day he was a jocular extravert, everybody's pal, the second he became argumentative and maudlin. By the third day, he was sodden, bitter, and downright dangerous. Cosgrove realized that he could no longer function as a police officer when he was drinking. And his gun and badge were all he had left, the very essence of him.

Which was why Strickland's threat of a third suspension triggered a spasm of fear that he hoped he had covered with his quick acceptance of the captain's decision. He pictured Steelegrave's handsome, arrogant face—a man who had killed an innocent, religious woman and never spent a day in jail. Cosgrove had read about it at the time and felt outraged. Now he would not be the man who brought the bastard to justice after all. Not if he obeyed Strickland's edict. Well, he still had some moves left. And it was no time for drinking.

The day had begun more auspiciously, full of challenge and opportunity! Marla Monday's butler had called the station at seven in the morning to report discovering the actress's body, and a black-and-white with two cops had arrived at the mansion within minutes to seal off the area and make a quick search in case the culprit was still lurking around. Cosgrove and his detective partner, Willy Danforth, were next on the scene, taking charge of the preliminary investigation. Practically on their heels came the SID people to take pictures and collect the forensic evidence. A coroner's unit followed them, sent in to pick up the remains. It was an orchestrated, efficient performance.

Cosgrove looked briefly at the small, pale body of Marla Monday dangling over a drying pool of blood. She was not impressive in death, he thought, no different from anyone else, no exception to the old truism which holds that death is the great equalizer, diminishing everyone. A set of diamond earrings sparkled cheerfully in the morning sun, lending to her naked corpse a touch of the absurd.

Cosgrove left SID photographing the body and the ambulance crew waiting around to unhook and remove it. While Danforth still prowled the mansion looking for clues, he went to the little house in back where Dieter Greim lived.

The man who opened the door to him must once have been very powerful, judging by his frame. Now he was sunken and gaunt, with big wrist and knuckle bones stretching his skin. Colorless hair was brushed flat against his skull and he stared at Cosgrove out of great hollows within a sallow face marked by a whitened star-shaped scar. Taken aback, Cosgrove thought he should be answering the door of Frankenstein's castle. "Sergeant Cosgrove," he said. "May I come in?" There seemed no point in flashing his I.D. when the place was teeming with cops.

The tall German moved aside and Cosgrove stepped into rather Spartan surroundings with dark utilitarian furniture brightened by surprisingly cheerful drapes and throw rugs in light, warm colors. A single painting on the wall depicted the battle of Jutland and a cluster of photographs stood together on a desktop.

"Would you care for coffee?" asked Dieter Greim formally. His English was correct but strongly accented.

Cosgrove shook his head and seated himself in the chair Greim indicated. For a moment he studied the man closely, giving him the cop look he had developed to intimidate suspects, witnesses, and law-abiding citizens alike. Greim merely gazed back at him.

"How long have you worked for Marla Monday, Mr. Greim?" he finally asked.

"Thirteen years. Since she was married to Mr. Evander. She received the estate when they divorced, and my wife and I went with it. Lotte died five years ago of diabetes. I have carried on alone."

"And what were your duties?"

Greim shrugged and Cosgrove thought he saw the trace of a smile. "General service. I chauffeured her, did some light cooking, supervised the day help. And I saw to her privacy."

"I see. Now, I would like to know when and under what circumstances you last saw her alive and then I'd like to have a brief summary of your activities from then until you found her body this morning."

Greim took a packet from the table next to him and extracted a long gray cigarette. He lit it and blew out a cloud of acrid tobacco smoke. It made him cough and he laid the cigarette aside. "Last evening about seven o'clock I served Miss Mondy a glass of Dubonnet before she went out. She was dressed elegantly in a sort of Grecian affair and wore some jewelry—the diamond earrings and ring she still had on when I found her. She took the Lamborghini you saw in the driveway, her favorite car. I assumed she had a social engagement but I have no idea with whom."

"Was it customary for her to go out like that rather than having someone call for her?"

"Yes, as often as not. She was most independent."

"What was her state of mind or mood last night, from what you could tell? Did she give you any idea where she was going, if not with whom?"

"She was in high spirits because she was starting a film tomorrow—I mean today. She told me she would not be late, that she had to get her rest. I don't know where she went."

Cosgrove leaned forward, his eyes intent on Greim's. "Did you hear her come home? Or perhaps see her later, inside or outside of the house?"

Greim hesitated no more than an instant. "I heard her arrive home," he answered. "At least, I believe I heard the car. I retired early because I have been ill, but I do not sleep well even with medication. I knew when she turned on the outdoor patio lights, for they reflect in my bedroom window. I would guess the hour at around midnight, but I cannot be certain. I stayed in bed."

"You stayed in bed? Wasn't it unusual for her to turn on outside lights at that hour? Unusual enough for you to check it out?"

"It was not unusual, it was almost habitual. Miss Monday frequently swam at night and then exercised or stretched on those bars I found her . . . suspended from."

"She did this naked? As you found her?"

Again the trace of a smile. "Did you know Miss Monday personally, Sergeant?"

Cosgrove looked hard at him. "No, I didn't. What makes you think I would?"

The German shrugged and relit his cigarette. "She was friendly with the police and donated to their causes. She was often given police escorts and she liked joking with the officers. But no matter. Yes, she exercises naked at night. And yes, I have seen her do so."

"You watched her?"

Greim seemed amused. "Not really. As you earlier suggested I should, I used to investigate when the patio lights went on. I could not very well help seeing her, could I? As time went on, I became familiar with her habits and simply assumed all was well without rushing out to see. It seems last night I should have done so." He began coughing again and ground out the cigarette.

"Well, what happened next, Greim?"

"I went back to sleep. In the morning I found her."

"Then you saw nothing and heard nothing—except for the light and the car?"

"That is correct."

Cosgrove hauled himself out of the chair and stood looking down at Greim from the advantage of height. "Who might have done this, Mr. Greim? Who were her enemies? You must have known many of the people who came to this house, many of the people she associated with."

Greim lifted his hands in protest and shook his head. "Too many, Sergeant, far too many. She was a famous woman, loved and hated, envied and even worshiped, if you like. She entertained, gave parties large and small. Everybody came. I can show you the guest books in the main house and you will have an idea of what I mean."

"Then, can you think of anything that has happened recently that is out of the ordinary? Any quarrel or change of relationship with friends or associates?"

The German pondered for a moment. "About two weeks ago, I drove her to her attorney's office. She went up alone, but presently came back down and asked me to accompany her. It seems they needed another witness to a document she had ordered prepared. It was her will and I could not help seeing that she left her fortune to her second ex-husband, the actor Rick Steele. I confess that I was surprised, but I also heard her laugh and tell the lawyer that she was only assuaging her conscience, she intended to live forever. Actually, I believe she wished to be certain nothing fell into the hands of her son, whom she really despised. When she told him, perhaps a week ago, he came to the house and screamed at her. She laughed at him."

Cosgrove felt a blip of excitement. He remembered Rick Steele, the actor who had killed a young woman while driving drunk and never done time for it. A Hollywood golden boy who could trample the lives of lesser mortals with impunity because he had been born with a handsome face and a graceful body. And because he could afford a good lawyer. Cosgrove felt a satisfying rush of hatred.

"I would like to know the name of the son and where I can find him. Also a location for this ex-husband, Steele," he said to Greim.

"Her son's name is Eric Deckar. I don't know the addresses of either of them, but she had a secretary who comes in several days a week. He should be here today."

Cosgrove's partner ambled through the open door with a casual salute in the direction of Greim. He was a tall thin man, more than ten years younger than Cosgrove at thirty-five, with a long hound-dog face contradicted by bright, merry eyes. He liked to refer to himself as a one-hundred-percent Florida cracker, a claim no one questioned.

"I might be able to throw some light on the sec'tary," drawled Danforth. "I was nosin' around the house up yonder, where it seems nothing was stole, when I looked out the window and seen this dude humpin' down the trail, away from the ol' manse. So I run out and collared him. Turns out he's the sec'tary—a very, very shy little man. Seen the police cars and changed his mind about comin' in. Didn't want to get involved, he says. That's 'cause he done a year in Leavenworth for embezzlement, as he confided to me after I hard-talked him some.

"Anyway, after we was through jawin' and I called his family to check his alibi, I liberated this here book from him. Reads like *Who's Who*."

Cosgrove took the leather-bound address book from his partner and opened it. Steele (with "Steelegrave" in parentheses) was listed with a Santa Monica address after two others, one in Rome, had been crossed out. He found nothing under "Deckar" so, on a hunch, he looked under E. There was an Eric with an address in Venice Beach.

"What is her attorney's name?" he asked Greim.

"Marius Markham."

He was also in the book.

Danforth shook his head and sighed. "House all intact

and her hangin' there with diamonds in her ears. Musta been one of them crimes of passion."

Cosgrove and Danforth reported briefly to Strickland, who had showed up in person and was busy dealing with the reporters who invariably get the word about such events as soon as they occur. By way of jungle drums, they'll tell you. For jungle drums, read anyone already on the scene who wants to make a fast fifty bucks and can get to a phone.

The captain, already harassed, told them to get on with it, so they went to the offices of Marius Markham in Brentwood, who confirmed the contents of the will but, despite blandishment and veiled threats, refused to show them the document. Back out on the street, they flipped a coin and, since Steelegrave won out over Eric Deckar, they drove down San Vicente to Ocean Avenue in Santa Monica. They located Steelegrave's bungalow in the jungle of Wisteria Manor but there was no one home, so they continued on in the direction of Venice.

South of the Santa Monica pier the city began to disintegrate. Crumbling stucco apartment buildings fronted on deep but unkempt beaches. Junk-food stands and roller-skate rentals competed for space along the ribbon of concrete that bordered the sand. Derelicts huddled in doorways drinking out of bottles hidden in brown paper bags, and clusters of shirtless punks in jeans lounged around littered parking lots, dealing drugs and fistfighting. Progress had been frozen by rigid building codes and strict rent control further discouraged landlords from improving their property. Detractors of the city government called Santa Monica Moscow-by-the-sea, but retirees blessed them for holding down rents and fending off an incursion of high-rises.

Cosgrove pointed to an old wooden house on the seaside of Pierson Avenue. "That's Jane Fonda's place," he told Danforth. "The one she uses when she's getting out among the common people."

Danforth gave a clenched-fist salute as they drove by. "Just want to make some points in case she's looking out the window," he explained.

They passed a lonely brace of tall apartment buildings

overlooking a nine-hole golf course that had been put up
before the freeze and drove into Venice, a high-crime area
where once-beautiful canals had become stagnant sewers
and the locals tried to disguise the blight by painting
everything that stood still in a riot of pastel colors. Cosgrove
liked Venice, with its smell of the sea and decay. It was all
that remained of Raymond Chandler's Bay City and he
imagined the ghost of Philip Marlowe still haunted the
mean streets for twenty bucks a day and expenses.

On weekends the ocean-front looked like a bazaar in
Marrakech, with tents and stalls selling flea-market hand-
me-downs, stoned musicians performing for free, dogs and
their by-product underfoot everywhere. People whipped
around on bikes, skateboards, roller skates, and unicycles.
Muscle men pumped iron on the beach surrounded by
groupies, and an open-air roller disco that was an ethnic
potpourri blared rock at the passersby.

Marlowe wouldn't have recognized the place on weekends,
Cosgrove thought, but today it was quiet enough. It was
as if the burning wind had driven everyone into the sea.

"Sure is hot," Danforth allowed. "Puts me in mind of
home. Shacky little town out by the tidewater flats. My
daddy had him a shrimp boat he worked on the gulf.
Saturday nights we used to go into Fort Myers and get
pissed on beer. 'Nother shacky little town. I tell you, friend,
that wasn't just life in the slow lane, that was life on the
shoulder of the road."

"You've come a long way, Willy."

"Yeah. Now I live in Sin City and work for a nigger. My
mammy knew that, she'd fetch me home by the ear."

They found the street they were looking for just north
of Washington Avenue and turned toward the sea, checking numbers as they went. Eric Deckar lived in a yellow
frame house distinguished from its neighbors by the painting of a reclining nude that spanned one side of the building.
She had orange skin and pubic hair in the shape of a heart.
The windows of the house with their peeling sashes looked
as if they had never been opened.

As they approached the door, a shrill voice within
proclaimed, "If you don't like the way I do it, you can
fucking do it yourself!" This ultimatum was followed by a

meaty *whack* and a prolonged howl that was cut off by the sound of Cosgrove's big knuckles against the wood.

A man in his early twenties opened the door wearing a tiny heart-shaped apron and nothing else. He had a mass of ebony curls, one very red cheek, and tears in his eyes. He held a spatula in one hand and behind him on the floor lay an overturned pan of scrambled eggs. "And just whatever the fuck do you want?" he asked petulantly.

Danforth showed him a badge. "We're from the police, son," he said mildly. "You mind if we come in?"

The young man looked at them defiantly, then suddenly brightened. "Police? Well, you're just in time, then." He gestured behind him with the spatula. "I want you to throw this prick out of my house!"

Another man of the same age lounged in a doorway facing the living room. He wore skintight jeans and his lean, muscular body had been oiled. He had lank yellow hair that fell to his shoulders, and small sinister eyes.

Cosgrove and Danforth stepped past the distraught young man and around the mess of eggs on the floor. "Eric Deckar?" asked Danforth, looking first at one man and then the other.

"That's him," said the long-haired man with a thin smile.

"Thanks ever so much, Tom," said the brunet. "Yes, I'm Eric Deckar and I suppose it's about the painting again. Well, it's not an obscene display, it's legitimate professional advertising. You can take me to court if you like. I've told you people before."

"Just what is your profession, son?" asked Danforth, perplexed.

"I'm a hairstylist."

"Pussy hair," sneered the one called Tom. "He braids the hair on women's snatches."

"It's a living," sniffed Eric.

Cosgrove reddened. No amount of violence or bloodshed fazed him. It came with the job, and so be it. But he could not abide degenerates and therefore could not deal with them tactfully. In these cases Danforth always played good guy and let Cosgrove be himself. "And what do you do?" Danforth asked Tom before Cosgrove could speak.

"I'm an actor."

"Oh sure, he's an actor," said Eric, giggling now. "A gay-porn star. He struts around like a macho stud, acting so terribly *HE* while he makes gay porn like *Golden Rod* and *Little Boy Blew*."

"I'm going to make you suffer for that," Tom promised him.

Cosgrove was disgusted. He had bought a videotape recorder primarily for the purpose of watching pornography. But *fag* porn! Jesus, that was sickening. "We'd like to look around the house," he said to Eric between his teeth.

"Why? Why should I let you do that?" Eric bridled suddenly. "You need a warrant for that."

"Listen, you little shit," Cosgrove grated. "We just witnessed a violent domestic quarrel and we have to be sure you don't have dangerous weapons."

"Hey, hold on, ol' hoss," said Danforth easily. He turned to Eric. "Don't mind if I use the toilet, do you, son?"

"We sure as hell do," Tom told him, but Danforth was already into the narrow hallway, where he found the bathroom and locked himself in. Tom hit the door once with his fist.

"Settle down," Cosgrove warned him, hoping he wouldn't.

Danforth emerged in about three minutes with several small plastic containers, which he placed casually on the dining-room table. "Coke, looks like." He opened one, then another. " 'Ludes here, and maybe this one's some kind of upper. Bet there's grass and amies around too, if I look hard enough. You boys got a license to run a pharmacy?"

Eric turned and left the room, his exposed buttocks dimpling as he flounced away. When he returned he wore a Japanese kimono and was much calmer. "What do you really want?" he asked. "You know you made an illegal search. Is it a shakedown?"

Danforth shook his head. "Want to know where you were last night. The whole time."

"I might tell you when you tell me why."

"Your mother died last night. She was murdered. We heard tell there was bad blood between you. Just want to ask a few questions, is all."

Eric actually staggered. He backed against a couch. "Marla? Murdered?"

Danforth took out a cigarette and lit it. "Mind if I smoke?" he asked belatedly. "Yes, son, murdered. Knifed to death. Now, I'd quote you your rights if we planned to arrest you or anything like that, and with all this dope lying around, that could sure be arranged." He turned to his partner. "Thing is, shit, this ain't a drug bust, is it, Cos?"

"I don't like either one of you," said Cosgrove with a quiet menace. "I can find a dozen reasons to haul you in without a warrant. I use warrants for shit-paper when I run into scumbags like you."

"Whoa, now, Cos," Danforth chuckled easily, the voice of sweet reason. "This boy here has just had a bad shock, losin' his mammy and all."

Eric had collapsed on the couch, looking crumpled within his kimono. "I can't believe it," he muttered. "The bitch!"

"What's that, son?" Danforth queried, not trusting his ears.

"He hated his mother," Cosgrove told him. "Isn't that right, boy? She cut you out of her will and you hated her guts. The butler heard you yelling at her and threatening her just a few days ago."

"I never threatened her." Eric looked up at Cosgrove steadily. "I told her what I thought of her, that's all. I never expected to inherit anything from Marla anyway. She's the type who lives forever. Buries everybody. It was just the idea of it. Leaving everything to that miserable actor she hadn't seen in years. Then telling me, just to see me squirm."

"Then you remember him."

"Yes, I remember him. I don't remember my own father, but I remember 'Uncle' Rick. I was eight or nine and they kept me out of the way in boarding schools most of the time. When I was home, he tried to make me play tennis or go surfing or some such stupid thing, the prick. Why don't you go harass him? He had a reason to want her dead. Why in God's name would I kill her, when I knew she'd left everything to him? Use your collective brains, you two!"

Danforth stepped between them as the big sergeant moved forward. "Now, as I said, son, we can take you both on down and lock you up in the Gray Bar Hotel for havin' all this shit here. We ain't going to worry about illegal search when we found all this evidence while investigating a disturbance. Or else you might just give some straight answers right here and walk away clean if they prove out."

"Just tell him what he wants to know, Eric, you asshole!" bleated Tom, alarmed.

"Good thinking," said Danforth; then, to Eric, "Now, where were you last night? The whole time last night."

"With Tom," answered Eric, adding quickly, "I didn't mean that about kicking you out of the house, Tom."

The yellow-haired man smirked and said nothing.

Danforth sighed. "Well?"

Tom crossed his arms and leaned against the wall. "That's true," he begrudged. "We were at Randy's until closing time. Then we were here."

"Fag joint on Rose Avenue," grunted Cosgrove. "Anyone who can corroborate that?"

"A *gay* bar, mister," snapped Tom. "The bartender, Stu, knows us. He saw us and so did a lot of regulars."

Danforth looked a question at Cosgrove, who shrugged. "Stay put," he told them both. "No traveling. I want to know that I can reach you on short notice." He started for the door, followed by Danforth, but turned back with his hand on the knob and looked at Eric. "Your mother married again, didn't she? After Steele."

" 'Uncle' Vandy. Justin Evander the Turd."

"And what was your gifted impression of him?"

"A rich sadomasochist."

"They were divorced, I understand."

Eric shrugged. "She divorced him. Took him for a pile."

"How did he react? That is, if you recall."

"I recall. He was very, very angry. That big German, Dieter, had to act as Marla's bodyguard. He never liked Uncle Vandy anyway."

*   *   *

When they got back to their car, the radio was squawking for Danforth to call the station. He complied at the first phone booth they found and came back white-faced, his eyes not at all merry. "Some Chicano kid knifed Danny on the playground," he said, tight-lipped.

"Jesus! Is he going to be all right?" asked Cosgrove.

"He just got nicked, but I'd better get home. He's shook up and Julie's having a fit. Shit, what a city! Ten-year-olds dealin' drugs and stabbin' one another at school. I should have expected somethin' like that, seein' it all the time, but somehow when it's your own kid you never do."

Cosgrove drove Danforth to the station on Butler Avenue so he could pick up his car. Then he went to a German restaurant in Santa Monica and sat down to a long, heavy, belated lunch. He ate ribs and potatoes and sauerkraut washed down with a half dozen cups of coffee. He would have much preferred beer and maybe a couple of shots of Jack Daniel's, but that was an indulgence of the past, a memory to be chased out of mind.

By the time he was finished, the sun was low in the sky, reminding him that it was late October despite the unseasonable heat. He drove toward the sea and parked his unmarked car on Ocean Avenue, a block from Wisteria Manor. Once again he knocked at the door of Steelegrave's bungalow, feeling the adrenaline flush he always experienced when he anticipated action. He was glad of the opportunity to confront the bastard alone. It simplified everything and he was keyed to the task, sharpened by his hatred.

Still there was no answer at the door, no sound from within. No car occupied the numbered slot allotted to Steelegrave. Disappointed, Cosgrave went back to wait in his car, which commanded a view of the alley. Suppose the man didn't return? Suppose he was out of town? Cosgrove didn't want to think about that. He waited as he had been trained to wait. Impassively and patiently.

Finally, of course, Steelegrave had come home. And after that everything had gone straight to hell.

11

Cosgrove drove home to his apartment a block south of
Santa Monica Boulevard in West Hollywood. He parked
in the underground garage and set the system on his car
that would beep a signal to him upstairs if the vehicle were
tampered with. There was no alarm to warn the intruder,
giving Cosgrove a chance to run down and apprehend or
shoot the son of a bitch. He had made three collars in the
last year using this tactic, beating one suspect enough to
require hospitalization.

His apartment was a one-bedroom furnished unit as
impersonal as a hotel room. The sofa was overstuffed and
mouse-colored. The vinyl easy chair was rump-sprung
from his weight and the rug around it was scarred by
burns from the cigars he dropped and ignored when he
was drinking. Even the prints on the walls preceded his
residence, reflecting a Holiday Inn–Hyatt House concept
of art. Cosgrove had no prized possessions besides the
books crowded on sagging makeshift shelves and the shabby
Olds that had been potently souped for him at the police
garage and, like its owner, was capable of a great deal
more than was outwardly apparent.

Once he was a different sort of man, ambitious and
acquisitive. He had been raised on the Texas flatlands
between San Antonio and the Mexican border by his
father, a hard-scrabble rancher who ran a few head of
cattle on three hundred parched acres of mesquite and

tumbleweed near the town of Durham. It was the kind of place you sank into or got the hell out of, and Ryan Cosgrove decided early to get out. His birth had cost his mother her life, a fact hardly resented by Coleman Cosgrove, who had never much cared for his drab, skinny wife. Her demise freed him to cross the border into Piedras Negras on Saturday nights and vent his libido on teenage whores. Usually he got back in time to clean up before attending service at the First Baptist Church in Durham on Sunday morning, but sometimes he ran late, and then he showed up disheveled and unsteady, reeking of tequila and Mexican pussy. On these occasions the congregation, outwardly horrified but secretly delighted, prayed aloud for their most reliable sinner while he knelt before the pulpit, the preacher's hand on his bent head, and listened to the Reverend Caleb Quisenberry verbally wrestle the devil for his soul. A firm bond grew between the old thunderer and his favorite penitent, whose misdeeds made him a challenge worthy of the preacher's most colorful rhetoric.

Young Ryan Cosgrove came in for his share of religion during the week, when Coleman passed on the message, pounding the Bible and inveighing against Satan in a style reminiscent of the good reverend himself. The elder Cosgrove was a lapsed Catholic who far preferred the fire and brimstone of the Holy Rollers to the more restrained sermons of the pope's emissaries. Using their vivid prose, he scorched the boy's ears with dire warnings about the wages of sin every night after supper and before bedtime. Except for Saturday, when the sap rose within him and he climbed into his old pickup truck for the trip south of the border.

Durham was a small town but it boasted a grade school and a high school, both of which Ryan Cosgrove attended with distinction. The boy grew up all bone and gristle, the most successful running back Durham High had ever had, less because of his speed than because of his indestructibility. His only competition on the football field was Bucky Lee Owens, the lean, sticky-fingered end who could catch about anything that flew anywhere near him through the air. It was inevitable that these two rivals for local-hero status would clash, because they had to decide who was top dog.

A pretext was provided when Bucky Lee removed an inch of hide from Cosgrove's ass by snapping a wet towel at him in the shower room. Even so, they didn't wrestle around naked on the slippery floor; that wouldn't have been proper. They donned shorts and went discreetly around to the back of the gym, where a crowd had gathered in anticipation. There they slugged it out for a long, bloody time, the advantage passing from one to the other.

Bucky Lee was much faster than Cosgrove. He danced in and out, peppering the slower boy with punches, loosening teeth and drawing blood. But now and then he got caught and went down. Cosgrove, puffy-eyed and bleeding, never went down, he just kept moving in and swinging. Finally Bucky Lee just couldn't get up anymore. Unlike Cosgrove, his face was unmarked. Ironically, he looked like the winner, who had just lain down to take a rest. But he had been put down by body punches that were later found to have cracked two ribs and caused internal injuries as well as multiple contusions. After that, even the elder Cosgrove's antics were no longer the subject of ridicule while the younger was within earshot. Though he was only fifteen, adults and juveniles alike had learned that he took offense easily and was quick with his big fists.

Off the athletic field, moreover, Ryan Cosgrove got top grades in school, excelling in literature and debating, the latter having been considered a "sissy" course until he became captain of the school's debating team. The town library was hard put to supply the quality of material he sought to read, and he had begun to surpass some of his teachers in his knowledge of the subjects they taught. Yet there was about him an air of abrasive righteousness that made him more feared than popular among his peers. He had learned at his daddy's knee that while the Lord was with him he could do no wrong, and he tended to interpret the Lord's will so that it coincided remarkably with his own. Being perceptive, he recognized the impression he made on others and, when it suited his purpose, he could alter like a chameleon, donning amiability like a spare garment. With a wink and an Irish grin inherited from

Coleman, the bully disappeared, to be replaced by the good buddy. It was a deception that fooled some but not all who knew him.

Given this diversity of talent, it is unlikely that Ryan Cosgrove would have remained mired in Durham even if oil hadn't been found on his father's land, but the discovery accelerated his chance to escape. When Coleman found that he could lease his land to a wildcatter and still run his herd on it, he signed a form contract with a small oil company and used the few extra dollars thus earned to pay his land tax. Happily, within a year the oil outfit had spudded in a pair of little wells, and Coleman, even with only the lessor's one-eighth royalty, had more money than ever before in his life. It was enough to expand his homestead, buy a new pickup, and send Ryan to the University of Virginia, where he stayed to complete both college and law school, graduating with honors the youngest man in his class.

By then the Korean war was over but the draft was still in effect. Not waiting to be called, Ryan Cosgrove joined the army, won a commission at Fort Benning, and was shipped to Germany. There, because of his law degree, he was assigned to the provost marshal's office in Hamburg, where he found out, once and for all time, what he wanted to do for the rest of his life.

He wanted to pursue and prosecute criminals. As an attorney, he had not the slightest interest in the role of defender. His loathing for crime and criminals was simple and obsessive. Sinners all, they were to be scourged or, when possible, eliminated. As prosecutor for the provost marshal's office, he sent his fellow soldiers to the stockade for misdeeds ranging from petty black-marketeering to murder. His record was outstanding; he prepared his cases meticulously and his zeal bemused even the hard-case officers who chaired the courts-martial.

At the same time, paradoxically, he was able to come to terms with his own sins, such as that of fornication. The Lord, he reasoned, must understand the weaknesses within a man's body, since he was responsible for the design. Certainly he would wink at an occasional lapse in the behavior of a good servant. This rationalization left Cosgrove free to enjoy the power his position gave him over the Germans, who, even a decade after the war, still found themselves much at the whim of the occupying powers. Comely Fräuleins were grateful for small favors at the hands of an officer and gave generously of themselves in return. Cosgrove learned that he liked his women submissive, even obeisant, as conquered people tend to be. When his tour of duty ended, he was sorry to leave Germany.

He returned to America and to Durham, at least, as a hero. The peacetime decorations he wore, such as the good-conduct medal and a markman's badge, went well with his captain's bars and no-nonsense crew haircut. Townspeople thought of him as the boy who made good, an attorney and an officer, sprung from humble loins to be sure, but living proof that an American could rise above his origins.

Perhaps it was inevitable that he came to the attention of Hiram "Bull" Durham, after whose granddaddy the town and county were named, even if he hadn't first come to the attention of his daughter, Elizabeth Ann. Bull, belying his nickname, was a lean, stringy man with wiry white hair and flinty gray eyes reminiscent of the actor Charles Bickford, who often epitomized the rugged westerner that Durham truly was. But in Texas if your name is Durham you're called "Bull," just as you're "Dusty" if your handle is Miller or "Muddy" if it's Rivers. To say Bull was a big frog in a small pond would be an understatement, for he had been a state senator and was an authentic power in Texas. If he was not exactly a self-made man, well then, his granddaddy had been, and that was close enough for him to appreciate a young man risen from poor beginnings who seemed destined to cut a wide swath.

Elizabeth Ann Durham was sole heir to Bull, for she was an only child like Cosgrove, and her mother was dead. She was no beauty, being too tall and angular, but she had lovely wide-set eyes and a shy intelligence. She knew that people deferred to her because she was her daddy's girl rather than for her own qualities, and it made her cautious and retiring. When she met Ryan Cosgrove at a coming-home party the town threw for him at the big grange where meetings were held, it was for the first time, even though they had been classmates and she had thrilled to watch him plunge through the opposing line at the football games of long ago. Now, perhaps because his father was dead and no longer a public embarrassment, or because of a dearth of heroes in Durham, he was man of the hour, and as the town's most prominent daughter, it was natural that she would attend his event.

They were introduced casually enough, but a few minutes of conversation sufficed to form a bond. She discovered a man of passionately held convictions and diversified interests who transported her a world away from the sunbaked plains of Durham. He found a young woman of intelligence who would listen to him, and whose education at Vassar College had left her mercifully free of the shitkicking regional accent he himself had struggled to overcome. That she was wealthy and prominent (at least locally) was an added boon to a young man who still had his ladder to climb.

Their relationship ripened without hindrance from Bull. Elizabeth Ann was twenty-four, growing long in the tooth for a single woman by his standards, and the wealthier bucks weren't exactly standing in line to ask for her hand. Hell with them! Why not an infusion of hardy new blood? He sensed this young Cosgrove fella was a comer, intelligent and sure as hell tough. Just purely kicked ass out there on the football field when he was a teenager and got top grades everywhere he went. He'd be grateful to Bull for giving him the main chance, and he'd be good to his girl, too. Maybe he'd go all the way, with Bull standing behind him calling the shots, responsible for it all, so to speak.

Still, the boy seemed to be dragging his feet just a tad with Elizabeth Ann. So one night after Cosgrove had dutifully kissed her good night at the door and was leaving, Bull ambushed him and steered him out onto the veranda, where they sat in the hot summer night with their boots hitched up on the rail, drinking bourbon and branch water and listening to nothing at all.

"Son," said Bull, a trifle prematurely, "you got to have some plan now you're out of the army. Mind my askin' what you're thinkin' on?"

"I thought I might try a big city. Houston, likely as not. It's a growing place."

"Lawyerin'?"

"Yes."

"Lawyerin' all by its own self is for shitheads, son. A law degree serves a purpose just as a steppin'-stone to better things. Now, if I were in your boots, I'd think about politickin'. You talk good and you think fast. You could go a long way."

"A lawyer can always hang out a shingle," murmured Cosgrove. "How do you start in politics?"

It was a question Bull was ready to answer. "You start from home territory. Big city's a fine place later along in life, but you don't want to start out there cold with no friends or contacts. That's not clear thinkin'.

"What you do, you get yourself a power base. For instance, Durham County. Now, you say to yourself, sure, but where do I start? In some country law office? Nossir! You got friends in Durham County. Leastwise, you got one friend. Me." He held up a hand to parry the younger man's reply. "I know how you feel about Elizabeth Ann, son, and I know how she feels about you. And I know sometimes it's hard to speak your mind to an older man like me, who might seem a mite forbiddin' at times. So I'm going to make it easy for you, my boy. I want you to know you'd be welcome in my family."

For once, Cosgrove was caught by surprise. He had thought he had more time. "You do me great honor, Senator," he managed.

"Call me Bull, like ever'body does who knows me. But now let's say you and Elizabeth Ann go ahead and tie the knot. You'll be a family man with responsibilities and the motivation to get ahead. I'll be right there behind you to give you a couple shoves in the right direction. You bein' a lawyer and a man with a law-abidin' bent of mind, suppose we were to start you out as county prosecutor? That's one of the best springboards to public office I know. After that, I'm thinkin' about the state legislature and the U.S. Congress and maybe someday you'll go all the way. You got the fire and I got all those friends in high places you hear talk of." Bull winked and patted Cosgrove's knee. "We'll be a team, you and I, but you'll be the one up front. I'll be behind you, nudgin' you along, ready to circle the wagons if there's any trouble."

Cosgrove's mind rapidly absorbed what the older man said and shifted nimbly over to the process of calculation. He had come back to sell the ranch he'd inherited from Coleman and get the hell out of Durham as quickly as possible. The oil play on his property had petered out and there were no practical or sentimental considerations to keep him in town. He saw his future in a raw, fast-growing city like Houston or Dallas.

What Bull suggested would delay his escape from Durham, but at the same time it presented tantalizing new possibilities. Politics! From Durham to the statehouse and beyond, with the implication of enormous power! It was a dizzying thought, but not at all out of his reach with the old senator behind him. Cosgrove had always harbored within him a sense of mission. He knew he needed only opportunity and direction to take off like a missile.

It was the thought of marrying Elizabeth Ann that gave him the longest pause. His feelings about her were ambivalent, to say the least, falling something short of love as he thought of it. His experience equated love with passion. Elizabeth Ann did not excite him physically, whereas the mere recollection of the jaded, tractable Fräuleins of Germany made his pulse leap. She was no more to him than a companion in the intellectual exile imposed by life in Durham, Texas. Yet as the wife of a politician she would be hard to improve upon. She had intelligence, character, discretion, and a regal bearing that commanded respect without suggesting snobbery—invaluable assets for the mate of a man in the public eye. On balance, marriage to her and full acceptance of the senator's plan were the only logical course for him to take. It was a shortcut to the inside track, a gift of years. The baser instincts could always find gratification elsewhere. Discreetly. The Lord knew of his needs and understood.

By the time he left that night, his foreseeable future had been decided. He and Bull shook on it.

12

The home Bull Durham built for Elizabeth Ann and her husband was a far cry from his own functional ranch house. He had come to think that a budding politician and the daughter of the county patriarch should live in imposing circumstances, so the building he raised looked like an antebellum plantation house with its facade of columns peering down a long cinder drive that fed into Route 85. Cosgrove was reminded of some of the more ostentatious fraternity houses near the University of Virginia campus. Certainly there was nothing else like it in Durham County.

Elizabeth Ann would have been happy with something less pretentious, but she wanted to please her daddy, so she oohed and aahed over her massive chandeliers and sky-high ceilings when he was visiting. Otherwise, she just looked around helplessly and sighed frequently. Cosgrove, who was shrewd enough to realize that his home was a monument to bad taste in the dusty little township, went around with an attitude of good-humored self-deprecation, making clear that none of it was his idea. It didn't matter, for no one blamed him or the senator. Truth be known, the townspeople were proud of the elevation of one of their own.

On the wedding day, before the house was complete, Bull had presented his daughter and his son-in-law with his-and-her Lincoln automobiles and simultaneously announced Cosgrove's appointment to the office of county prosecutor. On top of that, the bride looked stunning in white and the groom was sure he saw a gleam of envy in the eye of more than one stud on the guest list who had passed up a crack at plain old Elizabeth Ann. And this was just the beginning, Cosgrove exulted to himself, the first step.

There was to be still another bonus for him. Elizabeth Ann, he discovered, came to his bed a virgin, shy, indeed terrified of the act of love. Cosgrove found that this fear in her acted as a strong aphrodisiac for him, surpassing even the self-abasement practiced by the girls he had dominated overseas in his army days. Thus stimulated, he remained erect as never before, became a bull. Throughout the tumbled night, during which he had no need to imagine himself back in the cribs and cold-water flats of Hamburg as he had planned, Elizabeth Ann cried out many times, in pain or pleasure—who knew? Nor would he ever find out, for they never discussed sex throughout their marriage. Cosgrove did not think it was proper, and Elizabeth Ann would never have been so forward as to initiate the subject.

As criminal prosecutor, Cosgrove became the bane of lawbreakers throughout Durham County. Within a year and a half, by the time his daughter Bettsy was born, his reputation as a relentless adversary had stretched beyond the county line and defense attorneys despaired of crossing swords with him, no less because of his skill and fervor than because most local judges were beholden to Bull Durham one way or another. The senator, radiating approval, had already begun to talk about a run for the state legislature. He and Cosgrove became nearly inseparable, Bull recreating his own youth through the burgeoning career of his protégé.

Working at his office or in court and drinking until late at night with Bull kept Cosgrove away from home and from a wife he was growing indifferent to. Little Bettsy, however, was the apple of his eye and he began coming home for lunch again so that he could spend an hour with her. He already foresaw her debut into high society and his own grave responsibility in screening her many beaux so that she would make the perfect marriage, achieve the totally happy life. That was the hard part, knowing that she must marry, for he had another vision of her, growing up beautiful and popular, but spurning all others in her singular admiration of him.

Before announcing for the legislature, Bull decided Cosgrove should meet some of the crowd back east, so he took him to visit the corridors of power in Washington and New York, where the old senator was readily and deferentially received. In the capital his friends were the old pols, the men who ran the committees and councils by right of seniority rather than brilliance. In New York they were the power brokers of big business, hermetically sealed in their executive suites high above the teeming streets. Bull kept his own two-bedroom suite on a year-round basis at the Beekman Tower Hotel near Forty-ninth Street and First Avenue, overlooking the East River. Regrettably, the recently constructed UN Building largely blocked his view of that estuary and was, for more than one reason, the object of his disdain.

Bull peered out at the huge, brightly lit glass tower with slitted eyes. "Monument to the stupidity of men," he grunted. It was nearly midnight and they had just returned from dinner at Sardi's after seeing *My Fair Lady*. "A Trojan horse right here in the U.S. of A. They got more Commie spies in there than in the KGB. Them that's not plain damn fools. Maid here tells me there's half a dozen African niggers from over there livin' here. They shit in the bathtub and in the sink, most anywhere but in the crapper, she says. Bunch of animals." He drew the curtains, blotting out the offending sight.

A discreet red light began blinking on the living-room phone. Bull picked it up, listened for a moment, and then said, "Send them up."

With a grin he turned to Cosgrove. "I've got a surprise for you, son."

The surprise arrived in the form of two very comely black girls, bittersweet chocolate and café-au-lait. They smiled easily, wore fur wraps, and carried outsize Vuitton shoulder bags that no doubt housed their kit. The senator greeted them courteously and showed them to the bedrooms, where they could prepared themselves. Then he came back and stretched out on the couch with a bourbon and branch water in his hand.

"Hope I ain't shockin' you any," he said to his son-in-law. "It's not like you were being unfaithful to Elizabeth Ann or anything like that. I'd whip your ass if I caught you porkin' a white woman, but this is just fuckin' for fun. They say you ain't a man till you split black oak. Besides, these two come guaranteed one hundred percent clean."

Cosgrove's surprise turned to anticipation. At the University of Virginia, he had never joined his fraternity brothers in their occasional sorties to the black whorehouses of Charlottesville. ("Shit, it ain't like we're going to school with 'em, Cos," they'd said, trying to persuade him.) But he had abstained for hygienic rather than racial reasons, and bedding a black woman had remained among his fantasies. Especially if she were well-paid and correspondingly pliant.

When the girls returned they were naked, and the darker one went directly over to sit on the couch next to Bull. She giggled and unzipped his fly, rooted around, and finally produced his joint. It was fully erect, an angry-looking red. She bent forward to meet it.

The café-au-lait girl, Melba, used a different approach, as though she could read Cosgrove's mind. She came to him almost shyly, eyes cast down, head bowed submissively. She had a firm lovely body, small breasts with erectile nipples, a narrow waist above the slightest swell of belly, long legs tapering from full hips. Cosgrove felt the excitement pulsing to his extremities.

In the bedroom he carefully locked the door behind him. Deep in his soul he was enough of a prude not to want the randy senator bouncing in calling for a foursome. The girl melted back from him to arrange herself on the bed while he undressed. Watching his eyes, she lay on her back and parted her legs. Then, slowly, anticipating him to an uncanny degree, she shifted her body so that her ripe buttocks were presented to him even while her torso remained breasts-up and her eyes stayed glued to his, the better to interpret his desires. He motioned her to turn all the way onto her stomach, then knelt on the bed and spread her thighs gently. He caressed the firm, unblemished globes of her buttocks, thrust his fingers into her, hearing her gasp, feeling his desire rise. When finally he plunged forward into her and she arched to meet him, he was at fever pitch, unable to contain himself more than a few moments. But for those moments he rode her hard, while she caught the pillow between her teeth to muffle her cries and gave back as good as she got. When he had spent himself with a great shout that distracted the senator in the next room and collapsed beside his lovely partner, it was with the sure knowledge that he had not even scraped the surface of her potential. Lying there, feeling her fingers kneading the nape of his neck, tracing the path of his spine down to his buttocks, he felt an uncharacteristic tenderness, tinged with regret. He realized that this splendid courtesan was just what he needed. Talented, unquestioning passion, available on call. But not in Durham, Texas.

It was hard for Cosgrove to adapt to the torpor of Durham after one of his infrequent trips to Washington or New York, where he felt himself to be at the hub of the universe, part of the vital force from which all progress and policy emanated. The flat, desiccated Texas landscape, perennially parched for rain and stretching around him into seeming infinity, was profoundly depressing, made bearable only by his love for Bettsy and by the promise of eventual escape. To distract himself as well as to bring the eventuality closer, he threw himself into his work with a single-minded purpose—to maintain a perfect record of convictions.

The violent death of Peggy Sue Gruenig, a local girl and niece of Sheriff Barton Gruenig, was the sensation of the year in Durham County, where lurid crimes were rare. Her body was found two miles south of Durham off Highway 85 by a pair of lovers looking for a place to make out. They had pulled off the road, opened a gate in the barbed-wire fence, and proceeded down a dirt track to an area used as the town dump. Almost immediately their headlights had picked out the body of Peggy Sue sprawled on a pile of rubble, no attempt having been made to bury her. An investigation revealed that she had been raped and then stabbed repeatedly in the abdominal and genital areas. Her panties, if she had been wearing any, were missing.

She had been there a day or so and the rats had already been at her.

The prime suspect was Jose Luis Hoyos, an apprentice mechanic with no family in the United States. He lived alone in a single room above Homer's Auto Repair, providing the premises with a live-in watchman and himself with quarters, and had been seen on various occasions dogging the footsteps of Peggy Sue Gruenig. This had not amused Peggy Sue's mother, who chased him off her lawn on Jackson Avenue with a horsewhip when she'd caught him hanging around. Then Peggy Sue's two big brothers moseyed over to the garage where he worked and told him earnestly that they would cut him up and feed bits of his mangy brown hide to their dogs if they caught him within a country mile of their sister. After that, there had been no further sightings of Jose Luis in the vicinity of Peggy Sue. But two weeks later she was found murdered.

The morning after she was discovered, a deputy was dispatched to search the area by daylight and see if some clue to the crime could be found. The deputy was Waylon "Bubba" Diefenbaker, the youngest, biggest, and probably the meanest (after Bucky Lee Owens) deputy working out of the sheriff's department. Bubba's close-set pale eyes had a psycho stare under a conical thatch of yellow hair that resembled a haystack. He liked to place beer caps between each of his spread fingers and then crumple all eight of them by merely closing his big hands, a trick he performed endlessly, long after losing his audience. Otherwise he had few passions unless you counted an abiding hatred of Mexicans, hardly a distinguishing characteristic in Durham County, and a bad case of hero worship for Ryan Cosgrove, the crusading county prosecutor he felt shared his antipathy for the ungodly in general and for greasers in particular.

Bubba took only about ten minutes to find the bloody kitchen knife wrapped in the missing panties which had been casually discarded under a mesquite bush some twenty yards from where Peggy Sue had been found. In his excitement, he was sorely tempted to hit the red light and siren for the two-mile trip back to town, before remembering that Sheriff Bart frowned on that kind of grandstanding.

As it was, he very nearly ran down Ryan Cosgrove, who had just stepped off the curb in front of the county courthouse.

Seeing who it was, Bubba pulled up to apologize despite his haste. "I'm purely sorry, Mr. Cosgrove," he assured the prosecutor, who came over to the car window. "Gotta see the sher'ff right away. I found the evy-dence!"

"Evidence?" Cosgrove raised his eyebrows.

"Just now found the knife that greaser used to kill Peggy Sue! Out by the dump, wrapped in her panties."

Cosgrove peered into the car. "You were alone?"

"Surely was."

Cosgrove watched while the deputy pulled his cruiser into a slot in front of the old brick courthouse building where the sheriff had an office two doors from his own.

"Bubba," he said, walking over to the hulking deputy who was climbing out of the car. "Got a moment to spare me? I'd like to talk to you."

"Gotta see the sher'ff. . . ."

"Sure, I know. But I've got to get the facts from you, too. No better time than right now." He took the man's arm and steered him gently toward the brick building. "Sheriff Bart's over having breakfast at the diner, anyway."

Inside his office Cosgrove closed the door behind him and motioned the deputy to take the chair facing his desk. He poured two cups of coffee from the pot he kept on a hot plate and sat down facing him.

"Figure there's any doubt about who did it?" asked Cosgrove, sipping.

"That fucking Mex did it! Jose Luis!"

"Has he been picked up yet?"

"Yeah. Bucky Lee brought him in first thing this morning."

"Anyone go through his place?"

"No. Just picked him up at the gay-rage and brought him in for questionin'."

"What did he say?"

"Says he ain't even seen Peggy Sue for more'n two weeks. Shee-it!"

"He going to stick to that? Even after going 'round and 'round with Bucky Lee?"

"Looks like."

Cosgrove shook his head and sighed. "Too bad there's no hard evidence."

"No hard evy-dence? I just found his blade wrapped up in her panties! It's gotta have his prints."

"Maybe not. Probably not. He probably used her pants to wipe them off. Look, Bubba, I'm a lawyer and I'm the one who's going to have to try this case. I know about the rules of evidence. There's not much to go on if there are no prints and he doesn't confess."

Bubba pondered the information. "You mean that copper-colored sumbitch is going to get away with this?" he cried finally. "God damn! She was so blond and purty!"

Cosgrove stared at the outraged deputy for a long moment. At last he said, "I think there's a way justice can be served. God helps those who help themselves." The word came out "he'p," for Cosgrove could slip easily back into the regional accent when it served his purpose.

Bubba looked puzzled.

"What I mean," Cosgrove went on, "we know Jose Luis killed that girl, but it won't do any good unless we can prove it. We need to help ourselves along some. Now, if that knife and those panties were found up in his place, there wouldn't hardly be any problems."

"But I found them out by the dump!"

Cosgrove closed his eyes for a moment, then continued patiently, "If someone, like for instance you, Bubba, went over to Jose Luis' place and put them there, maybe in a drawer or, say, under the mattress, then that's where they would be found when anyone looked. Of course, you'd want to be real sure no one saw you coming in or going out.

"Meanwhile, when Sheriff Bart comes back from breakfast, I'll go in and suggest to him he get a warrant and send someone over there while he's still hanging on to Jose Luis." Cosgrove leaned back in his chair. "If you were to do something like that, I sure wouldn't tell on you. That's because you'd be aiding justice. And doing the Lord's work, too." He winked at Bubba and gave him his friendliest grin.

Bubba found it hard to speak for a moment. Here was

the county prosecutor making him a full partner in his fight against crime! "Reckon I could do that," he said when he was able. "Know for a fact old Homer's over to Crystal City gettin' car parts. Bucky Lee said so when he got back with the Mex. Shouldn't be anyone around there. Yeah, I reckon I could do that, Mr. Cosgrove."

When he finally got up to leave, Cosgrove said to him, "I'm sure I don't have to tell you this is just between us, Bubba. Sheriff Bart, well, he just wouldn't understand. 'The Lord works in wondrous ways his miracles to perform.' Today you are his instrument."

Jose Luis Joyos was duly charged with murder and Cosgrove proceeded to compile the case against him. Bubba himself had been sent to search the suspect's room, a fortunate happenstance for the conspirators, as he had left signs of forced entry on his prior visit, a fact that another deputy might have found suspicious. It was the only good luck they were to have.

On the third day of the trial, when Cosgrove already had Jose Luis Joyos practically strapped into the electric chair and was anticipating the renown this colorful case would bring him, a semiretarded drifter from Beaumont named Roy Bob Dexter confessed to the murder of Peggy Sue and to four other similar butcheries. He was arrested in Shreveport, Louisiana, after bragging of his crimes to a bar patron who promptly turned him in to the police. Roy Bob obligingly waved extradition and was returned to Texas, where he recounted how he had stolen a kitchen knife from a home out on Farm Road, a fact confirmed by old lady Buford, who owned the place and missed the knife. A partial print of Roy Bob's thumb was lifted from the murder weapon and he furthermore convincingly testified that he had never known any Jose Luis Hoyos. In fact, he had never before committing the crime been in the vicinity of Durham County. As for Peggy Sue, he had chosen his victim haphazardly, ambushing her as she biked home from a friend's house. After raping and killing her he had thrown the knife and panties into some bushes near the dump.

Sheriff Bart Gruenig smelled a rat very quickly once he

realized that Deputy Bubba Diefenbaker was not likely to have found the knife and panties in the room of Jose Luis Hoyos. He moved fast, before Cosgrove had a chance to instill a spirit of resistance in his shaken confederate. Cloistered with Gruenig and the persuasive Bucky Lee Owens, Bubba, who was only slightly less retarded than Roy Bob Dexter, opened up like the brand-new drive-in movie down at Eagle Pass. He spilled his guts, naming Cosgrove as the instigator of the plot to frame Jose Luis and confessing his own complicity in detail. Sheriff Gruenig, taken aback by this turn of events, felt obliged to call on Senator Bull Durham for advice.

Cosgrove did not appreciate the extent of his undoing until he stood before Bull's massive oak desk in the paneled den of the senator's ranch house. Bull sprawled facing him in his old leather chair, booted feet up on the desk, drinking bourbon which he did not offer to his son-in-law.

"That dumb peckerwood, Bubba," the senator began, sipping. "He told Sheriff Bart all about how you and him set up that Hoyos boy."

Cosgrove felt the shock wave hit his guts. He had not known the situation was so far out of hand.

Bull shook his head sadly. "Now, Bubba bein' the town dummy, it's not hard to attribute any kind of damn fool act to him. You, on the other hand, bein' an educated man and, by way of the office you occupy, one of the county's prime upholders of the law, are a mite harder to understand." He nailed Cosgrove with eyes the color of steel filings and added softly, "Any ideas about what we ought to do now?"

"Maybe it's time to circle the wagons," Cosgrove ventured.

The senator nodded. "I thought you might have in mind something like that." He finished his bourbon and poured some more, straight. "Well, let me tell you something. Even if the girl hadn't been Sheriff Bart's niece, makin' him specially riled about this particular case, and even if I could clap a lid on the whole thing and make it just quietly go away—I wouldn't lift a finger this much to help you." His forefinger rose a scant inch off the polished wood it rested on.

"Oh, you're not goin' to jail or anything like that," he

went on. "But that's not helpin' you, really, that's just helpin' Elizabeth Ann and the little girl, so she won't have to grow up knowin' her daddy was a yard bird. No, Sheriff Bart and I figured another way. Bubba, he's goin' to join the army tomorrow and you're going to leave the county of Durham and the state of Texas tonight. When you leave this house. No goin' home first, no whinin' to Elizabeth Ann, blowin' snot and tears, lyin' and deceivin'."

"For God's sake, Bull!"

"Call me 'Senator'!" the old man shouted, then settled down again. "I was wrong about you, boy. You're small-minded and petty. This country doesn't need any more of your kind in high places. Got enough deadwood already. Riggin' evidence to win a two-bit case . . ."

"I was sure he was guilty! Everybody was. You know how many of these bastards get off on lack of evidence every year! Christ, Bull . . . I mean, Senator, are you saying you never cut a corner in your life? I've heard stories—"

"I've cut corners," Bull interrupted quietly, leaning forward. "I've brought pressure and I've traded favors. I've even given and received considerations, meanin' bribes. That's the way bi'ness is done in statehouses and on the Hill. That's the way things are accomplished, made to happen. Not all the time, but some of the time. But I've never known nor heard tell of a man that would frame another man into the electric chair for the sake of winnin' a court case." He leaned back in his chair again. "You came from nothing. I treated you like my own, gave you my only daughter, and showed you how to get ahead in the world. But I was mistaken about you. You talk righteous, but you're crooked. So crooked, when you die they're probably gonna have to screw you into the ground. You came from trash, and trash is what you remain. I was tryin' to make a silk purse out of a sow's ass."

Cosgrove took an instinctive step forward. The senator's right hand plunged below his desk and reappeared holding a sawed-off pump shotgun, which he laid across his lap, pointed casually at Cosgrove. "You know," he said conversationally, "I make my own loads for this piece. Don't use double-ought buckshot or anything like that. That stuff can go right through the wall, injure a servant or a family member. No, I make a load usin' bits of rusty nail and wire. It doesn't go beyond the room, but when it hits a man it's downright disfigurin'. You'd purely have to scrape the remains off the wall with a trowel.

"Now, I'm goin' to ask you to haul your sorry ass out of here. When you're clear of Texas and settled somewhere, we'll ship you your gear."

Cosgrove's surprise and frustration were replaced by cold anger. "Listen to me, old man," he grated, "now that I've listened to all your holier-than-thou bullshit. Your daughter happens to be my wife. She's free to make her own choice."

"She's already spoken," snapped Bull. "She said, 'Tell him I don't want to see him again. Ever.' "

"I'll hear it from her, not you. If she feels that way, fine. Amen. But Bettsy is mine as much as hers. You can't take her away from me by your decree, like some goddamn feudal lord. Even you're not that big, Senator."

Cosgrove turned deliberately away from the senator and his shot gun. A broad area of his back crawled in anticipation of the savage impact one of the old man's murderous loads would make, but he made the long trip to the door of the study intact. As he opened it, he heard Bull call after him, "Don't you go over there! I'm warnin' you . . ."

But there was something uncertain in the old man's tone now. Cosgrove closed the door on his querulous voice. The moment for shooting had passed.

He went directly, unhesitatingly home. It was night but the porch lamp over the front door was out, as were the downstairs lights. A dim glow came from the upper rooms.

He shoved his key in the lock, to no avail; Elizabeth Ann had simply thrown the inner bolt. He rang the bell and pounded on the big hand-carved door.

"Get away from here!" Elizabeth Ann's voice reached him from an upstairs window.

Cosgrove looked up, squinting his eyes to see her in the dark. "Open the door," he told her. "Get down here and open this goddamn door right now!"

"You've got two minutes to leave before I call the sheriff."

This was a new Elizabeth Ann, no longer the submissive if increasingly remote woman he had taken for granted over the last two years. He recognized cold hatred in the level tone of her voice, and it shocked him.

Cosgrove looked around him. The downstairs windows were mounted with wrought-iron bars to discourage intruders, so he walked around to an outbuilding next to the garage where the yard man stored his tools. He chose a heavy ax from several racked on the wall and returned to the front door, where he shed his jacket and went to work.

Chunks of wood flew before his blade, and he never heard Elizabeth Ann come down the stairs. He did hear her shout, "Damn you!" before she fired twice through the door at the very point where his assault had thinned the wood.

One shot went wide; the other caught him high on the left breast and felt much as if one of his robust drinking buddies had slapped him playfully on the chest. He took two steps backward and dropped the ax. Behind the door he heard Elizabeth Ann make a sound that may or may not have been a sob. Well, he thought with astonishment and a touch of rueful admiration, she's her daddy's daughter after all. He'd dismissed her long ago as an ineffectual partner he was chained to through the circumstance of necessity.

Cosgrave opened his shirt to assess the damage. By starlight he could make out a dark spot on his chest that oozed a quantity of blood. He touched it, wincing, and felt a hard lump. The bullet, largely spent by its passage through the door, seemed to be lodged in the pad of pectoral muscle over his breastbone. Nothing serious, but he had cause to regret that he had chosen the hardball ammo for his thirty-eight revolver instead of hollow points that would not have been able to punch through the heavy wood at all. Where had he recently listened to a lecture on the merits of using the right ammunition?

In the sudden quiet of the night, he thought he heard the cry of a child inside the house. Bettsy! The sound, imagined or otherwise, renewed his determination. No one in the world could deny him access to Bettsy. Very calmly he reflected that Elizabeth Ann had three rounds left in the revolver. If she were wise enough to hold her fire and shoot him after he got through the door, that would be that. To hell with it! He bent to pick up his ax.

The police cruiser with Bucky Lee Owens and Wally Morgann in it turned slowly and quietly off Route 85 onto the cinder path leading to the Cosgrove place. Not until their headlights picked up the man on the porch holding an ax in his hand did Bucky Lee touch the siren, which emitted a low, warning growl.

"Sure God is ol' Cos, gettin' ready to commit some kinda mayhem," said Bucky Lee happily, uncoiling from the driver's seat. He was six-three, lean and leathery, a man who seemed to be made out of spring steel and rawhide.

" 'Pears so," sighed Wally Morgann, staying where he was. His big belly bulged over his gunbelt and his massive shoulders hung slack. Wally was an insurance broker who served as a reserve deputy for the fun of it. He was a drinking buddy of Cosgrove's and godfather to Bettsy. The present situation distressed him.

"Now, you drop that toothpick and come down off'n there, Cos," Bucky Lee called pleasantly. He stood casually, hands on his hips, rocking on the balls of his feet.

The man on the porch laid the ax carefully against the side of his home and walked steadily toward them. As he neared, they could see the dark stain against the white material of his shirt.

Wally struggled out of the police cruiser, lugging a long flashlight, and moved out to meet him. "You hurt bad, Cos?" he asked, concerned, playing the beam of his light over the bloody shirt. They hadn't heard the shots.

"Not bad," said Cosgrove. "Hello, Wally. Bucky Lee."

"That a gunshot wound?" Bucky Lee peered at Cosgrove's chest.

"Spent round. Barely broke the skin. She shot me through the door."

"We better get you over to Doc," said Wally.

"No need. You boys go on home. This is family business."

"You shouldn't have come back here, Cos," said Bucky Lee, shaking his head. "The senator says we got to pound on you some, we catch you doing something like this. Didn't he say that, Wally?"

Wally looked down at his feet. "Yes, but I'm not going to beat on a hurt man. We'll take you in to Doc, Cos, let him patch you, and then escort you to the line."

"And that's gettin' off easy," grunted Bucky Lee, disappointed.

"You really want to try me again?" Cosgrove asked Bucky Lee softly. Then he looked at Wally Morgann. "Bettsy's in there, Wally, and I'm not going anywhere until we've settled what hapens to her."

"Don't be crazy, Cos!" cried Wally. "You already been shot once!"

"We're just wastin' time," said Bucky Lee, pulling his stick out of its loop.

Wally caught Cosgrove by the shoulders to protect or restrain him, but the wounded man half-turned and buried his fist in the deputy's flaccid belly. The air whooshed out of Wally's lungs and he sat down abruptly. Cosgrove used the same fist to backhand Bucky Lee across the face, staggering him, then bulled him back against the squad car where he could use his blocky weight to best advantage. He was heavier than the deputy and very solid in those days.

But the gunshot wound had taken its toll in shock and loss of blood. Bucky Lee used his sinewy strength to wrench loose, then punched his stick viciously into Cosgrove's diaphragm, stunning him with pain. Free again to maneuver, he slashed at the big man's forehead, opening a cut that sent a river of blood into his eyes.

"Been waitin' a long time for this," Bucky Lee grunted as he worked, half-paralyzing Cosgrove's arms with blows to both elbows. "College boy, huh? Fuckin' army officer! County prosecutor, huh?"

Cosgrove lunged blindly, unable to land a solid punch, gasping for air. The blows came from every angle, rackingly painful, calculated to torment rather than finish him. He was so tired. It would have been good to give up and lie down, as common sense strongly suggested he do, but something deep inside him would not allow it. He wallowed around, absorbing the punishment trying to the last to get his hands on Bucky Lee.

When he finally went down, it was for the first time in his life. Tiring of his sport, Bucky Lee cracked him hard behind the ear, putting an end to it. Then he kicked the fallen man in the crotch, but Cosgrove was already unconscious.

He awoke at false dawn, stretched across the front seat of his Lincoln. His shirt was glued to his chest with congealed blood, his body was a mass of pain from his groin to his battered head. His coat containing his wallet intact had been thrown over his upper body. The car was parked on the shoulder of Route 85 under a sign that read: "YOU ARE LEAVING DURHAM COUNTY."

Cosgrove didn't like to think about his journey out of Texas. Mercifully, there was much he couldn't recall. He had awakened feverish, and had driven to Crystal City, where he roused a veterinary doctor he knew to extract the slug from his chest, give him a shot of penicillin, and patch him up. Then, concussed and semidelirious, driving with the exaggerated care of a drunk, he made it all the way to Gila Bend, Arizona, where he had collapsed in a motel and slept for two days. When he roused, somewhat recovered in strength but still in agony and with his testicles swollen to the size of oranges, he drove on to California.

For nine months he lived in the San Diego area on proceeds from the sale of his ranch, drinking. Finally he had to sell the Lincoln too. Near the end of his resources, financial and emotional, he caught himself at the edge of the brink and worked slowly back to fitness. In the spring of 1961 he joined the Los Angeles Police Department, passing through the academy with ease, and was assigned to duty. He was twenty-nine years old.

Cosgrove never returned to Durham. It was not that he was afraid; he no longer cared much what happened to him. He simply recognized the futility of such a gesture. Bettsy was only two years old when he left. She would be guarded for years, but someday would have to be given freedom of action. And freedom of choice. Then he would go back.

*   *   *

Now, twenty years later, the trip to Texas was no longer necessary. That was because Bettsy had come to Los Angeles.

He learned that she had arrived when he saw her on the cover of *People* magazine almost a year ago. It was not exactly that he recognized her, simply that something about the beautiful wide-set eyes seemed familiar, compelling him to open the magazine. Inside there were more pictures and an article about the promising young actress who had left the New York stage to star in a West Coast soap opera and was now ready to put that behind her for a career in feature films. Her name was unfamiliar to him until he read that she was the former Elizabeth Durham Leeds, granddaughter of the late senator from Texas and daughter of the prominent Elizabeth Ann Leeds, now of Houston, Texas. Leeds would be someone Elizabeth Ann married later and who would seem to have adopted Bettsy. There was no mention of her real father.

He stared at the pictures in shock. Bettsy had her mother's lovely hazel eyes and so much more! Even on the glossy cover she had a clear, uncluttered beauty seldom associated with Hollywood. The article stressed that she was a serious, dedicated actress who shunned the drug-and-disco culture of the show-business crowd. Cosgrove, who despised that whole element of society, hoped fervently that this was true. She had to be an exception!

He got her unlisted number without difficulty, using his police connection, but did not call her immediately. He did not want to act on impulse, jar her needlessly with an emotional overture. Instead he strove to relax and deliberate his approach calmly. Finally he picked up the phone.

Her recorded voice bade him leave his name, number, and any message he wished to include. She would call back. The voice was cool and melodious, no freaky music in the background, no cretinous gibes about lost nickels. He hung up at once, conscious that his hands were sweating.

On his next attempt, she answered in person. "Hello?"

"Bettsy?" He could not bring himself to use her stage name.

There was a silence. "No one calls me Bettsy except my family," she said at last. "Who is this?"

"This is your father. Ryan Cosgrove."

Another silence; then she said. "My father is Orin Leeds. I'm sorry, Mr. Cosgrove."

"Bettsy . . . please listen to me. Please give me a moment of your time." He hadn't rehearsed it this way at all. She would be stunned, yes, perhaps even angry for what she might think of as his willful neglect. But deep down she would be happy to hear from him, insatiably curious about her real father.

"All right. But I think this is a mistake."

He pulled himself together. "Bettsy. There's so much you don't know. I never left you. I was forced away from you."

"I know that."

"Then you must know that I fought to stay with you. But your grandfather had the power, the police, everybody. I had no way of winning . . ."

"I know that you had to leave. And I know why." He heard her take a light, quick breath. "Mr. Cosgrove, this must be painful for you and I don't think there's any purpose to be served. You see, I was only two years old when you left and I don't remember you at all. I only recall being brought up by my parents. . . ."

"Bettsy, I am your flesh and blood!" Cosgrove tried for a firm, commanding tone. This talk was going all wrong. "I want to see you. At least agree to meet me. That's not very much for a father to ask." Jesus, he was begging!

"No, Mr. Cosgrove," she said very gently. "It would be very wrong. For both of us. I'm very sorry if I am hurting you, but I must ask you not to contact me again."

"But, I love you . . ."

The phone was dead.

13

The furnace heat of his apartment struck Cosgrove like a blow as he crossed the threshold, driving Bettsy out of his mind. There was no air conditioning and he crossed the living room to turn on the heavy-duty fan before he laid the cassette and album taken from Steelegrave's bungalow on the end table by his easy chair. Then he went into the kitchen to put on coffee. He planned to stay up late and needed to combat his weariness.

Steelegrave's album was full of yellow clippings and old glossy prints charting his career in tennis and on screen from the early fifties through the mid-sixties. Marla Monday figured prominently in the later entries, smiling and incredibly beautiful next to or across from a young and handsome Rick Steele. Often they were joined by the smooth-haired Lang Desmond, an actor Cosgrove remembered from boyhood. They were invariably sleek and stylish, being photographed in fashionable surroundings and in the company of other celebrities. A golden couple, Cosgrove thought sourly, whom you could not imagine having acne or bad breath or even natural bodily functions. He saw their faces as beautiful arrogant masks through which they surveyed the rest of the world with disdain. Faces with neither pity nor patience to spare for the unfortunate, the ugly, or anyone less God-gifted than themselves. He felt the bile of hatred rise in his throat and welcomed it. It made him feel righteous to be the hunter of such as these.

The album seemed to contain nothing dated later than 1965, as though Steelegrave, or at least Rick Steele, had died then. Cosgrove was about to set it aside when he spied the edge of a loose photo poking out between the last pages.

It was a fresh five-by-seven print of a young woman with a stunning figure and incredible legs. She was in a bikini, standing hipshot on the beach with the Santa Monica pier in the distant background. She was relaxed and smiling, a girl who was at ease in front of a camera. The photo was signed "Yours—For now! Erin!" Cosgrove turned it over and saw a recent date stamp over the logo of the Shutterbug Camera Shop in Pacific Palisades. He laid it carefully to one side.

After finishing a large pepperoni pizza delivered by a local Italian eatery, he popped Steelegrave's cassette into his Betamax, grateful that it was the same make as the actor's machine and would accept the cartridge. The stereo tape player was a luxury he had bought to indulge his taste for pornography. He watched his porn movies on Wednesday nights with his maid, a small, timid Mexican girl who catered to him in ways unrelated to the weekly housecleaning for an extra twenty dollars. Generally he settled for oral sex but now and then it amused him to lift her astraddle his huge belly (planting her on the peg, as he thought of it). She was gratifyingly submissive and cried easily at his small cruelties, providing him with exactly what he needed in a sex partner.

Fall Guy was a slick detective yarn casting Rick Steele as a man on the run, having been falsely accused of murdering his wife, effectively played by a very young Marla Monday (the irony was not lost on Cosgrove). Lang Desmond was the wartime buddy who hid him from the cops, at one time disguising him so that he could move around freely while trying to solve the mystery. In the end it developed that Desmond himself, unbalanced by the war, murdered the wife, knowing she was no damn good and would ruin his pal's life. He finally caught a bullet intended for Steele and died in his friend's arms with a line ("Got a match? I think my light's going out") that made Cosgrove wince.

Cosgrove tried to suspend his antagonism toward the man and look objectively at Steele-Steelegrave. The picture was entertaining, if dated. The pace was fast and Steele had physical grace and considerable presence. Cosgrove caught himself rooting for the man on the screen and could understand how he'd made it to the top as an actor. Yet he was willing to bet Steele was not so much acting as living a role he had created for himself and managed to project to the public. The man he had met today was too similar to the man he saw on the screen. Even to the rash act of making a run for it when the goddamn dog had jumped Cosgrove.

He watched the film twice even though he was not sure there was anything to be gleaned from screening it. Other, perhaps, than to hone the edge of his hatred. Several times he stopped the tape, freezing Steele in mid-action to study an expression or a characteristic in the instant of its execution. Know thine enemy, he thought. It might help you to get to him first. Which is exactly what Cosgrove intended to do.

14

By the time Steelegrave drove Erin's little red Fiat off the San Diego freeway toward Corona del Mar he was very sober and assailed by doubts. Finding himself with only sixty dollars upon leaving Erin's, he had gone to his bank in Brentwood and furtively used his express-stop card to withdraw his limit of four hundred dollars from the instant teller. That gave him enough money to lie low somewhere until this whole crazy business got sorted out. If it didn't take too long.

Why, then, go to Laguna Beach and confront Vandy at all? Would the bastard just up and confess? Could he be conned or threatened, somehow, into telling the world he had murdered Marla Monday and framed Richard Steelegrave? It didn't seem likely. So why not just go on to Mexico? He could cross the border at Tijuana and hole up in some fleabag in Ensenada until everything got straightened out. They weren't looking for Erin's car, and the border handled a lot of traffic.

He refused to feel guilty about using Erin's car, though she would be in trouble if the cops caught him. Her romantic escapade of the night before had cost him an alibi as well as a measure of his pride. Not that he could really blame her under the easy terms of their relationship. Perversely, what angered him most was that her damn car radio didn't work, only the stereo tape deck, and he could not find out what was going on. That was typical of Erin, to disdain the radio. As long as there was music.

But he was already in Corona del Mar, driving the little Fiat with the rag top up despite the heat. He also wore the panama hat to disguise his bright hair, and discovered he had on sunglasses at nine-thirty at night. Was he losing his mind? He would look sinister as hell to anyone pulling up next to him. He snatched off the glasses.

He was hungry and thirsty and presently found a liquor-store deli that was open and uncrowded. The streets of the seaside resort were mercifully empty, too. Just a few beach types wandering aimlessly here and there.

Steelegrave screwed up his courage and went into the deli still wearing his hat. Better to look eccentric than recognizable. The pimply clerk behind the counter seemed to inspect him closely. Two big surfer types playing electronic video games gave him the bad eye. They both wore tank tops and bulged with muscle. They had arms like sausage skins stuffed with baseballs and seemed remarkably alike, though one was Anglo and the other Latino. Steelegrave felt that anyone who played Pac-Man had to be a cretin, but he forced himself to smile at them before he turned to the shelves that held the liquor. It was his imagination, of course, that people were paying him undue attention.

He selected a fifth of Cutty Sark and two large submarine sandwiches and took them to the counter. The clerk accepted his money without comment and the surfers drifted past him and out of the store with hostile sidelong glances.

Steelegrave took his purchases gratefully out to the car, fighting back an urge to uncap the bottle right away. He was backing out of his parking slot when he heard a howl of anguish that made him hit the brake automatically. One of the big surfer clones, the Anglo, limped dramatically over, resting a hand on his buddy's shoulder.

"What's the matter?" Steelegrave asked, bewildered.

"You ran over my fucking foot, you fucker!" the boy cried.

Steelegrave had a feeling they were playing a game. He had sensed no object whatever under the wheels of the light car. He forced another friendly smile. "Sorry about that. No harm done, I hope?"

"No harm done, my ass! My foot could be broke!"

A few people began to move idly toward them. They were going to gather a crowd! Steelegrave shoved the car in gear, but the big young men were fast. They moved swiftly behind the little Fiat, bent to grip the rear bumper, and hauled both back wheels free of the ground, where they spun uselessly in the air. They stood spread-legged, muscles straining, and laughed uproariously. So did an increasing number of bystanders. Steelegrave clenched his teeth over a groan, appalled by his luck.

"Hey, man, how about that?" shouted one of the surfers. "You ain't goin' fuckin' nowhere!"

Steelegrave could see it all happening. Someone would come over and stare intently at his face. (With his luck, probably a cop.) There would arise a great cry. Here was the murderer being featured on all the TV channels for the last hour. He would be hauled out of the car. Beaten. Arrested. Suddenly anger overwhelmed him. He jammed down the clutch and pushed his gear lever into reverse. Then he gunned the engine and stuck his head out the window. "All right, you pricks! It's in reverse now. Put it down anytime. It'll run right over you!"

The surfers looked at each other, grins fading. The crowd was laughing with Steelegrave now. He made a show of lighting a cigarette and settling back in his seat, which wasn't easy at that angle and in his state of mind. He kept the engine roaring.

"Bet ten bucks they can't hold her up there five minutes!" someone hollered.

"I'll take it!" another shouted back. "Fuckin' Donny can hold it up there five minutes all by his own self!"

Donny was evidently not so confident. "Fuck that!" howled the Anglo surfer over the engine noise. "You win, man. Let us put it down, huh?"

Steelegrave was shaking as he drove south out of Corona del Mar. He kept his eye on the rearview mirror but nothing was following him. A few minutes later he arrived at the gentle S-curve where Marla had smashed Ugolini's big Cadillac into the Volkswagen so long ago. In all the intervening years he had never driven this section of the coast road again, until now.

It was too much. He pulled off the highway near a deserted fruit stand and followed a secondary dirt road that ended abruptly on a bluff above the Pacific. He killed the lights and stepped out of the car carrying his bottle of Scotch.

Below him the surf pounded the rocks at the base of the cliff. It wasn't at all like that other night. Tonight there was no fog and the bright stars looked near enough to touch. The hot wind from the desert blew against his back, as if trying to nudge him over the cliff into the sea.

He drank deeply of the Scotch, listened to the surf, and watched the stars. Slowly he relaxed, feeling the ghosts disperse, unable to haunt this gentle night. The whiskey sharpened his appetite and he went back to the car for one of the huge sandwiches. He ate and sipped whiskey. When he finished the sandwich he smoked a cigarette and drank a little more Scotch.

Soon he felt fortified, alert, and competent. He was ready to deal with Vandy. Memories of his old "friend" came flooding back, dispelling any doubts about his guilt. Vandy had been ruthless and devious from the day they had met.

That had been almost thirty-five years ago, on a bright fall afternoon in Connecticut, the first day of the school year at the Colton Academy for Boys.

Colton Academy was a vast, brooding Tudor structure built of brick and smothered in dying ivy. The school grounds had a deceptively pleasant air and included an eighteen-hole golf course, playing fields for baseball, football, and track, tennis courts, and a tiny lake used as a hockey rink in winter. Within the walls the aspect was grim and institutional. The functional organs of the school—dining room, auditorium, classrooms, gym, and study halls—were connected by long flagstone corridors under high vaulted ceilings that echoed the heels of scurrying students relentlessly. Narrow, leaded-in windows like the defensive slits in the turrets of old castles peered out at intervals, and below ground level a maze of subterranean tunnels linked biology lab, school-supply store, locker and shower rooms, storage and trash-disposal facilities, and a dismal windowless rec room containing two pay phones where homesick boys could call their parents collect.

The second, third, and fourth floors housed the students according to grades—there were Lower Middlers, Middlers, Upper Middlers, and Seniors—the equivalent of high school—with two faculty apartments on each floor from which teachers could effectively spy on student activities. Maintaining discipline, however, was in the hands of upperclassmen called monitors who formed a sort of inmate Gestapo and were selected by the headmaster and the faculty. Aside from low grades, smoking, drinking, and masturbation were among the cardinal sins they sought to ferret out. Monitors descended upon their victims in midnight raids and hauled them down to empty classrooms in the bowels of the school, where they were browbeaten and interrogated with their backs to the blackboard and a flashlight aimed into their eyes. Further punishment ranged from demerits, called black marks, to expulsion.

The buildings and grounds were maintained by students through assigned tasks for all and additional chores for those unfortunates working off black marks. The exception was maid service, which was provided by a corps of hags known as "wombats," who were generally graduates of jails and mental institutions willing to work cheap and unlikely (though not unknown) to stir the libidos of two hundred or more sexually deprived and horny teenagers. Toward this end, too, the food was liberally spiked with saltpeter and the younger married faculty members grew gaunt avoiding the milk, mashed potatoes, and gravy within which the stuff lurked.

The student labor system saved the school a fortune and understandably upset many parents, who were paying high tuition fees. These were told that the condition existed because of wartime manpower shortages, until the Japanese surrender. After that they were assured it was part of a program to build character. Locals thought the long lines of Colton boys shouldering shovels on their way to clear away snow looked like prison work gangs.

Scholastic and athletic competition were encouraged and

stimulated by the fact that all boys upon joining the student body were arbitrarily divided into rival organizations called Alpha, Beta, and Gamma. These were distinguished by the wearing of different colors on the intramural athletic field—blue, gray, and shit-brindle—and were supposed to inspire fierce partisanship. Higher loyalty was due only to Colton itself, in reverence to which the entire student body and faculty joined together as one voice raised to sing the school anthem or shout on the school team. This phenomenon was known as "school spirit" and was deemed a vital ingredient of character in anyone who would succeed at Colton Academy.

Though Richard Steelegrave did not yet know the worst, his first impressions left him depressed and with a deep sense of foreboding. He stood in the doorway of the room assigned him, clutching his valise in one hand and his tennis racket in the other, and peered around at the peeling yellow walls, and protruding cast-iron radiator, the leaded windows which had to be cranked open. It seemed no place for a fifteen-year-old California kid who mostly liked to play tennis. He had been happy going to high school in San Diego and could not fathom why his parents had banished him to the Ivy Leagues. He felt very much alone.

In fact he was not alone, for another boy lounged on one of the two narrow beds in the room. He was swarthy, with jet-black hair and ebony eyes. Even lying still he exuded the lazy grace of a cat, and he seemed enviably at ease. He had already laid claim to the most desirable portion of the quarters to be shared.

"So you're my new roomie," the boy said without rising. "My name's Vandy."

"Richard Steelegrave." He dumped his valise on the bed nearest the window and the radiator, where he suspected he would alternately freeze and swelter.

"I was here for summer school," Vandy volunteered. "That's because I was thrown out of Choate and had to make up the spring term."

"Why were you thrown out?"

"Got caught fucking a townie in my room," Vandy said casually, proud of the status of his offense. Associating with townies, as members of the local population were called, was frowned upon in all eastern prep schools. Fucking them was absolutely forbidden. And remained the number-one student fantasy.

"My roomie turned me in," Vandy added.

"Get even with him?"

Vandy shrugged. "I didn't have much time and I couldn't find him. They had me on the next train out of town. I did shit in his bed, though. Then I made it back up real neat. Wish I could have seen him climb in that night."

Richard winced. He sat down on his bed gingerly, testing the springs under the mattress. The middle section sagged. He read an inscription on the wall over the bed. "Lucy takes it up the ass" someone had scrawled with a soft lead pencil.

"Who's Lucy?" he asked.

"Music teacher's daughter. I'd like to suck her pussy. You better get that off before lights-out."

"I didn't put it there."

"It's on your wall," smirked Vandy, the most likely author of the graffiti. He stared at the racket still clutched in Richard's hand. "You play tennis?"

"Yeah."

"You won't play much around here."

"Why not?" asked Richard, alarmed. "I saw the courts out there. They're not bad."

"You like to play in the snow? Starting next month we're all going to be up to our ass in snow until next April."

Richard was appalled. He knew it got colder here in the East, but no one told him it was that bad. The distress must have showed on his face.

"Tough shit, Ricky."

"You can call me Richard or Rich. I don't like Ricky. My mom calls me that."

"I'll call you anything I like unless you want to try to whip me."

The days and weeks passed miserably. Colton was a prison. The boys rose in the morning to the same strident bell that told them when to go to class, to meals, to gym, or to the athletic field. Long periods in study hall were the norm, room study being a privilege accorded only to honor-roll students. Afternoons were allocated to sports, with long cross-country runs or work details for those who didn't make a team. The snow arrived in late October, as Vandy had predicted, and fell monotonously.

Richard stood bundled in heavy clothing watching the horrible white stuff blanket the tennis courts he had gotten to use only half a dozen times. He wished he were not too old to cry. A cold glob slammed against the back of his neck and oozed down inside his collar before he could get a hand up to wipe it away. He whirled to see the jeering face of his roommate.

"What's the matter, Ricky?" Vandy called. "Can't hack a little cold weather?"

Richard covered the ground between them in several swift bounds. He tackled his tormentor around the middle and brought him down, punching at the hateful dark face as he straddled the fallen boy's body. Vandy managed to get his knees up against Richard's chest and throw him off. On their feet again, they flailed with their fists in the manner of untrained youngsters, hampered from inflicting much damage by their heavy clothing and gloves.

They soon gathered a crowd. Boys walking to and from the Snack Shack, an on-campus hamburger joint where they were allowed to supplement their tasteless diet for a price, paused to watch. As did the basketball team, which was jogging monotonously around a nearby wooden track. No one interfered. Unwritten law maintained that belligerents be permitted to fight it out. Even faculty members seldom intervened. Fights provided entertainment and a release of frustration.

Richard and Vandy fought for a long time. When they could hardly lift their arms to swing, they switched to wrestling. No one had won the punching. Gouging and kicking on the ground were about even. They began to lose their audience as the weak November sun went down and spectators started drifting away blowing on their frozen mittens. Soon they were barely moving, locked together grunting and shifting to gain the slightest advantage.

"Shit," Vandy said at last. "I'm willing to call it even if you are, Rich."

Richard thought about it. The knees and seat of his breeches were soaked through. They were all alone now and it was cold. There didn't seem to be anything more to prove.

By the time they had cleaned up, they were late for study hall, earning one black mark apiece. An hour of shoveling snow. But they had formed a bond that would pass for friendship for many years.

Justin Evander III, known as Vandy, was the son of enormously wealthy parents, but that did not distinguish him at Colton among the offspring of beer barons, movie moguls, an oleomargarine heir, and the biggest name in French perfume. Nor did the fact that he had been expelled from Choate. Colton acted as an institution of last resort for "problem" students cast out of such prep schools as Choate, Taft, Andover, and Exeter. Discipline was stricter, the regimen more demanding. What set Vandy apart was simply that he was more cunning and ruthless than his peers. Promised by his father that another expulsion would result in dire consequences for him, he was motivated to work within an unforgiving system. He became adept at securing his own comforts and gratifications by any and all means.

Richard learned a great deal from Vandy, all of it extra-curricular in nature. He learned to make a crude, undistilled liquor out of the sweet cider the boys were allowed to keep, by adding sugar, raisins, and yeast, then, after a month of fermentation, suspending the brew out of a window on a freezing night and draining off the alcohol that rose to the top. This was kept out in the open in a huge hair-tonic bottle, by Vandy's decree. He had read "The Purloined Letter" by Edgar Allan Poe and concluded the best place to hide any object of search was in plain sight. Richard had had his doubts, but sure enough, the monitors who turned their room inside and out during regular searches never found the contraband.

Far more profitably, Vandy had found a way into the files where exam forms were kept. These he boldly removed and mimeographed in the nearby city of Waterbury, returning the originals and keeping copies. Thus he assured his grade average and augmented his allowance through discreet sales. Richard was privileged to receive his copies free.

Not even the faculty was safe when Vandy felt himself wronged. A mathematics teacher named Professor Comstock had the temerity to flunk him in the first term of his middle year, Vandy being hopelessly inept at math. Comstock, who lived with his wife in a small house just off campus, prepared his exams at the last moment and kept them at home rather than in the files Vandy had breached. With no chance to cheat, Vandy failed the exam and the term miserably.

He planned his revenge with care, waiting until he heard that a death in the family would keep the Comstocks away for an entire week. Then he enlisted four cronies, Richard among them, and explained the trick he wanted to play on the professor. Part of it, anyway.

By stealth and at night the five boys procured a cow from the stables of a neighboring farmer, led the animal to the Comstock residence, and by heaving and shoving, finally forced it through the door into the living room. There they all collapsed in hilarity, imagining the mess the animal would make and the difficulty Comstock would have getting it the hell back out the door.

As the laughter began to subside, Vandy pulled out a thirty-eight caliber pistol and shot the cow in the ear, dropping it instantly. In the horrified silence that followed, he explained his reason to the others. The dead cow would bloat and be ever so much harder to remove, he said between giggles. Indeed it was. The Comstocks had to have the reeking animal butchered and taken out in sections. None of the boys ever squealed on Vandy. They were too deeply implicated. And much too scared of Vandy.

In the spring when the tiny lake that doubled as a hockey rink finally thawed, it swarmed with fat docile goldfish. One among them stood out for its huge size, its distinct personality, and the fact that it was a favorite of the headmaster, Dr. Van Alstyne (called "creeping Jesus" by Vandy, who had a nickname for everyone). The doctor, an austere disciplinarian who was frosty to the students and held himself aloof from the faculty, nevertheless loved the fish he had named Wilson, after his favorite president.

Every afternoon at precisely four o'clock, save during the frozen winter, he strode out to feed Wilson, and the fish, sensing his presence, materialized like a friendly submarine. The authoritarian figure of Van Alstyne casting bread upon the waters like some modern-day Moses provoked snickers among the faculty and students alike, but the doctor did not care if they knew, and clung faithfully to his ritual of throwing handfuls of crumbs to the gobbling fish.

All of the goldfish were far too well-fed to respond to a baited hook, and anyway, it was strictly forbidden to fish them. As the lake stood under the dark windows of the school, any boy would be foolhardy to try.

Catching Wilson became an obsession with Vandy, who had come to regard Dr. Van Alstyne as a symbol of oppression and the fish as his creature. On his first attempt he used a sharpened stake with which he tried to spear Wilson when he caught the fish swimming near the surface and close to shore. But the big carp was canny and veered away. Next, Vandy tried hurling the stake like a javelin, only to miss repeatedly when Wilson took evasive action.

The solution came to him shortly before school let out in June, at the end of his upper middle year. The weather was warm, the water tepid, the fish lethargic. Vandy strolled past the little lake frequently until he found himself alone and unobserved. In his pocket he carried a powerful cherry bomb, the round firecracker with a fuse that could detonate underwater. He located Wilson finning in place among several smaller fish, near the surface, where they all seemed to stay during hot weather. The cherry bomb arced out, fuse lit, and splashed gently into the water on top of Wilson. Contemptuously the fish moved aside as it brushed by and sank beneath him. The explosion was an underwater "cru-u-ump," barely audible, but the concussion was devastating. Three fish including Wilson turned belly-up and floated to the surface. There to be discovered by Dr. Van Alstyne at precisely four o'clock in the afternoon. Vandy was only sorry he would never be able to tell the good doctor exactly what had happened.

Richard had always known that Vandy was kind of a

shit. Had he been asked why he continued the close relationship, he would have said it was because Vandy was never boring. Things happened when he was around.

The Evanders had a home (one of several) near the town of Washington, Connecticut, and Richard was invited when the school granted a free weekend and for vacations as well. Before making the long trip back to California by train, he often spent a week at the estate, a two-hundred-acre spread that boasted a fine tennis court, a large swimming pool, and a private forest. The boys could hunt the surrounding hills, fish the lakes and streams, and explore the forest. Tom Sawyer and Huckleberry Finn with perks.

Vandy's father, Clayton, was a distant, preoccupied man who didn't understand his younger son and even secretly doubted that the boy was sprung from his own loins. His elder son by a wife now deceased was tall and blond like himself and already in training to someday take over Evander Enterprises. The father's hopes for his empire and family reposed entirely in Clayton Jr., to the total exclusion of Vandy. But Katarina, his darkly exotic and beautiful wife, doted on Vandy, her mirror image. In her eyes, he could do no wrong. Those same dark eyes swept over Richard in a very different way. He sensed her interest at once and returned it. She was no more than thirty-five, twenty years his senior, and swiftly found a a place in his more erotic fantasies.

Vandy liked to hunt or, more accurately, to kill. Neighboring farmers encouraged the boys to hunt woodchucks in their fields because the burrowing creatures dug holes that cattle could step into, breaking a leg. Both Vandy and Richard became crack shots with the twenty-two rifles Mr. Evander provided, and they imagined themselves great white hunters on safari as they roamed the countryside decimating the population of small furred animals. But while Richard limited his prey to the outlawed woodchuck, Vandy shot at anything that moved, from squirrels and sparrows to beehives and butterflies. He also trapped quail by balancing a box on a twig over a handful of grain. The feeding quail would nudge the twig, which would drop the box. The cook then dressed out the birds and served them to the family.

In the evening after dinner the boys often repaired to the deserted stables to enjoy an illicit cigarette. Empty stalls were still stenciled with the names of the riding horses that had been banished after Vandy's sister was killed in a fall that broke her neck.

They were smoking in the tack room when the flutter of Vandy's captive birds distracted him. He walked over to their cage and reached in to pull out a bird. "Now we're going to have a display of aerial fireworks," he told Richard.

"How's that?"

Vandy rummaged in a chest with his free hand and came up with a small packet of firecrackers. He used his teeth to separate one from the string that held them together. "Well, you light a firecracker and you shove it up a quail's ass. Then you let the bird go. The firecracker's got a six-second fuse, like a hand grenade. He gets about fifty feet in the air and—bang! Shit and feathers all over the place." He laughed and held out the firecracker to Richard. "Light this with your butt, amigo."

Richard stood absolutely still for a moment. Then he took the cigarette from between his lips and pushed the glowing end carefully against Vandy's thumb. Vandy yelled and jumped back, dropping the firecracker and releasing the bird, which streaked out the barn door with a whir of wings in the night.

"You son of a bitch!" shouted Vandy.

"It was dark. I couldn't see."

Vandy stared at him. "I've got another bird in there," he said softly.

"Forget it, Vandy. Don't do it."

"So you did it on purpose."

"Just leave the bird alone."

Richard visited the Evander estate for the last time over a year later, after their June graduation from Colton Academy. He and Vandy had been roommates for two full years by then, a time of wary camaraderie. They were more allies against the school system than friends in the true sense.

Richard, the more popular among their peers, had captained the tennis team, managed a fair grade average, and quickened the hearts of faculty daughters and their mothers alike with his blond good looks. But it was Vandy who actually managed to seduce the music teacher's daughter (who, it developed, did *not* take it up the ass) and her mother (who did). Sly and cat-quick, he was the school's best wrestler and, with heavy reliance on cheating, got good enough grades to be admitted to Yale. His graduation from Colton was a tribute to the arts of cunning and duplicity; had even a fraction of his transgressions been traced to him, he would not have survived the first term of his enrollment. Neither he nor Richard was selected to be a monitor in their senior year, having both been judged lacking in school spirit.

Leaving Colton, they felt reborn into freedom, even though the Evanders had arranged summer jobs for them at their country club on nearby Lake Waramaug. Rick, who had parental permission to spend the summer in Connecticut, would be assistant to the tennis pro and Vandy a lifeguard on the club beach. Both jobs were sinecures, leaving plenty of free time.

At seventeen the boys had laid aside their hunting rifles to race around in Vandy's Buick convertible in search of different prey. They had little difficulty. The shores of Lake Waramaug fairly teemed with nubile teenagers. As did the Saturday-night dances at the country club, where the boys cut elegant figures in their white dinner jackets, swarthy pirate and blond princeling.

Vandy had been a renowned cocksman since the tale of his episode with mother and daughter had spread throughout the student body of Colton. Secure in his own legend, he operated among the girls with the assurance of a veteran. Richard walked more cautiously and usually turned aside locker-room queries about his sex life with a wink and a grin which were mistaken for nonchalance. Actually, his experience was limited. A summer ago he'd had a few frustrating encounters with an exceptionally pretty neighbor in Mission Hills who had a deserved reputation as a cock-teaser. Determined to preserve her virginity, she nonetheless had a lively interest in sex and regularly manipulated Richard beyond the point of control. Then she delicately handed him a handkerchief. He had progressed somewhat further with a distant cousin of Vandy's named Cindy. But once again too much inexpert and protracted groping had brought him to premature orgasm. He could say he had accomplished the deed. Barely. He knew there was a lot more to it.

The summer flew by pleasurably and without notable incident until the middle of August, when Vandy lost his job at the club for nearly letting a pair of infant twins drown. No one had been in the water for weeks because of a polio scare. There was no such thing as Salk vaccine in 1949 and the discovery of several cases of the dread disease in the vicinity of Waramaug made everyone suspicious of the lake. Vandy's job became a mere formality and in boredom he drank a couple of gin and tonics every day with his lunch at the clubhouse, where even underage members were never refused. Then he returned to the beach to doze in the lifeguard stand.

He wakened to an urgent tugging at his leg and peered foggily down to see a frantic woman shouting and gesticulating toward the lake. She was a certain Mrs. Hollinger and he had noticed that she and her children were the only occupants of the beach when he had climbed sleepily onto his perch. Evidently she had dozed off like himself, leaving the toddlers to entertain themselves.

Vandy squinted in the direction indicated by her flailing arm and saw the two tots at least fifty yards out on the lake clinging to an inner tube and splashing water merrily at each other. They were a year and a half old.

He leapt down onto the sand and raced for his rowboat, hauling it into the lake. A dozen yards offshore, the boat, uncalked and neglected for a year, filled rapidly with water, leaving him no choice but to swim to the rescue. He swam hard and even prayed. Prayed the little bastards would not let go of the inner tube before he could get there, and prayed that he would not get polio from the fucking lake.

He was lucky and managed to coax the kids into hanging on to the tube while he towed them in. Mrs. Hollinger was not impressed by the performance. She reported that he had been asleep on duty, jeopardizing the lives of her children, and since the Hollingers were almost as important as the Evanders, managed to get him fired.

Vandy did not take his dismissal with good grace. He grew sullen and spoke darkly to Richard of burning down the club. Alarmed because he was fully aware of what Vandy was capable of, Richard stuck close to him, inventing projects to distract him. He gave up his own job and spent a week honing Vandy's tennis game, which improved markedly before Vandy quit, tired of taking instruction. They put together a raft and spent three days in the Housatonic River having some good times, but still Vandy sulked.

And he drank.

They had taken their dates to the movies in nearby New Milford to see *The Champion* with Kirk Douglas. During the show Vandy swigged from a silver flask he had stolen from his father, and he was already loaded when they drove to Lover's Leap, a promontory high above a fork in the Housatonic River where local youngsters went to neck. But the girls wouldn't put out much and Vandy rammed the car into gear in disgust. He almost drove over the cliff trying to turn around.

"Shit, Vandy, let me drive!" cried Rick.

"Hell with that noise." Vandy completed his maneuver perilously and got onto the narrow dirt road that snaked down a steep hill leading back to town.

"God!" exclaimed the girl sitting next to him. "My mother told me not to go out with you."

"Yeah," said Vandy nastily. "I bet she told you that thing's just to pee out of, too."

He tore down the hill, swaying from side to side, scraping the convertible against the underbrush at either edge of the road. The girls screamed but Richard kept silent, knowing that anything he said now would simply goad Vandy to further recklessness.

Against all odds they reached the bottom of the hill without mishap, but their luck ran out at Gantry's Bridge, an obsolete structure that had been preserved as a historical landmark despite serious doubts as to its safety. There was a modern span farther downriver that handled the heavier traffic, so the old single-lane wooden bridge was used almost exclusively by sightseers and local residents.

Vandy missed the narrow approach with room to spare and plunged down the steep bank into the river. The water deepened abruptly beyond the edge of the bank and the convertible sank like a monkey wrench. Fortunately, the top was down and the occupants simply floated clear. They all reached shore safely amid a lot of screaming and crying on the part of the girls.

Richard leaned down to help them stumble up the bank in their sodden dresses, and then he reached for Vandy, who was last. He jerked Vandy forward by his lapels and drew back his fist.

"Not now," Vandy protested, and buckled over, holding his chest. "Jesus, I think I busted something inside!"

They tramped the mile and a half back to town, soaked and angry, with Vandy moaning every step of the way. Mrs. Evander came for them with the chauffeur but Richard returned with him alone, Vandy having been hospitalized for observation. Katarina, distraught, was allowed to spend the night in his room. She arrived home the following morning with the news that Vandy seemed to have a couple of fractured ribs. He would be kept in the hospital for tests and return the next day.

Richard was curiously relieved to be on his own, able to plan his time without regard for Vandy. He went to the club and sailed, swam, and lay on the beach alone. Late in the afternoon he played two sets of tennis with the pro he had assisted earlier in the season. He won both sets beating the man for the first time, and went home feeling deep satisfaction. In three days he would be returning to California. He could hardly wait.

Richard and Vandy shared a room called the sunporch because it resembled a veranda with its many tall windows. They caught the breeze from any direction on a hot summer night, and the stars were visible from either bed.

Richard lay on the outside of the sheets wearing a pair of shorts, bathed in the moonlight. It was almost bright enough to read, and he never ceased to wonder at the clarity of these eastern nights, so rare on the California coast where he lived. He smoked a cigarette, luxuriating in the unaccustomed privacy, feeling an edge of restlessness he knew how to assuage, and wondering if he should hunt up the Vargas Girl calendar he kept under his shirts in the bureau drawer.

The tap on his door caught him by surprise, and he crushed out his cigarette automatically. He could imagine no reason for anyone to visit him at this hour. "Come in," he called, perplexed.

Katarina Evander came in wearing a light robe that ended above her knees and carrying a tray with a glass of milk on it. There was no need for anyone to turn on a light. They could see each other clearly.

"A glass of warm milk is good for the digestion at night," she said gravely, approaching his bedside with slow gliding steps, taking care not to spill the milk.

He lay gaping at her, finally remembering to close his mouth. He felt naked in spite of the shorts, vulnerable and more than a little stupid, for he could not think of anything to say. His instinct told him immediately why she had come; this was the moment he had dreamed of. In those dreams he had been suave, witty, capable.

Katarina put the milk carefully down on the bedside table. "May I sit down for a moment?"

Richard managed to nod. He looked sideways at the glass and choked back a wild impulse to laugh. Milk! According to everything he had read, it should be champagne. Or maybe cognac.

He felt the warm bulge of her buttock touch his thigh as she sat next to him on the bed. To his horror, he felt himself begin to harden. Soon it would be obvious. But worse, if she did anything, even touched him, it would quickly be over. He knew that he could never contain himself, never make it as it always was in his fantasy, where he dominated her, made her plead and perform and wait for him.

She held the glass out to him. "Please drink it," she said.

He took the glass from her. He hated warm milk. It nauseated him. Then he realized he would drink piss if she asked him to. She watched carefully while he swallowed down half the glass and grimaced.

"All of it," she said, unrelenting, watching him drain

the last drop. When he was finished she took the glass from his hand, while he tried not to gag.

"There," she soothed. "That wasn't so bad, was it?"

Richard lay back on his pillow and closed his eyes, fighting to keep the milk down. Why in hell had she made him drink the Christ-awful stuff? Suppose he threw up all over her? God! Don't even think about that! Presently he felt her hand brush lightly across his forehead, miraculously banishing his queasiness. Her voice came to him softly from far away. "Rest awhile. . . ."

He did not know how much later she put her hand on him, but when she did he no longer felt panic or even doubt. Only a smooth, growing strength within him. He opened his eyes and saw that her robe had parted, revealing her firm breasts, the slight swell of her belly, the dark triangle below. He reached up and drew her down to him.

Then he was living his fantasies. She writhed beneath him and he was strong. He asked her to do things and she did them. She did things he would not have thought of asking her to do. She didn't leave him for a long time and when finally she did, he felt like raising his head and howling at the moon.

Years later he guessed that she had put something in the milk.

Vandy returned from the hospital in a foul mood, his ribs strapped with tape. Mr. Evander said little and seemed more taciturn than ever. Richard felt sure his skull was made of some transparent material and his thoughts were public property. He could not meet Katarina's eyes to see the amusement lurking there, but he watched her covertly. And lustfully. He was torn between an urge to flee the premises at once and a far less logical impulse to declare his love to Katarina's surly husband and damn the consequences. In his dreams that night he fought a sword duel with both Evanders, father and son, while Katarina looked on in fear for him. Leaping around as nimbly as Errol Flynn, he forced his clumsier opponents back, back . . . out of the castle into which the Evander estate had been transformed, into the black moat that had sprung up around it . . . out of their lives.

But he left on schedule two days later with only a polite

good-bye to Mr. and Mrs. Evander. He did bring himself to look Katarina full in the face.

"I want you to feel welcome here anytime," she told him with a slight smile. "I would love to have you again."

15

Steelegrave saw that the whiskey bottle was about a quarter down. Enough. He took a final drink, capped the bottle, and walked back to the car. He tossed the Scotch onto the seat and took Erin's revolver out of the glove compartment.

The gun was a comfortable weight in his hand. When you had a gun, people were supposed to do what you told them. He dropped the gun in the side pocket of his windbreaker and stepped away from the car, but when he tried to draw fast it snagged in his pocket, making a burlesque of his effort. He shoved the weapon down into his waistband and tried again, a smoother motion this time, crouching slightly as Hawke always did, keeping the piece centered on an imaginary target. He'd learned the technique long ago from an expert who had coached him in preparation for *Love–Forty*.

"Don't move, Vandy, you son of a bitch," he mouthed, drawing again and then again. He was getting better and faster. He pushed the revolver back under his belt, where the barrel lay cold against his belly and pointed ominously at his groin. Remembering that it wasn't loaded with blanks this time, he pulled it out and dropped it back in his pocket so that he wouldn't accidentally blow his balls off. Hawke had always worn a holster.

Back in the car he took one last drink of Scotch; then he was ready to go. It was ten forty-five and Vandy lived five minutes away. But suppose the bastard had company? Christ, he might even be giving a party! Steelegrave pushed the thought aside. Vandy had always used the place for a retreat. The odds were that he would be alone. In any case, Steelegrave would find a way. He was ready for anything.

The private entrances to Emerald Bay had proliferated since he had last been there, and they were protected by gate guards in little cubicles that bisected the access roads. The colony had grown impressively, expanding across the highway into the mountains away from the ocean. Steelegrave knew a moment of panic before he located the gate that had served the original community, which was tucked down in a little cove by the sea.

He cruised past the guarded entrance along a low wall looking for a place to park inconspicuously, but could find nothing suitable and finally pulled off the highway as close to the wall as he could get. A passing cop might get curious about an abandoned car, but it was a chance he would have to take.

The homes beyond the wall were screened from the road by a stand of trees, and Steelegrave used them for cover as he moved along inside the wall to a point as close to the entrance gate as he dared come. Crouching low, he darted through a draw thick with foliage and picked up the road beyond sight of the gate guard. Then he strolled down toward the sea, knowing anyone who saw him would take him for another resident out for a late walk.

Vandy's place was ranch-style, low-slung, and almost hidden in a cluster of trees. A nine-foot hedge surrounded it, broken only by a tall gate fashioned out of wrought-iron spears to discourage trespass. There was a black Lincoln in the driveway and the garage doors beyond it were closed, so Steelegrave could not guess whether it belonged to Vandy or to a visitor. Dim light showed at the windows as if they were heavily draped.

Steelegrave remembered the gate and the hedge from the old days. He moved away from the driveway along the hedge, certain he would find a place where he could breach the shrubbery. He was not worried about dogs. Vandy hated dogs and wouldn't have one around.

Well away from the gate, he thrust his arm into the hedge, looking for a way to force himself through. His hand caught in the mesh of a chain-link fence which was concealed by the hedge and rose to the same height. He let go immediately, afraid that the damn thing might be electrified at time intervals. That would be like Vandy. The fence was something he did not remember, a formidable obstacle. Even if it wasn't charged with current, it would be a real bitch to climb. He stepped back, swearing to himself.

He looked along the length of the hedge and then followed it around a corner. In a *Love–Forty* script there would have been a tree or some goddamn thing he could scale leaning against the fence, but there was nothing like that to be seen. Silently he stole back toward the gate. Perhaps there was some access on the far side of the property that he had not yet examined. He was beginning to feel an edge of frustration as he had in the past when someone suddenly changed the script.

Justin Evander locked the desk drawer containing the kit he had used to test the shipment. The pile of white packets wrapped tightly in cellophane he left stacked casually before him. As a matter of form and because Ekhardt insisted on the discipline, he had tested four of them at random. He knew the merchandise would be as described. Ekhardt and his source were completely reliable. And Ekhardt, after all, had been his sponsor.

The pilot sat before him with a tumbler of whiskey in his big fist. He had been an adventurer all of his life, a soldier of fortune when there were wars to fight, a smuggler when the mercenary business was slow. He looked the part, tanned and crinkly-eyed, his white hair cropped close. At sixty, he owned and operated a school for pilots near Palm Springs, and he was wealthy. Though the school turned a good profit by itself, he could never think of it as anything but a cover. There wasn't enough excitement in it.

As a much younger man, Ekhardt had had a brief, legitimate career as a commercial pilot for Avianca Airlines in Colombia. He met and married a Colombian girl of good family over the strong objections of her parents, who were grooming her for a more prestigious match. Yet such was Ekhardt's rough charm that in time they came to accept him, and when his wife died tragically in a car accident, he remained one of them even after he left Colombia, crushed by his loss. For years he remained a drifter, fighting other people's wars, running any kind of contraband. When he finally returned to Colombia, he found his brother-in-law had gone into the cocaine trade. They became partners.

Ekhardt had recruited Vandy after Katarina Evander died two years earlier. With his mother's death Vandy had lost the only person he had ever loved completely, including himself. He had also lost his principal source of income.

His father's will had left the management of Evander Enterprises to his older son, Clayton, along with half the assets of the estate. The income from the other half went to Katarina for the remainder of her lifetime, after which everything reverted to Clayton. There was no mention of Vandy.

Katarina provided for Vandy out of her enormous income, but she wanted him to have something to call his own. She bought real estate, yachts, and even businesses and gifted them to him outright, hoping he would build his own capital structure, knowing he would have no resources when she was gone. But the businesses failed and Vandy squandered money. In making him independently wealthy Katarina had also left him vulnerable. His divorce from Marla Monday was a constant drain, for she had been granted a huge alimony for life as well as the house on Antelo and a cash settlement. Shortly after his mother's death Vandy called Marla to report that he was destitute (an exaggeration) and could no longer afford to make payments.

"How about the house and the boat and the property in Hawaii?" Marla wanted to know.

"If I sell all that, I've got nothing left. You get a fortune for every picture you make. Why do you have to bleed me?"

There was a shrug in her voice. "I have expensive habits, just like you do. You've literally thrown away millions. Is that my fault?"

"I'll declare bankruptcy. Then you'll never get another dime out of me!"

Marla laughed. "You? Declare bankruptcy? Why, they'll take away all your toys, luv—houses, boats, everything. You can't keep anything if you go bankrupt, you know."

Vandy had received word of his mother's death aboard his yacht, the *Satyr*, in Acapulco. He flew back to Los Angeles, which was a mistake. In accordance with her wishes, it was a Greek Orthodox funeral, complete with keening and wailing. He didn't even know the hags dressed in black who were making all the noise, and the sight of his mother in her coffin undid him completely. The whole affair had been staged by Clayton in the vacuum created by Vandy's inability to function. Clayton was not even blood kin to Katarina, and Vandy suspected he had arranged the whole circus with cold cynicism, realizing the effect it would have on his half-brother. Clayton had always believed Katarina had driven his father to an early death with her infidelities, and there had been no love lost between them.

Back in Acapulco, Vandy surrendered to blackest despair. Not only because of Katarina's death and the plunge of his own fortunes, but because in his mid-forties, life had suddenly lost its savor. Very little amused or distracted him. His jaded palate had produced a junkie's dependence on ever-greater injections of thrill to sustain even a moderate interest in his surroundings. He had sampled every pleasure and vice available to the idle rich, and everything seemed to pall now. If life held no zest for him even with the trappings of wealth, what would it be like in the reduced circumstances he was facing? It was too late to opt for accomplishment or eminence in any field. He couldn't very well become a brain surgeon or a diplomat at his age. He couldn't get any kind of position in Evander Enterprises because Clayton wouldn't let him in. His prospects seemed incalculably bleak.

The ninety-foot yacht *Satyr* rode at anchor in Acapulco Bay between the Swedish liner *Kungsholm* and a lean American destroyer that shifted restlessly in the lightest swell. Shore boats plied to and from the *Kungsholm* loaded with people dressed to dine aboard or bound for adventure in the city while the destroyer looked on like a gaunt wolf exiled from the pack. *Satyr* had her share of guests as well, transported out in a Boston whaler by the Amazon, a gigantic young woman currently in charge of Vandy's entertainment and personal safety.

Vandy seldom joined the endless boat party. When he did, he burst among his random guests with the frantic energy of a manic-depressive on the uppermost sweep of the curve. He looked more than ever like Lucifer, for his black hair had receded slightly at the temples, accentuating his widow's peak, and swaths of white curled above his ears like horns. A hairline mustache and a trim Vandyke beard enhanced the satanic resemblance, which his behavior did nothing to contradict. Upon his command the Amazon occasionally pitched a guest overboard to swim the mile to shore, dodging ski boats in the daytime and heavier traffic at night. In the local discos, Vandy's giantess awed Acapulqueños and tourists alike as she cleared his way to a table or expelled an interloper. The very concept of a female bodyguard offended Mexican machismo, and the Amazon's undeniable beauty added to the provocation. It was only a question of time before there was trouble.

They were taking the sun at the Villa Vera, a semiprivate club overlooking Acapulco Bay high above the Costero Miguel Alemán with its cluster of condos, Holiday Inn, Hyatt Hotel, and fried-chicken, pizza, and hamburger joints—all the deritus of another civilization cast haphazardly along the shores of the once-pristine resort. From this aerie one could almost imagine the place as it once had been, a range of jungled mountains plunging down to meet wide white beaches and an azure sea, thatched huts sheltering fishermen and bleached nets spread on the sand between the sturdy wooden boats that hauled them.

The Amazon reclined on a chaise by the pool, her magnificent six-foot-two-inch body oiled, the long smooth muscles gleaming brown, burnished by the sun. Her breasts jutted majestically upward, rising above a narrow waist and taut, sculptured legs. She wore the bare minimum, a bikini that could have been stuffed into a thimble, and her Indian-black hair fanned out over the cushion beneath her.

Vandy sat on a barstool submerged in the pool and

drank Bloody Marys. He stared at the bay below him without really seeing the sailboats running gracefully before the wind or the big snow-white liner putting out to sea for other exotic, tropical ports. A perfumed breeze stirred the tall palms above the Villa Vera and caressed his body, but he did not notice. Everything was spoiled for him by the knowledge that it could not last much longer.

It was the beginning of the end. To afford the *Satyr*, her upkeep, and her crew (not to mention the Amazon), the house in Emerald Bay would have to go. Then, before long, the property in Hawaii. There were a few other odds and ends to liquidate, but nothing that could buy him the kind of time he needed. If the bitch goddess Marla didn't have to have her regular pound of flesh, he might have been able to string it out. As things stood now, the years of graceful living were coming to an end. Panic welled up within him as he considered his future. He took a pull at his drink to hold it down.

A blonde swam up to claim the stool next to him. Vandy noticed idly that she had black eyes and dark skin and that she wore water-resistant makeup. The man who hoisted himself up beside her had the lighter skin of Spanish forebears but the flat profile and obsidian eyes of an Indian. He was wide and muscular with a spectacular collection of scars that he seemed to wear proudly. A ridge of raised tissue bisected his profile from one temple to the corner of his mouth, and his deep chest was crisscrossed with ancient weals. Two heavy chains weighted with trinkets circled his thick neck, and he wore three rings, a wide gold wrist bracelet, and a gold Rolex. Vandy stared at the ornaments that dangled from his chains: they included a phallic symbol in graphic detail, a vial of white powder that was probably cocaine, and an elaborate golden figure of Christ affixed to the cross. The man was named Ramon something but he was called El Choques, "he who breaks heads," and he functioned as a bodyguard to the wife of the president of Mexico. Vandy had been around the Villa Vera enough to know who he was, as indeed did almost everyone. Waiters hastened to serve him well and the manager frequently inquired after his comfort. El Choques was a very dangerous man.

It didn't take El Choques long to notice the Olympian figure of the Amazon stretched out a few scant yards away. He tossed back the thick, shiny hair that hung before his eyes and said something so swiftly that Vandy didn't catch it despite his considerable knowledge of Spanish.

"*Es la guarda espaldas de un gringo rico,*" the woman with him replied. "She is the bodyguard of a rich American."

Vandy was somewhat piqued that they did not recognize him as that American.

"*Ay, pues claro que sí!*" exclaimed El Choques. The Amazon was becoming something of a legend around Acapulco herself. "*Cosa más ridícula. ¡Que pendejada!*" He lit a cigarette and blew out a stream of pungent smoke.

Not so ridiculous, the blond ventured, considering the Amazon must be at least as tall and nearly as heavy as El Choques himself. Even so, countered the bodyguard, she was still only a woman and therefore good for only one thing. His big hands came up to grip a pair of imaginary shoulders and he humped his pelvis forward a couple of times by way of illustration.

The woman showed a flash of anger. "*Ya estamos en el siglo veinte,*" she snapped. "We are in the twentieth century and women are no longer the personal property of men."

El Choques gave her a look that was downright sinister and she laughed nervously, as if to deny her brief show of independence. The laughter turned to a squeal of pain as he caught her upper arm in his big paw. Then he told her what he would enjoy doing to the Amazon and how she would beg him first to stop and then never to stop, this bitch with her tits in the air like the twin mounds of Ixtacihuatl. He also reminded the blond how she had pleaded with him for respite on many occasions in the past and would again tonight if he chose to favor her, a development he considered unlikely in the light of the demands far more beautiful women made upon his time. He released her arm with a shove that toppled her off the barstool into the water, and dropped his cigarette in her drink.

Vandy, who had followed the exchange, was mildly intrigued despite himself. Any diversion from the dark train of his thoughts was welcome. He looked away to where the Amazon lay supine, all unaware of the turmoil she was causing. "Pardon me," he said to El Choques in Spanish. "I could not help hearing what you said. It happens I know the *señorita*. I would be glad to arrange an introduction."

The bodyguard scowled at him. "I need no help in these matters, *señor*."

Vandy gave him a friendly smile. "*¡Claro que no, hombre!*" he said. "That's obvious. But sometimes it makes things easier. You know. A friendly gesture from one man to another." He winked.

El Choques looked at him disdainfully. But finally he shrugged and barely nodded.

Vandy picked up his drink and waded through the waist-deep water to the edge of the pool and climbed out. He squatted next to the Amazon and lit a cigarette, blowing the smoke down at her, knowing she hated the smell of tobacco. She wrinkled her nose in distaste but kept her eyes closed. He knelt down until his lips were close to her ear and told her exactly what El Choques had in mind for her, adding a lurid detail or two from his own rich imagination. The Mexican had overlooked some of the finer perversions.

The Amazon's eyes snapped open, green irises surrounded by the blue-white of perfect health, and she sat up. "Where is the son of a bitch?" she demanded, glaring around her.

"Easy. Take it easy. The one with all the gold in the water over by the bar."

With a lithe, swift movement she brought her legs beneath her in a crouch. "The greasy . . . pig!" The Amazon was a lesbian in the purest sense. She hated men. She tolerated Vandy because he paid her well, and even procured for him when she could share the prize, but neither he nor any other man could as much as touch her.

"Easy," Vandy cautioned again. "First you need a Spanish lesson."

"I don't need anything."

"I will teach you a few lines you can use to express yourself."

In less than ten minutes Vandy was satisfied that the Amazon could repeat the speech he had taught her in intelligible Spanish. Her cold rage made her an apt student.

She flung her long legs over the edge of the pool and slid into the water.

El Choques watched her move toward him with appreciation. True, her expression seemed strange, totally lacking in warmth or friendliness. Even so, what a magnificent woman! He snarled at the blond, who vacated her seat immediately, and rose, arranging his features into a smirk of welcome.

The Amazon halted directly in front of El Choques and looked down into his eyes. She stood about two inches taller than he and she had moved very close to him. A few drinkers at the bar looked up curiously and waiters paused in their rounds. The Amazon and El Choques were an impressive pair.

"Eres un pinche naco impotente," said the Amazon, and the bartender dropped a glass. *"Y además un hijo de la gran chingada."* She spoke slowly and clearly, rendering Vandy's string of mortal insults in very understandable Spanish.

El Choques blanched and made a strangled sound in his throat, but his recovery was quick. He lashed out at the tall woman with his right fist, a blow intended to knock her cold. The Amazon moved her head back slightly to avoid the punch and brought her hands up with blurring speed, snapping them down around his wrist and hand, twisting them aside, and simultaneously dropping her own weight. El Choques slid to his knees with a cry, his head barely above water, his arm now high above him, clamped in the Amazon's grip. She wrenched the arm higher, forcing his face under the surface, and placed her knee down on his neck to hold him there.

People around the pool sat up to gape, while the waiters froze in place. The blonde woman who had been with El Choques screamed and scrambled gracelessly out of the pool. Vandy sat dangling his legs in the water, amused for the first time in weeks.

The Amazon held El Choques under until his frantic thrashings diminished and a great stream of bubbles broke the surface of the pool. Then she swiftly changed her grip, kneeling to catch him in a headlock and straightening again to haul him above the level of the water. Holding his neck firmly in the crook of her arm, she buried her free hand in his thick hair, got a grip, and pulled. El Choques screamed

hideously and the Amazon's face grew red with effort.
Finally she jerked out a fistful of hair, which she cast upon
the water, where it floated like a discarded black toupee. A
patch of bare lacerated scalp appeared on top of El Choques'
head. The Amazon reached for another handful.

"Enough!" Vandy called out, putting an end to the
depilatory process before she could snatch him completely
bald. He had lost his enthusiasm for the scene. This bull
dyke took enough pleasure in the humiliation of men to
make him uncomfortable.

The Amazon released El Choques on command and
stepped away from him as two waiters leapt into the pool
to catch him under the arms and hold him afloat. The
water around him pinkened with the blood that streamed
from his head. More staff appeared on the run and guests
rose from their chaises to crane for a better view. Vandy
paid his check and left the Villa Vera, followed by the
Amazon.

Acquaintances in Acapulco warned Vandy not to leave
the yacht if he valued his life. He valued it not at all, but
he stayed aboard anyway, too apathetic to go ashore.
People kept coming out to party, filtered by the Amazon
for his protection, but he no longer joined them. He
secluded himself in his stateroom on the upper deck, forbidden territory.

Through the big bronze porthole he could see the neck-
lace of lights strung around Acapulco Bay, masking the
shabby commercialism that daylight exposed. Sounds of
the ongoing party reached him from below, the writhings
of his court jesters. He sat at his burnished mahogany desk
ignoring the glass of Scotch at his elbow, the burning
cigarette that had rolled off an ashtray to scar the fine
wood.

Finally he reached into the desk and took out a long-
barreled .357 Magnum revolver, the kind of weapon that
could pierce the engine block of an automobile. After
making sure that it was loaded, he put the barrel in his
mouth and cocked the hammer. The steel was cold against
his lips and tongue, an utterly impersonal tool awaiting his
command. The gun had been customized and the trigger
pull was very light. A touch of his finger would cause his

brains to splatter on the wall behind him. The slightest pressure and he would experience the ultimate adventure. The thought gave him almost sensual pleasure. He moved his finger into position.

"Go ahead and pull the trigger, asshole," said a voice from the passageway, and Vandy, startled, nearly did just that. Still holding the gun cocked and pointed at his head, he turned slightly to see who had invaded the proscribed area of his stateroom.

A tall man lounged against the bulkhead holding a rich-looking drink in his big hand. He had broad shoulders, short gray hair, and a weathered face. He wore an embroidered Mexican *guayabera* shirt that hung loose, almost disguising a slight paunch. Not in the best condition perhaps, but he gave an impression of physical power.

Vandy carefully laid the revolver on the desk in front of him, still cocked. "And exactly who are you?" he asked. It cost him an effort to speak evenly. His thoughts reeled in turmoil.

"Johnny Ekhardt," the big man said. "I just dropped by to talk some business. Pardon me all to hell if I interrupted anything."

Vandy retrieved the cigarette smoldering on his desk and stubbed it out with exaggerated care. He needed time to pull everything together. Everything he had been ready a moment ago to blow apart. As his numbness dispelled, he began to feel red anger and humiliation. This Ekhardt was dabbling with his very soul. He picked up the revolver and pointed it at the big man.

"You did indeed interrupt," he said softly. "You see, I'd gotten to thinking I've been everywhere and done everything and life has become as dross to me. No kicks left, to put it into language more intelligible to you.

"Then you came on the scene uninvited, crassly assuming you have business that could conceivably interest me." He smiled unpleasantly at Ekhardt. "You've made me angry and at the same time you've done me a favor, because you have reminded me that there is still one thing I have never done."

Vandy aimed the revolver at the bridge of Ekhardt's

nose. "I've never killed anyone before, and what better moment than now?"

Ekhardt, apparently undaunted, ignored the threat. He ambled into the stateroom with the gun tracking him and reached for the chair in front of Vandy's desk. "Mind if I sit down?"

"I was going to insist."

Ekhardt set his drink on the desk and took out a cigarette which he lit with steady hands. "It's hard to keep a secret in Acapulco," he said. "I mean, everybody knows everybody's business. Especially in the crowd you run with.

"For instance, they say you're a rich man's son. Blacksheep type. Got cut out of the really big bucks by your brother and pissed away what you had. Down to your last couple of million is what they say. 'Course, some people would figure that wasn't anything to shoot themselves about, but I can see how it could cramp a life-style like yours. Anyway, you're shooting yourself 'cause you've done it all and you're bored, right?"

"Right." Vandy held the gun steady.

"Ever deal drugs?"

"Are you some kind of cop?"

"I'm a pilot," Ekhardt said. "I fly cocaine into the States from Colombia, sometimes Bolivia. A lot of it."

"Fascinating."

"I planned to be more subtle. You know, feel you out. Beat around the bush. Not many of us come right out and tell a stranger we're in the trade. But when you find a man with a gun in his mouth, you figure you might as well come to the point fast."

"The gun's not in my mouth anymore, friend." Indeed, the gun pointed steadily at Ekhardt. "But, by all means, come to the point."

"What we've got," the pilot went on, unperturbed, "is a family operation, and by that I don't mean Mafia or anything like that. I mean brother-in-law and kissin' cousins. We gather it together down south and fly it out. Don't mess with strangers on our end, don't leave ourselves open for a cross."

"You must do very well," Vandy told him. "But you're

boring me. Remember, I kill when I get bored." The gun didn't waver.

"It gets better. Anyway, I've been flying to Florida, like everyone else. It's like no-man's-land on that end. The minute I touch down, I've got to deal with greedy, murdering bastards who hijack one another's goods and sometimes rather kill you than pay for a shipment. There's Mafia, too, gunning for the independents. It's no good for us anymore.

"I've been in plenty of wars, but this one's not my kind. I'm a pilot in the supply business, that's all. So I found me a new, safe route through Mexico to California, where I can land and refuel on the way, no sweat. I even bought a flying school in Palm Springs for cover, where I run a legit operation, hire and fire employees, have Hollywood celebrities for clients . . . like that."

"How jolly for you. Now . . ."

"What I don't have is the market. And a middleman. A buyer to take the stuff off my hands and distribute. I can't supply and distribute both, and because of past experience, I don't want to go with any organization, I want to build one. Small and tight. I need a key man."

"And you just naturally thought of me."

Ekhardt ignored the sarcasm. "From everything I've heard, you fill the bill. You've got money but you need more. You've got all those rich friends in the nose-candy set. You know the music freaks and the creepos who run the clubs. You were about to pull the plug because you can't figure anything to do. How about dealing some coke?"

Vandy sighed. He put both hands around the revolver, which was getting heavy. "Me? Scamper around hustling drugs to my friends? I ought to shoot you just for suggesting it. Maybe I will."

"Hold it! I don't mean you run around laying off dime bags in discos. I mean you make a big buy from me and you pass it on to the distributors who take it from there. We'll be partners. You know the market. The market is your high-rolling friends and their friends. And the distributors are the punks you know who run the discos and dives you've spent the last twenty years in. You just put the two together."

"You're being dense, Ekhardt. You know I'm going broke, right?"

"Right. And I also know you can still raise a million. Now, it's not like in the stories, where a million in snow has a street value of twenty million and you make the difference every delivery. But you'll do well, very well. And very fast."

"Why me? I don't know anything about selling cocaine." But the gun sagged, forgotten by both of them.

"That's why you. Because you're an amateur. I don't want any more mob connections. They're the kiss of death. I'll show you how to set up an organization, alter the product, all that crap. I'll teach you the trade because you have the contacts I don't have the time or background to set up. We won't have to trust each other because we'll need each other.

"And think of the new kicks, Evander. No more dross in your life."

"I know a few hoods myself. There's Mafia on the west coast too, you know. What makes you think they'll let us alone?"

"We don't get greedy. We keep a low profile and keep our organization small and tight, like I said. The mob take is billions. We'll settle for millions."

Vandy laid the revolver down and stroked his neat spade beard. "I sell everything to give you a million so you can go off and find cocaine? I may be suicidal but I'm not crazy."

"I bring you a sample free of charge and hold your hand while you push it. We'll see how you do."

"Sounds like the way you get people hooked on junk."

"Something like that."

"You appeal to the felon in me, I admit. But everything I've heard and read tells me this is a damn dangerous game for beginners. A fellow could get killed."

Ekhardt stared at Vandy for a moment and began to chuckle. Then he banged his glass on the desk and roared with laughter. "Well, if anything goes wrong, you won't have to shoot yourself!" he finally managed.

Even Vandy had to smile.

*   *   *

Vandy was well-suited to the cocaine trade. The gross illegality of what he was doing stimulated him and he applied himself to business as never before. Following Johnny Ekhardt's blueprint, he culled his distributors from among the nocturnal citizens who ran the dives and discos of Hollywood; he never peddled directly. Then he let his moneyed friends—the actors, playboys and girls, musicians, and assorted big spenders he ran with—know where they could find the best stuff. His product was of premium quality, minimally adulterated, and sold for top dollar. Money was no object to Vandy's customers; they just wanted to be sure they wouldn't unwittingly freak out on speed or any of the other dangerous substances commonly used to cut street coke. The small integrity paid off and his first big buy brought him enormous profit. Encouraged, he expanded the operation to include the affluent beach communities south of Los Angeles.

As his partner had predicted, Vandy's fortunes thrived. If anything, his life-style became more profligate than ever. He traveled by private Lear jet, bought a hotel in Cannes, a bordello he stocked with Scandinavian girls in Taiwan, and a movie company in Italy. The businesses eventually failed, but he was well sustained by the flow of cocaine from South America. He could even afford Marla.

Johnny Ekhardt's decision to quit the trade had stunned him. "But, goddammit, why?" he burst out when the pilot had told him of his decision a month ago.

"I'm sixty," Johnny Ekhardt said placidly, "and I'm rich. It's getting too hard to hide the money around here. I want to go somewhere I can enjoy it. Lie back and damn well enjoy it."

"It's only been two years. We're just getting started."

"Two years can be a long time in this business. Things happen fast. For instance, in Bolivia the new government's trying to shut down the trade, or at least take it over themselves. They shot General Vasques Muñoz just deader'n a smelt the other day and he was our man in La Paz. My brother-in-law is pulling out in Colombia, along with the rest of the family. Most of them are older and richer than I am. Tell the truth, I can't even leave you with a source, Vandy." Ekhardt sighed. "If I were younger . . ."

"You're cutting me off at the knees!"

"Come on, kid, you've made a pile."

Vandy thought of the perpetual hemorrhage of wealth to Marla, the closure of his whorehouse in Taipei, the French hotel running in the red, and smiled bitterly. "I've got extraordinary expenses."

"You don't live within your means."

"How inadequately you put it."

"Look, there's one last shipment, like I told you. Augusto says it's the biggest score yet, more than a hundred pounds. After you lay it off, your end should carry anyone for life. Even you."

Vandy shook his head. Not with Marla sucking his blood. "I doubt it. In no time I'll be back to square one. How do I find a new supplier? I can't advertise in the L.A. *Times*."

Ekhardt shrugged. "They're around. A lot of action is switching from Florida to California. But it's dangerous, chum, and I don't think you want to commit suicide anymore. They could get a lock on your market and eliminate you."

Vandy felt a chill. It was true; he had not felt suicidal lately. Murderous, to be sure, when he thought of Marla's greed forcing him to stay in the drug trade at increased risk, but not suicidal. The old panic began to well up within him, the fear of sliding from his privileged perch to the level of lesser mortals, driven there by the loss of his money and possessions.

That had been a month ago. Marla's death had changed everything. Now he could lounge back easily and contemplate the packets that covered his large desk, smiling like a happy devil. As promised, it was a huge shipment. The biggest ever.

Ekhardt looked at him curiously. "I thought you were going to wig out when I told you I was through. You're handling it well today."

Vandy shrugged. "This is a big score, just like you said. I plan to invest the proceeds wisely this time. Anyway, I just got rid of an expensive habit."

The pilot studied him more closely. "I heard on the news your ex-wife got murdered yesterday," he remarked casually. "My condolences."

Vandy's eyes narrowed at the implication in Ekhardt's tone. "That's right. You must also have heard they are looking for another husband, my old friend Rick Steele."

"Hey, you don't have to explain anything to me, old buddy. I was just remembering something you said once. You know, about there being that one thing in your life you never did yet. Occurred to me you might have finally gotten around to scratching that itch."

Vandy licked a trace of white powder from his finger. "That's a crude suggestion, Johnny. Coming as it does in my hour of bereavement."

Ekhardt laughed. He finished his drink, put down the glass, and rose. "It's nothing to me one way or the other, partner." He looked at his watch. "Well, I'll be getting along. Mustn't intrude too long on your grief."

Vandy walked him to the door and opened it. They stepped out into the hot breeze together. Ekhardt said, "In North Africa they used to call this kind of wind a sirocco. Claimed it drove men mad, made them capable of anything." The pilot grinned.

"Oh, I wouldn't need an ill wind to inspire me." Vandy smiled back. "Well, it's been a fascinating two years. Hardly a dull moment."

Ekhardt nodded. He turned and walked to the Lincoln. The men didn't shake hands. They had never really been friends.

Vandy went back inside and sat behind his desk staring at the stacked packets of cocaine. They represented a respectable fortune even by his standards, one he would not squander this time. He could cut his losses in Europe and Formosa and still have enough to support the elegant trappings without which his life was not worth living.

Now that Marla was dead.

Steelegrave was easing past the front gate when the men stepped out of the house into the driveway. He moved swiftly back into cover behind the hedge as Vandy's voice came to him, clear and unmistakable. Then he heard a car door slam and an engine firing up. The heavy gate opened electronically, swinging outward, and the big Lincoln came backing out. Steelegrave froze in panic, aware of his error. He would be pinned by the headlights when the car cleared the gateway. It was too late to run. Shit, he thought, Hawke would never have been that dumb. He tried uselessly to melt into the hedge, but the tough shrubbery resisted and he could feel the chain-link fence against his back. Undeservedly, the driver reprieved him by choosing not to hit his lights until he had backed out onto the road and swung away from the house. Then, with a thrust of power the big Lincoln slid away into the night.

The gates began to close. From behind the hedge Steelegrave couldn't see whether Vandy was still standing in the driveway or not. The hell with it, this was his only chance to get inside. He jerked the revolver out of his pocket and darted between the gates an instant before they swung shut.

The driveway was empty, the house silent and waiting. Now, of course, he was effectively locked in. He stood in the lighted driveway holding the gun, feeling exposed and, for the second time in minutes, inept. He ran past the front door and around the side of the house to the patio and pool area, not knowing when he might trip an unseen alarm or collide with someone he had already alerted. Adrenaline coursed through his system, nullifying the comforting effects of the liquor he had consumed. His heart pounded so heavily he thought someone might hear it.

No one came out to investigate. The pool lights were on but the patio was dark. Steelegrave made an effort to relax as he began to remember the setup. Sliding glass doors led to a party room off the patio, with a bar, a billiards table, and deep sofas. Beyond that, doors at either end of the room gave onto a corridor that led to Vandy's den, three bedrooms, and an equal number of bathrooms.

Steelegrave peered into the party room, empty and lamp-lit. The glass doors were closed against the hot night, but not, as he had feared, locked. He pulled them silently apart and slipped into the air-conditioned interior.

Everything seemed to be as he remembered it. A portrait of Vandy's mother dominated one wall, looking down on him with mild approval. She would be somewhere in every room, he knew. Above the bar was the mounted head of a water buffalo Vandy had shot on some long-past safari. Framed photographs cluttered the walls.

Steelegrave crossed the room to the corridor. From there he could see the front door, the anteroom, and from an oblique angle, Vandy's den. A light reflected from the den and he could hear the murmur of stereo music. He took a deep breath, crossed the anteroom, and walked in.

Vandy sat at his desk in profile to him, staring down as though lost in thought. He did not look around until Steelegrave stood beside him with the gun pointed at his head.

"You're dead," said Steelegrave. Years ago when they were kids they used to go out after dinner, and starting at either end of the Evander estate, stalk each other with pellet guns. A successful ambush and kill was followed by the ritual cry "You're dead!"

Vandy stared at him with wide, unbelieving eyes. "Wait a minute, Rich . . ." He lifted his arms in a defensive gesture.

"Put your hands on the desk!"

Vandy lowered his hands slowly, until his fingertips rested on wood. He began to breathe deeply, the air sawing in and out of him, as he brought himself under control. When he spoke, the words came out in a tumble.

"Listen to me, Rich. . . . After what she did to you, I don't blame you. A jury wouldn't either—if I testify for you. Tell them how you took the blame for that accident and how she dropped you afterward. How you sacrificed your whole career for her. . . ."

"You sure know about that, Vandy."

Vandy's head jerked up and down. "I do, and I'll bear witness. You'll get off with a wrist slap. They'll understand. But you don't get two for the price of one, Rich. If you kill me too, that'll tear it. You'll go to the gas chamber. And what for? That was years ago, and I—"

"Cut the shit, Vandy! I'm supposed to be the only actor here. You killed Marla and planted that goddamn knife at my place!"

Vandy seemed genuinely astounded. "I don't even know

where you live, Rich! Sweet Jesus, I'm glad she's dead, but I didn't kill her."

Steelegrave, who was holding the gun with both hands, police-style, cocked the hammer with his thumb.

"Don't!" screamed Vandy. "I can prove I was right here! I've been here for a week!"

"You can pay someone to lie, just like you buy everything else. This thing's got your name all over it. Only a sick, sadistic son of a bitch like you would be capable of it. You're going to sign a confession!"

"All right! All right! I'll write out anything you want. But it won't change anything, because I didn't do it. Go ahead, dictate whatever you want. I'll write it out and sign it." He reached toward a desk drawer.

"Keep your hands in sight!" Rick yelled. He felt suddenly weary and unsure of himself, but he couldn't let Vandy know it. He needed a drink badly. With the liquor dying in him, he could gauge the extent of his folly. What had made him so sure Vandy would cave in and confess? Guilty or otherwise, nothing he signed under duress would be worth a damn. All the bastard had to do was play along with him and deny everything later. Unless Steelegrave was prepared to execute him, which he certainly was not.

His gaze fell to the material stacked on Vandy's desk, nearly covering it. Cellophane stretched tight over white powder, exactly like the props they used on *Love–Forty* when the show was about a drug bust.

"Well, now . . ." He picked up a packet with his free hand. "Seems you've got a new business."

"That has nothing to do with you," Vandy said swiftly. He leaned forward, keeping his hands carefully on the table. "You came here for something and I've agreed to give it to you, although I had nothing to do with what happened to Marla. I thought you killed her, like everyone else does. When you walked in, it scared me to death because I thought you were going to make it double or nothing.

"But you've convinced me, Speed." "Speed" was his old prep-school nickname for Steelegrave. "You really think I did it, which means you didn't. And I believe it. You're just not that good an actor."

"I'm not buying any of this." Steelegrave tried to express conviction he didn't feel. He was no longer certain of anything. Vandy's fear of him had been genuine enough, the fear of a man confronted by a homicidal maniac. Perhaps he could even produce an alibi. Still, there had to be a way to get at the truth.

Out of the corner of his eye. Steelegrave saw a wet bar and a tempting array of bottles. His thirst raging, he edged backward, keeping Vandy covered, and put down the packet of cocaine to select a fifth of Chivas Regal. He poured into a tumbler and drank quickly, relishing the instant, heady jolt. Vandy was watching him catlike, a hint of contempt stealing into his eyes.

Steelegrave poured a second drink more casually. He set it down after swallowing half of it and picked up the white packet. Tearing a corner open with his teeth, he poured a steady stream of cystals into the sink and ran the water.

Vandy leapt to his feet with a cry of anguish. "Don't do that!" He started around the desk.

Steelegrave raised the gun. "Get back or I'll blow you away, so help me!"

Vandy was trembling with anger and frustration. "Rich, listen to me. You don't know what you're doing! You just drowned thousands of dollars. It could have been yours, Rich. I'm willing to share—"

"I don't need money. I'm rich, didn't you know? Marla left me everything she had."

Vandy gaped at him.

"Get back and sit down, Vandy." As the shaken man complied, Steelegrave walked toward the desk. A test had occurred to him. "I'm going to dump this stuff into the plumbing one bag at a time until you tell me how you did it. How, when, why . . . all the details." He picked up another packet and backed away.

Vandy groaned. "I can't tell you . . . I can't make something up, just like that. . . ." Then something behind his eyes shifted and he went on quickly, "But wait . . . there is one thing I can tell you. If you didn't kill Marla and I didn't . . . then I know who did." His eyes veered to the gun. "Rich, uncock that thing, can't you? It can go off very easily the way you've got it now."

Steelegrave pointed the revolver upward and eased the hammer down, leveled it again. "Done. You've got a minute to kid me." He flipped the packet of cocaine in the air, catching it in his palm, tossing it again.

"I'm not kidding. Hear me out. I know who must have done it."

Steelegrave had started to laugh at him when he felt a sharp blow to his right wrist which instantly numbed his fingers. The revolver fell harmlessly on the rug. He was spun around to face a lithe black figure an instant before a precise punch to the diaphragm dropped him to the floor in unspeakable pain. He knelt there with his head bowed and his hands pressed against his upper stomach to contain the hurt. Through flooded eyes he saw a foot sweep out to kick away the fallen gun. The same foot gently shoved him from his prayerful position onto his side, where he curled up as though back in the womb.

Outside of his cocoon of pain he heard Vandy say, "Where the hell have you been, you silly sand nigger? I've been standing on the buzzer for ten minutes!"

"Sorry, Sahib, I was in the can," replied a distinctly feminine voice. The English was very precise, slightly British despite the Americanism. "He's a real amateur, this one. Standing with his back to the door."

Steelegrave opened his eyes as sharp agony receded into dull ache, and looked up to see a tall, lean black woman dressed in a halter and short shorts. Taut muscles quivered with her slightest movement, like a horse twitching off flies. She had pronounced cheekbones, an aquiline nose, and thin, fine lips.

"Meet the Watusi," said Vandy. "She's from the deserts of Ethiopia, so she tells me. She's pretty good when she finally gets into action."

"Only . . . call . . . people . . . Sahib . . . in India," Steelegrave managed to gasp.

"You're right, Speed. She's probably never been east of Harlem. Now, do get up off the floor. We shall have to decide what to do with you."

Steelegrave rolled painfully onto his stomach and pushed back up to his knees. The Watusi yanked him the rest of the way up with ease and deposited him on a short leather couch facing Vandy's desk. He noticed that she had a fascinating face close up, a sculpture in ebony. A suggestion of veiled humor lurked around the bold slanted eyes and there was a sensual curve to her lips. None of this did much to ease the humiliation which was replacing his pain. In the old days he had thrown out any script in which Hawke was bested by a woman.

He became aware of Vandy sitting behind his desk, which was cleared now, save for Steelgrave's revolver. The Watusi stood apart from him as a sentinel might, but there was little diffidence in her proud stance. She had the air of a mercenary one could hire in body but never in spirit.

"If I call the police . . ." Vandy began.

"How about letting me finish my drink and maybe smoke a cigarette."

Vandy nodded and the Watusi brought his glass and lit his cigarette. He watched the play of muscles in her tight, round haunches as she moved away from him.

"If you call the police," said Steelegrave, returning to the subject, "I will tell them that I saw you with enough snow to cover the slopes up at Mammoth. Maybe you can hide it or get it out of here before they come, but you better believe they'll be watching you. I would think that might be a handicap in your line."

Vandy sighed. "I thought you might say something like that." He lit a cigarette of his own. "Well, there's another solution. Let's see if you like this scenario.

"You came down here to kill me after you disposed of Marla. For old times' sake, since the game was up for you anyway. You were motivated by hatred over my taking Marla away from you years ago. The Watusi caught you skulking around the grounds with a gun in your hand and she shot you first. She's a licensed bodyguard, so she would be acting entirely within the law. Case closed."

Vandy picked up the revolver. "If you try to jump me, of course I'll shoot you with your own gun. Then we'll say you tried to kill me, but I got the gun away from you and did you in. Better yet. A clear case of self-defense." He leveled the revolver at Steelegrave. "Yes, I think I like that

better than hiding behind a woman's skirts. Or hot pants."
He smiled, but his eyes became very cold. "Get up, Speed."

Steelegrave looked at Vandy's eyes and saw that he
meant it. Suddenly he was more afraid than he had ever
been before in his life. This was the real thing. How many
times had he been in a simulated situation not unlike this?
A hundred? He could hear the director say, "Okay, Rick,
a little tension in the eyes. . . . You're cool and wary,
never afraid. You're getting ready to move fast. Great!
That's the look I want! Remember, throw the glass right at
camera and move out after it fast, okay? Ready? A-a-a-and
roll 'em! . . ."

But this was no studio set with spun-sugar glassware,
breakaway furniture, and blank cartridges. There was no
stunt man to make the bone-jarring dive across the desk,
and no director to yell "cut!" His stomach still hurt and he
was not sure he could even get up, never mind launch
himself across the room. Even so, he felt himself tensing,
bracing against the couch, gathering himself as unobtru-
sively as possible. He had to try to take them out. Anything was better than being slaughtered like an animal.

It was the Watusi who intervened. Her black eyes were
suddenly huge but very determined. "I didn't sign on for
anything like this, Sahib," she said quickly. "Not for
murder. Not even for cover-up."

Vandy never took his eyes off Steelegrave. "Not even
for a bonus? A big one? Suppose he tells about all the nose
candy? They'll put me where I can't pay your salary
anymore. Ever think about that?"

The Watusi shook her head. "I won't go along with it
for anything."

Steelegrave broke in. "I won't tell anyone about the
goddamn dope!" His voice had gone husky, coming out as
a croak.

Vandy glanced at the Watusi, a look of sheer malevolence.
But when he turned back, he had changed, one of the
mercurial changes Steelegrave remembered from long ago.
He laid down the revolver and began to laugh. He laughed
until tears came. "I really had you going, didn't I, Speed?"

Steelegrave downed the rest of his drink in a single gulp.
The Watusi did not smile, and her eyes remained wary.

"How do you think I felt when you came in here and stuck a gun in my ear?" Vandy asked between chuckles. "Call this my little revenge."

Steelegrave didn't trust himself to speak. He knew that he had come within an inch of death. Vandy would have shot him without a qualm. He owed his reprieve solely to the black girl.

"Admit it, I fooled you," Vandy insisted with a broad smile.

"Not for a minute," said Steelegrave truthfully.

"Get me a vodka on the rocks and go back to the can or wherever you were when this guy was about to blow my head off," Vandy said to the Watusi.

The girl served him and walked out with her back straight, almost disdainfully. Steelegrave could appreciate the clench and roll of her marvelous buttocks even now, though her departure caused him some apprehension.

But Vandy was leaning back in his chair, away from the gun, relaxed. "Of course you knew I wouldn't shoot you. How could I, after all the giggles we've had together? Remember the time we shoved that cow into old man Comstock's house?"

"And you shot it."

Vandy laughed. "Of course, but that was only a cow. Who were the guys with us? I've forgotten."

"Junglebreath and Liverlips." Once again, nicknames bestowed by Vandy.

"Of course!" Vandy was delighted. "Seems like yesterday, doesn't it?"

"It seems like a hundred years ago."

Vandy changed the subject abruptly. "I meant what I said before—when you were waving the gun around at me."

"What was that?" Steelegrave was ready to get the hell out of there. Where to, he did not know.

"I know who killed Marla if you didn't. It had to be Dieter."

"The butler. Like in a bad movie."

"Oh, he's no ordinary butler, friend Dieter. Marla had something on him, I don't know what. But she laughed when I told her I would use him against her in any divorce action. She said she knew where his skeletons were buried.

Literally. He was her slave, she said. And she wasn't
lying, because Dieter turned down a lot of money rather
than testify for me. He did quite the opposite, as you may
have read. And all I wanted him to do, at considerable
profit, was to tell the truth."

"Maybe she outbid you."

"She couldn't in those days. Not with money."

"I don't see a motive for murder."

"Suppose he got tired of being a slave?"

"What makes you think he was?"

"I saw him in action."

Katarina Evander and Marla Monday had hated each
other on sight, a circumstance neither of them troubled to
conceal. The older woman treated her rival (Vandy's women
were all her rivals) with silky arrogance and Marla returned her malice with amused contempt. They had met
at the wedding and subsequently only once again. After
that Vandy made no further effort to bring them together.

As Katarina preferred to live on the east coast, either at
the Evander estate in Connecticut or at her Park Avenue
apartment, Vandy traveled between them. He visited his
mother at least half a dozen times a year at one residence
or another. Two years after his marriage to Marla, Katarina
noticed the sudden lack of reference to the actress in her
son's conversation, the blank look that had replaced his
resentment when she delivered one of her own occasional
gibes.

"It's not working, is it?" she asked.

They were sitting alone at either end of the long table at
the Evander estate, dressed formally for dinner as she
preferred it. The butler had served brandy and retired.
Vandy played with his glass in place of making a reply.

Katarina sighed. "I know a cheap tart when I see one."

It was a remark that would once have prompted an
angry reply. "A tart perhaps, but hardly a cheap one."

"I stand corrected." Katarina fitted a cigarette into her
holder. "I'm sure she's extremely costly."

Vandy looked across the table at his mother. In the
candlelight she looked far younger than her fifty-odd years.
Her black eyes and olive-hued beauty were not unlike his

wife's, and he wondered if it wasn't this very similarity that had attracted him to Marla in the first place.

"She's a diamond-hard little bitch for certain, Kat," he said. "What is sometimes referred to as a ball-breaker."

Katarina expelled a plume of smoke that made the candles flicker. "Pity you didn't learn anything from the way she treated your handsome friend Richard. But of course, you were a party to that yourself."

Vandy shrugged. "I was a victim of my own fascination. Couldn't help myself."

"And that fascination has waned?"

"The music stopped."

"Which is when you pay the piper. I've made a very serious mistake with you, Justin." Only his mother called him that. "I could easily have put you on an allowance instead of assigning you stocks and property. Then no one could get at you because you would have nothing in your name. Of course, under those circumstances you would be penniless if anything happened to me. Your father's prejudice against you began at birth, you know. As soon as he saw that dark skin and those black eyes, I suspect. In any case, I had a dreadful time even persuading him to name you after his own father, though he had already named Clayton for himself. I wanted you to have an old family name."

Vandy closed his eyes, having often heard tell how he had become Justin Evander III. "That's old news, Kat."

"Of course it is, but do you know why he felt that way? Have I ever told you he suspected you were not his child?"

Vandy's eyes opened. "I am, aren't I?"

"Damned if I know."

Vandy was obviously shocked for the first time in her recollection. He was speechless.

"Don't brood. It hardly matters. You *are* mine. Unfortunately, however, you were raised without a loving father's discipline, brought up by me to be ornamental and reasonably amusing. Saving graces, to be sure, but hardly the equipment needed to deal with the harsher realities. Since I felt responsible for this lapse in your education, I've tried to correct it by making you financially independent in the hope that you would learn to manipulate your assets to show profit, become a successful entrepreneur like your brother."

"Since when has Clayton been an object of your admiration?" said Vandy, finding his voice.

"He is definitely not, but some of his business acumen would have served you well. Do you know that I secretly hoped you would one day eclipse Clayton and Evander Enterprises, found an empire of your own? Not a very realistic hope, I admit."

"We hot-blooded Greeks against the pale-eyed Nordics?"

"Something like that. I've made an enormous investment in you, Justin."

"I'm sorry to be a disappointment, but I'm something of a hedonist. And quite comfortable, thanks to you."

Katarina sighed. "I know, but back to my dilemma. If I had put you on an allowance instead of making you independently wealthy, you would be quite safe from that predatory little bitch you married. And, unfortunately, quite insolvent once I am gone."

"Don't talk like that, Mother," Vandy said sharply. "You're younger than anyone I know." He seldom called her "mother." It was a measure of his concern.

She smiled at the distress in his eyes. "Thank you for that, my dear, but the elder generation generally precedes the younger out of this life. We have to think and plan realistically. I did what I thought was best for you at that time. Now I wonder."

"I'll manage."

"Will you?" She sipped her brandy thoughtfully. "Is this marriage over, then? And if so, who wants it that way?"

"She's acting restless and defiant. She provokes me on purpose. She's getting ready to make some kind of move. I know the signs."

"And how do you feel?"

"I can live without her. The world is full of women." Not quite like Marla perhaps, but at least more manageable. Vandy preferred to administer the lash than feel it himself.

"Then I suggest you move first. That shouldn't be too difficult. Her attitude suggests she has something going on that you could catch her at."

"Catch her *in flagrante delicto*? With witnesses and cameras, et cetera?" Vandy felt a desire to laugh, which he suppressed. "She wouldn't be that stupid."

"I read her differently. She may be clever, but I doubt that she is wise. There is also a recklessness about her, a don't-give-a-damn sort of daring. You are probably wearing a set of horns to rival a Siberian elk's."

Vandy flushed. "We had a strong thing together physically." And sometimes together with others, he remembered. It was nothing he wanted to explain to Kat, but the idea of trying to gain leverage over Marla with evidence of her moral turpitude would be the ultimate irony. And irony always appealed to Vandy. He smiled.

"I notice you use the past tense. In any case, remember how much is at stake. Rich men's divorces do not come cheaply. Remember also what she did to Richard." Katarina rose from the table, indicating that the conversation was coming to a close. "Do as you like, Justin, but bear in mind that my advice has served you well in the past. When you've bothered to take it. Now I'm tired." She came to him along the length of the table and leaned over to kiss him lightly on the mouth. "I'm going to bed."

Vandy flew back to Los Angeles a day early without calling Marla. His plane landed at nine-thirty in the evening, considerably before the hour when he wanted to return home. He picked up his car at an airport parking facility and drove to Matteo's in Brentwood, where he had several drinks and a long, leisurely Italian dinner. It was nearly midnight by the time he finished.

He had mulled over his mother's suggestion and decided to make a dry run to satisfy his own curiosity. Chances were, Marla wouldn't even be home. After all, there was an endless variety of places where she could rendezvous for a tryst or even an orgy, if she were so inclined. The way to get sound evidence would be to employ a private detective, a tactic he had under consideration. Tonight he was merely game-playing.

He parked his car on Antelo, well short of the big house, and got out to walk the rest of the way. The music hit him at once, loud and portentous. He recognized

Wagner's *Gotterdämmerung*, hardly a piece he would have thought to Marla's taste. But then, no one could presume to know everything about Marla.

Her Lamborghini, which she seldom troubled to garage, stood alone in the driveway, so there would be no guests, to Vandy's vague disappointment. Dim light glowed from the upper windows, but it was dark below. He used his key in the gate and the front door and then climbed the stairs quietly, though the music would have covered an invading army.

At the head of the stairs, the smell of marijuana reached his nostrils and he followed it along the hall to Marla's bedroom. They had separate accommodations by mutal preference and her suite was at the end of the upper corridor, giving onto a semicircular terrace with a view of both the valley and the distant sea to the west.

The bedroom door was slightly ajar and Vandy nudged it farther open. No one in the room noticed his presence. They were in a tangle on the big bed—Dieter, Marla, and Lotte—naked except for the visored officer's cap Marla wore. It was black with a silver eagle over skull and crossbones and looked both saucy and sinister perched on her dark head. The rest of the uniform—trousers, belt, and a tunic with badges of rank and decorations—hung neatly across the chair in front of Marla's dressing table.

Vandy was more taken aback by Marla's choice of lovers than by the scene itself. The presence of Lotte, especially, jarred him. He had thought her a guileless creature, wholesome and cheerful, obviously in awe of her massive husband. Now she sprawled loosely like an obscene rag doll, her pleasant, stubby features grotesquely rouged and lipsticked. A rustic milkmaid transformed into a soiled mannequin. It angered Vandy to have misjudged anyone so completely.

He stood in the doorway engulfed by the stentorian music and the reek of marijuana. Still nobody noticed him until he rapped his knuckles hard against the doorjamb. "Knock, knock," he said.

The German reacted swiftly, shoving Marla aside and rolling off the bed in a single lunge, surprisingly graceful for a man so large. He was even more impressive naked than clothed, for he was heavily muscled, with no trace of

softness. The right arm, which he always carried slightly
bent, was terribly scarred, patterned with thick ridges of
white tissue from elbow to shoulder. He stood like a
soldier at ease, body relaxed and eyes wary, awaiting the
next development. He seemed conscious neither of his
nakedness nor of the awkwardness of his situation.

"Vandy!" cried Marla. "What a surprise! Why, how sly
of you!" She swung her legs over the side of the bed and
rose. He could see that she was stoned but, as always,
under control. "We've been rehearsing a play I've been
thinking of doing. It's all about decadence in Nazi Germany." She walked over to turn off the music.

"This sort of thing will ruin the servants, you know."
Vandy looked at Lotte, who lay spatulate, the makeup
smeared across her face, her eyes open but not tracking.
She seemed to be heavily drugged.

Marla laughed. "Don't be such a snob. Anyway, Dieter's
not really a servant, he's an aristocrat of some sort. And
you've got to admit the casting's absolutely perfect." She
turned to the big German. "Dieter, put on the uniform for
Mr. Evander. I want him to see for himself."

Dieter plucked the black jodhpurs off the back of the
chair and stepped into them. Then he pulled on gleaming
boots and shrugged into the tunic, all without taking his
eyes off Vandy. He smoothed his hair and accepted the
peaked hat from Marla, placing it on his head at a perfect
angle. He cinched his belt and pulled on leather gloves.
The black uniform with its silver piping was a perfect fit.
Moreover, so was the man within. He belonged there.

"You see?" Marla exulted. "Perfect! I couldn't find a
thing to fit him at Hollywood Wardrobe, so I had the
whole thing tailor-made. Dieter told me about the emblems and all that."

"I hope you didn't go to old Nate Landau." Vandy
didn't want to lose his favorite tailor because of a macabre
joke.

"Of course not! What do you take me for?"

Vandy evaded the question tactfully. He had begun to
see how he could use the situation to his advantage. "Then
this is just a bit of theater . . ."

"Of course, luv. It's a pity I can't use Dieter in the

actual play, but he'd have to belong to the union. And there was a perfect part for you, if you had just let me know you were coming." She giggled and he saw that her pupils were dilated with drug. She was mocking reality, working deeper into her fantasy world. When acting, Marla always had to convince herself first. It was her method.

"May I assume that we are discharged?"

Vandy turned to face the immaculately uniformed Dieter, who stood impassive save for a trace of irony in the spit-colored eyes.

"Assume nothing. Return to your quarters," said Vandy, playing his part now. He gestured toward the inert Lotte. "And take that slut with you."

Something came into Dieter's eyes that convinced Vandy he was looking at death. Then it was gone and the big German stooped to pick up his naked wife as though she were weightless.

When he was alone with Marla, Vandy opened the French doors leading to the terrace and breathed deeply of the night air. A hint of night-blooming jasmine replaced the smell of marijuana in his nostrils. He had stumbled on a perfect situation; his mother could not have asked for more. Of course, there were no witnesses except for the participants, but they could provide the most effective testimony of all. Given an incentive.

When he went back into the bedroom, Marla was in a dressing gown smoking a cigarette. "Carrying on with the servants is quite unforgivable," he told her. "I'm something of an elitist, you know."

"You're just pouting because you feel left out. I saw the way you were looking at Lotte."

"No, I'm crushed. I think I'll divorce you."

Marla puffed her cigarette, unfazed. "That's interesting. How do you plan to go about it?"

"Dieter and Lotte will testify to your degenerate ways and confess to their own participation. It'll be lurid, but any judge or jury will be in complete sympathy with me. About the only part you'll be offered after it's over will be Mary Magdalene. Of course, you can avoid all this by agreeing to an uncontested divorce."

"And renouncing any property settlement?"

"Exactly. You'll be all right. You make a good living, to say the least."

"You'll bribe Dieter and Lotte to testify for you, is that it?"

"Generously. You won't be able to match me."

Marla started to chuckle; then the laughter bubbled out of her. Her eyes still reflected the drug in her system, but her defenses were well in place now. "Oh, poor Vandy! Well, it was a good idea, anyway. But, luv, what you don't understand is that Dieter is my creature. He belongs to me. I know where all his skeletons are buried. Quite literally. He will never, never give evidence against me, no matter what you offer him.

"But you've given me an idea. And you've made it easy for me. Picture the script you just described in reverse. With you as the defendant. Do you see what I mean?"

"Did you try to use Dieter against her?" asked Steelegrave.

"Oh, yes. I offered him fifty thousand and went up to a hundred. Not bad for a servant in those days. He stopped me there and said it was no use. At any price."

"But he testified for Marla?"

"They both did. Made me look like the devil incarnate. You must have read about it."

"I heard that she took you big, but I didn't get all the details. I was out of the country."

"Ah, yes. Making spaghetti westerns in Italy."

"Until Umberto Ugolini found out about it and had me blackballed. But go on."

"Well, they simply turned it all around. I had seduced and corrupted Lotte, beaten and threatened my wife, engaged in all manner of perversion, et cetera, et cetera, ad nauseam. The settlement Marla got was some sort of record at the time. No judge would ever rescind it. I've been paying ever since. Until yesterday."

"And now you want me to believe that Dieter killed her in order to get out from under some kind of blackmail. Maybe he was having a ball."

"I don't care what you believe, Speed. But I saw the ten-o'clock news tonight and everybody else believes you killed our ex-wife. I'm not at all sure you can correct that impression by running away.

"Where are you going to go? Mexico? They described that flashy car of yours on TV, but even if you're driving something else, they can stop all traffic going south with just a few units. Maybe put a control just below San Clemente like the one they've got to catch wetbacks going north. Where you can't even turn around to get away. Forget about getting on a plane. So what are you going to do?"

"What do you suggest? That I go and try to beat a confession out of Dieter?"

"You came tearing down here to do exactly that to me." Vandy got up to mix two drinks at the wet bar, leaving the gun casually behind on his desk. He brought one of them to Steelegrave.

"Listen, Rich. I saw him in that uniform. It was eerie. He told Marla about the right emblems, remember? She said he wasn't a servant but some kind of an aristocrat. She said she knew where his skeletons were buried. Now, we have this aristocrat turned servant who knows all about Nazi uniforms and refuses a hundred thousand dollars or more just to go into court and confess to a little hanky-panky. Suppose, Rich, that the good fairy, in my somewhat unlikely form, appeared before *you* with an offer like that. Would you turn it down? No, I think she had him where the hair grows short. I think he's some kind of war criminal."

"You're just blowing smoke. And why would he plant the knife at my place? If it turns out to be the right knife."

"You told me that Marla left you everything in her will. It sounds strange to me, but if it's true, then Dieter probably knew about it. If he did, then he'd found someone with a strong motive. You. How hard would it be for him to find out where you live and leave the knife there? Just the way you thought I did. He knew the cops would check you out. Maybe he gave them the idea."

Steelegrave drank half the Scotch in his glass and shrugged. "Anyone could get in by jimmying a window. You or him. There's still nothing to go up against him with." But the idea seemed less preposterous with the

Scotch spreading its soothing glow. He downed the remainder of the liquor.

"Not for the police, maybe. But you could lead him to believe that Marla told you about his past. In Nazi Germany. It's only a guess, but it's got to be damn close to the truth. You're supposed to be an actor. If you're totally convincing, it could panic him into making a mistake."

"It could panic him into killing me. I remember the bastard. He's a giant."

Vandy sighed. "I've been telling you all this to help you. For old times' sake. I don't want to see you take a fall for that Nazi. But I can't tell you what to do." He turned back to his desk and picked up the revolver. "Consider your options. Keep running and they'll catch you. Give yourself up and they might convict you. If, on the other hand, you decide to visit Dieter, maybe you'd better take this with you." He handed over the gun.

Steelegrave put it in his jacket pocket and rose. "I guess I can trust you not to call the cops on me. I'd have to tell them about your sideline."

"Fear not. This visit will be our secret. Even if you get yourself caught, eh?"

"Sure. As long as it wasn't your doing."

Vandy led the way to the front door. As they passed through the corridor, Steelegrave caught a glimpse of the Watusi standing just inside the party room. He turned to Vandy. "One thing more. Why would this clever Nazi aristocrat tell Marla anything that would give her such a hold on him? Have you thought of that?"

Vandy smiled. "Oh, I imagine it was pillow talk. Have you forgotten how marvelous she was in the feathers? I believe she was the best I ever had. Don't you agree?" He opened the door for Steelegrave and pressed the button that swung open the gates.

"Almost. I can think of one better."

"Who?" asked Vandy with immediate interest.

"Your mother," said Steelegrave, and walked out.

16

The phone jarred Cosgrove out of shallow slumber. When he was sober, his sleep was seldom more than a thin layer of unconsciousness easily shredded by the faintest sound. But at least he wasn't plagued by the night sweats he suffered during his drinking bouts. He rolled over heavily to reach for the phone, noting that it was 1:05 A.M. by the luminous hands of his electric clock.

"Yes?"

"Hello, Cos." It was Marsha Wing. "I'm sorry about what happened today. That's the first thing I want to tell you."

Officer Wing was a coworker at LAPD, a widow, forty-five years of age with a handsome face and a thick mane of red hair. She was tall and large of breast and buttocks, but Junoesque rather than fat. Cosgrove was the object of her unrequited lust and she did not hesitate to show it, for she had no way of knowing she was simply not his type, being in fact the antithesis of the bruised, tractable women he was drawn to. He had to use all his cunning to parry her straightforward overtures and keep their relationship on a casual slap-and-tickle basis. So he was bluff and hearty with her, quick with a wink and a joke. He wanted to keep her happy. Privy to everything that went on at the station, she was extremely useful to him.

"At this time of night, there better be more," growled Cosgrove, playing their game.

"I've got the switchboard, Cos, so I thought I'd call and let you know what's happening. You want to hear, or enjoy your leave in peace?"

"Shoot."

"Nothing exciting. A lot of volume on the Monday thing. They're relaying me the calls from downtown. People who think they saw Steelegrave. Nut calls and a confession or two. One old bat says Steelegrave raped her but she's got him locked up in her garage. Captain's got units checking out everyone but the real space cadets."

Cosgrove grunted. "Usual crap. No real leads on Steelegrave at all?"

"I don't think so. The captain went home, but I've been passing all this along to him. He's not getting excited."

"What about Nash?" Al Nash was the detective third-grade who headed the burglary-homicide detail.

"Nash is out in Santa Monica after a crazy who bladed his wife for leaving the cap off the toothpaste or something and is threatening to kill the kids too. SWAT's there by now."

"Leaving Fletch on top of the Monday kill."

"Yeah."

"And nothing coming in."

"I don't think so. . . . Well, there was a woman called, said she was a cop, a narc working undercover. Told me there was a good chance Steelegrave was going back to the Monday place tonight, that we ought to move on it. She wouldn't give me any I.D., said it could blow her cover, so I thought, balls, another kook. But I got to admit there was something in her voice—an urgency, you know? And she was talking low and fast like she didn't have much time."

"When did this call come in?"

"Maybe an hour ago."

"What's Strickland doing about it?"

"Well, he's got Kalb and Grady staying up at the Monday house. He had me call and tell them to keep the lights out and hide their unit. Just in case. But he's not hot on it."

"Neither am I. Is that it?"

"That's about it. Listen, Cos, I know how you must be

taking this. It's really a bum rap. So if you get feeling down, don't hesitate to call." A throb came into her voice, telling Cosgrove she was on the threshold of emotion. "I mean, if you want to talk . . . well, you know I'm always here. If you like, I could come over tomorrow, fix your breakfast."

"Thanks a million, angel," Cosgrove interjected swiftly, "but I think I'll get out of town for a few days. Leave early and maybe go to the mountains. Catch a few trout. I'll save you some."

After he hung up he lay awake and went over it in his mind. How in hell would a lady narc on assignment stumble over a fugitive like Steelegrave? The percentage of likelihood seemed nil. He thought of the countless hours of policework wasted shagging false leads. On a case like this, all the fruitcakes came out of the woodwork and had a field day. The book said you had to check them all out. Have fun, Fletch.

But he wished he had heard the woman's voice. Marsha said she sounded urgent and to the point. That wasn't like a space cadet; they all loved to talk. Had he heard her, he could have made a judgment. He trusted his instinct to interpret nuance behind the spoken word.

Why would Steelegrave return to Marla Monday's place? It made no sense to him. What could he hope to accomplish there that would change anything? His options were to run or surrender. Still, as Cosgrove well knew, desperation often resulted in bizarre, unpredictable behavior. Fair enough, but it was more of a challenge to imagine how Steelegrave had happened across this female narc and confided his plans to her. Unless maybe she was his girlfriend and he didn't know she was a cop. Marsha had said she was undercover.

Within fifteen minutes Cosgrove knew he would not be able to sleep. The multiple ironies of the day haunted him, compounded by the old cop habit nagging him to follow up the slimmest lead. He turned on the light and struggled out of bed. Any activity, no matter how inane, was preferable to lying sleepless, reliving his frustrations. Soon he would start to thirst, and he didn't trust himself in that situation. He dressed and went down to the garage, sure

that he was on a fool's errand. Things to do to keep from
drinking.

When he turned on the car radio, he learned that
Steelegrave was still at large but no longer topped the
news. A fire had broken out in Malibu and was racing
down Latigo Canyon toward the luxury homes seaside of
the highway. Another was scorching the hills along
Mulholland, west of the San Diego freeway. Fed by dry
brush and driven by the Santa Ana wind, neither had been
contained. Cosgrove listened with instinctive dread. Fires
were the bane of cops as well as firemen. They meant
danger, long hours, and shit details.

The night was still bright and starlit when he reached
Mulholland Drive by way of Coldwater Canyon, but
he could see the smudge of smoke and the glow of fire over
the distant hills to the west. He wound along the mountain
ridge, alert to the danger of nocturnal drag racers who
forced other cars off the road and sometimes left the twisted
skeletons of their own littering the steep ravines on either
side of the thoroughfare.

Antelo Drive branched off Mulholland at a steep angle,
bisecting with a narrow dirt road called Antelo Lane, and
was posted "NO TRESPASSING—PRIVATE PROP." Cosgrove
stayed on the paved road and climbed the hill, passing
Marla Monday's house slowly. He saw that the lights were
out and the gate had been left invitingly open. Kalb and
Grady playing "spider-and-the-fly" in the unlikely case
that Steelegrave showed up. If they had not already taken
him, an assumption he had to make for the sake of the
exercise.

Antelo Drive dead-ended two properties beyond at the
wooden gates of a ranch-style home that was deserted and
for sale. Cosgrove turned around in front of the gates so
that he was facing downhill and killed his lights. The
brightness of the night favored him, for he could see well
beyond the Monday mansion and remain inconspicuous.
Not at all a bad stakeout. Now, if he only had a drink and
a cigar.

Exhaustion crept up on Steelegrave as he drove north
toward Los Angeles on 405. Again the buoying effects of

alcohol had worn off, leaving him with a furred tongue and sluggish thought processes. He had trouble keeping his eyes open and would have fallen asleep at the wheel without the staccato cadence of his tires rippling over the lane buttons when he strayed. He concentrated on holding the car steady, knowing he couldn't pull over to rest. At this time of night, the cops would check anything alongside the road.

He didn't know where he was going. He was just driving, heading north because they would be less likely to check traffic going in that direction. Vandy had convinced him he couldn't make it across the Mexican border, so he was following his homing instinct through Long Beach and back toward Santa Monica. He wanted to return to Wisteria Manors and go to bed, to hell with the whole thing. Better yet, go to Erin's, let them find him there. Suddenly he missed her terribly. Of course, he knew he could do neither of those things. It was all like a bad script. Nothing made sense. He simply drove.

Near the airport off-ramp he almost ran into the guardrail, then straddled three lanes, overcorrecting. He jerked upright, the adrenaline shooting through him. Christ, he had fallen asleep and nearly crashed! He peered through the rearview mirror and saw no one behind him. A single set of headlights burned far up ahead, giving him a feeling of infinite isolation. He was driving alone through a great void, following this gray ribbon, swaying back and forth.

He had to get off the freeway.

Sepulveda Boulevard was seedy and deserted. Steelegrave found a closed gas station and pulled in, turning off the lights. Before he cut the engine he noticed that the gas tank was almost empty. Fighting his urge to sleep, he got out of the car and drank his fill from the drinking fountain. Then he checked the gas pumps, finding them securely locked. Back in the car he allowed himself a swallow from the Scotch bottle and wolfed down his remaining sandwich. The return of strength was encouraging, and he sipped again, knowing he had to ration himself. The lift that booze gave him was reliable but impermanent. Perhaps just one more, but that was it. He made it a long swallow.

Now what? He couldn't pass out on the apron of an

economy gas station, to be hauled in by the first cruiser that came by. What kind of headline would that make? A Mexican bullfighter had once told him all you needed was *"un kilo de corazón y dos kilos de huevos"*—roughly, a big heart and huge balls. Steelegrave had to believe he qualified. The house on Antelo was not that far away. What the hell? he thought, go for it.

He turned off Mulholland, taking Antelo Lane, the dirt road he knew would lead him directly beneath Marla's house. Beyond there, the path meandered another quarter of a mile to an estate half-hidden by a stand of tall pines. Steelegrave drove the Fiat as far off the track into the bushes as he could and got out. Marla's property began above him, beyond a riot of stunted trees and scrub brush. A steep climb, but he elected the indirect approach, realizing the police might have left someone behind to discourage looters or the morbidly curious.

He worked his way up the bluff at a point he calculated would bring him out behind the servants' lodging occupied by Dieter. The only obstacle he encountered was a chain-link fence much lower than Vandy's, probably designed to keep animals in or out. He negotiated it easily and stepped out of the bushes onto an edge of manicured lawn.

The big house was dark but a light still burned in Dieter's quarters, although it was two-thirty in the morning by his watch. He moved carefully along the side of the building, passing curtained windows on his way to the front door, dismayed by the brightness of the night. Someone looking out from the main house could probably see him.

Worse still, a bulb burned above Dieter's door, casting a patch of light he could not safely step into. Steelegrave retreated into the shadows and was debating rapping on a window when he saw a fuse box recessed into the wall. He got his fingers under the metal casing and pulled it open, then yanked down all the handles he could find. The lights went out and he edged back toward the front of the house.

The door opened slowly and Dieter's voice called to him in a guttural whisper, "Mr. Steele? Is that you out there? I have been expecting you."

Steelegrave froze, his hand around the revolver in his pocket. Expecting him? How the hell could that be?

"There are two policemen over in the other house, Mr. Steele," whispered Dieter. "We must be very quiet."

Steelegrave looked at the tall, thin silhouette of Dieter etched against the night. He could see the man was much diminished, not at all the brute figure he remembered. He stepped forward cautiously.

"Come inside," said the German, seeing him now. "I will tend the lights." He moved past Steelegrave toward the fuse box.

Steelegrave stepped into the house and away from the door, keeping his hand on the gun in his pocket. In a moment Dieter was back, closing the door, making certain the curtains were drawn before he turned on another lamp.

"Sit down," said Dieter. "No? Then forgive me if I do. I have not been well. That is why I was still awake."

Steelegrave studied Dieter more closely. The man was gaunt and slightly unsteady on his feet, lost in the folds of the robe he wore. "How could you have been expecting me?" he asked.

"Because I received a phone call saying you were coming here in a desperate state of mind, armed and prepared to kill me."

"Who from?" Steelegrave was dumbfounded.

"Why, from Mr. Evander, of course. He said that you had learned all about me from Miss Monday and that you realized I had to kill her to stop the blackmail. He urged me to defend myself. I found his concern quite touching."

Vandy! The slimy bastard. "Why didn't you call the cops? Or did you?"

"Of course not. And I'm certain Mr. Evander guessed I wouldn't have anything to do with the police. He thought I would kill you or, better yet, we would kill each other."

"I don't get any of this. You just sat there waiting for me to come and kill you?"

"Death holds no terror for me. Quite the contrary. I'm amused to be part of this little adventure. In any case, it will be my last. Well, then, is it true that Miss Monday told you all about me? About the death camps? Everything?"

Steelegrave took his cue. "That's right, she did."

Dieter smiled a death's-head grin. "I had nothing to do with any camps, Mr. Steele. But no matter, I knew she had told you nothing. Despite her final generosity to you, a peculiarity that I witnessed, I doubt you have seen her in years. I would have known." His expression was smug.

"Nevertheless, I shall satisfy your curiosity. Your guess, or Mr. Evander's, misses the mark, but the consequences for me are much the same. I am former Stürmbannführer—Major, if you prefer—Freiherr Gerd von Mannstein of the Liebstandarte Division of the Waffen SS. My father was an army officer of some distinction, a cousin to Field Marshal von Mannstein. He was disappointed in my choice of services, but I was intrigued by the elite nature of the SS, the glamour if you like. The Armed SS were strictly combat soldiers, unlike the scum that guarded the camps—a distinction that was unfortunately ignored after the war. I graduated from the officers' academy at Badt Tolz at the beginning of hostilities and served in France and Poland. I was a seasoned officer of twenty-one when we invaded Russia. . . ."

He paused to light a long gray cigarette, which instantly brought on a spasm of coughing. "Russian cigarettes," he explained. "They are truly foul, but I developed a lifelong taste for them. Now they have killed me. So, one way or another, Ivan has got me at last. . . .

"But not to digress. Russia was a hellhole and Liebstandarte suffered appalling casualties. They always threw the SS into the worst of the shit, you see, because we got the job done at any cost. Finally we went back to Paris to refit in June 1942. Then, after a bit of the good life and a stint at the Atlantic wall to show us off, it was back to the Russian front. Kursk, a year later, was the greatest tank battle in history, and I was a tank officer. We very nearly won it, nearly turned the war in the east around. But Hitler panicked when the allies invaded Italy and transferred the best SS units out of Russia. Including Leibstandarte. By then it no longer mattered to me. I took a tree burst of shrapnel at Kursk while I was outside the turret of my tank, and that was the end of my war." He smoked and coughed some more.

"When I left the hospital, my right arm was useless. I

was finished as a combat officer. But the war was going badly and no one could be wasted. I was transferred to Paris and to an SS police battalion. I did not like the posting and I reported for duty wearing my tanker's combat uniform and decorations by way of protest. This earned me a reprimand but no change of assignment—"

"What has this got to do with anything, Dieter?" Steelegrave interrupted. "I haven't got time for a history lesson."

"Very well, I'll be brief. In late summer of 1944 the fall of Paris was imminent. As you may recall if you were old enough, we declared it an open city and simply marched out, so there was no bombing or shelling. A humane decision, I thought, for I loved Paris—"

"Come *on*, Dieter."

"To the point, then. . . . My final assignment and the only one I had of this nature was to see to the execution of twenty-seven partisans. I found the task distasteful but I did not balk. These people shot German soldiers in the back for a pastime. The Geneva convention clearly states that men fighting out of uniform can be shot out of hand as spies. But then, one man's terrorist is another man's hero, eh? Well . . . I supervised the execution myself and helped deliver the coup de grace, for I won't ask a subordinate to do what I will not." Dieter leaned back, lost in reminiscence.

"They were a sullen, defiant lot, those Frenchmen, except for one who was jumping about protesting his innocence. I quickly recognized him as a fellow named Boucher, a sorry lout we all knew. He was a pimp and a gigolo, but certainly not a terrorist. I suppose he stepped on the wrong toes and some policeman, French or German, had put his name on the death list. The others were not helping him, hoping he would die along with them. Anyway, on my own authority, I told the idiot to get the devil away from there. He ran as though he thought we would shoot him in the back. We laughed then, but I wish we had shot him.

"Well, of course Boucher later denounced me by name, becoming something of a Resistance hero in the process. He described his harrowing escape, dodging bullets all the way. The French put me on their list of war criminals, where I have remained ever since."

"You told all this to Marla?"

"Hardly. My wife Lotte was a simple little peasant whom I married to bolster my new identity. I became fond of her and she adored me. She also worshiped Miss Monday, who managed to seduce her with assurances that women loved each other in a different way and their kind of love could never constitute infidelity to a man. Convoluted logic, perhaps, but effective enough with Lotte. In the course of their affair it seems Lotte could not resist boasting about her husband, an aristocrat and war hero. Miss Monday became intrigued to know why such a man would change his name and become a servant. Having guessed the nature of the matter, she made extensive anonymous inquiries about Gerd von Mannstein. Early on she was frustrated, I gather. I wasn't wanted by Weisenthall or any of the Nazi-hunting Jewish organizations. But finally her inquires reached the French. *Et voilà!*"

"I thought you were an American citizen. Doesn't that protect you?"

"Not at all. In fact there is a law that voids your citizenship if you received it under false pretenses. Such as using an assumed name. I could be extradited to France to stand trial."

"This is interesting, Dieter. It gives you a perfect reason to kill Marla. Now, why are you telling all this to me?"

"Because it doesn't matter anymore. Just today the doctors told me that my condition is terminal. The tumor in my lung cannot be removed. I have only a short and painful time left to me. I had rather hoped you would come in here bent on murder and resolve the situation for me. But, alas . . ."

"Dieter, I don't want to seem cold-blooded at a time like this, but if you only found out today, you didn't know you were out of time when Marla was killed."

"How perceptive of you. However, Miss Monday—I, also, called her Marla when we were alone—told me she had prepared a document and left it with her attorney, Mr. Markham, in case anything untoward happened to her. I doubt that she really did, but we shall soon find out, no?"

"So Marla *was* blackmailing you."

"It pleased her to think so. She loved Hollywood melodrama. It was a game we played, really. You see, I could never have killed her or even left her, because she fascinated me. Especially after Lotte died. I generally find Americans a dull lot—in constant conflict with their tedious morality, stupefying themselves with drug and drink to feel deliciously wicked. They are such amateurs at wickedness. But she was so imaginative and sensual, so refreshingly degenerate. I wonder if you understand what I mean?"

"Go on." He suddenly lost any sympathy he had begun to feel for Dieter.

"She became my whole world. I have led a very restricted life here in America, being a fugitive—a feeling I am sure you are beginning to understand. Of course, I had to share her, but we were closer than you could ever imagine. We laughed at the world together. She told me everything, perhaps because she knew so much about me. Did you know that her mother was Mexican?"

"No. What difference does it make?"

"I'll tell you a story. Marla was from a small town in Arizona. Her Mexican mother left her father and the child. But he didn't want her either, so he took her across the border to some wretched village and sold her to the local chief of police for fifty dollars. The man tied her up and raped her for six months before she could escape. She was fourteen at the time."

Steelegrave had not heard that one. He tried to imagine Marla at fourteen, skinny and brutalized, in place of the glittering woman he remembered. It wasn't easy.

"Now that she is dead," he heard Dieter say, "I will find it much easier to go. . . ."

Steelegrave felt the conversation was becoming maudlin. And leading nowhere. His head was beginning to ache and there was a taste of ashes in his mouth. Somewhere, sometime, he was going to have to sleep. Unbidden, he took a cigarette from Dieter's packet. It was a king-size hollow-tube with about an inch of tobacco at one end. He lit it and gasped over the acrid smoke, crushing it out at once.

The German laughed. "Another Russian hoax, eh?"

Suddenly Steelegrave didn't want to go on. He doubted that Vandy, for all his treachery, had killed Marla. Nor had this wasted Nazi, who clearly had little reason left to lie. He parted the curtains and peered out at the big dark mansion. Had he gone there himself last night, drunk and filled with old resentment after watching their picture, and cut Marla's throat? He didn't think himself capable of it, but she might have provoked him beyond endurance. Marla could do that.

"Do you have an interphone?" he asked, dropping the curtain.

"Yes."

"Then call those people over there. I've had enough."

Dieter got to his feet painfully. "You are sure you want that?"

"Yes."

The German lifted a receiver from its wall mount and dialed two digits. He waited, then broke the connection and dialed again. Finally there was an answer. "Mr. Kalb? You had better come over to my quarters with your partner."

The receiver squawked in protest.

"I realize it is very late, but it is a matter of importance." He hung up and turned to Steelegrave. "I hope you can prove your innocence."

"What makes you think I'm innocent?" Steelegrave slumped down in a chair. "I was drunk last night. I can't remember anything."

Dieter smiled. "Because I saw who killed her."

Steelegrave sat in utter silence for a moment. Then he lunged out of the chair and caught Dieter by the lapels of his robe. "Why didn't you say anything? What kind of game are you playing?"

"Take your hands off me, Mr. Steele. What can you threaten me with?"

Steelegrave dropped his hands reluctantly. "You watched someone kill her and you didn't do anything, didn't tell anyone?"

"No, I didn't watch her killed. I was awake when the terrace lights went on. I often can't sleep because of pain. I got up and saw her walk out naked to her equipment. A moment later someone followed, walking right through the light. That was not unusual. She often had company. I went back to bed and neither heard nor saw anything more."

"Why didn't you tell the police?"

"No one would have believed me. I hardly believe it myself. I would have been questioned and harassed."

"You're an eyewitness, goddammit!"

"I would have been investigated."

"You said yourself it didn't matter anymore!"

"I will not spend my last days under interrogation."

Steelegrave felt the sweat trickling down his side. He didn't have much time. "You say you cared for her, but you'll protect her murderer?"

"Nothing will bring her back, no matter what I do."

Steelegrave took the gun out of his pocket. "You're going to tell them the truth."

The German gave his taut smile. "Or you'll shoot me, Mr. Steele?"

"At least tell *me*, Dieter!"

"I owe you nothing. However, I shall do what I can to avenge Marla. I shall write a statement and leave it with the attorney, Marius Markham, that custodian of interesting documents, to be opened upon my death. It shouldn't be too long."

"I can't count on that. You're telling me I've got to keep running until you die!"

Dieter shrugged. "They should be coming over soon." He looked out through the curtains just as floodlights lit up the terrace. The gaunt German turned out the table lamp and the light over the front door. "You can still slip out. I will invent a story about a prowler."

"Damn you!"

But he left, easing out the door as two figures emerged from the big house into the wide circle of light. They carried flashlights but it was unlikely they could see much until they stepped out of the glare.

Steelegrave could not return the way he had come. It

would have meant exposing himself even if he clung close to the wall of the small house. He darted to the right instead and bulled his way through the hedge that bounded Marla's property. The neighboring lot was empty, a tangle of shrubbery and puny trees, colorless in the pale night.

He followed the hedge until he reached the road, and then started past the house toward Antelo Lane and the Fiat. Almost instantly a set of headlights stabbed the night behind him and switched to high beam, skewering him. An engine roared to life and the lights bore down on him.

Pounding along the pavement, Steelegrave knew he had to get off the road, out of the shaft of light getting close enough to warm his back. He flung himself to the left onto Antelo Lane, racing toward the Fiat in the bushes. The car behind him slowed, brakes squealing, trying to negotiate the ninety-degree turn. The headlights disappeared into brush, backed free, and came after him again.

Trying for the Fiat was out. He would have been trapped even if he had left it heading in the right direction. He plunged off the trail and down a draw, stumbled across a dry, rocky creek bed and then he was climbing again, pulling himself up through the shrubbery toward Mulholland.

Behind him the car stopped, a door slammed. "Halt! Stop, goddammit!"

Steelegrave kept going, his back muscles tensed for a bullet, praying the foliage covered him. There was no shot. Instead, the car door slammed again and the engine revved, backing.

Steelegrave staggered out onto Mulholland and ran west. Looking back, he saw the car's lights filtered through the trees as it backed onto Antelo Drive, then shot forward toward Mulholland. He threw himself off the road before the lights could pick him up again and rolled into the sparse shrubbery beyond the shoulder, lying still, not knowing if he was visible or not.

The car turned onto Mulholland and came on slowly, a spotlight sweeping back and forth in front of it. Steelegrave held his breath and stared at the thin beam as if it were a deadly laser. It flirted around him, skipped over by inches, finally passed on. The car rolled by, a nondescript model

without police markings. Steelegrave watched the taillights
recede, then brighten as the car stopped. Someone got out,
carrying a flashlight now, and walked back toward him.
He saw the glint of a gun—shit!—watched the malevolent
yellow beam probing nearer. A yard short of him it stopped,
faltered, and reversed itself, preceding its owner back to
the car. This time the taillights continued on out of sight.

He waited for the car to come back. Waited through five
minutes that seemed like an hour. But he could not stay
here. Cops had radios even in unmarked cars, and the area
could soon be crawling with them. He got up cautiously
and walked west toward a distant glow in the night sky.
A fire, he thought. It figured with this damn wind.

He had no objective now; he was on automatic pilot,
operating on basic survival instinct like an animal in a
hostile environment. Nor did he try to make much sense
out of anything beyond assuming it was some kind of
ambush. Vandy had obviously alerted both Dieter and the
police. Maybe the army and the Marine Corps, too. It
must have been that crack about Katarina.

Beyond the next rise he would be looking down on the
San Diego freeway. There was no point in going in that
direction, trying to cross eight lanes of highway that could
see traffic at any hour. Roscomare Road fell away to his
left, winding through Bel-Air. He could lose himself there,
among the small residential streets. Until when? Until it
got light? Until Dieter died? He would think about that
later, when he didn't have to worry about the car. He
started to cross the road.

The car nearly got him then. It came rushing out at him
from where it had lain in wait, blending with the night.
First the engine roar, then the blinding lights, trapping
him in brightness. Steelegrave dived to his right, feeling
the wind of its passing. He landed painfully on asphalt,
rolled, and got back on his feet. He ran, not looking back
at the car but hearing it screech to a stop, whine in
reverse, lunge forward burning rubber for another try.

He left the road and plowed through a lot of dry, spiky
shrubs, running downhill on the valley side of Mulholland.
He fell heavily, bruisingly, and rolled, tearing his clothes
and scratching his skin. He could hear the car on a parallel

course, confined to the road, gearing down on the sharp turns. It occurred to him that this son of a bitch was trying to kill him rather than arrest him. He turned away from the sound and broke out of the trees onto someone's property, leapt a fence, and bolted across the lawn, nearly falling into the pool. A dog came after him, a large one, and lights appeared in the upper windows of the house.

Steelegrave crossed a driveway and went haring down the street with the dog behind him. It caught up and tore a piece out of his chinos before abandoning the chase, content with its prize. Steelegrave turned a corner and ran another block before he paused to look around. There was a chorus of barking behind him as neighborhood watchdogs roused themselves, and lights were blinking on. He glanced at the street sign above him. Intersection of Longbow and Nightingale. Who was it that used to live on Nightingale? He ran on.

It was Lang Desmond.

Steelegrave had lost track of Lang Desmond years ago, after he quit *Love–Forty* and the show had been canceled. The cancellation was hard on Desmond, who had been enjoying a revival of his career. He had been pissed off, and Steelegrave, who didn't blame him, had avoided him out of a feeling of guilt. They had drifted apart by the time Steelegrave left to try his luck in Italy.

The turmoil behind him began to subside. He left the street and moved furtively along the sidewalk, looking back over his shoulder for car headlights. Desmond had lived around here somewhere, back in the old days. Once he had been honorary mayor of Sherman Oaks, a flamboyant star the locals took pride in. Steelegrave had been his guest many times, to hoist the wassail cup, as Lang called getting ripped. By now he might have moved away—you never saw him on the tube anymore. Hell, he might be dead.

He found the place almost by accident, recognizing the brick wall and the fountain at the center of the cobblestone driveway beyond the gates. The house was dark and the fountain was dry. There was a feeling of neglect.

Steelegrave pushed the button above an ancient voicebox. He remembered that used to set off a medley of chimes inside. He hoped it still did. Something came into his peripheral vision, tugging him around. Far down the street a set of headlights materialized, moving toward him slowly, the spotlight playing along the hedges and among the driveways. He groped in his pocket, but the gun was gone, lost somewhere on the hillside.

He kept his finger down on the button. Please, he said, please . . . He did not think he could run any farther.

Finally, "Who the hell is it?" in the unique gravelly voice of Lang Desmond, older now or distorted by the antique squawkbox.

"Hawke! Let me in!"

A pause. "Give the password."

Oh, shit. But that reminded him. "Bandini is the word for steer manure," he said, as had been their custom.

The car was getting close, the yellow rays reaching for him. "Come on!" he yelled.

The old gates began to part and he squeezed between them. Inside, he turned and used his weight to force the gates shut against their electronic will. It took his remaining strength, but slowly they closed and stayed that way, to his relief, their circuits confused. He leapt behind the protection of the wall an instant before the beam of the spot filtered through the gate to splash over the cobblestones. It swept around, exploring the recesses it could find, then continued on its way.

Steelegrave sat heavily on the ground and rested his head against his knees. Wiped out. There was one thing, though. He hadn't killed Marla.

17

By the time Cosgrove gave up and went home, it was nearly dawn. He didn't go to bed, knowing he wouldn't sleep—just sat listening to early-bird reports on the news station. He kept himself under control through an effort of will, refusing to surrender to rage or self-disgust. There were positive aspects to the failed chase, and he concentrated on those.

There was no doubt in his mind that he'd nearly taken Steelegrave. The man had been in his lights twice, only for seconds, but it was enough time to recognize the fair hair and the way he moved. He ran exactly like Steele did in *Fall Guy*. The clothes were different from what he remembered, that was all. He wished to hell he could have talked to Kalb and Grady. Had they even seen the bastard? But he could not let them know he was hanging around. Strickland would shit-can him for sure.

The radio had nothing new on the case. They rehashed Marla Monday's career and said that the suspect, her ex-husband, was still at large. The big story was the spreading fire licking at the shoulder of 101 in Malibu and nearing the San Diego freeway inland. No containment in sight. The Santa Ana wind was driving the flames before it and would until it abated.

Cosgrove took what satisfaction he could from the fact that he had followed his true instinct about the lady narc's tip and come closer to Steelegrave than anyone else. He had to believe it was destined, even ordained, to happen again, that he was programmed to avenge an innocent woman who had died fifteen years ago, crushed into a metal coffin by one of Hollywood's decadent elite. Therefore he would not be deterred by the edicts of that asshole Strickland. He was heeding a higher authority.

When the Shutterbug Camera Shop in Pacific Palisades opened at nine o'clock, Cosgrove was its first visitor of the day. He handed the five-by-seven glossy he had found in Steelegrave's apartment to a chubby young woman wearing thick glasses that magnified her blue eyes out of all proportion.

He was trying to find this young lady to offer her a job modeling, he said. She had sent in her photos—what a fine job the Shutterbug had done on them, incidentally—and his fool secretary had lost the manila envelope with the return address. So he had just gone ahead and done a little detective work and looked up the address of the photo shop on the back of the print. Maybe he ought to be a cop, ha-ha.

The girl looked down at the print and up again. Why, of course, she would be delighted to help. That was Erin Englund in the photo, a lovely person who had a dance studio in Venice, only she lived in Santa Monica somewhere. The Shutterbug seldom did that kind of work, leaving it to the Hollywood outfits that had a lot of show people for clients, but Erin liked their stuff better and always came to them for everything. What kind of modeling job? Well, said Cosgrove, they wanted to fly her out to Hawaii to do a layout for a big new hotel. A week's work, at least.

The girl sighed. Cosgrove thought he could read her fantasy, that she could be slim, poised, and beautiful, just like Erin Englund, and then they would ask her to go to Hawaii. . . . She just needed to get in shape, maybe do some jogging. She would begin tomorrow.

"Do you have an address on her?" asked Cosgrove, breaking the spell.

"I bet she's in the phone book," said the girl, and reached under the counter for a western edition. "She spells it E-n-g-l-u-n-d."

She was there, listed by address. It was as simple as that.

The house was on Wellesley Avenue near Montana in Santa Monica. It was small and hedged in by oleanders on one side and a palmetto thicket on the other to give it a cozy look. A weathered wooden fence covered with ivy stood in front. Both the house and the adjacent garage were painted slate gray and had been built to last.

Cosgrove rang the bell and knocked. No answer. He walked around to the garage and tried to lift the door. It wouldn't budge, was probably operated by a Genie. He circled the garage, squeezing himself between the oleanders and the building, and found a small, high window in the rear. Climbing on a discarded concrete block, he peered inside.

The green Thunderbird Steelegrave had escaped in was parked with the top down, as he remembered it. He returned to the house, more cautiously now, a hand on his revolver, though he was almost certain he would find no one there. The lock was a simple affair, not even a dead bolt. Cosgrove opened it with a shim and stepped inside.

He moved through the rooms as quickly as his ponderous bulk would allow, making certain he was alone. Once sure of that, he could search at leisure. He reached the kitchen last, checking out the utility room near the back door.

Something heavy hurled itself at the screen door leading to the backyard, rending the mesh. There had been no warning, not even a growl. Seeing the huge brown dog, Cosgrove recoiled, fumbling for his gun. The animal drew back to spring again, certain to break through this time. For an instant Cosgrove considered shooting it; then he turned and fled into the living room, slamming the door behind him. The dog exploded into the kitchen and began throwing itself repeatedly against the closed door.

Ignoring the animal as best he could, Cosgrove began to search the house. The bedroom yielded nothing out of the ordinary, a female wardrobe suggesting an athletic lifestyle, a variety of sports equipment. In a laundry hamper in the bathroom, however, he found the navy-blue polo

shirt and white slacks he had first seen Steelegrave wearing.
Which explained why the man he had caught in his headlights was wearing something else. Carrying the clothes,
he moved to the living room.

A car turned into the driveway, startling him. Through
the window he saw the girl in the photo get out, dressed in
leotards and carrying a canvas bag. Cosgrove would have
preferred to confront her later, on his own terms. Here, he
felt caught like a thief. He threw the shirt and slacks on
the couch.

She stood in the doorway and looked at him, poised to
bolt if he moved toward her. "Who are you and what are
you doing in my house?" There was more outrage than
fear in her voice.

Cosgrove reached for his badge. "I'm from the West Los
Angeles Police Station. My name is Cosgrove."

"That doesn't give you the right to break into my house!"

"Miss Englund, it does if you have Richard Steelegrave's
car in your garage and I have probable cause to believe he
could be here. Please come in."

She stepped inside, leaving the door open, concealing
her surprise as best as she could behind a neutral expression.

"I found evidence that he changed clothes here," Cosgrove
said. "It's a crime to harbor a fugitive."

"I didn't know he was a fugitive when he came here. I
just heard it on the radio."

"When did he come?"

"About seven o'clock last night."

"What did he want?"

"He wanted to leave his car and his dog." She started
toward the kitchen. At the sound of her voice, Junkyard
had begun throwing himself even more violently against
the door.

"Don't open the door!" cried Cosgrove, alarmed. "That
dog jumped right through the screen."

The girl shrugged. "All right, Junkyard, settle down!"
she called.

When the dog subsided, she turned to Cosgrove. "It
sounds as if you owe me a screen door."

"You don't seem to understand that you're in trouble."

"Shall I call a lawyer?"

"Miss Englund, I don't want to arrest you. I'd like to take your word about not knowing that Steelegrave was wanted. But you're going to have to be entirely truthful with me."

She shook her head. "I don't want to say anything. Richard and I were . . . are . . . close."

Cosgrove sighed. "I can appreciate loyalty, but in this case it's misguided."

"Richard wouldn't kill anyone. I know that."

"Up until now, the evidence indicates otherwise."

"I begged him to give himself up, but he wouldn't, and it's not for me to help anyone against him."

Cosgrove's eyes suddenly crinkled in the friendliest way and he gestured with his hand. "Please sit down and let me explain something to you."

Erin put aside her bag and sat warily on the arm of her couch. Cosgrove tried to keep his eyes off her splendid legs. "Miss Englund, you have, as I'm sure you know, every right to remain silent. I wouldn't want to coerce you if I could. But if you say nothing, I'll have to hold you as a material witness. Then you can consult with an attorney, but of course you'll be under arrest."

She shrugged helplessly. "I don't know where he is anyway. I couldn't help you if I wanted to."

"Let me be the judge of that, but first I want to tell you something. As a fugitive and a murder suspect, Steelegrave is assumed to be armed and dangerous. Maximum force will be used to apprehend him." He paused, letting it sink in, seeing the concern in her eyes. "Now, let me tell you something else, confidentially and off the record.

"There is a new breed of Los Angeles policeman on the streets nowadays. This new officer, male or female, lacks proper training and experience. The police academy is graduating illiterates and even felons because we've got a civilian commission that says you can't turn down certain minority applicants. These people hit the streets green. They're insecure and trigger-happy. Believe me, I don't enjoy telling you this. Police work has been my life, and this situation makes me ashamed."

Erin stared at him, wide-eyed. "And you expect me to help people like that find Richard?"

Cosgrove pulled up the footstool Richard liked to prop his feet on and sat down. He looked up at her with boundless sincerity. "No. I expect you to help *me* find him—before they do. I can bring him in without violence. I want him in protective custody so we can get this thing straightened out. If he's innocent, it will become apparent. If he keeps running, some nut might very well shoot him."

Erin blinked back the moisture in her eyes. "Oh God, it's true! The one who came to arrest him shot at him!"

Cosgrove nodded, unperturbed. "Help me and you can be sure he'll be safe. I'll make that a promise. And of course, I won't have to bring you in."

"But what can I tell you? I don't know where he went."

"How did he leave? Not on foot, I imagine."

She hesitated. "I gave him my car. That's a rental I just picked up out there."

"What kind of car? Save me calling Sacramento."

"A Fiat convertible. Red."

Cosgrove took out a notepad and pen. "Year and license number?"

She told him.

"Where would he go?"

"I've already said I don't know."

"He must have friends, Miss Englund. You said you were close to him. Weren't there people you went out with? Had dinner or played cards with?"

"Not often. Sometimes we had a drink with one of his clients from the tennis club where he worked. The Malibu Tennis Club."

"Who were they?"

"The Colemans, Heidi and Tom. Phil Riley. They were casual acquaintances. He would never impose on them."

Cosgrove made a note of the names. "He had no close friends at all? No pals?"

Erin smiled wryly. "Maybe a bartender or two. No, no one I can think of. Richard is kind of a loner."

"A celebrity without friends?"

"Former celebrity."

"How about an actor named Lang Desmond?"

"That was someone he worked with years ago. I don't think he's seen him since."

Cosgrove closed his notepad and put it away. "Is that your working costume, Miss Englund?" He permitted himself a long look at her legs to accompany his question.

"Yes. I have a dance studio. I came home because I'm too upset to work today."

"After you heard the news."

"Yes."

Cosgrove heaved himself to his feet. He dug a card out of his pocket and jotted a number on it. "I want to leave this with you. In case Richard gets in touch. Don't use the number at the station, just the one I wrote down. You can leave a message on the machine if I'm out. Will you call me?"

"I'm not sure."

Cosgrove looked down at her and smiled—a tight smile because his teeth were bad, but avuncular and totally reassuring. "I understand, but I want you to consider carefully. I think you're a loyal, decent person, and I don't believe Richard is a criminal. They've put me in charge of his case and I'm giving it my complete attention. I only want to bring him in peacefully, clear everything up. But remember what I said. There are a lot of overeager, undertrained cops out there. If they get to him first, or if he runs . . ." He shrugged his massive shoulders.

Erin put her face down into her hands. "Oh, please don't let him be hurt," she said just above a whisper, more as a general supplication than to Cosgrove.

He rested his big hand lightly on her shoulder. "I'll do everything I can. . . ."

Lang Desmond had changed in the same way his house had. Everything was in the same place, only older now. His hair had gone snow white, but he still wore it parted near the middle and smoothed back like a thirties matinee idol. The sudden smile still flashed boyishly across his creased, tanned features, revealing teeth as white and even as ever. He wore a monogrammed dressing gown over pajamas with a silk scarf knotted at the neck, his perennial lounging outfit, and smoked his customary unfiltered Lucky. Steelegrave knew he had to be well over seventy.

They had finished a large breakfast of papaya, *huevos rancheros*, and Mexican beer served by Conchita, an ancient crone who had kept house for Desmond throughout the half-century of his career. Steelegrave was amazed to find her alive and spry, eyes twinkling and toothless mouth agape with the thrill of seeing him again. He had always been a favorite of hers.

He lounged back in the terrycloth robe Desmond had lent him and nearly fell asleep in his chair. It was in reaction to his ordeal, he guessed, for he had slept heavily for six hours and might have slumbered indefinitely if Desmond hadn't bullied him out of bed. He had showered, sitting on the marble bench in the old-fashioned stall, letting the hot water beat down on him while he fell asleep again. Finally he had made it downstairs, where he had to tell the whole story to Desmond over breakfast, while the older man badgered him for details, treating it all as some kind of high adventure.

"It's right out of *Fall Guy*, Rick!" Desmond slapped the table, jarring Steelegrave back into focus. "Like someone followed the script! Marla dead, for real this time, and you on the run, framed for her murder. I mean, what a hell of a coincidence."

"Yeah." Steelegrave looked at him blearily.

". . . And you come to me, your old buddy, who hides you from the cops. . . . Can you believe this?"

Steelegrave didn't reply, his eyelids drooping.

"We need a Bloody Mary," said Desmond. He pulled a golden whistle on a chain from under his scarf and blew on it. No sound emerged but Conchita came shuffling in from the kitchen.

"Dog whistle," explained Desmond. "Only thing she can hear at a distance. She must be about a hundred and seven now." He raised his voice almost to a shout. "Conchita, you desiccated old hag, bring us *dos* Bloody Marys! *Rápido!*" She started out, but he stopped her. "Conchita! You remember Señor Hawke? My *gran amigo* and hero of the American *televisión*?"

Her head bobbed violently, bright old eyes alive with excitement.

"Well, he is wanted by the police and I am hiding him.

You are telling no one—*nadie*—or I am going to jail and no longer paying your salary!"

Nodding and cackling, she pushed out through the pantry door.

Desmond sighed and made a gesture that took in the old house in its state of genteel neglect. The faded pictures on the wall that depicted his past went undusted and a ceiling fan whickered overhead, barely displacing the overheated air. "God, how I miss the old days! I've had this place since 1935, when I was making two-reelers for Paramount. Had maybe a platoon of servants, including Conchita. Used to have a hundred people partying on the patio and around the pool, whole place lit up with torches, fountains that spouted champagne. I had a Duesenberg I raced against Gary Cooper's down Sunset Boulevard . . . planes I flew myself from a hangar I owned not five miles from here. Now there's no one in the pool but frogs. Shit. . . ."

Steelegrave nodded, having heard it all before. Somehow Desmond's past glories seemed trivial to him today.

"I made millions, Rick. Several. Where it went, not even the fucking Shadow knows. Dames. Oceans of booze. Wives with kids I could claim, others I couldn't. I spent like there was no tomorrow. Well . . . there's only Conchita left now. A relic of the past."

The Bloody Marys arrived, delivered somewhat unsteadily by Conchita. Steelegrave lifted his glass and toasted, "To the old days." The drink was surprisingly good.

"To yesterday." Desmond drained half his glass. He lit another cigarette and wheezed, his shoulders lifting. He patted his chest. "A little emphysema. No sweat, you can go on forever with it."

"Long life." Steelegrave drank again.

Desmond put aside his Bloody Mary and leaned across the table. "Listen, Rick, what I was just talking about was make-believe. Bullshit. Ephemeral. Here today and gone tomorrow. You're living right now what we used to fake on screen. This is the real thing, sport, a unique opportunity! We've got to make the most of it!" He was as eager as the Hardy Boys.

Steelegrave slammed down his glass, slopping the red drink over his hand. "Cut it out, Lang! You're as bad as the Nazi. Making it a game. You read the paper this morning. The lab tests show the blood on the knife was Marla's. I'm in a box!"

Desmond reached down and snatched up a section of the L.A. *Times* that lay scattered at his feet. "You're front page for the first time in twenty years, Rick! You'd have made the headline if it wasn't for the fucking fire! Not a bad picture, either." He tossed the pages across the table. "Once we solve this mess, all you'll need is a good agent."

Steelegrave blinked at the older man. "We?"

"Hawke and Travers, sport."

"That was in the *movies*, Lang! Now I need a lawyer, not an agent."

"The actor living his picture! That's what you're doing, don't you see? You'll be proved innocent just like in *Fall Guy*. Think what the media'll do with that!"

Steelegrave shook his head, thinking that Desmond might be getting senile. He looked down at the newspaper lying over his plate. The column on him was printed under an old studio still with the caption: "FORMER STAR OBJECT OF WIDESPREAD MANHUNT." It sketched his career up to the manslaughter conviction that ended it, and went on to describe his escape from the arresting officer when confronted with the evidence of his alleged deed. Under a glamour shot of him and Marla together was a long tribute to her career and a rather lurid description of her murder. He did not finish reading the coroner's detailed conclusions. Then there was a photo of the kind of young stud currently referred to as a "hunk," with brooding eyes and dark ringlets hanging down to his shoulders. The caption read: "RANCE EVANS. LAST TO SEE HER ALIVE." He had come forward to volunteer that he was her lover and had been with her on Sunday night.

"Who is this Evans?" Steelegrave asked.

"Her latest. She was getting to like them young."

"Maybe he killed her."

"No way. She got him a part in *Star-crossed*. Shoved him down Braski's throat. Without her he'll be back hustling chicken hawks on the Strip." He finished his drink and raised the whistle to his lips. Conchita answered the silent summons, carrying two more Bloody Marys.

"What do you know about *Star-crossed*, Rick?"

Steelegrave shrugged. "What everybody else knows—that it was going to be Marla's next picture. I don't read the trades anymore."

"You knew our old friend Gil LaFarge adapted the script from his own novel and that he's producing and directing too?"

"I think I read that someplace."

"Well, did you know that he wrote the leading part for the love of his life, Neva Morgann? It was going to be her big break—the perfect part for her."

"I read Marla replaced somebody."

"Marla was obsessed with playing Jana ever since she read the book. She thought she *was* Jana, a kid who came out of nowhere to grab the world by the tail. She acted like it was her biography, so who else could play the lead? She waltzed in and stole the part."

"How could she do that with LaFarge producing?"

"Because the money man is Mel Braski and Marla got to him. Gil thought he had a good deal with Braski. He even got final cut in writing, but he didn't nail down casting because they'd all agreed from the beginning that Neva had the part of Jana."

"Who's Braski, anyway?"

"He's just an individual. A financier with a couple of associates. Forms a different company for every picture— 'Star-crossed Productions,' in this case. He got up the money and that gives him the power. It's often done that way nowadays, sport." Lang chain-lit a fresh cigarette.

"Well, when he gave Gil the word, LaFarge kinda went to pieces. Neva's twenty-three years old, a comer if I ever saw one, a real talent. She's perfect for *Star-crossed*, and that picture could take her all the way. Gil's crazy about her, and vice versa, I guess. Anyway, suddenly he saw it all going down the tubes—his picture, Neva's big chance, everything. Marla was still gorgeous, but much too old for Jana. She'd have blown it for everyone."

"Couldn't this Braski see that?"

"You know how much imagination the money men have. They just see dollars, and what Braski saw was one of the biggest names in the business offering herself to him. In more ways than one. She was all over him like a wet dream. I can hardly blame him. She was a great lay . . ." Desmond broke off, embarrassed.

Steelegrave stared at him. "You too?" he asked finally.

The old man actually reddened. "Easy, sport. Not when you were married to her—or even living with her."

"When?"

"Well, when we were making *Fall Guy*. It was no big thing . . . I wasn't the only one."

"Who else?"

"Well, I think maybe Gil LaFarge."

"How about Lars Vincent and George Barth? And maybe the crew?"

"No, no, Rick. Nothing like that."

"So it was just you and me and Gil. Well, I guess that's okay, then."

"Aw, come on, Rick . . . it was a hundred years ago."

Steelegrave sighed. Desmond was right. What the hell did it matter now? "How come you know all about this picture, Lang?"

"Because I've got a featured part in it. My comeback after a long absence from stage and screen, as they say. I almost lost it, but I got it back."

"Congratulations. What do you mean you almost lost it?"

"Marla threw me off the picture. Exactly one week ago."

At MGM Lang Desmond gave his name to the gate guard, an old-timer, and received a broad smile. "Back with us for a while, Mr. Desmond?"

"Right you are." Lang smiled back, wishing he could remember the old guy's name. He used to make a specialty of that.

He followed the blue line past the sound stages to the suite of offices Mel Braski had taken for the duration of *Star-crossed*. They were housed in twin bungalows and Lang parked his old Caddy in the first reserved slot he found empty.

He was attending the meeting with more curiosity than trepidation, though Gil's invitation had been abrupt and mysterious. Why would a mere featured player be summoned to Braski's office for an executive session? he wondered. He got out of the car, shrugging off his misgivings, and walked into the building.

As always, Lang had dressed with care. He wore a blazer with a crest he had designed himself, his ever-present silk scarf, and cream-colored flannel slacks. He earned the same look from the secretary behind the reception desk that women had been giving him for over fifty years.

"Go right in, Mr. Desmond," she smiled after a murmured consultation with her phone.

The instant he entered Braski's office he knew something was very wrong. Mel Braski sat scowling behind his desk, a beefy man with a heavy jaw and an uncombable thatch of gray-black hair. He looked like the truck driver he had been when he started out with a single rig to build the third-biggest truck fleet in America. He got out in time, too, just before the OPEC fuel-price hikes nearly crippled the industry. In recent years he had financed films, sometimes in association with others, and hadn't had a loser yet. Lang had met him only once before.

"Who died? Anyone I know?" Lang asked, stretching his smile to include everyone.

Neva Morgann sat alone on a leather couch placed against the paneled wall. She was lovely from any angle, without being Hollywood pretty. Her hazel eyes, solemn now, were wide-set beneath unplucked brows and her shoulder-length auburn hair framed a face that was strong without being indelicate, a photographer's dream. Her lips were full and could have been petulant, but that was never her attitude unless the script called for it. Then she could be anything she had to be. In that one sense, she was like Marla Monday.

Lang winked at her. Just the trace of a smile touched her lips, for she liked him, found him a charming old rogue and an engaging liar.

"Sit down, Lang," said Gil LaFarge, who had opened the door for him. "This concerns you, too, which is why I asked you to come. Of course, there's nothing you can do about it, but you've got a right to be here."

Puzzled, Lang sat on the couch next to Neva. He took out a pack of Luckies and shook one out.

"Oh, not in a closed office, Lang, please," said Marla, who sat in a leather armchair next to Mel Braski's desk. Of them all, only she seemed at ease. She was dressed almost primly, with a white blouse peeking out of a tailored suit jacket, very much the businesswoman. Lang marveled again at her ability to slip into any role. He put the smoke between his lips but didn't light it.

"My associate, Phil Parkhurst," said Braski shortly, nodding at a tall, pale man in a loose-fitting double-breasted suit who sat on the edge of his desk. He had an eastern look, out of place in a city full of palm trees.

"All right to go on now?" asked Braski with an edge of sarcasm.

Gil LaFarge strode to the center of the room and stood there with his fists thrust deeply in his trouser pockets. "You're ruining my picture," he said to Braski. "And people along with it. Shitting on five years it's taken to bring *Star-crossed* to the screen." He looked drawn and harried, his thin, sandy hair sticking up in wispy disarray. Once, when he was younger, he'd looked like a romantic's idea of an American artist exiled to the Left Bank. The years and the intensity of his talent had worn him down.

"Let me rebut that point for point," said Braski. "First, it's not your picture if I'm financing, because it's like I bought the biggest piece of it. I don't like to put it that way, but you couldn't get any of the majors to make it, so you're stuck with me. Second, I'm not ruining *your* picture, I'm saving it. I find a lot of the time you artistic types gotta be saved from yourselves. Third, I'm not out to hurt people. Neva Morgann's a kid with a lot of talent and I'm sure she coulda given us a great performance, and she'll get another chance. Lang Desmond's been around about a hundred years and you can't hurt a legend." He smiled at Lang. "Right?"

Lang kept his own smile in place with an effort. He liked the part about being a legend and he'd nearly agreed before he grasped the import of the words.

Braski went on. "I just seen a chance to make a big picture with a major star and I'm taking it. Miss Monday has agreed to play Jana and I want her to do it. We need her name and, of course, her great talent. Hugh Magnus isn't big enough yet to carry the picture." Magnus, the leading man, was a TV sensation making his first feature.

Gil turned to Lang. "That's why I asked you here, Lang. You're off the picture. I just wanted these pricks to have to tell you themselves."

"It was my idea, Lang," Marla put in. "You're too old for the part."

"You know I can play sixty with a dye job, honey," Lang said lightly. He didn't want to beg. "I'm playing Jana's old sugar daddy, after all."

"I want to go with a different concept for John Cornish. More contemporary. I want him younger and more of a villain. So Jana is justified in doing him in."

"I can play heavy. Christ, I did about a hundred heavies when I was finished with leads."

"You're a nice old fellow, Lang. I'm sorry. I know what's right for me."

Lang stared at her. So much for a relationship that went back more than twenty years. He lit the cigarette he held between his teeth. Fuck Marla.

Gil said to Braski, in measured tones as if speaking to a child, "Jana is twenty when the picture opens, twenty-five tops. I'd hate to be hanging since Marla turned forty. I know because I wrote her her first picture. If you're so hot for talent and fame, why don't you get Bette Davis?"

"Watch yourself, Gil," said Marla.

"It's not that big a problem, LaFarge," said Braski. "They used Audrey Hepburn in that picture from Sidney Sheldon's book, playing a girl half her age. Marla don't look her age any more than Hepburn."

"But twenty-five years old, for God's sake?"

"Why do you keep fighting, Gil?" said Marla. "It's all decided. I'm being reasonable price-wise because I really want this one. You wrote a wonderful book and a good screenplay. Neva seems very sweet and I'm sure she's capable but you need a name to sell this picture. Hugh Mungus, or whatever he's called, isn't going to do it."

"I don't want your name! I want my picture back, with my concept and my cast!"

Braski sighed. "My associate, Mr. Parkhurst here, he's the marketing expert. Maybe he can explain."

Parkhurst cleared his throat and straightened up. "It's really all computerized, the way we evaluate the markets these days. Practically a matter of feeding the robot names and programming him to answer. Such and such a star, so many tickets sold—that sort of thing. If you want a detailed report on how we decide—"

"Shit no," Braski stopped him. "They get the drift. Look, we're just making a bigger picture now, more expensive with Marla in it, but maybe fifty times more salable."

"More expensive, yes," said LaFarge bitterly. "It'll probably cost an extra million just to light her so she'll look anywhere under thirty-five."

Marla's look should have incinerated him where he stood, but her voice was cold. "That's enough, Gil. You'll learn to live with it or you can shop your work of art around and try to raise the fifteen million Mel pledged you somewhere else. End of discussion."

"I'm truly sick and tired of all this." Neva Morgann spoke for the first time from the couch. "Gil, either do the picture with them or we'll start all over and try to raise financing elsewhere. I don't know how hard that will be, so I want you to make up your mind without thinking about me. I'll be all right, believe me. Just don't beg these people."

"Spoken like a trouper," Marla smiled.

Neva rose and walked over to stand in front of her, next to Gil LaFarge. "I've admired you on screen since I was a kid, Miss Monday, which is a real tribute to your acting. That's because I don't like you one damn bit in person. Whatever happens to me in this business, I surely hope I'll never get to be like you." She turned to LaFarge, touched his arm lightly. "Do what you think best, darling. I'll wait for you outside." Then she strode out of the office without looking back.

Marla applauded lightly. "I'll watch for her on the *Amateur Hour*."

Lang thought he saw Gil start to reach for her neck and then check himself. "You sorry bitch," he said tightly. "Keep your mind on your lines if you can. When you're not thinking, a giant spot might drop on you, or a piece of the set . . . or maybe I'll just direct you into oblivion!"

Marla laughed at him. "You couldn't do that if you tried, and you won't try. This is your masterpiece, your baby. And I _am_ Jana, you know. I've lived her life!"

"She always fantasized her parts," said Steelegrave.

"Maybe not. Jana comes out of the sewer to be a star. So did Marla."

"There seem to be a few things she didn't tell me."

"A Portagee fisherman took her off the streets in San Diego when she was seventeen."

"She told me she married a fisherman who was lost overboard. Eric's father."

" 'Lost' is the delicate way to put it. Anyway, he didn't marry her, just knocked her up. He used to come home drunk and burn his initials all over her ass with a cigarette about once a week. Took a lot of plastic surgery to get rid of the scars, she told me.

"Well, one day she contrived to meet one of the guys on his boat who didn't like him too much. Used her charm on him, as you can imagine. After some fun and games, she promised him that they could always be together if only old Felipe or Julio or whatever was no longer around. And presto! He's 'lost' at sea. Right after that she left town, came to Hollywood with the kid, and picked new names for both of them."

Steelegrave shook his head. He had never really known her, it seemed.

"Don't feel bad," said Desmond. "She didn't want you to know her sordid past because she wanted you to marry her. I didn't matter. She could talk to me, because we had something in common. I wasn't a preppie, you know. I had to hustle. Lifeguard in summer, ski bum in winter. Sounds plush, but I starved a lot. I got into pictures when a carload of Hollywood hotshots ran down my motorcycle and broke both my legs. They put me in movies because they didn't want to get sued."

Steelegrave thought he remembered another version, but then, Lang was always inventive. "So now that she's dead, you'll go on with the picture as if nothing happened?"

"Sure. Braski's a practical man. Even pressured the coroner to request an immediate autopsy so she can be buried today. He already lost two days of shooting. Time is money."

"You and Neva Morgann both back on the picture?"

"Sure."

"What if it turns out Gil killed her? He had the most reason, according to you."

"I like Gil and I need this picture. But I want you clear and I'll do anything I can to help. Fact is, I've got a couple of ideas. Hell, like I said, it's Hawke and Travers, sport."

18

A pall of smoke from the multiple fires burning out of control around Los Angeles polluted the atmosphere and darkened the skies so recently blown clean by the Santa Ana winds. Staring out of his office window, Fletcher Strickland took it as an ominous sign. All of his available units were already involved in traffic control around the Mulholland area where the flames were threatening to jump the freeway.

He had slept little the night before, having asked to be kept plugged in on the Marla Monday murder. His wife had stayed up with him, a soothing and reassuring presence. She was a Vassar graduate and a practicing psychologist, a handsome woman with amber eyes and skin the color of coffee ice cream, little altered by eighteen years of marriage and two children. Strickland had remained in awe of her, never really certain why she had married him in the first place. He had been a rookie cop then, meagerly educated and with an apparently limited future.

Just yesterday, it seemed, he and his partner had spotted the tan Chevy two-door weaving erratically down Fairfax Avenue near Wilshire. It was just after midnight and they were winding up their tour of duty, heading for the station. They U-turned and closed in on the car, their headlight beams picking up shadows of a struggle going on inside. His partner, Gilman, who was driving, goosed his siren and hit the red light.

The car speeded up for a couple of blocks, but someone must have yanked at the wheel, for it yawed suddenly to the right and jumped a curb into a Mobil station, narrowly missing the gas tanks. The Chevy ran over a metal trashcan, dragging it along in a shower of sparks, and plowed into a cast-iron pillar supporting the Mobil sign.

Two figures spilled out of the wreck and took off with Gilman behind them, gun in hand. Strickland grabbed his baton and ran to the car. A third man was trying to extricate himself from the back of the two-door. Strickland caught him by his thatch of black hair, threw him on the ground, and put a foot on his neck. "Stay right down there, boy," he cautioned.

The girl who remained inside was half naked and sobbing. She managed to tell him that three Latinos had swarmed into her car at a stoplight and tried to rape her alternately while one drove. She had fought them off, but they had been trying to beat her unconscious when the cruiser intervened.

Though still a novice policeman, Strickland was well inured to violent crime. He had seen it on the streets of his childhood and avoided its temptation, first in the ring and then by joining the police force. Somehow the sight of this lovely girl in fear and pain triggered a disproportionate rage in him, a desire to vent on one individual the accumulation of his ire against a cruel, uncaring society. He looked at the kid lying on the ground with the white skull and crossbones on his black leather jacket and wanted to stomp on the back of his head. Instead he put the cuffs on extra tight, knowing the hands would quickly go numb, then ache excruciatingly when the steel was removed and the blood flowed through them again.

Afterward he kept in touch with the girl, Laura, shyly at first, then with more confidence as she encouraged him. He married her not quite believing his luck, then or today. Even his sons, teenagers now, were straight kids, incredible considering what he saw in the streets and schools. In fact, they were much impressed by their father, having found no one they could admire more. Had he only known it, Laura felt exactly the same way.

The light on his private line blinked and Strickland answered with his name.

"Willy Danforth, Cap'n. I thought I better walk this one right around Al Nash and call you direct."

"Well, go ahead."

"Cap'n, you did furlough ol' Cos, didn't you? Put him on leave of absence?"

"I did."

"Well, now, you know Grady and Kalb found that little Fiat car in the bushes after all that ruckus around the Monday place last night. I checked out the plates and found it belongs to a little lady lives right here in Santa Monica. Turns out she's Steelegrave's honest-to-God girlfriend. Purty thing. Made my chin all spitty just lookin' at her."

Strickland felt a tug of excitement. "Good work, Willy! She talk to you?"

"Oh, yeah. Claims he come by and left his car and dog last night before she heard the news. Lent him her Fiat without askin' any questions, she says, and she's got no idea where he'd go."

"Balls."

"But that ain't why I'm callin' you personal, Cap'n. This Erin Englund, she was surprised to see me on account of another cop come callin' on her maybe an hour before I got there. She didn't get his name, but he was a big, heavyset dude with orange hair and a limp."

"Goddammit! How did he find her before we did?"

"Beats me. She couldn't understand why we sent two people around, one right after the other, to ask the same questions. Makes us look kinda dumb when you think about it.

"Well, I laughed it off, sayin' we got ourselves double-booked or some crap like that. Said I wanted to tell her we had her car. We can't really bring her in or nothin'. She claims she just heard the news before Cos come by and she's still in shock."

Strickland felt a patch of moisture spreading between his shoulder blades. His mind raced furiously.

"Anyway," Danforth was saying, "that's why I circumcised Al Nash and called you direct. Knowin' you and Cos go way back, and all."

"I think it's 'circumvented,' Willy," said Strickland, his mind elsewhere. He gripped the phone tightly, marshaling his thoughts. "Willy," he asked finally, "who's riding with you?"

"Detective Gutierrez." He pronounced it "Gooty-aries."

"Now, listen to me, Willy. I think Cosgrove's flipping out and we got a loose cannon on deck. I don't want to go public with this, just want you to find him and bring him to me. Gutierrez can follow up on this Erin Englund and any other witnesses. You've got to know better than anyone, even me, where Cosgrove hangs out nowadays. So go find him, Willy."

After he hung up, Strickland went into his bathroom and splashed cold water over his head. He wiped his face and hands meticulously and went back to his desk. What did he know about Cosgrove, anyway, after all the years since they had met in Hollywood division? Just what the man had told him, that was all. When he picked up the phone again, he was very angry. "I want all the records from downtown on Detective Ryan Cosgrove," he said into the receiver. "I want them now."

The huge condominium at the corner of Doheny Drive and Burton Way had all the amenities of Southern California living—saunas, gyms, pools, and tennis courts. It was a high-security building, with a uniformed guard and a receptionist in the lobby twenty-four hours a day. Even so, a party seeking admittance had to dial the desired apartment from the outside and the resident had then to advise the guard by way of the receptionist before entry was permitted. Once inside, the visitor moved soundlessly over thick wall-to-wall carpeting that covered every inch of floor space including elevators and lavatories.

Neva Morgann hated the place. Her apartment was on the floor below the penthouse suites, facing west. It was a one-bedroom affair, starkly modern with a miniature terrace. She leased the apartment from its owner and thought of it merely as a place to sleep and hang her clothes. Aside from a bed, a bureau, and a dinette table, she had not even bothered to furnish the unit, such was her dislike for condo living. She'd had every intention of moving long since, but somehow she had always managed to put it off. That was because moving meant marrying Gil LaFarge, or so she had promised him.

Gil was twice her age and somewhat manic-depressive, a driven talent given to bouts of uncontrollable enthusiasm alternating with periods of darkest despair. She put up with his wildly fluctuating, occasionally dangerous moods not only because he was brilliant and she could learn from him but also because he had the touching, irresistible quality of really needing her. At times she felt older and stronger than he, and she wryly guessed that she was subject to a mother instinct she would not have expected to find lurking within her. As she saw it, the sum total of her emotional feelings for him amounted to love. That he loved her in return was something that she could not doubt.

But lately she had found herself waffling, making excuses in order to postpone the final commitment. She was so young and there was so much to do! She wanted to succeed in films and then graduate to theater, which she thought of as a total dedication. What would be left for Gil with his endless needs and demands? If only his brilliance and energy were blended with strength and self-dependence! What a pity you couldn't construct your lover out of component parts you chose yourself—the mind of this one, the heart of that, the phallus of yet another. Have your mate tailor-made instead of off the rack. She chuckled at the idea. It was a fantasy that might have a viable future someday.

She and Gil didn't live together. That was part of the arrangement, that each had space and independence to function in separate careers until they were married. They did, however, spend several nights a week together, and Sunday night was to have been one of them. Gil had called to cancel, saying he was too depressed to come over. Shooting was set to start the following morning on *Starcrossed*, with Marla in place of Neva. The film was going to be a painful ordeal for him. He simply wanted to stay home and go to bed early. Familiar with his moods, she did not press him. She felt she could use some time alone with her thoughts, too. Losing the part of Jana had left her stunned and lethargic.

He called her a little after ten the following morning. "She's dead," he said. "The Dragon Lady's dead."

Neva was confused. She supposed he meant Marla, but she didn't understand whether he was speaking literally or whether he had managed somehow to get her off the picture.

"What I mean is that someone cut her throat." He spoke in a studiously even tone, as if afraid he would shout at the sky if he lost control. She sensed the exultation behind his words. "She didn't show up on location, so I sent someone to find her. The place was swarming with cops. Fritz had a hell of a time finding out what happened. But when he said he was production manager on her picture, they told him. I don't know if it's on the news yet."

"My God!"

"I'm coming over." He hung up.

Gil arrived an hour later, while she was searching the TV channels. He was riding a manic high, face flushed and eyes glittery, not an unfamiliar state for him but disturbing under the circumstances. He banged the bottle of chilled wine he had brought down on the dinette and caught her by the shoulders.

"The unnatural bitch is dead," he said between his teeth, still holding himself in check. "You're Jana, just as you've always been. I want you, Jana. Now." She could feel his excitement hard against her.

"No, Gil . . ." That he had hated Marla, she could understand. But this tasteless celebration of a grisly murder was repugnant to her.

He held her tight, pressing against her, and she was surprised again by the strength in the thin, frail-looking man. "Don't deny us, my sweet. Let's savor this moment . . . be bonded together as we come back to life! You and I and Jana . . . inseparable." He brought his mouth down on hers, hard and insistent, far removed from the tender lover who had endeared himself to her.

She wanted to shove him away but she hesitated and the chance escaped her. Abruptly she was caught up in his wiry arms, carried into the next room, and tumbled onto the big bed.

He made love to her selfishly, without concern for her feelings. Usually so attuned to her subtlest shift of mood, he seemed suddenly indifferent to her lack of response, striving only for himself. She submitted, most disgusted with herself when she began unwillingly to share some of his excitement. But the emotion lapsed quickly when she remembered that the occasion for this lovemaking was someone's death. She wanted to tell him that he was spoiling everything, doing the opposite of what he intended, but some instinct cautioned her to play the detached observer instead. She was learning about Gil.

Finally he sprang out of bed and brought the wine with two long-stemmed glasses. He uncorked the bottle and poured. "To the renaissance of *Star-crossed* and the rebirth of Jana."

She drank the wine because she needed it, without acknowledging the toast.

Gil lay down next to her. "I've already talked to Braski. It took him maybe five minutes to get over the shock—a very pragmatic man, Mr. Braski. I pointed out that we don't have to lose more than two shooting days if we get Marla into the ground right away, and I suggested he ask his good friend the coroner to do his autopsy or whatever immediately so she can be buried tomorrow. Then we pay our obligatory respects with the usual pomp and go on with the show." He rolled onto his back and rubbed the base of the cool glass against his sweaty forehead. " 'That don't hardly give me time to gather a crowd,' " he mimicked Braski, then giggled. "I convinced the slob a couple of media announcements would take care of that if he got on it right away—"

"You knew her a long time, didn't you?" Neva interrupted. She didn't want to hear any more about the callous nature of the arrangements.

"I knew her before you were born. I wrote her first picture, *Fall Guy*. Rick Steele starred in it. She married him and then dumped him when he got in trouble. She had no time for losers."

"Was she always the same? Tough and selfish?"

"Always. She went through people's lives like a wreck-ing crew."

Finally she asked, "Who do they think killed her, Gil?"

"They don't know. A cop told Fritz there was no robbery."

"Who do *you* think did?"

"Someone who hated her, baby. Someone who really hated her."

After he left, a feeling of horror began to steal over her. She tried to immerse herself in the script of *Star-crossed*, though she was already letter perfect. It was no use; the pages blurred before her eyes. She could not stem the dark, nasty runnels of suspicion that were seeping into her consciousness.

Who had more to gain by Marla's death than Gil? Unsta-ble and tempestuous as he was, had he finally put himself completely beyond the pale and committed murder? He might well convince himself that he had a justifiable, even lofty motive. To save her and *Star-crossed*, not to mention himself. She could imagine him worrying the idea like one of his scripts, polishing and rationalizing it until murder became some sort of public service.

The story burst on TV around noon, in shocking detail but with no mention of a suspect. Nothing seemed to have been stolen, so robbery was ruled out as a motive. Neva spent the afternoon and evening miserably, watching the news, veering between refusal to believe the worst of Gil and a persistent, growing conviction that he was capable of it. At least the stranger who had burst in on her this morning was.

A ten-o'clock late-news bulletin finally released her. An ex-husband of Marla's, the actor Gil mentioned, had re-sisted arrest and fled after a knife thought to be the murder weapon was found in his home. Neva felt an overwhelming, guilty relief. Whatever else he was, temperamental genius or borderline lunatic, Gil was no killer. Which meant that murder had not been committed in her name. She went to bed and thanked God in prayer for the first time since she was a little girl. Then she slept dreamlessly for ten hours.

The funeral was scheduled for three o'clock and Gil was coming to pick her up. With unparalleled hypocrisy, he had agreed to be a pallbearer. She had nearly refused to go, repelled by the whole scenario. The spectacle of Marla Monday being buried with unseemly haste surrounded by cynical mourners did not appeal to her. She remembered the magic the woman could weave on screen, all the hours of rapt, wide-eyed pleasure she had given a stagestruck kid. Even if she was a rotten human being who had nearly cost her the opportunity of a lifetime, Neva could take no satisfaction in her death or in the Hollywood rites that would accompany it. At the same time she knew that her absence would be misinterpreted as spite and used against her by a horde of columnists, making it a gesture she could not afford. So once more she would accommodate.

Neva loathed the glitzy, fast-lane life of the film community as much as she loved acting. Gil assured her that so did he, but the two went together. At least at the beginning. When she was established and no longer needed that kind of exposure, she could withdraw into relative privacy and concentrate on her art. With that promise in the future, she found herself yielding more and more to a life-style she detested. She accepted the Hollywood invitations, laughed at the glib dialogue, traded insincere cheek kisses, tolerated the snorting, smoking, and drinking. When anyone leaned on her too heavily, she could hide behind Gil. Not that he was strong, far from it, but he was respected and would not be transgressed. In that sense, he served as her shield.

Now she suddenly felt naked. Gil was not possessed of even those modest virtues she had credited to him. He was just another Hollywood schemer, shedding crocodile tears over the grave of the enemy, hiding his glee, happy to scuttle after his dream over someone's dead body. She wished for the first time she were back in the suburbs of Houston where her mother presided over genteel, boring entertainments and her stepfather expounded for hours on the manufacture of oil-storage tanks. She missed the soft Texas accents she had worked to eradicate from her own speech, and even the humid, mosquito-filled nights by the Gulf of Mexico. Anything that was light-years away from Los Angeles.

The pang of nostalgia surrendered to the urgency of the present. *Star-crossed* started shooting tomorrow. She would play Jana and do it well, but it would not be the same now. Her good fortune had cost someone else too dearly. And she would be alone, for the episode with Gil was irrevocably over. Working with him now would be more difficult, but they could handle it. They were both professionals.

She walked out on her tiny terrace and leaned on the railing. At night she could see a carpet of lights stretching to the rim of the bay. Now the city looked drab and seamy under darkening gray skies that smelled of smoke. It was a good day for a funeral.

Luis Alcalde believed that the massive influx of illegal aliens from Mexico represented nothing less than the repossession of California by its legitimate owners. Though he was American-born to modestly well-to-do parents in West Los Angeles and spoke only limited Spanish, he sympathized fiercely with the new arrivals and resolved to dedicate his career to their aspirations, once he passed the bar. His parents, both dedicated Americans, baptized him Louis, but he scorned the Anglicization and dropped the "o." Flaunting his Latino origins, he despised the pale-eyed Anglos, whose reaction to his attitude ranged from condescension to outright hostility.

Their women were a different matter.

Luis rolled away from Erin and propped his head on his hand to look down at her naked body, believing it to be the most lovely he had ever seen. He was tormented by desire and regret. "What's the matter?" he asked her.

Erin shook her head, not sure she could explain it to him. She knew that she was passionately fond of Luis, perhaps on the brink of falling in love. At least she loved the way his mind worked, the depth of his feelings, and the honesty with which he expressed them. He didn't play games and he never acted. There was about him a lack of superficiality, as if he didn't have time for such things, just as he didn't have time to muscle or tan his lean, sallow body. He channeled his energies into specific projects, each one a challenge for him. There was no waste.

She decided that his dark eyes were intense even when they were sad, as they were now, in disappointment. By way of apology she reached up and tousled his brown, curling hair. "I'm sorry," she murmured.

"We Latinos are all macho men," said Luis. "We can't stand rejection. We consider it a slur on our manhood. Rejection makes us go out and do crimes in the streets." He smiled. "You're endangering the neighborhood."

"You're sweet," she told him. "Very understanding."

"I'm holding my volatile nature in control. Trying to."

Even in bed, he gave the impression of being stretched taut. She wondered if he would be the same way after making love. She didn't know yet, despite the lie she had told Richard in anger. There hadn't been much time for relaxation in Luis' world, but perhaps she could change that. By way of contrast, she pictured Richard lolling there as he so often had, lazy and self-satisfied, probably smoking a cigarette.

That was the trouble. They were in bed with Richard's ghost. Maybe it would be different if he weren't out there running for his life. Then maybe she could blot him from her mind and be what she wanted to be for Luis. In the meanwhile it was just no use. Which made her angry at Richard.

After the second detective left, she had called Luis and asked him to come over. Not to sleep with him, just to have him near at a time when she couldn't bear to be alone. One thing led to another and they had ended up in bed. She found she simply could not function as a lover and had probably ruined his day. The Latin girls he must be used to were no doubt much less neurotic.

He reached over to touch her intimately. "If at first you don't succeed . . ."

She intercepted his hand and removed it gently. "Not now, Luis. Really."

He got to his feet and slipped on his shorts, then sat back down on the edge of the bed. "I'm safer from myself here." He grinned. "Now tell me about this Anglo, Steelegrave."

She smiled at him. "He's everything you're not."

"Tall, blond, and handsome, as I remember."

"Selfish, conceited, and insensitive is what comes to mind."

"But you're in love with him."

"He was kind of an addiction."

" 'Was' sounds encouraging, but he's still got a lot of influence around here, I think. Kind of like an evil spirit that needs to be exorcised."

Erin got up and took a robe from the closet. "That's pretty close. I guess he's still under my skin. The trouble is, I can't help it. I'm very worried about him and I just can't think of anything else." She sat next to him on the bed.

"If he's innocent like you think he is, why doesn't he just walk into the nearest police station? We've got a reasonably competent criminal-justice system, when the cops aren't all out bashing spicks and niggers."

"He lives in another world. Right now he's acting out one of his old movies. The one where his wife is murdered and he's the suspect. He's got to solve it to clear his name. Just like in the script."

"You're kidding."

"Oh not, I'm not."

"Then he's crazy."

"He's an actor, which is maybe the same thing. Anyway, now he's running around playing a part, and everyone's after him for real. The policeman said they'll shoot him if he tries to get away, which is just the kind of thing he'll do." She was coming close to tears.

Luis took her hand gently. "I'll be around when you need me. If I were qualified I'd defend your friend in court myself. I want him home-free, proved innocent." He leaned to kiss her lightly on the lips and smiled. "Then I can compete with him. There's something too romantic about an outlaw. When this Anglo's off the hook, he better look out. I'm after his girl." He stood and finished dressing.

The phone rang five minutes after he left.

"Hello?"

"Hi, hon. This is the knife-wielding maniac."

"Richard!"

"The same. I just wanted to hear the dulcet tones of your voice."

She was sure he'd been drinking. "Richard, listen to me!

The police have been here. They know you drove my car."

"Damn . . . then they found it. I was calling to tell you where I left it. Are you in trouble?"

"Never mind that . . . *you're* in trouble! The police officer practically told me they'd shoot you on sight. With real bullets, not blanks! You've got to give yourself up, you idiot!"

"They cannot shoot him whom they cannot find," said Richard loftily.

"Richard, have you been drinking?"

"Before noon? Never! Well . . ."

"Where are you, for God's sake!"

"In good hands, never fear."

"Please, Richard . . . please go to a police station and give up."

"Can't. I've got to go to a funeral."

Erin had read that the funeral of Marla Monday would be held at the Westwood Village cemetery at three o'clock this afternoon. That must be what he was talking about, but she couldn't understand what he meant to do. It sounded like a publicity stunt. "Then you'll give yourself up there?"

"They'll never know I was there," said Richard mysteriously.

"You're drunk!"

"I am not drunk," he replied with dignity. "We're about to get this whole thing solved. I'll call you later."

After Richard hung up, Erin sat very still for several minutes. Then she found the card Cosgrove had left her and dialed his number.

Maybe he was a little drunk at that, Steelegrave admitted to himself. He and Lang Desmond had had several Bloody Marys while Lang outlined his plan.

"The way I see it, it's our last chance," Desmond said, pacing the floor. "Our" he'd said, and he was beginning to pick up Travers' mannerisms, getting into the part. "You can't go back to Marla's with the cops around there, and if Dieter's that sick, he might never come out again. But you can bet he'll go to the funeral if he was in love with her.

Then we'll both confront him playing cops. Tell him we've got Steelegrave in custody and he told us the whole story. It'll knock him right off balance. Whoever killed Marla's gonna be there too. All Dieter'll have to do is point a finger."

"What makes you think the killer has to show up?"

"Braski invited everyone on *Star-crossed*. It's a command performance. Somebody on the picture must have done in Marla. They all hated her. Would a thief leave her hanging there with diamonds in her ears? Could anyone she didn't know come up on her like that?"

"Suppose the disguise doesn't work and someone spots me? You know there'll be at least one cop at the funeral."

"But it *will* work! I'm an expert, remember?" He rubbed his hands together. "We'll do just what we did in *Fall Guy*. Only much better."

"This isn't a movie, Lang," Steelegrave reminded him again. "I don't think Dieter will buy your act even if I can get past him. He'll probably recognize you."

"I've never met him and I haven't made a picture for years. And I never worked with white hair." Desmond blew his silent whistle for more drinks. "Look, Rick, let me work on you . . . then you decide. One way or the other, you've got to change the way you look if you're gonna stay at large, right?"

Steelegrave remembered Vandy's theory. The best place to hide something was in plain sight. Maybe it worked with people, too. They carried their drinks upstairs and Desmond sat Steelegrave in front of an ancient makeup table. The mirror was bordered with bulbs that threw a bright, merciless light. The older man began to pull a variety of bottles and tubes out of the drawers.

"You're going to be my nephew," Desmond said. "I've got one, you know. Works for UPI in Hong Kong and hasn't been back for years. He met Marla when he was a kid, so it's logical he'd come with me and pay last respects if he was in town." He brought out an electric razor and plugged it in.

"What's that for?" Steelegrave wanted to know.

"I'm going to shave your head. The front and the crown. I'll leave you a fringe."

Steelegrave sprang out of his chair. "The hell with that!"

"C'mon, Rick, sit down. This has got to be a complete change."

"We didn't shave my head in *Fall Guy*."

"Like you said, that was just a movie."

"Aw, hell . . ." But he sat down.

Desmond sheared off his hair and razored the scalp smooth. He applied Pan-Cake makeup, matching the bald areas to Steelegrave's tan, then dyed the remaining hair mouse brown, leaving the sideburns white. Two inserts of sponge rubber puffed out his cheeks, breaking the lean line of face and jaw, while a third gave him a longer upper lip. From a selection of mustaches Desmond chose one he found suitable and dyed it to match Steelegrave's remaining hair. He coated his upper lip with a sticky adhesive and pressed the mustache on carefully, then stood back to admire his handiwork.

"I can fix everything but the eyes," he said. "Don't happen to have any nonprescription contacts, but we can use some glasses I've got with a light tint. No dark lenses, that'll make you look like a fucking mafioso, attract attention." He told Steelegrave to hold his head back and shoved a slim tube of tightly packed cotton up either nostril.

"Damn!" Steelegrave mumbled through the sponges. "I can hardly talk and I can't breathe at all." He looked sadly at the clumps of hair in his lap.

"Breathe through your mouth, it's not forever. You're not going to have to talk that much."

"Thit!" lisped Steelegrave. But the transformation was remarkable. He peered into the mirror and saw a bald, squirrelish-looking man with a rather wide nose and a prominent upper lip that suggested buck teeth. He didn't recognize or like himself at all.

He spat out the sponges and reached for his Bloody Mary. "What am I going to do for clothes? I'm taller than you are."

"Conchita's letting the sleeves and pants down on one of my suits. Couple of inches should do it. The shirt'll be okay, you don't have to see the cuffs."

Steelegrave drank some of his Bloody Mary, being careful of his new mustache. Conchita arrived with a charcoal-gray suit, cackling and breaking into a little jig of amusement when she saw him.

"The rest is acting," said Desmond. "I don't still have to tell you about that, do I? Stoop a little, maybe shuffle. Don't, for Christ's sake, limp. It's too obvious."

Steelegrave put on the suit. It fit well enough, considering. There were barely visible creases where the sleeves and trousers had been let down that no amount of ironing would completely erase. The shoes pinched, contributing a rather strange gait. He practiced shuffling around the room with his shoulders hunched, camping it up. Lang and Conchita howled with laughter.

When Conchita bustled away to make more drinks, Steelegrave placed the call to Erin. "She thinks I'm drunk," he said to Desmond after he hung up.

"She's right, sport. Otherwise you wouldn't have told her you were going to the funeral. Hawke'd never do that. You can't ever figure exactly what a dame'll do."

"You don't have to worry about this one."

"That's what you thought about Beverly in *Fall Guy*, remember? You trusted her for true blue and she almost got you caught trying to help you."

Steelegrave decided Desmond was the one who was drunk. "You're getting a little carried away about that movie, Lang."

"Can you blame me? The similarities are downright eerie."

"Remember who did the killing in *Fall Guy*? It was you, old pal."

Desmond looked offended. "That's a terrible thing you're suggesting, sport."

Steelegrave laughed at the expression on his face. "See what I mean? It was only a picture, Lang."

Only a picture. But Steelegrave suddenly remembered something else. Years ago he had inadvertently scuttled Desmond's career when he quit *Love–Forty* and the series was dropped. Last week Marla tried to cancel the old actor's comeback after a decade out in the cold. Lang had reason to believe they had both wronged him. To murder one and lay blame on the other would be both a balanced and a theatrical revenge. If someone showed him a script like that, he'd probably buy it.

Fletcher Strickland had to read through the file on Ryan Cosgrove twice before anything bothered him. All the facts and documentation he found corroborated what Cos had told him over the years in casual conversation. If anything, the man was substantially overqualified for his job.

Cosgrove had been born and raised in Durham, Texas, son of a small rancher who had found a little oil on his property. He went to high school in Durham and had graduated from college and law school at the University of Virginia. He served three years in the U.S. Army, mostly as a legal officer in occupied Germany. Photocopies of his diplomas and his discharge with the rank of captain were appended to his file. In 1958 he returned to Durham to manage his property there. It was not until 1961 that he moved to California and entered the police academy in Los Angeles. He had evidently never married.

Cosgrove's record as a police officer was more colorful. In 1965 he had won a citation for bravery by foiling the holdup of a liquor store, shooting to death two armed suspects. During the Watts riots he was cited again for his conduct while responding to a call by an officer in need of help. The man was trapped in his car, surrounded by a mob that was trying to set it on fire. Cosgrove and his partner broke through to the car and held dozens of rioters at bay until more units arrived. A year later he had shot and killed a robbery suspect fleeing a supermarket. No citation this time. In fact the captain at Hollenbeck division had reprimanded him and commented in writing that he was "overzealous."

Starting with his transfer to Hollywood division, Cosgrove's career was more familiar to Strickland. He remembered when Cos had been shot in the leg while off duty drinking in a bar. He had prevented an attempted robbery and the suspect fled with a bullet in his shoulder, to be picked up within the hour. His wound left Cos with a limp, and his assailant, a man with a long record, served four years in prison. He was dead a week after his release, the victim of an unsolved murder.

Cosgrove's record was sprinkled with commendations and reprimands. The reprimands were invariably for unnecessary use of force. His first suspension came when he surprised an illegal alien trying to steal his car and pistol-whipped the man half to death. On that occasion his promotion to sergeant was canceled. After a year of exemplary work the rank was restored, but Cosgrove earned a second suspension almost immediately, this time for blowing away a knife-wielding attacker with illegal hollow-point ammunition.

Strickland put aside the dossier and sighed. The suspension he intended to lay on Cosgrove for direct and willful disobedience of an order would finish his police career. Just as well, thought Strickland, because Cosgrove was a bomb waiting to go off. Years before, when cops had more room to maneuver and fewer civilian committees keeping them under surveillance, an officer like Cosgrove had his uses. Now he was a liability that could cost a city millions in lawsuits. Not to mention the grief he could cause a superior.

Still, something nagged at Strickland. What the hell was it Cosgrove was supposed to be doing from the time he left the army to his enrollment at the police academy? He opened the file again and studied the bit about personal-property management. This army officer and attorney had returned to his home town (Cos had once told him Durham was just a wide spot in the highway) and pissed away three years managing his property. Instead of getting a job or raising a family.

Strickland only knew what he had read about small towns. They weren't part of his experience. Everybody was supposed to know everybody else, as he understood it. At least he supposed they kept records. He picked up his phone and told the operator to get him the sheriff of Durham, Texas.

"Sheriff's office," drawled a young female voice.

"I'm Captain Fletcher Strickland of the Los Angeles Police Department. I'd like to talk to your sheriff."

"Sure thing. Hang on a sec." He heard the girl call out to someone, "Bucky Lee in his office?"

The reply was garbled. He hung on.

"Sheriff Owens," said a voice presently.

"Sheriff, this is Captain Fletcher Strickland calling from Los Angeles. I was wondering if I could trouble you for some information about a former resident of your city. Or maybe you could direct me to someone there who'd keep records."

"Shoot, Cap'n, this ain't hardly a city. Anyone within the last thirty years or so, I can probably tell you personal."

"Name's Ryan Cosgrove."

A pause. "Hoo-ee! Ol' Cos? What's he gone and done now?"

"He's an officer on my staff," Strickland said cautiously. "We have a review board and we conduct periodic background surveys when our people come up for promotion," he added inventively.

"Do tell? Cos is an officer of the law now?"

"Yes, he is."

"Well, now, you called the right man. I known Cos since we was both knee-high to a grasshopper."

Strickland blessed his luck. Small towns were the way he had imagined them. "I'd just like to fill in a couple of blanks. Our records show he came back to Durham after he was discharged from the army in 1958. Then there's not much until he joined our police department. Just that he managed some property he owned down there. Hell, I sound like a nitpicker, Sheriff, but I thought someone in Durham might be able to plug that hole for me."

"That what he told you? That he managed his property? That's all?"

"Well, that's what's on file."

Another pause, longer this time. "Cap'n, I honest-to-God don't want to bad-mouth anybody. But one lawman to another, I feel I got to be honest. . . . Shit, I don't know where to begin."

Strickland tried not to sound too eager. "Just tell me what you think I need to know, Sheriff."

"Well, Cos come up dirt poor like most of us here, but his

daddy struck a little oil and he got his schoolin' at the University of Virginia and studied the law."

"I know all that. What about when he came back from the army?"

"Well, he came back an officer and a gentleman. Bars on his shoulders, all that. . . . First thing he done was marry old Senator Bull Durham's daughter. Now, Bull, he liked Cos real well and he was goin' to put him into politics, big politics. Started him out as county prosecutor. . . ."

Strickland felt his interest mount. He'd known there had to be something.

"Thing is, Cos, see, he got too ambitious. He had him the senator's daughter and the senator behind him and he got to thinkin' he was too good for a hick town like Durham. He figured if he done perfect as county prosecutor he'd move up and get out of here faster. So he got to kinda riggin' the odds. . . ." Bucky Lee paused, enjoying himself.

"Go on, Sheriff. What did he do?"

"Well, he planted evidence, Cap'n, on a suspect he'd be prosecutin'. Him and a deputy he had in cahoots with him."

"What kind of evidence?"

"A murder weapon. A bloody knife."

Strickland felt a chill steal along his back. He welded the phone to his ear.

"Only it didn't work out," Bucky Lee went on happily. "Some drifter confessed he done the rape and murder and left the knife he used near the body in the town dump. Not where it was found, under the mattress of a Mex kid lived above a garage. Which is where ol' Cos had the deputy plant it for him." Another puase, during which Strickland thought he heard the sheriff strike a match. He waited him out with dogged patience.

"That deputy was a dumb ol' boy. I.Q. you could roll on a pair of dice. Sheriff Gruenig had me bring him in—I was a deputy too, in those days—and we worked on him some. Took us maybe an hour to get the whole story." Bucky Lee puffed in silence for a few infuriating seconds.

"Now, the sheriff, he had a lot of respect for the senator and he told him about it first thing. Asked him what he oughta do. Old Bull, he didn't hardly hesitate. He told his daughter he was goin' to throw Cos out of the state, and she said, good, she'd had a bellyful of him too. Cos fought it and we had to pound on him some before we dumped him over the county line, but it worked out all right. Ain't seen hide nor hair of him since."

"So that's why he's got no criminal record," Strickland said, mostly to himself.

"He had a little girl. Senator didn't want his granddaughter, or his daughter neither, mixed up with a jailbird. So we just kinda eased him out of Texas."

Strickland sat tensely, holding the phone tight to his ear. Let it be a coincidence, he prayed. Don't let it be a repeater. But how could it be? Cos had no motive.

"Family ain't a total loss, though," Bucky Lee was saying. "We sent his daughter out there to you in L.A., too, now she's growed up. Back here ever'body used to stop ever'thing at three o'clock to watch her in the soap opera. Neva Morgann, she calls herself now. After her godfather, Wally. We're right proud of her. Read she's on her way to bein' a big star."

19

Bringing the little Fiat back to Erin was a pretext on the part of Willy Danforth. He'd had no luck locating Cosgrove at his apartment or at any of the fast-food joints they frequented on duty. Leaving Gutierrez staked out in front of the apartment, he used the phone to check Cosgrove's favorite restaurants—Musso's in Hollywood and the Black Forest in Santa Monica—though it was barely noon. No one had seen him. Finally it occurred to Danforth that Erin Englund had been the last person to see Cosgrove, and there was a meager chance he might have mentioned something to her.

Danforth drove the Fiat, followed by a cruiser with two uniformed cops inside. One went to the garage and hot-wired Steelegrave's Thunderbird, driving it away to the police impound lot. The other waited in the car for the detective.

Erin stood in her doorway and watched him approach with unwelcoming eyes. "You again," she sighed.

"Afraid so." A smile lit his sad hound-dog face. "Thought you might be wanting your car."

"Thank you." He stood awkwardly before her but she made no move to invite him in.

"You remember my partner, Cosgrove? Big fella who came to talk to you before me?"

"How could I forget?"

"Did he, uh, say where he was going after he left here?"

Erin looked at him with frank surprise. "Don't you keep track of each other with radios or something?"

Danforth looked so sheepish she thought he would kick at the turf next. "Fact is, miss, we can't seem to locate Cos anywhere. There's a real urgent message for him at the station."

"And you want me to help you find him?" She almost laughed.

"Just thought he might have said where he was going next, something like that."

"What he said was that he was in personal charge of this case and he was giving it his full attention." When Danforth didn't reply she asked, "That's true, isn't it?"

"Well, in a manner of speaking."

"What does that mean?"

"Uh, there's other officers on the case now. It's just Sergeant Cosgrove feels strong about it because he was the one originally tried to arrest Mr. Steelegrave."

Erin's eyes widened. For a moment she couldn't speak. Finally she said, "He shot at Richard." It was a flat statement.

"Well, now, it seems—"

"He did. Richard told me. The radio and the papers didn't even mention it." Her voice rose. "That Cosgrove is the same man who shot at Richard!"

"Miss Englund—"

"And he told me most of the other police were trigger-happy but I could trust him to bring Richard in safely!"

Danforth gulped, his prominent Adam's apple bobbing.

"He gave me his own number to call in case Richard got in touch with me. He wanted to make sure nobody else could find him before he did. . . ." She stopped abruptly and stared at Danforth. "Now you can't even find *him*. What's the matter with you people? Are you all crazy?"

"Miss Englund, Sergeant Cosgrove was relieved of duty yesterday because of the way he handled that attempted arrest. He had no authority to question you this morning." There, I've gone and done it now, thought Danforth. But she has a right to know.

"Then why is he chasing after Richard? Why is he so eager to be the one to find him?" Erin heard herself becoming shrill and tried to calm down. "Is he looking for revenge? Or another notch on his gun?"

Danforth thought of something. "Did Steelegrave get in touch with you?"

Erin said nothing.

"And if he did . . . did you call Sergeant Cosgrove?"

No answer. She just stared at him.

Danforth contemplated her gravely. "We've got to know anything you might have told him. You see, we think Sergeant Cosgrove might be kinda losing control."

There were two messages on Cosgrove's answering machine. The first was from Captain Strickland—abrupt and to the point, matter-of-fact in tone. Would Cosgrove please report to him immediately. Something's come up. Thanks, Cos.

Cosgrove shifted uncomfortably in the stifling phone booth, squinting his eyes in concentration as he tried to interpret the intention behind the words, his antennae out and probing. Strickland sounded elaborately casual, almost breezy, an atypical attitude for the captain when he was on duty. It was more like his happy-hour mood, when it was time for the first drink on an off-duty evening. Or like when he was jacking a suspect around, jollying someone to put them off guard. He decided to ignore the request.

The second message made him smile broadly, his faith in the righteous order of things restored. Erin Englund was telling him that Steelegrave planned to attend Marla Monday's funeral today. Please don't hurt him, she added. He's not dangerous to anyone.

He didn't doubt that she was telling the truth. Steelegrave had run out of gas and decided to end the chase with a dramatic gesture. It fit the man's conception of his make-believe world. The trick now would be to get to him first. Strickland was sure to have the funeral covered. There had been a lot of publicity and there would be a mob scene around the cemetery. Maybe within, too, if Cosgrove were lucky. He needed a crowd to lose himself in.

Cosgrove pocketed his beeper and stepped out into the hot, smoky wind. The graying stubble on his chin itched and his damp, soiled shirt clung to his back. The shapeless

linen suit he wore was wrinkled and bagged at the knees
and he could smell the sour odor of his body. It was a
great temptation to return home for a shower and a change
of clothes, but something in Strickland's casual message
spoke to his instinct, telling him to forget it. The place
could be staked out. He knew the evidence would sooner
or later lead them to Erin Englund and expose his own
maverick behavior. He counted on his hunt being over
long before that, but something could have gone wrong. If
the captain was onto him somehow, he didn't want a
run-in with him now. Not yet. When he brought Steelegrave
in on ice, okay. Let them try to knock him down then.

He looked at his watch and saw that there was still an
hour and a half to kill before the funeral, and he was
within fifteen minutes of the Westwood Village Mortuary
where it was scheduled to take place. It might be a good
idea not to stand around the street in home territory where
all the cops knew him. Limping with exhaustion, he crossed
Lincoln Boulevard near Pico and went into a flyblown
restaurant. Excitement gave him a craving for greasy food,
the way hangovers once had. He ordered two double cheese-
burgers and a pot of coffee.

Before he was finished eating, he had decided how he
would do it. He would use the throwaway gun he always
kept in his car.

20

The Westwood Village Mortuary had been planned to accommodate Westwood when it had been a village in fact as well as in name. It was a small compound contained within a three-acre lot, personal and cozy compared to the vast green sprawl of Forest Lawn. A rectangular drive bordered gravesites shaded by wide pepper trees and tall pines. On two sides stood marble mausoleums containing crypts and bearing names such as the Sanctuary of Peace and the Sanctuary of Tranquillity. The Armand Hammer family had a mausoleum of their own and famous Californians were represented across the spectrum, including film stars such as Marilyn Monroe and Natalie Wood.

Unhappily, no one had foreseen the proliferation of high-rises that had transformed the village into a city, and now the glassy towers of AVCO and MCO frowned directly down on the little cemetery, providing a platform for photographers intruding on the privacy of celebrities. No one could hide from the zoom lenses they used to catch every detail for their viewers, who could watch and smugly say, See? They were famous but I'm still here. The interments of both Monroe and Wood were covered in close-up, though both services were strictly private.

Today the photographers were already in place up in the towers and hanging over the ivy-covered fence that hedged the cemetery off from a neighboring parking lot. There was no light to reflect off their lenses; the sky was dark and sooty. A large, polite young man had been stationed at the black wrought-iron gate with instructions to admit all recognizable celebrities and filter out the general public, while his twin stood farther down the driveway charged with traffic control. Inside the modern chapel, Marla's casket was watched discreetly by dark-suited private security men assigned to guard the body from the time of the autopsy through burial. Two mortuary directors stood by, solemn but not morose, supervising every aspect of the arrangements from car parking to the placement of floral tributes numerous enough to perfume the small chapel with a cloying mélange of scents.

Vandy watched the early arrivals to the funeral on live TV from the back of his stretched Mercedes limo. High angle shots of a lot of long black cars not unlike the one he was riding in. He had sent to L.A. for the limo and his trusted chauffeur, Vejar. It was appropriate to the occasion of the largest and last drug delivery of his criminal career that both the Watusi and Vejar were along to ride shotgun on the transaction. There was an unholy amount of cocaine packed into the trunk compartment.

Vandy poured champagne for the Watusi and himself and smiled, relaxed and comfortable in the cool, ample interior of the car behind the dark, opaque windows. He had forgotten about the funeral; that was a bonus. All in all, this was a most gratifying day.

An idea struck him and his smile became absolutely mischievous. He hit the switch on the intercom. "Vejar," he said. "Get off the freeway at Wilshire and turn east. We're going to a funeral. At the Westwood Village Mortuary."

"Ten-four," replied Vejar, who was addicted to police jargon.

The Watusi looked at him in surprise. "We've got a meet at three o'clock, Sahib. It's half-past two."

"Plans are made to be changed."

"You can't just cancel," the girl said uneasily.

"Can't I? Watch me." He reached for the car phone and requested a number from the operator. "Vandy here, Cass," he said presently. "I can't make it at three. Let's say six and make it at Fala's." He hung up.

The Watusi was puzzled. "Where's Fala's?" she asked.

Vandy raised a single eyebrow. "And what, little darlin', is that to you?"

"Nothing, only it doesn't seem like a great idea to drive around all day with a trunkload of coke in the car."

"We're not driving around. We're going to my ex-wife's funeral."

"You *hated* her!"

"Maybe I want to make sure she's dead."

"But look at me. I'm not dressed to go to a funeral!" She wore skintight white jeans that came to just below her knees and a skimpy scarlet halter. Her painted toenails poked out of espadrilles.

"True. You can wait in the car with Vejar."

"This is a crazy idea!"

Vandy studied her with cold eyes. "Since when do we make decisions by committee around here?"

The Watusi subsided.

Vejar turned right off of Wilshire at Glendon, where two motorcycle cops were directing traffic. The entrance to the mortuary was behind the AVCO building and there were a half-dozen cars lined up in front of them, inching toward the gate. A crowd of the curious pushed as close as the guard would permit, craning to see into the cemetery or leaning over to peer into the arriving vehicles. Finally they were opposite a towering young man with set, pleasant features. Vandy let down the window and smiled winningly. "Ex-husband," he said. "The name is Evander." He sipped from his glass of champagne.

The man bent down and looked into the back of the car, letting his eyes rove over the luxurious appointments and then linger on the Watusi. "Go ahead, sir," he said finally.

He was still looking after the Mercedes when a doleful-looking man in a seersucker suit walked up and showed him a badge pinned into a leather wallet. "Police officer," he said laconically as he sauntered past. The guard did not find that unusual either.

Willy Danforth strolled around the mortuary grounds watching the mourners climb out of their cars and greet each other. In little knots, they moved slowly toward the chapel, a sleek beige-colored A-frame with a steep shake roof. Danforth looked carefully at their faces, famous and otherwise, but saw no one that resembled the photographs he had studied of Steelegrave. There was no sign of Cos either.

He went into the administration office, which was housed in a low building adjacent to the chapel. A youngish balding man in a three-piece dark suit looked up with mild disapproval. "Yes?"

"Police officer." Danforth displayed his badge again. "Wonder if I might share your space here. This being a murder case, we got to take some routine precautions."

"You mean you think this Steelegrave might show up?" The man's eyes went round.

"Never can tell." Danforth pulled out a small two-way radio called a Rover that was clipped to his belt and thumbed a button. "Come in," he said, and waited for an answer to filter through the static.

Fletcher Strickland was sweltering in an unmarked car two blocks away on Wellworth Avenue, along with two other plainclothes cops. "Had to pick one without air, didn't you?" he said disgustedly to the one behind the wheel, named Gannon.

"I didn't know it didn't have air," said Gannon defensively.

"You could have looked."

"I guess I wasn't thinking, Cap'n."

"Shit."

The instrument on the seat next to him began to crackle and spit. He picked it up. "Strickland here," he said. "Over."

Danforth's voice came tinnily to his ear. "Got me set up at the mortuary office. Thought I better stay out of sight on account of Cos. Don't want to spook him. I can see anyone comes in from here, with or without a car. Over."

"Okay. If there's any action, do like we planned. Over."

There was a pause. "I got to take Cos the way you said? In cuffs? Over."

"If he won't come any other way, yes. Over."

"What if Steelegrave shows up about the same time? Over."

"Just get Cosgrove out of the way. The rest of us will handle Steelegrave once you spot him for us. Over."

"Ten-four. Over and out." Danforth lowered the Rover

and shook his head. It seemed to him the captain was overreacting.

He had left Erin Englund with the distinct impression that she knew more than she was telling. She'd gone pale when he asked if she had heard from Steelegrave, and frozen on him completely when he wondered if she had passed the information on to Cosgrove. Assuming just that, he went back to pick up Gutierrez and persuaded the building manager to let them into Cosgrove's apartment. The light on Cosgrove's answering machine was blinking away, so he played back the messages, and there it was. Strickland went into high gear when he phoned him about it, and seemed more excited about finding Cosgrove than picking up Steelegrave. It just didn't make sense. He was staring out the open door of the administration office when he saw a pink Volkswagen bug drive by. It was a convertible with the top down and that fruity kid of Marla Monday's was in it with his boyfriend. They were laughing as if they were going to a party.

From his vantage point on the sixth floor of the AVCO building, Cosgrove watched through binoculars as Willy Danforth went into the administration office. With the services due to begin in minutes, Willy was the only cop there except for traffic control, which meant Strickland had no clue that Steelegrave might actually show up and was just taking a routine precaution. Moreover, it meant that his own unauthorized activities remained undiscovered and he was still way ahead of the game. Cosgrove smiled and lowered the binoculars. He wasn't worried about Willy Danforth and there was no restriction on his attending funerals anyway.

His plan made it vital for him to spot Steelegrave before Willy or anyone else did. That was the dicey part. That and getting Steelegrave alone or at least away from the crowd. The rest was razzle-dazzle, legerdemain, a matter of passing him the throwaway gun without anyone seeing. It would take some luck but Cosgrove felt he had that going for him now. The force was with him, as the kids liked to say.

The secretary who had finally let him into the suite of

empty offices was twitching around the room nervously. She had balked at his request even after seeing his I.D., for though he had washed up as best he could in the greasy-spoon restaurant and shaved with the electric razor in his car, he looked pretty funky for a cop.

"I won't steal the furniture, don't worry," said Cosgrove, irritated by her attitude.

"It's just that Mr. Stevens gave me strict orders. No photographers in these offices. They're everywhere else in the building today. I think it's morbid." The secretary had a bad complexion, hair like steel wool, and the face of a sheep.

"I'm not a photographer, I'm a police officer." He raised the binoculars to scan new arrivals, but there wasn't much to see until they alighted from their cars. It was time for him to get down to the gate, where he could catch Steelegrave coming in, probably on foot, maybe wearing dark glasses or a hat, figuring to con his way past the guard.

"I didn't know they had police officers spying on funerals," bleated the woman.

"Miss Monday was murdered. We have to follow certain procedures."

"I *know* she was murdered. I *know* how to read. But even if that man who killed her was fool enough to come to the funeral, how would you catch him from up here?"

Cosgrove sighed. He lowered the binoculars again and turned to face her. "Ma'am, I never would have thought of that," he said. "Maybe you should have been a cop. You kind of look like one I used to know. We called him Jack the Dripper. He's dead now—died of third-stage syphilis. Had it so bad that it even broke out on his face. Then he bloated all up and finally he just exploded. We had to hose him off the walls down at headquarters. It was terrible to see." Shaking his head in recollection, Cosgrove walked out of the office.

Erin Englund told the man at the gate that she was Marla Monday's close friend and choreographer. Since she was obviously distraught and very pretty, he waved her by without argument, not even fazed by the large dog sitting next to her who curled a lip to show his long yellow fangs. He was used to Hollywood people and their eccentricities; he had worked funerals that were *for* dogs.

Erin's distress was not feigned. She knew that her stupidity had put Richard in mortal danger. That fat policeman had played her like a violin, using the fear he had instilled in her about the quality of the Los Angeles police force to get exactly the information he wanted. To discover that he himself had been the one who had tried to kill Richard when he went to arrest him had stunned her and she had very nearly told everything to the officer who brought her car back. Perhaps she should have, but it seemed to compound the betrayal. What a pushover she had been! Because of her, Richard was walking into a deadly trap.

She had to reach him first, intercept him, and warn him off. Persuade him to surrender if she could, but not to the man who had shot at him. If she were with him as a witness, they would not dare harm him. Her mind made up, she was locking the back door when she spied Junkyard's nearly completed escape tunnel. The animal had been trying to dig his way out since his arrival and she had been filling in the holes as soon as she found them. There was no time now, so she just harried him out to the car and took him along. Damn dog!

Following directions, Erin parked her bright car among the preponderance of black sedans, left the top up, and lowered the windows a couple of inches to give Junkyard air. She walked toward the chapel, not at all out of place in her simple gray dress with black belt and matching handbag, passing little groups solemnly greeting each other, trying not to stare at famous faces while searching for Richard's. Would he try to disguise himself? He had said no one would know he was there. Maybe he wouldn't show up, she hoped. Maybe it had just been drunken bravado.

She hesitated to go inside the chapel, stationing herself instead between two tall, bearded palms that guarded the entrance like sentries. She felt self-conscious standing alone like that, but from there she could watch the cars arriving and the people filing into the chapel. No one seemed to be in a hurry. They stood around socializing like old friends who hadn't seen each other in ages.

Steelegrave shrank back in his seat as they rolled past Erin. "Nammid!" he spluttered through the sponges in his mouth. "Aff Ewin!"

"Keep quiet, sport," said Desmond, who hadn't understood him. "When I stop to talk to someone, I'll introduce you. Just nod and try to look sad. Point to your throat if anyone asks you something. Laryngitis. I'll cover for you."

They were arriving late, partly by accident and partly because traffic was being diverted away from the San Diego freeway due to the fire. The smoke was heavy on Mulholland Drive between Longbow and Roscomare roads and a highway-patrol unit blocked access to the freeway. Lang drove down Roscomare with inebriated caution past scenes of imminent evacuation. These people had been burned out less than twenty years ago and they were poised to flee again.

On Veteran Avenue near UCLA a woman in front of them driving an ancient Packard faked a left turn and then swung abruptly hard right. Lang, his reflexes dulled by the half-dozen Bloody Marys he had consumed, raked her front fender with his bumper and then wedged himself against the curb trying to go around her.

"Ged uff ourahere," mumbled Steelegrave, but it was already too late. The other driver pulled ahead of them and stopped, blocking escape.

"The miserable old coot," said Desmond, but he smiled pleasantly as he climbed out of the car.

The old woman who bore down on them looked formidable. She had flaring nostrils and a combative underslung jaw. Everyone circled the cars for a moment in silence, inspecting the damage. It was slight indeed, a mere crease in the massive fender of the vintage Packard.

"Look what you've gone and done, young man," the woman said to Desmond, pointing at the scratch. "I've had this car since 1939 and nary a mark on it. Why don't you look where you're going?"

"I'm extremely sorry, ma'am." Lang took out his wallet.

"I'll be glad to give you the name of my insurance company. They'll fix everything up for you in a hurry."

"Oh, no you don't." She pointed her shelf of jaw at him. "There are no witnesses except your friend here. Later you'll say it was my fault. I think we'll wait right here for the police."

That was all they needed, Steelegrave thought. Lang was smiling and looking at the woman with slightly glazed eyes. He seemed to be in a genteel alcoholic fog, a condition most cops would recognize. "It *was* your fault, ma'am," he said mildly, to Steelegrave's horror.

"What? What did you say?" The woman seemed truly not to believe her ears.

"Hake 'a bwame, Wang," Steelegrave pleaded through the obstacles in his mouth.

The woman rounded on him. "What's the matter with this man?" she asked suspiciously.

"He has a cleft palate."

"Oh."

Lang looked at his watch, seemed to pull himself together. "We're late for a funeral, ma'am. Marla Monday's funeral."

"The actress? The one who was murdered?"

"Yes. We were about to make a picture together," he said solemnly. "Now . . ."

The woman peered at him closely. "I say, aren't you . . ."

"Lang Desmond, yes. At your service."

Her eyes popped. "Why, of course. I used to see you in the movies all the time. Your hair was black then. . . ."

Lang handed her a card. "Please call me anytime. We can straighten things out about your car."

She took the card reverently. "I remember *Front Line* and *Morgan's Folly* especially well. You were very dashing." She shook her head, rippling the wattles under her big jaw. "You know, I haven't seen a film for twenty years. There's nothing but obscenity and gore on the screen nowadays."

"No illusions," Lang agreed. "Nothing left to the imagination. Why, when I made *Morgan's Folly* with Loretta and we did that bedroom scene, the Hays office said there had to be two beds and, not only that, the beds had to be no less than three feet apart. . . ."

Steelegrave caught his arm and steered him toward the Caddy. They backed up and pulled away with a lot of waving and smiling. The old woman would probably preserve and cherish the blemish Desmond had left on her car. He was a living reminder of the way things used and ought to be.

Though they were ten minutes late, people were just beginning to file into the chapel. Some still lingered in groups on the lawn as if reluctant to acknowledge the reason for their reunion. Whether the deceased had been loved or hated, funerals were an intimation of mortality and film celebrities were rumored to die in batches of three.

"Will you look at ol' Blue Eyes holding court," said Lang when they were out of the car. The singer was surrounded by a clutch of the ultrafamous, who were laughing at something he'd said.

They walked slowly across the turf, timing themselves to be last into the chapel, and Lang paused to greet Lars Vincent. He introduced Steelegrave, saying, "This is my nephew, Willis Clay."

The director's formerly red hair was the color and texture of cotton. He had the leathery skin of a man who had spent years in the sun shooting westerns and he squinted at Steelegrave through clear blue eyes that showed no trace of recognition. "Pleasure," he said shortly, as always a man of few words.

Steelegrave nodded and looked beyond him at a small man who had paused in hobbling past them. The man brought his face close to Desmond and blinked at him with watery eyes. "That you, Lang?"

"Yes, Malcolm." Lang shook his frail hand. Steelegrave recognized Malcolm Webley with shock. His small frame had shrunk to diminutive proportions. A fringe of white hair surrounded his bald pate and the flesh hung loosely from his jowls. Incongruously, he was as nattily dressed as ever.

Webley turned toward the chapel and said vaguely, "I discovered her, you know."

"I know."

"I made her a star."

"I know," said Lang. "And you discovered Rick Steele, too."

"Eh?"

"Rick Steele. You discovered him too."

Webley made a feeble, irritated gesture. "Oh, that bloody idiot, never could act, you know," he said. Then he shook hands with Steelegrave playing Willis Clay. "How d'you do."

"See," Desmond said as they walked away. "It's a piece of cake."

Steelegrave knew that Lang was enjoying himself, milking the part, and it annoyed him. He looked around, trying to spot Dieter among those entering the chapel, but he was nowhere in sight. Neither was Erin, who must already be inside. What in hell had gotten into her anyway, coming here? What, for that matter, had gotten into him? Back at Lang's house drinking Bloody Marys, the old actor's scheme seemed to have a sort of desperate logic. Out here, he felt naked and alone, ridiculous in his masquerade. Even Lang was an unknown quantity who could simply be engineering an elaborate trap. He no longer seemed to know where the script left off and reality took over, a state of mind that might lend itself to anything.

They entered the chapel at the end of the line and slipped into the last row of seats, ignoring the ushers, who were winging it anyway, seating the best-known faces closest to the front. The interior was modern as the rest, with parquet floors and comfortable benches made of blond wood. There was a matching podium equipped with a microphone, and a robed minister who looked right out of central casting was already in place behind it. Music from an invisible harp rippled through the room as he prepared to speak.

"Braski's giving her the deluxe sendoff," Desmond said, sotto voce. "Casket'll be bronze, I bet."

Steelegrave saw Dieter immediately, a scarecrow figure in a loose black suit, towering three rows ahead of them. It was harder to find Erin, but he finally located her farther down on the opposite end of the aisle.

"Four down to the right," whispered Desmond. "On the end. That's Neva Morgann next to our old friend Gil." Steelegrave followed directions and saw a rich fall of auburn hair, then a flash of lovely profile when the girl turned briefly toward LaFarge. The crown of Gil's head was balding, and tendons stood out sharply on his neck. His skin looked bright and flushed.

In the silence, Malcolm Webley's voice quavered from someplace, "I discovered her, you know."

Someone shushed him.

The minister began to speak in the rich, full tones of a TV anchorman. In effect he said that the life of the spirit was eternal and physical death merely the passing of one's soul beyond a horizon where it could no longer be known to those who remained behind on shore. ". . . So even as we grieve for Marla and say, 'There she goes,' someone beyond that horizon waits to greet her, saying, 'Here she comes.' "

Despite himself, Steelegrave was moved. Though he realized now that he had not seen her for years, he had always known Marla was there somewhere, to be loved or hated. Now she was irrevocably gone. How could he ever have believed he'd killed her?

Cosgrove waited until the guard was ready to close the gate before he passed through. He limped down the drive toward the chapel, disappointed that he had seen no sign of Steelegrave but not yet ready to despair. There was a good chance he had missed him either while he was scanning the crowd from the AVCO building to see who Strickland had assigned, or while he was in transit from the office on the sixth floor to the gate. He had a gut feeling the bastard would show. He had to. It was in his character as Cosgrove read it, and in the ingenuous sincerity of the girl's voice on his answering machine. He was never wrong about voices.

He entered the chapel and stood silently just inside the door, letting his eyes roam over the crowd. Their backs told him little and he resigned himself to waiting until the service was over, when they would have to file out to the gravesite. . . .

"How you doin', Cos?"

Cosgrove jumped. Intent on the crowd, he had let Willy Danforth sneak up, and it irritated him.

"He's not here, Cos," Willy went on. "I seen everybody that came in."

"Shhh!" A woman in the last row turned to glare at them indignantly.

Danforth touched Cosgrove's arm and lowered his voice. "Let's step outside a minute, Cos."

Cosgrove shrugged and followed him. They stood near the chapel door, through which the minister's voice emerged as a murmur.

"You're gonna have to come in with me, Cos. The cap'n wants to see you."

Cosgrove narrowed his eyes. "I already got the message. So I'll go see him. Why do I have to come in with you?"

"That's what he told me."

"Why?" Cosgrove repeated.

"Probably because he knows you're out nosin' around on this investigation after he put you on leave of absence." Danforth shook his head sadly. "You're in more trouble than an egg-suckin' hound, Cos."

Cosgrove did not ask how they had found out; it didn't matter. He smiled his tight, lipless smile. "And for that he told you to *bring* me in?"

"That's what he said."

Cosgrove studied him for a moment. Willy seemed guileless enough, yet something was wrong here. His antenna was quivering again. "After the funeral," he said shortly, and walked back into the chapel.

Willy Danforth followed him in.

The harp played in the background as the handsome minister spoke on. His voice washed soothingly over the audience, telling about a place of infinite peace where all secrets were finally unlocked and shared and one became part of the universe and therefore of everything. . . .

Dieter Greim didn't believe a word of it. When you died your body rotted and putrefied unless you had it burned, and finally returned to common clay. There was no residual spirit to waft about in the atmosphere, no reincarnation,

no memory of the past, no future of any kind . . . nothing.
For himself he was willing to accept this and marveled that
others couldn't. He should have been killed many times in
Russia, especially at Kursk, where the shrapnel burst finally got him. Instead he had survived, and every day
since then had been a gift, for whatever it was worth.
Which was not much, in Dieter's judgment. A life spent
hiding under an assumed identity hardly fulfilled the promise of the early years when he had been a Waffen SS major
at twenty-five and the bearer of a distinguished name.
How different it might have been had Germany prevailed.
How far he might have gone! Instead, he had merely
existed, masquerading in the role of a servant.

The police patrol had arrived shortly before noon to tell
him he must leave his quarters within the hour. The fire
had jumped the San Diego freeway and was moving east
along Mulholland at an alarming rate, fanned by the desert
wind. All residents in the area were being urged to evacu-
ate as soon as possible.

The order had little meaning for Dieter. Only yesterday
the doctor who had diagnosed his case as hopeless suggested he enter the hospital as soon as possible. The medication he was taking on his own could no longer control
his pain. He would need closer supervision and frequent
injections if his remaining time were to be spent bearably.

The big house was empty, Kalb and Grady having
already left. Dieter went to Marla's bedroom suite and
stepped onto the balcony. To the west, the smoke was
thick and he could hear the shouts of firefighters and the
babble of their radios as they retreated before the crackling
flames. There wasn't much time.

He went back inside to sit at Marla's desk and covered
three pages of her business stationery with his precise
handwriting. Simply and clearly, he put down everything
he had seen on the night of her murder. Then he folded
the pages into an envelope and put it in his inside coat
pocket. In the drawer of the night table next to her vast
bed, he found the small .25-caliber pistol he knew she kept
there. The police had left it behind, probably because it
had no bearing on her death. He made certain that it was
loaded and dropped it into another pocket.

It would be simple to stay behind and let the fire have him, a private Gotterdämmerung of his own. Use the pistol if the smoke didn't overcome him first. He had no intention of ending up helplessly drugged in a hospital. The idea was tempting, but it would mean the destruction of the document he had just written. There was no way to mail it, no longer anyone to give it to. Marla's killer would be forever free.

A sharp spasm caused him to sit down weakly on the big bed. He fumbled for his medication and swallowed two capsules, then waited for the worst of the pain to subside. Defiantly he lit one of the long, foul Russian cigarettes he blamed for his condition. He calculated that it would take the last of his strength to attend Marla's funeral, but Marius Markham was sure to be there and he had to deliver the letter.

Dieter had lost track of what the minister was saying, but he realized the oration was coming to an end with an invitation to come forward and view the deceased for the last time. For no reason he could have explained, he joined the solemn queue that filed past Marla's open casket and glanced down at her, like the others. She looked like a beautiful doll, her lips red and shining, her face glowing with makeup. She wore something white and frilly that reached to beneath her chin, hiding the ghastly wound made by the assassin's knife. He felt nothing whatsoever, as if it wasn't Marla at all, but merely a painted replica. He half-expected to turn and find her standing next to him, laughing at her own elaborate joke.

He had turned away and started up the aisle when he saw Marla's killer. For an instant he stopped in mid-step, so complete was his surprise. Their eyes locked until Dieter forced himself to look away, breaking the contact. Even so, he thought he might have betrayed his feelings by the expression on his face. He reached his place and turned his back, watching the rest of the people pass by the coffin without really seeing them, feeling a profound and growing elation. There was something left for him to do after all, but he no longer would need Marius Markham. It had occurred to him that the letter he had written might not suffice to convict the murderer. It was only the word of a man who might be exposed at any time as a fugitive and a war criminal. Even if it bore weight with a court of law, he knew the punishment would be inadequate. Death penalties were seldom invoked and virtually never administered in America. Therefore he would impose and carry out his own sentence. There were certain advantages in having nothing to lose, he decided. He touched the little pistol in his pocket and smiled. It was simply a matter of getting close enough.

The idea of peering into Marla's coffin didn't appeal to Steelegrave. He watched Lang work his way down the aisle, patting a shoulder here, shaking a hand there, acting like a goddamn politician. Farther down the line he noticed a man in a beautifully tailored suit the color of vanilla ice cream. There was something familiar about the coal-black hair with its dramatic streak of white, but he didn't recognize Vandy until he turned his head. Steelegrave wasn't surprised that he had showed up. It was a gesture Vandy would find irresistible, a last chance to gloat.

Almost everyone in the chapel had gone forward and Steelegrave felt exposed standing there alone. Sensing someone still behind him, he turned and found himself face to face with the bulky orange-haired cop who had shot at him yesterday. The man was staring directly at him with slitted, expressionless eyes. With an enormous effort, Steelegrave turned away from the compelling gaze, willing himself not to bolt. He stood with shaking legs, hoping the tremor didn't show, much as he had in Stella Harvey's class so many years ago. He could feel the cop eyes on the back of his neck, peeling away the elaborate disguise.

Minutes crawled by before Desmond was back. "I was wrong," he said out of the corner of his mouth. "Coffin looks like mahogany. So does Marla."

Steelegrave didn't dare try to tell him about the cop behind them. They watched the pallbearers start down the aisle, Gil LaFarge and Mel Braski among them. "Mel's the one looks like he could carry the box himself," Desmond commented. He glanced sharply at Steelegrave, who had begun to sweat profusely, expecting a hand on his shoulder or a gun in his back at any second. "Relax, will you?" said Lang.

Finally everyone was in the aisle, moving toward the front, ready to follow the casket out of the chapel. Steelegrave chanced a look behind him, and to his immense relief, the big cop was gone. He must have left by the back door. Probably gone for reinforcements, Steelegrave thought bitterly. He felt trapped here, hemmed in by the high walls, and had to fight off an urge to shove his way to the entrance.

When they got there, Orange-hair was waiting, standing next to a lean, dour man who had to be another cop. They carefully scanned everyone that emerged, and again Steelegrave had to conquer an impulse to run. He forced himself to shuffle by, shoulders slumped as he had practiced it back at Lang's house. Up ahead he could see Vandy walking next to Erin, talking to her and smiling. He remembered the elaborate trap Vandy had set for him last night and would have considered trading his freedom for five minutes alone with the treacherous bastard.

"Now, here's the plan," Lang was saying as they walked along. "After they say some words out here, the party's going to break up. We stay with Dieter, follow him back to his car. It looks like he came alone, which is perfect. I'll flash my phony buzzer at him and go into my act. You just keep quiet and give him the hard eye. He'll cooperate because he's got nothing to lose. You said he wouldn't talk because he didn't want to be hassled, wanted to die in peace or something. Well, here he's got two cops in front of him who know the whole story. Why should he hold out any longer?"

To Steelegrave, sober now, the idea sounded ridiculous. Especially with a couple of genuine cops obviously checking the crowd for him. Suppose Dieter spotted them for fakes and raised hell? The best thing to do was cut bait and get out of here. He tried to say as much. "Won' work, Wang," he mumbled. "Coff aw ower'a pwafe."

"Don't try to talk. Just follow me when I make my move." It was a line right out of *Love–Forty*. Only it was Hawke's line.

Marla's casket was placed on a platform that held it

suspended over the grave, which was surrounded by flowers. Everyone gathered around as the minister opened his book. Steelegrave heard the harp again and finally located the player stroking away behind the bole of the large pepper tree that spread its branches above them. He was playing "On a Clear Day."

" 'We brought nothing into this world and it is certain that we can carry nothing out . . . ' "

In front of Steelgrave a young man with glossy black hair, dressed in mauve satin trousers and matching halter, commented, "That's really going to piss Marla off." His companion, in a tight jeans outfit, snickered. The dark one looked familiar to Steelegrave. It took him a minute to recognize Marla's son, Eric. The years hadn't eradicated his dimples.

"That's Rance Evans over there, pretending he wants to jump into the hole with Marla." Desmond indicated a tall young man with long curls, swaying close to the excavation. He wore a black armband, a white suit, and a frilled white-on-white shirt. His expression was a study of Actor's Studio anguish and his neighbors were giving him plenty of room.

Fine cinders drifted out of the leaden sky, coating their shoulders like dandruff from heaven as the steady hot wind stirred the branches of the pepper tree. The smell of smoke was strong in the air.

" 'Ashes to ashes, dust to dust . . .' "

Steelegrave saw Erin turn and walk away before the ceremony was over. There was something in the carriage of her shoulders, a grace and pride, that made his heart go out to her. He knew she had come here to find him and to help him. She cared. And what had he done when she pleaded with him earlier to do the sensible thing and give himself up? Why, he had made a few drunken wise-ass remarks and hung up on her. Suddenly he needed to talk to her, at least to try to explain if not excuse himself. There might not be another chance. He stepped away from the cluster of people and started across the cemetery after her.

*   *   *

When Cosgrove saw Neva Morgann, who would always be Bettsy to him, he nearly forgot his mission. He followed her with his eyes, drinking in her grave beauty. He loathed the profession she had chosen but knew that she had risen above it. As much was there in her face, for all the world to see. She was incorruptible, impervious to the evil all around her. For that reason he had helped ensure her success and perhaps rid the world of some of that evil as well. Now he should be walking beside her, ready with comfort and counsel when she needed it, her anchor in the devious world she inhabited. If only he could tell her what he had done for her. Then she would finally understand and be grateful to him, return his love as she had when she was a little girl. But he wasn't finished yet.

He brought his attention back to the task at hand, studying every face with care. There was no one who looked remotely like Steelegrave, and he began to feel a bitter disappointment. He had been so sure he would show up. When he recognized Lang Desmond despite the white hair, he watched him closely. But Desmond was with some bald-headed guy who had turned around and given Cosgrove a dirty look in the chapel, probably because of his rumpled attire. The guy seemed horrified. Well, screw the lousy snob.

Then he saw Erin Englund. She could have only one reason for being there—to find Steelegrave. She caught his gaze upon her and looked quickly away. He saw the startled fear in her face and wondered about it. After all, she had left the message for him, and that should have meant she trusted him.

"I guess that's it," Willy Danforth said softly at his elbow. "He's a no-show. Let's go see the cap'n."

Cosgrove didn't reply. His eyes were back on the bald-headed citizen standing next to Lang Desmond. The man seemed restless, rocking slightly on his heels, his left hand clasping his right wrist. Watching him earlier, Cosgrove got an impression of chronic illness, a slouch about the shoulders, a shuffling walk. Now the man seemed almost jaunty. And where had he seen that familiar stance before, one hand holding the opposite wrist, the slight flexing of the legs? He concentrated on the elusive characteristics.

dredging up recent memories and running them through his mind.

It came to him suddenly, as such things do. The figure had been on his videotape machine just last night, swaying with that easy arrogance, a half-smile on the handsome features, playing out a scene. Rick Steele! Except that this man had puffy features and a bald pate, a thicker nose, and a long, prominent upper lip. . . .

Then he recalled something else about the picture. Lang Desmond, playing his buddy, had made Steele up so that he could get around even with every cop in the city looking for him. Cosgrove kept staring, but it was too far-out. That they would have the sheer audacity to try the same trick for real was something out of Sherlock Holmes, the stuff of fiction. He couldn't buy it. Until he remembered that they were both actors. . . .

The bald man wasn't paying attention to the service. His chin came up, and though Cosgrove couldn't make out his eyes behind the lenses, he seemed to be looking out above the heads of the crowd. Turning slightly to follow his gaze, Cosgrove saw Erin Englund walking away through the field of markers and tombstones. He watched her for a long moment as the pieces fell in place in his mind. When he turned back, the bald man was gone and Desmond was standing there alone, looking angry.

Cosgrove peered around and saw him at once. He was moving after the Englund girl, or at least in the same direction. There was no shuffle to his walk now, no slump to the shoulders. It was a springy, remembered stride. Cosgrove felt quickening exultation. You almost pulled it off, he thought. You almost fooled me. He spun around and broke out of the circle of people around the grave, limping rapidly after the bald man.

"Hold on, Cos . . ." Willy Danforth was trotting along beside him. "Where you think you're going?"

"Personal business, Willy. Give me a minute, can't you?"

"No way."

Cosgrove walked at an oblique angle to the bald man, who was obviously following the girl. With Danforth beside him, he left the cemetery grounds and crossed the driveway to the lawn in front of the chapel. That put about fifty-five yards and a row of cars between them and the funeral.

Cosgrove stopped and turned to his partner. "I'll explain later, Willy." He drove his fist deep into Danforth's belly, then clubbed him hard on the temple as he bent over. He used his foot to roll the unconscious man under a car.

That should buy him the few minutes he needed. There would be time enough for explanations when he had terminated Steelegrave. No one would question his disobedience to Strickland or anything else. It might even be worth a commendation. Danforth would look ridiculous making a complaint, and anyway, he'd make it up to Willy. Maybe buy him lunch at Musso's.

Limping painfully, he came out from behind the cars and closed in on the bald man. They were both far behind the Englund girl, who had reached her car and was opening the door, her back to them. Cosgrove shot a sideways glance to his left at the people gathered under the pepper tree, intent on the ceremony. There would never be a better moment. He put his left hand in his pocket and pulled out the throwaway gun, an unidentifiable thirty-eight revolver. With his right, he reached for his service revolver. He was only ten yards behind his target now.

"Steelegrave!" he called in a harsh whisper.

Steelegrave turned automatically, and Cosgrove flung the revolver in an underhand toss. "Catch!"

Steelegrave caught the gun instinctively, grasping it clumsily by the grip, staring down at it uncomprehendingly. Beautiful! thought Cosgrove. It had all come together perfectly, as he always knew it would. Everything in life was a matter of timing. He raised his revolver, aiming for the heart.

The shootings turned the afternoon right around for Anse Quinlan, a cameraman on KILTV's electronic newsgathering team. He had set up his videotape camera on its tripod and aimed at the caravan of sedans arriving for the funeral, zooming in on a few celebrities as they got out and headed for the chapel. Then he shut down and gagged it up with the secretaries in the fifth-floor office he had obtained permission to use, waiting for them to come out again. Unlike the bigger networks, which had full crews zeroing in from other office windows, he was working alone. Not even a goddamn videotape operator to help with the equipment.

Celebrity funerals bored Anse, but it beat stumbling around in the boonies covering the fire. He thought that excessive smoke inhalation probably caused cancer, not to mention the discomfort and even danger such assignments sometimes involved. Anse didn't think he was less daring or enterprising than anyone else, just more practical. Given a chance at two jobs, neither of which promised much in the way of dramatic possibilities, he would always angle for the more convenient. Which was why his peers did not concur with his self-assessment, deciding instead that Anse Quinlan at thirty-two had gone about as far as he ever would.

The casket emerged from the chapel borne by pallbearers and followed by the mourners. Anse zoomed in again, lingering on famous faces and strafing the rest of the column with his camera. Later they'd patch in the commentator's narration and be ready for the evening news. The day was so dark and dreary that the quality of the tape would suffer, Anse knew, especially since he was shooting through a hermetically sealed window. It looked like early twilight out there.

He taped the ceremony under the pepper tree, more of it than he needed, and noticed that the crews shooting live from down behind the hedge were already wrapping. He was about to do the same when he decided to add a little background. He followed a girl with a svelte figure as she picked her way among the markers, apparently leaving early. Then he panned along the driveway, establishing the compound of the mortuary, planning to end on the chapel. He picked up another early departure, a bald man in a gray suit, and behind him, still another. Even as he was shooting them, the second man, a bulky individual with a limp, seemed to shout at the first, then, when he turned, throw him something. At the same time, he drew a revolver and prepared to fire.

"Holy shit!" said Anse, and kept the camera rolling.

*   *   *

As he began to squeeze the trigger, Cosgrove felt twin slaps against his back at the same instant that he heard two sharp reports and knew that, incredibly, he himself had been shot. He took a short step forward, then spun awkwardly on his game leg. The tall, cadaverous German who had been Marla Monday's servant stood there aiming a small pistol at him, grimacing with effort as he tried to squeeze off another round. Cosgrove shot him once through the chest and the man flew backward and collapsed on the ground. Cosgrove turned back toward Steelgrave as if Dieter Greim had been only a minor diversion. He stumbled slightly, steadied himself, and began to bring up his gun again.

Erin stood frozen, holding open the door of her car. Hearing the shots, she had turned to see the tall, thin man fall to the ground and the heavy policeman she recognized shift his attention to the bald man. Even as she tried to interpret what she was seeing, the big dog shot out of the car past her and bounded away across the grass. At first he ran toward the bald man, then hesitated and veered away. He ran with teeth bared and hackles raised, his paws thrumming against the turf.

Cosgrove saw the big animal coming and reacted to the immediate danger. He whirled and fired at the dog, catching him in mid-bound, no more than a dozen feet from his throat. Junkyard collapsed almost at his feet and rolled onto his back. He pawed at the air briefly and was still.

Steelegrave used the seconds Junkyard bought him to full advantage. He suddenly saw everything in sharp focus, the mind's instinctive reaction to mortal danger. It occurred to him that the gun might not be loaded, but he didn't hesitate now. Holding the weapon at arm's length, legs slightly bent in the classic stance he had used so many times in *Love–Forty*, he shot Cosgrove twice in the chest.

The big policeman rocked back and sat down heavily, dropping his revolver. He stared incredulously at Steelegrave.

"Freeze! Drop it!"

Steelegrave turned his head to see a wiry man aiming at him very professionally from twenty yards away, and dropped the gun as though the steel burned his fingers.

Out of the corner of his eye he saw Erin approach, at first tentatively and then on the run. Farther away, from under the pepper tree, a frozen tableau of famous, fearful faces stared at them across the cemetery.

Willy Danforth spoke into the Rover, never taking his eyes or weapon off Steelegrave. Erin knelt quickly next to Junkyard and looked up at Steelegrave with puzzled eyes. He took a step toward her and heard Danforth yell, "Freeze, I said!"

Steelegrave took the sponges out of his mouth and dropped them on the grass. "I want to look at my dog."

"Richard?" Erin stared at him, unbelieving.

"Is he dead?"

She looked back at the dog, saw his eyes blink and his chest heave. The big shaggy head was bloody. Feebly he began to paw at the air again. Erin wiped gently at his wound with a handkerchief she took from Steelegrave's breast pocket. "No," she said.

Cosgrove sat on the grass, his bad leg bent awkwardly under him. He felt dull pain replace the numbness in his chest and back and knew it would soon get bad. It was hard to breathe, and a little salty blood was already coming up into his throat. He looked at the gun next to him on the grass, moved his hand toward it.

"Steady, Cos." Danforth knelt beside him and picked up the revolver, still covering Steelegrave.

Two police cars with lights blinking and sirens screaming came down the cemetery drive, followed by an unmarked sedan and the motorcycle troopers who had been directing traffic. Uniformed cops spilled out of the squad cars with weapons drawn, and Fletcher Strickland jumped out of the sedan, followed by two plainclothesmen.

Strickland ran up to Danforth. "What the hell's going on here, Willy?" he demanded.

"Fuckin' O.K. Corral is what."

"Who's this?" Strickland indicated Steelegrave.

"Steelegrave . . ." said Cosgrove from his place on the grass, and coughed delicately, as though clearing his throat.

"Cuff him," said Strickland.

Danforth holstered his revolver and reached for handcuffs. "I'd like to say something first," Steelegrave protested.

"Get your hands behind your back," snapped Danforth. "Move!"

Steelegrave complied reluctantly and felt the cold steel go around his wrists. "He threw me the gun and then he was going to shoot me. That's what would have happened if the other guy hadn't shot him first. And if my dog hadn't jumped him."

Cosgrove shifted his weight painfully and tried to smile through bloody lips. "Bullshit!"

Strickland squatted next to him. "Take it easy, Cos. Ambulance is coming." He looked up at Danforth. "You see what happened?"

Danforth fingered the swelling bruise on his temple. "No . . ."

"We've got another one down over here," a booted trooper shouted, standing by Dieter Greim. "He's trying like hell to talk."

Strickland stood up and walked swiftly over to the German, who was sprawled on his back at the edge of the driveway. If his eyes had not been open and his lips working, the captain would have thought he had been dead for some time. "You want to say something?"

Dieter Greim gave up trying to speak. He fumbled weakly inside his jacket and brought out an envelope stained with his blood. He tried to extend it to Strickland, but it fell from his fingers.

The captain picked it up and read it, standing over him. He read it carefully, taking several minutes, and when he looked down again, the man on the ground was dead, eyes staring up sightlessly, mouth dropped open. There was no need to search for a pulse, but the trooper knelt to do so all the same.

Strickland folded the letter carefully and put it back in the envelope. It told him what he least wanted to know, confirmed his worst fears. He considered destroying it. For about a second. Slowly, heavily, he walked back to where Cosgrove lay. The wounded man had fallen over on his side and begun to curl up. Danforth was trying to stanch the flow of blood from his chest with an emergency medical kit from one of the squad cars. An ambulance wailed in the distance, getting closer.

Strickland knelt down next to Cosgrove once more. "He wrote it all down, Cos," he said softly. "The German was an eyewitness."

The wounded man gathered himself. He drew a deep, slow, ragged breath. "I'll make a statement . . . One condition . . ."

Strickland hesitated only briefly. Cosgrove was in terrible shape, but he wanted badly to hear what he had to say. "Tell me."

"Want to see Bettsy . . . Bring her to me."

Danforth threw Strickland a puzzled look, thinking Cosgrove must be delirious.

"Go ask Neva Morgann to come over here," the captain told him. "Be polite."

21

Neva Morgann stood looking down at Cosgrove without comprehension. The thin policeman had simply asked her to step over, will you please? It's important. She saw a big man who was obviously badly injured, a large bandage turning red over the center of his chest. She had heard the gunfire and supposed he had been shot. Gil LaFarge followed uninvited and stood beside her, hovering protectively. She was confused and a little shocked and wanted to ask what she was doing here.

Danforth had propped a leather medical kit behind Cosgrove's back so that he could sit up a little. Moving hurt like hell. Cosgrove felt himself slipping away toward blackness, but seeing his daughter, he rallied by sheer effort of will. "Bettsy . . ." he said.

Neva's eyes widened at hearing the name but she still did not make the connection with the wounded man.

"What I did, I did for you, Bettsy . . ." Cosgrove spoke as clearly and precisely as he could, but blood kept coming up into his throat to garble his words. "When I read what she was doing to you, I went to her and begged her . . . she just laughed. She was an evil woman. I executed her so that you could fly free, reach for the moon and the stars, as you were meant to. . . ." He tried to smile through his bloody lips.

Neva stared at him in growing horror, suddenly remembering the voice on the phone, the man pleading to meet

with her, claiming to be her father. So now murder had
been committed in her name after all, not by her lover but
by her natural father, this perfect stranger. The irony
came home to her and she swayed as if she had been
struck, prompting Gil to steady her with his hand. Could
it all have been prevented if she had met with this wretched
man? She closed her mind to the possibility, unable to
absorb more guilt. With an anguished cry she whirled
around, tearing free of Gil's grip, and plunged away,
careless of the direction she took, simply escaping. LaFarge
went after her.

"Bettsy . . . !" Cosgrove called out. She doesn't understand, he thought. I was so sure she would understand. . . .

An ambulance came careening down the driveway, guided
by police hand signals, and bounced over the curb onto
the manicured mortuary lawn, coming as close as it could.
Two men and a woman in white uniforms sprang out of
the cab.

Strickland knelt again beside Cosgrove. "There isn't much
time, Cos. Why did you plant the knife on Steelegrave?"

Cosgrove tried to focus his eyes on the captain. "Steelegrave or the pansy . . . didn't matter to me. . . . One's a
degenerate, the other one's corrupt, rotten . . . ran down
an innocent woman and got away with it . . . Hollywood
scum . . ."

"Why Steelegrave?" Strickland insisted.

"I had the knife with me all the time . . . Deckar had an
alibi, Steelegrave didn't. So . . ." Cosgrove swallowed and
stopped speaking.

"Why not just throw the knife away? Why frame either
one of them?"

Cosgrove could see Strickland only dimly now. Still, he
wanted him to understand. Somebody had to understand.
"Just retribution, Fletch. . . . I was . . . instrument of the
Lord. . . . Remember the punk . . . shot me that time? You
can close the book on that one. . . ."

"You killed him too?" Strickland was incredulous.

Cosgrove nodded.

The two ambulance attendants unlimbered a stretcher
and came jogging over with the woman. They jostled

Strickland aside almost brusquely as they prepared to load Cosgrove onto it, intent on their own duties.

"One more thing, Cos." Strickland pushed back next to the wounded man. "You planted a throwaway gun on Steelegrave, too, didn't you? You were gonna take him out and claim self-defense."

Cosgrove managed to shake his head. "Oh no . . . just tried to arrest him. He shot me. You've got him for murder. . . ." Again the bloody smile, then he closed his eyes. The paramedics hefted him and rushed him into the back of the ambulance. The woman and one of the men leapt in after him and the other man slammed the rear door shut and ran around to the cab.

Steelegrave stood with his hands cuffed behind him, watching the ambulance leave. He had sent Erin to take Junkyard to the nearest veterinary hospital. If the dog survived, he would feast on sirloin forever, he vowed. If they both survived. He had heard Cosgrove's last vindictive statement. His legs felt rubbery, as if they would bend either way. He had been on the run, shot a man perhaps fatally, and very nearly been shot himself. It was hard to believe it all began less than twenty-four hours ago.

From behind the cordon of police keeping them politely corralled, the people who had attended the funeral stared at him accusingly. He saw Lang vainly trying to get through and Vandy in his cream-colored suit watching with what seemed to be satisfaction even at this distance.

A black girl in tight pants with a red scarf around her breasts came running down the driveway toward them and Steelegrave recognized the Watusi. She stopped in front of Strickland. "You a police officer, brother?" she asked him.

Strickland frowned at her. He disliked racial terminology, wherever it emanated from. "Yeah. Captain Strickland to you."

"Well, I'm a federal narcotics officer, Captain. There's a Mercedes over there with a load of cocaine in the trunk that weighs more than I do. I've been on it undercover for six weeks so I don't carry I.D. or even a weapon, but you can make a phone call if you don't believe me. We were going to bust the guy this afternoon when he made the drop, only he changed the location to I don't know where, and I can't take him alone. This is like the only chance left."

Strickland shook his head and massaged his eyes with thick, strong fingers. It was turning into quite a day. "Where is this guy?"

"Over there in the white suit. Not the one with the armband." She did not point. "He wanted to go to the funeral, so he changed everything. He's an ex-husband of Marla Monday named Evander."

"Honey, this honest-to-God better not be some kind of gag." He turned to Danforth. "Willy, take Gannon and Fleiss"—he gestured toward the two plainclothesmen who were leaning against the unmarked cruiser, smoking—"and check this thing out. I want a thorough search, on the grounds of reasonable suspicion."

"Watch the driver," the Watusi said. "He's got a gun and he's crazy enough to use it."

"That doesn't make him different from hardly anybody else around here today," said Strickland sourly. "Keep an eye on the guy in the white suit, Willy, and stand by to grab him if this is a straight story."

Danforth collected the two plainclothes detectives and they began to amble purposefully in the direction of Vandy's long, custom Mercedes. On the way, they paused to talk to a brace of dismounted motorcycle cops who then wandered off toward Vandy. It was all very subtle.

"Hi, there," Steelegrave said to the Watusi when he could catch her eye. She stared back at him blankly.

"Last night at Vandy's. Richard Steelegrave."

The girl obviously couldn't believe it, so Steelegrave said, bobbing his head, "Look, Ma, no hair." He felt suddenly lighthearted, almost carefree. There was nothing left to go wrong. He smiled.

"So that's what this is all about," the Watusi said to Strickland. "You got Steelegrave. I wouldn't have known him."

"You the one phoned the tip on him? The narc working undercover?"

"Yes."

Strickland smiled at her. "We're going to have a talk."

Steelegrave watched the representatives of the press move in, climbing the hedge from the parking lot, dodging around cops trying to head them off, agile despite their equipment. He asked Strickland, "What about me?"

The captain had the grace to look sad. "Going to have to book you," he said. "Attempted murder, for now."

When the first two shots cracked out, bitter little puffs of sound, the ceremony under the pepper tree faltered. The next report, a loud, high-caliber roar, was clearly a gunshot. Almost everyone crouched instinctively. One of Hollywood's foremost celluloid heroes threw himself flat on the ground. The minister hunkered down behind Marla's coffin, dropping his book. Vandy stepped discreetly behind the trunk of the pepper tree which already sheltered the harpist. He was about to peer out when he heard one, two, three more shots.

No one moved until the police cars and motorcycles came with sirens screaming to interpose themselves between the cemetery and the sound of gunfire. Then they began milling around with reviving curiosity. Vandy pushed his way to where he could see what was happening. He experienced a moment of horror, thinking it might have something to do with the Mercedes' cargo and someone was shooting it out with Vejar. But the car was well away from the action and he could make out the Watusi and Vejar peering out of the open windows.

Two men were down on the lawn near the chapel. One lay on his back next to the driveway; the other was crumpled up but moving on the grass beyond. A bald man stood with his arms partially raised in the accepted manner of surrender, while a cop in civvies (Vandy was sure) covered him with a pistol. More cops were jumping off their motorcycles and piling out of cars.

"Christ . . . they've got Rick," said a familiar-looking man with white hair who stood next to him. The man seemed to be speaking to himself.

Vandy turned on him. "What? Who?"

"Never mind."

"You said 'Rick.' Are you talking about Steelegrave?"

The man sighed. "Doesn't matter now."

Vandy was confused. He couldn't see anyone who looked like Steelegrave. "Where . . . ?"

"They just handcuffed him." The silver-haired man walked away distractedly.

Vandy looked closely at the bald man with the mustache. The stance and the cast of his face were familiar, though he couldn't make out features that far away. Rich in disguise! Vandy smiled and inserted a cigarette in the jeweled holder that was a legacy of his mother. It had taken balls for Rich to come here, he had to admit. Idly he wondered why the damn fool had done it, but it wasn't really important. He would have preferred him dead, as he had planned it, but this would have to do for now. They had the bastard who had defiled his mother! Just thinking about it summoned an image he had to suppress immediately or go mad. He cooled his rage with the sweet knowledge that Marla was dead and Rich would pay for it. And before the afternoon was over, he would be a few million richer.

On the chapel lawn, they fussed around the wounded man until an ambulance came to take him away. The other man, obviously dead, was left lying there for the time being. Vandy studied the body and recognized Dieter. His heart leapt and his smile grew broader. Sheer good fortune had brought him here to see all his enemies buried or vanquished at a stroke! It was indeed a perfect day. My cup runneth amok, he thought.

His enjoyment of the spectacle was interrupted when he saw the Watusi spring out of his Mercedes and come running down the driveway toward the cops around Steelegrave. Vejar got out, started after her, and then stopped cold, the idiot. She ran right up to the black cop who seemed to be in command and started talking to him. Vandy suddenly felt cold. She could have been asking directions to the john, but he didn't think so. Still, he wasn't willing to accept the idea of betrayal. He watched with narrowed eyes, puffing furiously at his cigarette.

The Watusi spoke at length and the black cop answered briefly, neither of them looking over at Vandy. It was Steelegrave standing handcuffed nearby who did that and gave the game away. He might even have smiled. Incredulously, Vandy watched three men start down the driveway toward his car. They stopped long enough to talk to a couple of uniformed cops who turned to look in his direction, then, hitching at their belts, began an elaborately casual approach.

Vandy didn't wait to see more. He stepped back out of sight behind the pepper tree, his mind churning. The black bitch had sold him out. Why, he didn't know, nor did it matter. He had to get away from here. If he could reach his lawyer, something might still work out. The laws of evidence were tricky. Maybe he could claim he'd been set up. If they got him here, with the stuff in his car, it was all over. There was no time to think of his staggering loss, only of escape.

He melted back toward the mausoleums, keeping the trunk of the pepper tree between himself and the cops. A quick glance told him the mausoleums themselves were traps, simply rooms full of vaults with no exit. Behind them a high cinder-block wall bordered the northern premises and reached to the gate. He made for the gate, breaking into a trot.

The cops saw him then. One jogged after him, angling to cut him off; the other ran back for his motorcycle. The big young man who had been stationed at the gate stepped forward to intercept him. The gate itself, closed now, was over seven feet high, a formidable obstacle even discounting pursuit.

The parking lot beyond the mortuary grounds was fenced off too, but the barrier was lower. A dozen or so media types with camera equipment were swarming over it into the mortuary compound, heading for the scene of the shooting. Vandy changed direction and sprinted toward them, trying for the fence. Behind him, one of the cops yelled for him to stop, but Vandy knew he couldn't risk firing a shot. The other cop had kick-started his bike and was roaring down the driveway toward the fence.

Vandy dodged nimbly between the reporters, never looking back. A cameraman directly in his path made no effort to stop him, just sidestepped and raised his hand-held Norelco, panning with him as he darted by, then did the same for the nearest cop, who snarled an obscenity in return.

Vandy reached the fence and vaulted it easily, gracefully. Before him was a lot full of cars, providing a maze of escape routes. Then, if he could get through to the street with any kind of lead, there were the big buildings on Wilshire to lose himself in. He didn't think beyond the limited goal of immediate survival. There would be time for that later. If he made it.

Burdened by his boots and equipment, the officer closest behind him faltered at the fence, losing precious seconds. By the time he had tumbled over into the parking lot, the Watusi was past him, clearing the barrier as though it were little more than a high hurdle. Striding out as she had when she ran the hundred for UCLA, she flashed down a lane formed by parked cars, closing in on Vandy. Her tackle was unorthodox—she simply landed on his back like a cat—but it bore him to the ground. They fell hard onto the asphalt in a tangle of arms and legs.

Vandy rolled with a wrestler's instinct, flinging her off so that she slammed against the side of a car, coming up quickly in a crouch. In an instant he was poised to run again.

Then he saw who it was. With a cry he leapt at her, all thought of flight forgotten. His hands snaked past the arms she raised in defense, catching her by the throat. He pushed her down beneath him and pinned her there with a knee on her chest, leaning forward to bring all his weight to bear, using the strength in his fingers to crush the firm column of her neck.

Coming upon them like that, the officer issued no warning. He clubbed Vandy hard on each shoulder, paralyzing his arms. Then he belted him once on the side of the head. Vandy crumpled loosely on top of the girl he had been strangling, and the cop reached down with both hands to yank him off. "Are you all right?" he asked her.

The Watusi sat up and raised both her hands to her aching throat. All in a day's work, she wanted to say. But the words wouldn't come out just yet.

* * *

They booked Steelegrave at the Santa Monica Police Station in a little room with one wall of wire mesh. He was read his rights and obliged to empty his pockets onto the counter. He was fingerprinted, asked some routine questions having to do with his identification, and finally submitted to a strip search, which included a thorough probing of his body cavities. His clothes were returned to him minus belt and shoe laces, his cigarettes without matches. He could ask the jailer for a light.

"I read somewhere I'm entitled to a phone call," said Steelegrave tightly.

"If you got a dime," replied the wit who had booked him, pointing at a pay phone.

Steelegrave called the veterinary hospital where Erin had told him she would take Junkyard.

"He's going to be all right," a Dr. Mariner told him. "He's lost some blood—head wounds bleed like hell. There's going to be another notch in his ear, near the base, and there's been some muscle damage, so he might not be able to hold the ear up straight. I couldn't find symptoms of concussion."

There was a pause. "You sure you want this animal back?" the doctor asked finally.

"Damn right. Why?"

"He's a rough customer. We've had a time controlling him since the young lady dropped him off. I think he's mostly wolf. Wolves don't make reliable pets."

"He's not supposed to be a pet. Just take good care of him."

"Well, all right. We'll want to keep him overnight and tomorrow for observation and to give him some plasma. You can pick him up late tomorrow."

"Someone will pick him up." Steelegrave hung up and they took him away to a holding cell.

Down the hall in a small lounge for police personnel, all the officers of the station except for the one on desk duty were watching the six-o'clock news on KILTV. Captain Strickland was also absent, busy dealing with the press.

KILTV's exclusive coverage of the shootings at Marla Monday's funeral would be compared with the famed clip of Lee Harvey Oswald's murder by Jack Ruby while he was in the custody of Dallas police. In some ways Anse Quinlan's footage was the more sensational of the two. It featured three protagonists in a real shoot-out as well as famous faces.

The station dedicated a full half of its allotted thirty minutes of news time to the sequence, running it at normal speed, then in slow motion, sometimes freezing a frame. Anse had the camera on Cosgrove when he tossed the revolver to Steelegrave and raised his own weapon. (Freeze-frame.) Then, when Cosgrove himself was shot, Anse whip-panned to Dieter Greim, widening the angle to keep both men in frame. Cosgrove shot Greim and turned back toward Steelegrave, preparing to fire again. There was Steelegrave, still obviously confused, and now there was the dog. . . . Anse had got it all—the dog tumbling, felled by Cosgrove's bullet, and finally Steelegrave firing, dropping Cosgrove to the ground. The tape was somewhat dark and grainy due to weather conditions, but everyone was easily recognizable. In those few minutes Anse Quinlan's career was assured, Richard Steelegrave was vindicated, and KILTV's call letters took on fresh meaning.

Al Nash, the detective in charge of Burglary and Homicide, shook his head. "Christ on a crutch," he said. "I turn my back for a minute and everything goes to fuckin' hell." Nash had been preoccupied with a homicide compounded by a hostage situation near Venice. The suspect had finally shot himself, sparing Nash and a SWAT team that was standing by considerable trouble. The hostages, the suspect's own children, were unharmed.

"You were busy, Al," said Willy Danforth sadly. "Anyway, it all went down pretty fast. We're gonna look worse than those valley cops that were running guns and whores and conspiring to kill that dame for her insurance."

Nash snorted. "We also just made the biggest cocaine bust in California history. That's tomorrow's headline. Fletch is gonna come out smelling like a rose." He switched off the TV. "Think all you guys can find something to do?"

"What about the prisoner?" Willy Danforth asked while the others were filing out.

"We hold him on the warrant," Nash said. "I want to talk to him tomorrow."

"I know that. I mean, you want me to tell him he's clear?"

"Hell, no. I want him humble when I get his statement."

Steelegrave spent a desolate night in the holding cell, sleeping sporadically. In his dreams he relived distorted segments of the last two days. One event played over and over during his semisleep with disturbing accuracy. That was the way Cosgrove looked when he had shot him. The big cop's brown eyes had snapped wide open and stared at him with surprise. They were in turn uncomprehending, offended, and finally angry. In the dream, Cosgrove would get up laughing and brush himself off, just like in the movies.

Awake, Steelegrave realized it hadn't been at all like the countless heavies he had dispatched on film. There was no dramatic fall, no snarling, defiant last words, no final attempt to squeeze off another shot. The big man had simply dropped his gun and sat down on the grass, staring up at him. He would probably never get up again. Steelegrave thought he might have died just before they put him in the ambulance. He knew he would never forget it.

They came to talk to him around midmorning, Al Nash and Willy Danforth. Actually, Nash did the talking. "You had a visitor, a Miss Englund, and a lawyer named Marius Markham came by to say you might want him to represent you. You're being held incommunicado to the general public, but you got a right to see the lawyer if you want to." Nash was a blunt-featured man with shrewd dark eyes and shiny black hair that grew low on his forehead and was slicked straight back. His voice was without inflection or emotion, like a bad actor reciting lines of memorized dialogue.

Steelegrave shook his head. "Ask me anything you want. I didn't murder anyone."

"Sergeant Cosgrove's dead."

Steelegrave felt dizzy with shock, though he had expected

the worst and tried to prepare himself. "I shot him in self-defense," he managed.

Nash took him through his story from the beginning. Twice. Steelegrave told him everything as it had happened, omitting nothing, answering every question without hesitation. The detectives left without comment.

They came for him again late in the afternoon, two unfamiliar officers this time. They took him to the showers, lent him gear to shave with, and returned his wallet, keys, belt, and shoelaces. Then they walked him to Fletcher Strickland's office and departed.

The captain looked weary and dejected. He had spent the night on a bunk in his office, napping between phone calls. "You are being released from custody," he said when they were alone. "Of course, your presence will be required at any inquest. On behalf of the department, I'd like you to accept my apology for your detention." Briefly he told Steelegrave about the remarkable tape on the six-o'clock news and about the contents of Dieter Greim's letter. "Until we saw that material, we had to act on the available evidence. Sergeant Cosgrove died claiming you shot him while resisting arrest. Sergeant Danforth didn't witness the incident."

"You knew all that last night and still you kept me in jail?" Anger moved in quickly to replace Steelegrave's sense of relief. "You could at least have *told* me!"

"We are entitled to hold you for seventy-two hours on the warrant issued for the murder of your former wife. The film had to be requisitioned from the station and studied. Also, I got corroborating evidence only this afternoon. The lab people found colorless nail polish on Cosgrove's fingertips. That's an old trick to avoid leaving prints. Kinda suggests he wanted yours to be the only ones found on a gun he might have handled, too." Strickland spoke of Cosgrove's guilt as though the words hurt his mouth. "On the basis of the evidence, I called the D.A.'s office and asked him to dismiss the warrant out on you."

"That was real white of you."

Strickland decided to overlook the remark. After counting to ten. The man had been through a lot, and anyway, he might have some actionable complaint. At least that goddamn Al Nash could have told him he was off the hook.

"Mr. Steelegrave," he said finally, "Sergeant Cosgrove was a cop gone bad. It happens once in a while because we're human too. We'll clean up our mess and try to keep it from happening again." He hesitated and then said, "I think you're a very lucky man. After reading the statement you gave Detective Nash, I think your dog saved you twice. Cosgrove could have tossed you that knife just the way he did the gun, and shot you right there in your house. That's probably what he planned."

"Some guardian of the law."

Strickland pushed several envelopes across the desk toward him. "Here's some mail we confiscated when you were a suspect. Never got around to opening it. Your car's two blocks away in the impound lot, if you can get to it through the reporters. You're a hero, Mr. Steelegrave," he added sourly.

Steelegrave shoved the envelopes into a pocket without looking at them. Reporters! "I've got a request, Captain. In return, I promise not to sue the city."

"Don't bet that you *can* sue the city, Steelegrave. What is it?"

Steelegrave passed a hand self-consciously across his naked scalp. "Lend me some kind of a hat, will you?"

When he left the captain's office wearing a long-billed navy-blue cap with a police insignia on it, the Watusi stood in the hall. She held out her hand. "I'm Gwen Longstreet," she said. "I'm sorry about what I did last night." But there was mischief lurking behind the bold, slanted eyes.

"You've got a hell of a punch, but I think you saved my life, too. So let's say we're even."

"I meant about calling the cops and telling them where you were going. Or didn't you even know about it?"

Steelegrave was surprised. "I thought Vandy did that."

She shook her head. "I heard him conning you to go after the German butler, so I did my sworn and civic duty. You were a fugitive and I knew where you might be headed."

"That was quite a show you put on, taking Vandy like that."

She touched the scarf around her neck. "He left his mark on me, the shit. Life with Mr. Evander was not all that charming, you know. The bureau planted me on him two months ago when one of his distributors plea-bargained. They found out he had a thing for exotic bodyguards. It took all that time to get him with the stuff. I didn't have to play house with him, but it was a close thing. Lucky for me, he had a couple of teeny-boppers around."

"Anything for the cause?"

She made a face. "Above and beyond the call of duty. I would have split. Evander was pretty weird. Besides, I didn't like the nickname he gave me."

Her accent intrigued him. "He thought you were African."

"American. Born in Jamaica to add spice." She put her hand on the doorknob of Strickland's office. "Got to compare notes with the captain now. See you around."

"You in the book?" Steelegrave asked.

She just grinned and opened the door. Maybe she nodded.

Lang Desmond was waiting for him at the desk downstairs, talking to the duty officer. Immaculate in a beige linen suit, he looked rested and fit. His sleek hair was tinted light brown, taking about ten years off his age. "The word's out you're not charged with anything, sport," he said, coming over. "Thought you might need an escort. They're laying for you out front, so the corporal here let me bring the car around back."

A few enterprising souls had figured that one out. Desmond and Steelegrave ran and ducked into the Caddy. Lang waved and smiled at the cameras from behind the wheel. Someone yelled, "How does it feel to kill a guy for real, Steele?"

When they'd pulled away, Desmond grinned. "See? They're using your name again. Like old times."

"Yeah."

"I was on location today. Way the hell out in Saugus, but they found us anyway. It was a bitch. We got about two setups all day and had to wrap early. Neva Morgann's a basket case, but she'll be okay, she's a pro. Tomorrow they're going to send a busload of cops to keep the fourth estate at bay." Lang took his eyes off the road to look at Steelegrave, a disconcerting habit he had when driving. "Now, listen to this, sport! I told Braski the whole thing and he got so excited he wouldn't leave me alone. He wants to do the story! Wants first shot at it. I told him you look good enough to play yourself. He wants to see you right away." He looked back at the road, swerving away from a parked car.

"What are you now, my agent?"

"You can have any agent in town. Look at that." Lang slapped the paper on the seat between them.

Steelegrave picked up the late edition of the *Times*. "MARLA MONDAY MURDERED BY L.A. COP" was the bannerline. Just below that, "ACTOR LIVES HIS ROLE," with a picture of himself taken long ago. On the center of the page, under a shot of Vandy's black Mercedes with the trunk open, "RECORD COCAINE HAUL AT STAR'S FUNERAL." He put the paper down without reading the articles.

"You're billed over the fire today," said Lang. "The Santa Ana quit blowing and they got it under control. Not until Marla's house burned down, though."

That seemed to fit somehow. Even her death had to be totally surrounded by drama—shootings, a cocaine bust, a fire. Steelegrave said, "Let me guess."

"What?"

"You gave the reporters the story, too."

"Damn right. I wanted them to get it down straight. You come out the hero on a grand scale. Like Audie Murphy. He did his own story, too."

"How about you?"

Lang shrugged. "Just featured, you're the star."

Steelegrave shook his head and laughed.

"Let's have a drink!" Lang suggested. "Celebrate! Where you want to go?"

"Home," said Steelegrave. "Drop me around the corner at the impound lot. I want to get my car and my dog. Then I want to get rid of this jailhouse stink and maybe go visit a lady."

Desmond looked disappointed but did as requested. "Sure, sport, I understand. But remember, you've got to move

while you've got the momentum. Today's hero is tomorrow's
bum. Right now you're the hottest thing in town." He
stopped the car.

Steelegrave got out and turned back to him. "Thanks,
Lang. For everything. I'll call you tomorrow."

The older man drove away looking slightly crestfallen.
Steelegrave supposed he could have tried to explain how it
felt to be on the run for two days, to kill a man and spend
the night in a jail cell waiting to be charged with murder.
But that would just have depressed them both.

He presented his receipt and went to find his car. It was
parked with the top down and covered with a layer of
dust. He looked at the scar left by Cosgrove's bullet and
vowed to send the city a bill. Just before he got in, he
noticed that the weather had changed. The hot wind had
stopped and the smell of smoke was gone. The air was
brisk with autumn, as it was supposed to be at this time of
year.

He drove to the veterinary hospital on Sepulveda. A
pair of attendants brought Junkyard out, muzzled and
choke-chained for their own safety. Otherwise they treated
him like a cross between Lassie and Rin-Tin-Tin. The
whole hospital staff turned out to get a look at Steelegrave
amid the kind of female giggling he hadn't heard since he
was a teen idol. Dr. Mariner gave him a fifteen-minute
briefing on the dog's condition and the nature of the care
he'd received, without once referring to his genealogy or
behavior. Junkyard wagged his tail when he saw his master,
which was about as demonstrative as he ever got. He
looked sheepish with his head neatly bandaged, one ear
dangling limply over his eye.

When they got home, no one was waiting in ambush,
probably because he wasn't listed by address in the directory.
Junkyard ranged through the bungalow making his own
security check, then settled down in front of the fireplace
with a yawn. The phone was ringing so Steelegrave switched
on the answering machine, turning up the audio to monitor the calls. As he lay on his bed with his eyes closed,
half-listening, three agents called, leaving urgent messages
for him to get back to them. A producer he hadn't seen in
fifteen years addressed him as "Ricky baby" and suggested

lunch. Mel Braski asked him to visit the *Star-crossed* location tomorrow and left directions. Marius Markham wanted to talk about Marla's estate. He turned off the machine.

The mail Strickland had given him lay on the table next to it. Three envelopes contained bills and he tossed them aside. The fourth was addressed in a vaguely familiar hand, so he opened it and read:

Rick, love,
    I doubt you will ever read this, for I am nothing if not a survivor. However, if you do, the unthinkable will have happened. In that event my attorney Marius Markham is instructed to mail this letter to you at once. He will explain the details.
    I am sorry for what I did to you, but of course I would do nothing differently given another chance. I simply did what was right for me, a habit acquired during my formative years, of which you know nothing. Just as well.
    If I chance to be reborn a more tender person and you will wait for me to grow up, we could try again, for I did love you. Until then, make the most of what I had no chance to squander. And crack your morning egg with care, for it might be

Your
Marly

Steelegrave laid the note aside, shaken. She could still reach him. Suddenly he didn't want to be alone. He wondered if Erin had called earlier, when the machine was off. They said she had come by the police station. More than anything else, he wanted to see her now.

It would be fun to surprise her. He took another shower and dressed in beige twill slacks and a navy-blue shirt. The unseasonable heat was over and a refreshing breeze came through the bedroom window. He decided he felt better then he deserved to under the circumstances. Until his mirror image stared back at him, bald-headed and baggy-eyed, dampening his mood. He had completely forgotten that Lang had shaved off his hair. Just yesterday. It seemed a year ago. He went to his closet, found a snappy panama and placed it on his head at a rakish angle. Much better. Pity he couldn't wear the damn thing to bed.

The sturdy oak bar beckoned to him, the bottles looking like an ad display against the rich wood. He could have used a drink—just one, to smooth things out—but decided against it. One would lead to a couple more, and Erin could tell when he'd had a few, even though he didn't show it. She was uncanny that way. Besides, he was going to quit drinking, at least cut way down. Tonight was a good time to start. There was so much he wanted to tell her.

Junkyard growled a complaint as he started for the door. It was dinnertime. Steelegrave fed him, throwing in half a pound of prime ground beef he had bought for himself. The dog looked so pathetic with his listlessly drooping ear that he decided to take him along. Erin wasn't overly fond of Junkyard, but she might as well get used to him. When they moved in together, he would be part of the household. Steelegrave would have to alter his life-style too, he supposed, watch the smoking and drinking, but that would be good for him. He felt he was ready for the give-and-take of living with someone now. And he had something to offer. Money and a resurrected career, if he wanted it. Or maybe they'd just travel, drift around the world for a year or two. They could talk about it tonight.

The night was cool and clear, the haze from the fires swept away by an ocean breeze. He left the top down, savoring the clean smell of the air. It was a luxury just to be able to drive around without all the cops in California looking for him. One he used to take for granted.

The spotlight mounted on Erin's garage bathed her driveway in light. An old Chevy convertible was parked there with the top down and Erin leaned into it with her elbows hooked over the window, talking to the driver. As he pulled up next to the fence, Steelegrave could see that the man was young and thin through the shoulders, with curly dark hair and Latino features. They both turned to look at him in surprise.

Finally Erin waved to him. Then she said something to the Latino and touched his arm, a gesture of easy intimacy. The young man smiled and gave the suggestion of a shrug.

He fired up his old car and eased out of the driveway. Without a backward glance he drove away, his porous muffler making flatulent sounds in the night.

Steelegrave got out of the T-Bird, leaving Junkyard behind, and walked up the driveway. Erin came to him and caught him by both hands, planting a light kiss on his cheek. "I'm so glad it's over and you're all right, Richard."

He looked after the retreating taillights of the Chevy and raised one eyebrow. "You hiring a gardener?"

Her face lost its vivacity. "Let's go inside," she said.

He followed her in, declining to take off his hat. That made her smile again.

"I tried to see you at the police station. They wouldn't let me."

"I know."

"Would you like a Perrier? Or a glass of wine?" she asked when they were in the living room. She never kept hard liquor around.

"Wine, please," he answered, imitating her formal tone.

She went into the kitchen. "You're all over the news," she called back. "They keep comparing what happened with that old movie of yours, *Fall Guy*. They even had scenes from it tonight on one of the news channels. Someone said you could make a great comeback."

"I haven't caught up with myself yet. Being in jail and all."

"Bill Stout said it would be life imitating art, if *Fall Guy* had been art in the first place."

"That sounds like him."

"Your friend Lang Desmond's been giving interviews."

"So I hear."

She came in and handed him his wine. "Cheers," she said, clinking glasses. "Your brilliant future."

"To us." It was time to change the subject.

She paused with the glass halfway to her lips, looking at him with solemn brown eyes.

He decided to ignore the signals. "The last couple of days have been an education," he began.

She didn't say anything.

"When they picked me for *Love—Forty*—God, it was more than twenty years ago!—I wasn't much of an actor. I got away with it because I *became* the guy I was playing. I used his dialogue, his mannerisms, his whole style, just the way the writer conceived him, both on and off camera. I convinced myself I was Hawke, and that made it believable on screen. After the series folded, I kept right on playing the part. For all these years. I didn't work at it, it just came naturally because I really believed it." He drained his wine but hesitated to ask for more. He knew much better than to light a cigarette.

"Then that crazy cop killed Marla and blamed it on me. And I ran. I was scared out there, Erin. I was no hero. It wasn't really like a script at all. I'd drink and try to be like Hawke, but the bullets were real and there were no retakes. I shot a man and he didn't get up again."

"It must have been terrible for you, Richard."

He saw the compassion in her eyes and it heartened him. "Now it's going to start all over again. They're going to hype this thing, casting me as Hawke in real life as well as on film. They'll want to do a picture about it with me playing myself that way. Only I don't believe it anymore, so I won't be able to do it. See, I'm not really an actor. The series and my pictures only worked because I really thought I *was* that guy I played. In *All for the Money* with Marla, they tried to get me to play someone else and I bombed. Am I making sense to you?"

"As much as ever, I guess."

"If they want to make a picture about what happened, great. But I'm going to make them do it my way, show the weakness and panic I felt and all the dumb luck that got me through it. No Hollywood heroics, just an honest movie. I've got some control, you know. They can't do the picture without me." He sighed. "The thing is, I want to be myself. And I can afford to."

She smiled. "Would I know you?"

"Erin, I'm serious. I know what I want now."

"To be yourself. And what else?"

"You."

She walked away from him and sat down on the sofa with a little sigh. He could detect no enthusiasm in her manner.

"We'll buy a nice house, travel whenever we want to,"

he said. "We can go anywhere, anytime. After I do the picture, of course."

"But the picture comes first."

He shrugged. "You've got to do that kind of thing while it's still news. People forget."

"Have you ever thought of what *I* might want?"

"Well, ah . . . tell me."

"I want a husband and kids. And pretty soon now."

Steelegrave was taken aback. It wasn't exactly what he'd had in mind. "Well, I thought we might begin by . . ."

"Shacking up? What do you think we've been doing?" She looked at him in a level, disconcerting way. "In other words, you were making a proposition, not a proposal."

Moment of truth. "We could get married. I do love you, Erin," he said awkwardly. "But I think I'm a little old to start a family."

"I'm not," she said bluntly. "I want to do other things, too. Go back to school, for one. So you see, I won't have time to be traveling around. Maybe when I'm older."

Which excluded him neatly from her plans. He began to feel angry, even betrayed. They were all the same. Show a little weakness, wear your heart on your sleeve, and they walk all over you with spike heels. He lit a cigarette without thinking, letting the smoke feather out of his nostrils. The eyebrow went up. "I don't suppose," he said evenly, "that all this could have anything to with that Mexican or whatever he is I saw leaving here."

Erin smiled. This was a more familiar Richard, one she knew well and could deal with. But she liked the other one better. "I'll get you some more wine."

She took his glass and went into the kitchen, staying there longer than the chore required. When she came back and gave him the wine, she said, "Richard, I'm probably going to marry that Mexican or whatever he is. Don't make me angry, please. Try not to be angry with me. We're only going to have memories of each other now. I want them to be pleasant and sweet."

She had caught him off balance. "I thought you showed up at the funeral because you cared."

"Of course I did. I was desperately worried. Now I know you're safe."

"And now you're free to leave me," he said with uncharacteristic insight.

She nodded. "It just happened that way."

"He's the one you were with the night Marla died. The reason you couldn't alibi me."

"Yes, but we just talked all night. I lied about the rest because I was angry."

"I guess it doesn't matter now."

"I wanted you to know."

He drank off his wine, swallowing the lump in his throat, and grinned. "Luck to you," he said. He was a good-enough actor to hide pain.

"Mean it?" Her own smile was quick and grateful.

"Sure. Just don't marry him until at least one full moon goes by. You never know."

They laughed together.

She walked him to the door. "Do the picture the way you said you would. I'll be watching for it." She kissed him lightly on the lips. "Good-bye," she said.

22

Rick Steele watched the screen so unblinkingly that his eyes stung. Or maybe it was smoke from the black cigarette he held clipped between his teeth. The film was choppy and lacked cadence, like any rough cut. Rick had never ceased to marvel at the difference between this crude footage and the final version with its smooth sequential flow. During all the weeks of shooting he had refused to watch dailies, afraid of what he might see, afraid it might tempt him to alter his interpretation so that scenes wouldn't match up. Now it was over except for postproduction— editing, looping, scoring—and they wanted him to see it.

Having considered his options, he had decided to take Braski's offer because Gil LaFarge would write the script and they promised to get Lars Vincent to direct. After all the years away from cameras, it was comforting to be surrounded by familiar faces. He had acquired a manager too—a coarse, deep-voiced woman who should have shaved more often and whose baggy pants he suspected of concealing testicles. But she was every bit as tough and cagey as Malcolm Webley had been before senility claimed him. Richard Steelegrave reverted to Rick Steele and she kept him before the public with talk shows and personal appearances until Braski could finish *Star-crossed* and start production on their project. He had to tell the story of the accident as it had really happened again and again, but the public seemed to believe him. There was no longer an eyewitness to confirm or deny it. Vandy had committed suicide, shot himself dead, on the day he was due in court for sentencing.

It was a week before Rick's fiftieth birthday, but the man on the screen looked much younger. With the white rinsed out of his fair hair, conditioned by months in gyms and on tennis courts, Rick could have stepped a decade or more back in time. Watching himself, he had an eerie feeling that he had done just that.

Liberties had been taken with the truth. Dieter Greim emerged as a sinister Nazi villain, exposed and finally dispatched in a harrowing fight by Steele in the course of his quest to clear himself of Marla's murder. Vandy was a Machiavellian psychopath whose *six* glamorous bodyguards tried to drown Rick in a swimming pool before he subdued them and went on to intercept the cocaine shipment. Of course, he got the girl in the end. (Neva Morgann refused to play that part or her own in order to star in a Broadway play.) Some names were changed, including Erin's. There was no dog in the script. Rick moved through the picture with an athlete's grace, unflinching and intrepid.

The lights went on and he sat staring at the empty screen. He told himself he'd tried, and it was true. He had fought against Gil's James Bondian script and run into a solid wall of opposition. Foiled there, he tried to rescue individual scenes. He balked at doing the underwater fight with the six Amazons. Overruled. He absolutely refused to shoot the murderous cop in the cool, detached way called for by the script, so Braski cunningly suggested a compromise. Let's shoot it both ways and see what comes out best, he'd said. Only the producer's version survived, of course. Rick's ended up on the cutting-room floor. But he should have figured that.

From the seat next to him, Mel Braski flung a heavy arm over his shoulders. "Aren't you glad we did it my way, kid?"

Rick said nothing.

"Listen, baby, it'll work. You know your job. I know mine. I used to watch *Love–Forty* back when I was driving a truck. Nobody wants to see Rick Steele acting chicken-shit or stumbling around drunk. You're a hero, stud. That's

all you ever been and all you ever will be. Never change a
winner." Braski winked and put the cigar back in his
mouth.

"It's pretty good, Rick. Better than we used to do."
High praise from the laconic Lars Vincent.

"It's not art, but it's commercial." Gil could afford the
remark. *Star-crossed* was running off the charts, a huge
success. It had done everything but get Neva back for
him. "A movie star solving the murder of Marla Monday
while he's both prime suspect and ex-husband. Playing
himself. We name names. How can it lose?"

Rick got up and left the projection room. He went down
a corridor and outside the building. The studio lot was
buttoned up for the night, the hangarlike buildings that
housed the sets locked and deserted. He stood on the street
taking deep breaths of the night air, making a game of
identifying the contents. There was the damp, salty tang
of a sea breeze moving in from the coast, a trace of
petrochemicals, the suggestion of semitropical vegetation.
Los Angeles summer smells.

Lang Desmond followed him out, lighting a cigarette.
"What do you think, sport?" He had thoroughly enjoyed
playing himself as Rick's debonair mentor.

"You know I wanted to do it differently."

"Sure, I know. You wanted to get up on the cross and
suffer. Show Rick Steele with his weaknesses and failings,
warts and all. I told you years ago, leave that to the guys who
do it well. Maybe Hoffman or Pacino nowadays. They
were born to suffer. People don't pay to see your warts.
Maybe in the *Enquirer*, but not on screen. They pay to see
you kick ass."

Rick bummed a cigarette from Lang. "Years ago, you
taught me to be Hawke. When I was on the run, I found
out I wasn't. I didn't think I could do that kind of part
again."

"But you did. Hawke or Rick Steele. One and the
same."

Rick shrugged. "It fit like an old coat," he admitted.
Maybe he was an actor after all.

"It's going to be big, you'll see."

They said good night and Rick walked to his car, parked

in a slot with his name on it. The T-Bird gleamed softly in the diffused glow of an overhead streetlamp. The blemish left by Cosgrove's bullet was long gone and a new high-performance engine nestled under the low cowling. Junkyard rose to his haunches, perking up his good ear. They had moved to a new house in the Malibu Colony, where there was a beach to run on. Rick had hired a live-in Salvadoran butler named Gerónimo who always wore white gloves and made excellent martinis. Junkyard tolerated him.

Rick started up the car, listening to the new engine's deep, even murmur. It was eleven o'clock, too early to go home. Especially when he was still strung out from sitting through the rough cut. Watching his own heroics had embarrassed him as never before. Maybe because he knew they were confined to celluloid. Not that it mattered anymore, but he hoped Erin wouldn't go to see the picture.

He decided to have a nightcap at the Guardrail. They still made the best Moscow Mules around and they deferred to him, having adopted him as their local celebrity. And why not? He had everything now.

Didn't he?

About the Author

Arthur Hansl was born in New York City in 1930 and raised in Connecticut, Florida, and Europe. He went to school in Switzerland and France as well as in the United States, graduating from Taft School in Connecticut, and Washington and Lee University in Virginia. After three years in the U.S. Marine Corps, he went to Mexico for two weeks and stayed for four years, becoming, he says, an accomplished beach bum. He moved from there to California and then on to Europe, arriving in time to enjoy the last years of the *dolce vita* in Rome, where he became an actor starring in some forgettable films and doing supporting parts in somewhat better ones. He returned to Mexico in the late sixties for another dozen pictures over half a dozen years. *Freeze-Frame* is his first novel. The author now lives in Pacific Palisades, California, with his French wife, Nicole, and two dogs and a cat in a house overlooking the sea.

Recommended Reading from SIGNET

**Buy them at your local
bookstore or use coupon
on last page for ordering.**

Thrilling Fiction from SIGNET

*Prices slightly higher in Canada

**Buy them at your local
bookstore or use coupon
on next page for ordering.**

SIGNET Mysteries You'll Enjoy